PEARLY EVERLASTING

A NOVEL OF THE ASPEN SILVER CAMP

BY
MARTIE STERLING

PublishAmerica
Baltimore

ISBN: 1-4137-4626-8
PUBLISHED BY PUBLISHAMERICA, LLLP
www.publishamerica.com
Baltimore

Printed in the United States of America

For Lee Uris, beloved friend and mentor

ACKNOWLEDGMENTS:

To Whit & Polly Whitcomb, my most valued critics.

To my cherished guru, Roddey Burdine.

To Larry Fredericks, Aspen history expert, who patiently corrected & recorrected details of the 1880s.

To Aspen Historical Soceity for their rich store of carefully preserved and collated pictures, writings, newspapers, and memorabilia, and the Pitkin County Library, the best library in the West.

To the Ute Mountain Tribal Council.

To the countless old-timers gone now: Tony Kralicek, Louise Berg, Lucille Baltizar, Prue Bogue, and Lizzie Callahan, who re-lived Aspen's pioneer times for me.

I am indebted to Dick Needham and Steve Cohen.

To Stefan Albouy and his successors in current Aspen mine projects, particularly Dana Knight, who have given me a reverence for—and understanding of—hard-rock mining.

To Karen Chamberlain's and my love child, the Aspen Writers' Foundation.

To Ron Carlson.

To Sue Brinkley Tatem, Jerry Airth, Jan and George Rogers, Belinda Frishman, Jim McPhee, and many others who read, suggested, and cheer-led.

To my agents Thelma and Jon Richard for their loving care.

To the memory of my dear long-time mentor, Robie MacCauley.

And not least to my beloved, zany children—and a long-suffering husband who often goes unfed.

Though the great silver strike and the Pearly Everlasting Mine are fictional, they are based on a real-life happening of the 1880s. Some actual personages intermingled with the story's fictional characters. Wyatt Earp and John Holliday spent time in Aspen, often en route from Leadville over Independence Pass to the sanatorium in Glenwood Springs, where the tubercular "Doc" eventually died and is buried. William Henry Jackson, famed chronicler of the West, photographed in and around Aspen. Maiden lady, Eppa Strait, died in a fall from Aspen's bell tower. The physical environs of Aspen and its mountain surroundings are in all ways accurate. Many incidental anecdotes are taken from newspapers and miners' and ranchers' writings of the period. However, this story and all its principals are purely fictitious.

BOOK ONE

PROLOGUE

Early in the War Between the States, the Rocky Mountains didn't count for much. Remote as the moon, men said. Teeming with graybacks. Stinking shaggies. No place, said women, for white folks. The inhabitants were half-crazed gold-panners and pock-faced Arapahos. Crafty, mahogany-skinned Utes disappeared like drifted smoke among high, snow-capped peaks.

In this faraway high country, summer was hotter than hellfire, and winter froze a man's eyewinkers shut. Rheumy-eyed dreamers stood in icy streams, feet wrapped in strips of rotted saddle blankets. Panned and sluiced for gold (silver would soon follow), ignored the war back in the States, and dreamed of hot-water hip baths and store-bought suit vests draped with gold watch chains.

On a bleak, rain-streaked Sunday afternoon in May of 1862, President Abraham Lincoln's Washington parlor was the scene of afternoon tea with Judge Elias Kershaw and his wife Alice, a genteel woman with fluttery hands. In her lap squirmed their squally infant Emma.

Child has a slight more gumption than her ma, decided the President dryly. When the tea cups were emptied, he adjusted his shawl and leaned forward in his rocking chair. "Elias, I am sending you west…." at which Alice Kershaw's pearly face turned white as wood ash, "to the mine country around Cherry Creek, out in the Colorado Territory."

"The fight goes against us, Elias. I fear it will be a lengthy, perilous affair. Our war chest is running low. We have levied new excises on the mine pickings out there. But those diggers are short on law, fractious as dogs in heat. You're an Illinois man, you know the frontier. I figure you're the fellow to bring them to order—collect the Union's tithe."

And so little Emma Kershaw was toted off to the middle Rocky Mountains, a country of high winds and hard blizzards and—for the few who leaned to operatic scale—of great beauty. Her days soon brimmed with the guffawing of rough-edged men, with the pawing of half-broke horses, with obsidian stares of curious Indians.

11

Though the child loved both West and Westerners, her timorous Bostonian mother did not. Alice Kershaw was terrified of the drum-voiced Utes who puked in the water barrel on her back stoop and crowded around her kitchen wood stove begging for "black water." She was aghast that dirt-encrusted pole-pickers spat greasy chaws across her Turkey carpets, that rouged women on Denver City's Larimer Street bared their hinders from open crib windows. Nightly, after hiking up her bed dress to squat on the chamber pot, the judge's wife prayed for an absentee God to deliver her from this barbaric hell.

Her wish was soon granted. She succumbed to the summer flux and was laid to rest in raw, red Rocky Mountain ground. Her grieving widower, like the governor and half the territorial legislature, he was consumptive. He'd hoped to regain his health in bracing mountain air, though his fine eyes were sinking deeper in their sockets, his big, muscular frame thinning to a spruce splinter.

With Lincoln in his grave, the West grew more unsettled than ever. Thousands of butternut and bluebelly veterans, unable to cease marching and shooting or to settle back on humdrum farms, invaded the Great Stonies. Many lived like wolves. Nowadays they shot hostiles, buffalo, and each other. There was more call than ever for law. The clamor for statehood was growing. The judge could not think of abandoning the miners' hard-won trust. With the black funeral wreath wilting on their front door, he'd hoisted his girl onto his lap. "How'd you like to ride circuit with your pa?" he'd asked.

Emma, recently arrived at her eighth year, her second teeth still overlarge in her mouth, looked startled. Her green-as-rimfire eyes shone. "Oh I would!" she declared.

"We'll need to find you a taller horse," said the judge thoughtfully. "Those are hellish high mountains out there."

"Can Polly come?" Polly Panakarpo was the Tabeguache Ute nursemaid brought to their door by young Nate Phipps, guide, prospector, and the judge's liaison with the six Ute Indian tribes. The gruff squaw had tended Emma since she ceased sucked her first sugar tit.

"We need Polly here to parlay with the politicians." The judge considered his girl chattered more than enough Indian. He did not plan on fitting her for missionary life or screeching out war cries in some raree Western show. He did, however, wish her to grow up with sand in her craw.

Thus, through spring to fall court sessions, father and daughter rode from

Bent's Fort to Hardscrabble Creek, from Black Hawk to Fairplay. The judge with his long, salty beard and the girl with her swag of honey-colored hair eagerly awaited sight in slab-log forts and tent-city mine camps.

The circuit was not so much broad as it was up and down. Close to the sky was where gold lode and silver outcrop lay. Many a mine shack balanced like a circus aerialist on steeps that mingled with overhung clouds. The judge's big Missouri mule and the girl's smaller Indian paint forded rivers roiling with rock-strewn snowmelt, skirted the suck of quicksands, crossed prairie so hot Emma's lips cracked and the judge's nose bled. They dismounted and slow-walked their animals along the oh-my-God route from Central City to the Idaho Hot Springs, clawed their way along treacherous twelve-thousand-foot clefts in the Great Divide, the night cold turning them blue in mid-July.

"At least no rattlers live in thin air," declared the judge. "Better frost-bit than snake-bit." When they hunkered down during late spring windstorms in the Great Sand Dunes of the Sangre de Cristos range, grit scoured their eyeballs raw. "I wished for sand in your craw, child—but I never meant this," he said. Prairies or peaks, the Colorado Territory was hard country.

Yet Little Emma, dressed in canvas britches and a straw boater with a cowhide chin-strap, took to all weathers. Her skin tingled at the bugling of bull elk in autumn rut. She was awed by summer sunsets blazing like brush fire run amok. She lay breathless beside the judge in the deep gramma grass of ten-thousand-foot high South Park, spying on great buffalo herds, gargantuan masses of curly, dung-caked wool and horns. A mingling so mighty it shrank the sky. The animals' rank smell made her gasp for air. Their bellows echoed away down bottomless canyons.

"May be our last look, daughter," sighed the judge. "Meat and hide-hunters are killing these short-horns off."

Emma could scarcely credit his words. So many thousands of roaring, bellicose bison were bound to cover the ground forever.

Territorial names, noises, sights, and smells became part of her memory. Every mine camp throbbed with the crash and thump of crude, powerful stamp mills pounding gold from its mother ore. In Buckskin Joe, there was a hotel with genuine Brussels carpet with roses big as cabbages. In Black Hawk, she rushed to the Elite Pool Parlor to get her pocket money down on a cheeky Cornish kid who whipped all comers at pocket billiards. Few camps boasted spare rooms, and she unfurled her blanket roll in the back of saloons or on jerry-rigged hoosegow bunks. The smells were always the same: kerosene, whiskey, boiled cabbage, coal, and smoke.

Men in mountain mine camps led a bone-wearing, mud-tinctured existence. In the bitter cold of winter, the younger ones wept into blankets that provided thin comfort. Amid these high lonesomes, a sprightly girl was a sight for sore eyes. When Emma rode into camp, men gathered, hats in hand, to gape reverently at hair that blazed yellow as aspen leaves in autumn. And at a young face glowing like a ripe peach under a raggedy straw boater. They inquired about her schooling and asked if the judge had planted her baby teeth to insure prosperity. Vied to shoe and curry her piebald.

Emma learned letters and penmanship copying court records, acquired a smattering of Latin and Greek, and conjugated verbs with former schoolmasters as they cobbled together long toms to catch flecks of gold in swift-flowing creeks. She comprehended workaday German and French, spoke Arapaho, though not as well as Ute, and knew Indian sign. Gold and silver-seekers were not only displaced professors, but also Alsatian farmers and American soldier boys, Garibaldi red shirts, Mexicans, and Texicans. Most were young, with military bearing. Fewer were greybeards, their teeth black as wet wood. Young or old, they shared their stories, touched her tender heart.

"H'it's the war drove them to chase the setting sun, honey. That and the panic. There's no jobs in the East, no work across the seas." The judge did not believe in mollycoddling. He told Emma of terrible conditions. Worldwide depression had made bad men murderous, decent men desperate. Back in Maryland, one bunch had knifed blooded racehorses, gulped down the meat half-raw. In Ohio, gangs torched whole farms, trying to keep warm. By the thousands, they moved on the Rockies—half-feral, clutching small, weak dreams of striking it rich.

These main chancers were as starved for news and entertainment as for fresh greens, and eventually Emma began reading aloud from eight-week-old copies of the *New York Tribune*. Southern boys, in particular, were poor readers. She owned a strong, clear voice and a flair for drama. By her twelfth year, she was gathering large, rapt audiences for her readings and recitations. When she neared the outskirts of a camp, men with fingers ratchety as unplaned boards reached for tin basins and yellow soap, passed the word from dig to dig faster than an Arap could drum. "Little Emma is reciting down to the Perry House tonight…the judge and Little Emma is due in Georgetown about Sunday…hear the girl has committed two new pieces to memory."

At thirteen, Emma could estimate a pinch of gold dust, case a boardinghouse for chinch bugs, pitch and trench a tent. At fourteen, she harnessed a four-horse team, shot a honker across a wide bend in the Purgatoire River. Yet, none of her considerable know-how was worth a piece of thin string when the judge's lungs took a turn for the worse. He grew too fragile to ride. They went to roost at the Denver place, Emma sick with worry, and Polly applying poultices of brown moss and goldenseal.

Willing himself to see his girl grown, the judge held on for nearly a year. On a late autumn evening amid the eerie quiet that presages snow, Emma sat in their caned rocker, a tangle of silk threads in the lap of her bombazine skirts, and said, "This damned embroidery keeps snarling on me."

The judge looked out the frost-limned front window and sighed. "Emma girl, I have not given you the upbringing I ought."

She looked up. "What did we forget? I wash behind my ears. Don't scratch, chew, or spit."

"Well, missy, you are whip-smart—but obstinate. You have yet to set a watch over your tongue. A blaspheming female is not welcome in polite circles."

"Oh I know my tongue needs gentled," she admitted sheepishly. "Reverend Hastings gave me what-for last Sunday after I yelled 'hellfire' across the vestry at Bill Scheinkopf."

"For another, you have not got mule sense. Here you are, nearing your first score of years—and still apt to go haring off over any new distraction." He paused for a fit of coughing that left him pale as hoar frost. "You need to exercise more caution. In particular, when it comes to finances." He feared his daughter, once on her own, would give away the coat on her back, empty her reticule for men down on their luck.

"You'll have ample—money, that is." He thanked his Savior that a handful of prospectors he'd grubstaked had stumbled on rich finds. *Plant enough seeds*, he thought, *and you were bound to harvest a few pole beans*. "But money's easier made than managed," he added severely. "For one more..." The judge paused to clear his throat. "You don't, er, bat your eyewinkers at men callers the way Lucy Metcalf and May Wiggins do."

"God almighty, judge, why would I do a thing like that?"

Her father paused to reflect. "If you cannot count on mule sense of your own, daughter, you had best catch you a man with a double supply." He looked critically at the young woman in the choker-necked dress. She was maybe a mite lean and hard-muscled for most tastes. And she had the Kershaw chin. But her nose and mouth were on straight. Her cat's eyes could make a man catch his breath. And that head of hair was glorious as sun on summer wheat.

15

He thought a minute more. "Your mother, God rest her, always held the back of her hand up, graceful-like, for a caller to kiss. When May Wiggins does the trick, she er—she bats her eyes."

Emma could not help herself. She shouted with glee. "Judge, if you don't beat all! Me—an empty-headed chicken like May Wiggins!"

Returning to her needle and embroidery floss, she looked ruefully at hands tough as boot leather from handling ropes and reins. "Oh, I know my rough edges show. But when I try to smooth my skin with verbena lotion, Polly gives me her hawkeye glare." She imitated the squaw's guttural tones. "Keep skin tough, Missy, rub plenty rock salt."

"The Ute way is not the civilized way," said the judge testily. "You need to be softer around men, Emma—and I do not mean lily-white, cushiony hands. I mean a sweet-toned voice, more tactful reasoning. In particular, do not get up on your high horse over this suffrage matter."

Emma closed that subject firmly. "I expect the frontier has made me feisty. And feisty I'll no doubt stay." She smiled and reached over to rumple his beard. "But I'll try to do better by you, Judge. That's a promise."

"This Garrett Sutton appears a comer, daughter." Her father's voice was hopeful. "And the Aspen mine country more your style than Denver balls and socials. I believe you'd take to it like a goose to a grainfield." Sutton, a prosperous mine owner from the new Aspen silver camp across the Great Divide had been paying her attention on his Denver visits.

"Now, Judge, there'll be no more talk of men or mine camps. Or of me leaving, either."

"But I am the one who's leaving, daughter. A little sooner than hoped, but then few of us may choose our time."

"Dammit, Judge," she'd wailed, her face streaked with tear shine, "I won't have it! I won't have you go!"

####

CHAPTER ONE

THE PEARLY EVERLASTING

Seventy-five feet under the Silver Queen cutoff in the Pearly Everlasting Mine, Calvin Krueger felt Aspen Mountain shiver. A mine, like a man, sometimes experienced an inexplicable shudder of foreboding. He paused to mop his broad brow with the back of his sleeve and took a hitch in the miner's lamp clamped to his rough linsey cap. The lamp's candle sputtered, steadied, shone dim on the headwall before him. That morning the blast tailings had lain deep. Tonight, wherever he moved the lamp, clean bedrock, cleared of muckings, glimmered slick as an iced-in tarn.

Despite the comfortable fifty-five degree underground temperature, Cal was sweating a rainstorm. Toward the end of the Pearly's last shift, Needle Newsome and Pete Beard, using a hefty sledge and drillers' steels, had pounded five core holes to hold new powder charges. The holes were drilled in a triangular pattern—edge holes at the top and both sides and a lifter hole at the bottom. Each core was fitted with a Bickford safety fuse or rattail. Before leaving the tunnel, Cal would use a lighted spitter to ignite the fuses. Then he'd double over and hasten through the gloom of the gallery where heavy timbers held the roof and the spaces between upright columns, which were crossed horizontally by smaller timbers called "lagging." Once in a well-shored side drift, he'd stuff his ears with cotton batting and hunker down against the explosion. The thunderous blast would break loose another three or four feet of hard rock. On the next shift the men would repeat the same arduous task of mucking out the released chunks of mountain, shoveling them into tram cars, then pushing them through the tunnel to dump down the hillside. If, miraculously, promising color appeared, samples of ore would go to Gus Ackerman, the town's assayer, to have their contents tested.

On their last go-round, he and the boys had mucked and trammed some thirty tons of ore. Then, just shy of five o'clock, he'd sent Pete, Needle, and Young Frank Parker topside. For more than three hours, he had worked on his own. He'd opened a new crosscut this side of the drift wall, the muscles of his broad shoulders rippling like the patterns of beach-breaking ocean.

Picking and mucking without a partner was like skipping rope with one leg, he thought wearily. He was so spent he could have slept in a dry creek bed. Mining was a business for young tigers. Edging fifty, a man's resolve, like his legs, weakened. Yet Calvin was still powerful in the manner of an aging pursefighter. Years on the march in the open—through the war and through the West—had left his strong-featured face and big hands as brown as an old hazelnut. He had none of the dead-white, blue-john look of soft coal miners who saw little sunlight for years on end. His wife Lavinia sometimes gasped wonderingly in the moonlight caressing their bed, "Calvin, you steal my breath away. I could be taken by a red Indian!"

Calvin's loins grew warm at the remembrance, though those times were far fewer of late. If only he weren't always so played out.

Needle Newsome hadn't wanted to leave. "Mine drift's no place for a man alone," he'd drawled, working his prominent Adam's apple to squirt a tobacco chaw in a well-aimed arc toward a far corner of rock. "Don't like them groans we been hearing. And the rats is restless." Taken on the whole, mine rats were a friendly lot, their small red eyes shining as they waited for lunch bucket scraps. Only when they sensed trouble would they scurry up a man's pant legs in search of shelter.

Needle, all beak, turkey neck, and a scraggly mustache, looked so pettish that Calvin said reassuringly, "I'll be moving topside while your tracks are still wet, old hoss. Figure on tidying up accounts. It'll be late. I'll bed down in the shafthouse."

"When you get to the place," he added, "tell Vinnie not to wait up."

Needle knew good and well Lavinia wouldn't like it. Calvin's wife already fretted that he was married more to the Pearly Everlasting Mine than to her. But Cal was a bullhead. Even when a quake struck, rumbling along Aspen Mountain's jigsaw of fault lines, Cal paid it no more heed than a gnat

"And if Nate gets in from the hills, let him know where I'll be." Nate Phipps, his long-time prospect partner, was due down from the high country for Aspen's July Fourth celebrations.

Cal stooped to pick up a burned-off rat tail from a powder charge. Many a mine man in a tight corner had grown careless about lurking, unlit charges—and blown himself to kingdom come. He might border on desperate. He did not hope to grow careless.

For nearly ten months he had toiled in this dig—ten months since that silk-cravated trickster Garrett Sutton had milked him of his life's savings for title to the Pearly. Not even clear title, but only a year's leasehold. His trouble had started the winter before last, when he, Needle, and Pete sold their prosperous Keystone dig. Silver had been going for around ninety cents an ounce, and Cal's share had come to $10,000. Enough for he and Lavinia to live out their days in some comfort.

But Calvin could not find it in him to retire from mining. He'd thought of the old bench boys idling on Aspen's telegraph office bench, spitting chaws, sipping whiskey from pocket ticklers, exchanging curses and remarks with passing lawyers. He preferred a good day's work, followed by the company of a companion like Deke Burdine. Deke kept a saloon and—unless asked—his own council. With little stomach for idling or empty talk, Cal had taken it in his head to tackle the Pearly Everlasting, the runt in Garrett Sutton's litter of mines. Word had it the owner was in a hard way for cash money and would let her out on lease.

"That Pearly holds silver. Top-grade silver or I miss my guess," he'd confided confidently to his wife Vinnie. Nate Phipps had first staked the Pearly claim, and he agreed. "The Pearly and the Columbine are sisters under the skin. Sutton has not been tunneling either dig where he ought. Your good belt of Leadville limestone comes across the hump from the northeast, and she angles through them mines on the oblique."

Few prospectors were able to trace gold float or silver outcrop to their source like Nate Phipps. He not only sighted good color, he smelled it. Men still told how, in the spring of '82, Nate had struck it rich right here in the Aspen camp. Sitting by an open sash in the new Clarendon Hotel dining room, he'd sniffed at a sharp breeze freshening off the first pasqueflowers in the snowmelt up Spar Gulch, set down his saucer of coffee, and announced to the boys at table, "I have just recollected something." Then he'd hightailed it up Mill Street, dug out a fair-sized rock tramped flat by herds of ore-seekers—and struck paydirt.

"A solid streak! Right alongside Deane Street!" Calvin had crowed, wiping his eyes in delight. "Smack under the noses of all the Welsh ore experts and that batch of Columbia College boys from the East!"

Gus Ackerman, camp assayer, had peered dazedly at Nate. "It beats all, Phipps. That there's the wrong damned configuration. The wrong exposure. The wrong host rock. Not a thing right about it. But she assays some thirty percent pure, near to translucent on the surface, with fine crystal facings." Gus had scratched his head. "If she holds true, you've made you a goddam mine. A mine that'll pay sixteen dollars a pound or I miss my guess."

Nate named his pride the Columbine, for the satiny ladyslipper that crowned these hills in summer glory. As an afterthought, he had staked and improved the next-to claim and called her the Pearly Everlasting, for the sturdy little bloom that camp women were so partial to. Dried, the tiny white flowers brightened parlors on dark winter days.

"The Pearly may not take any garden show ribbons," said Nate, "but that Columbine's a jewel beyond price."

"Word of the assays has spread. The freebooters will be on you faster than hogs on offal," Cal warned.

"Well sir, that thief Sutton is already bound and determined to have her."

And have the Columbine Sutton did, despite Nate tweaking him for twice the price to any other operator—though he threw in the Pearly to lighten the sting.

"When the Lord calls me to account, I reckon I'll tot up my share of sins," Nate said to Calvin. "But I am not envious…I ain't mean…and up to now you could not call me greedy. I don't rightly believe our Maker will mind me sticking that cold-eyed jasper."

Garrett Sutton may have pulled the wool over the eyes of bankers, senators, and not a few maiden ladies, but Nate Phipps knew him for the polecat he was. The man sawed his horse's mouth with a hard bit, shorted his help on wages, was suspected of salting a claim and unloading it on unschooled investors.

"Say the skunk even wallops Little Emma." Nate had looked bleak at thought of Sutton abusing his young bride. Nate had bounced that lady as a tot on his knee, back in Denver City.

The mine price turned out higher than Garrett Sutton, or even Nate Phipps, figured. The Columbine petered out. A mine would do that to you. Turn empty and heartless as an old whore. After months of sinking shafts into nothing more than low-grade lead and zinc, Sutton dropped his thin coat of Missouri charm. He cursed Phipps for a Quaker cheat. Fired two shift foremen. Whomped his chief engineer with a shovel while the man was lowering a digger down in the skip. Having a mine cage plummet eighty feet before being jolted to a stop had made a Christian of many a miner. The man quit the Columbine on the spot. The engineer was hard on his heels.

Calvin, having made up his mind to try his hand with the Pearly, had had a good wash, put on a Sunday shirt, and marched on the slab-sided cabin that served as quarters for Sutton's attorneys, Dunbar & Black.

The first thing Sutton did was throw him a high-handed look like he was there to empty spit buckets. "Krueger. What manner of name is that?"

It wasn't so much the man's words, it was the insolent tune they played to. In the second Manassas fight, in a hospital tent where Calvin had carried a gut-shot companion, he'd come close to throttling a surgeon for a like tone.

"German. High German," he said levelly. "Great-grandpap settled in Pennsylvania with William Penn's crown deputy. Leader of the Stoberfulst Guild. Starved-out Irish came later." Calvin admitted to a surfeit of pride over his family's roots in the great Hanseatic League. But Sutton was so annoyed that Calvin regretted his haughty tone. "*Angstau nicht,*" he murmured under his breath. It served no purpose to bait a mean bear.

In truth, Garrett Sutton appeared more high horse than cross bear: tall, well turned out, his coat brushed, pointy beard, and boots glossy with pomatum and polish. He owned not only hands white as a tea-pouring woman's, but also a bearing as stiff-necked as an Episcopalian divine's. Calvin had never encountered a nicer-looking fellow he so disliked on sight.

Still eyeing Calvin like he was a menial, Sutton dickered over the Pearly leasehold. Cal knew the popinjay must be in a tight corner. It pained him like toothache to dicker at all. "The Columbine is not for rent," Sutton said coldly.

"The Columbine was not in my plans."

"Though the Pearly has been paying well, I'll let her go. For a price."

"The Pearly has been paying less than tolerable. I have seen the reports."

Sutton was a shrewd negotiator. He would not sign the lease papers until he'd extracted the best portion of the $10,000 Cal had deposited in Big Gabe Tacker's river rock-fronted bank.

"Did it smooth as a four-bit dentist," Calvin groaned later to Nate. "That hornswoggler knew my balance to the penny."

"Did you ever doubt it? Tacker is in cahoots with him." Nate was seated at the Krueger kitchen table feeding fresh-roasted coffee beans through Vinnie's patent grinder. He turned the handle harder. "Aspen needs us another banker."

Calvin nursed his head in his hands. "He even suckered me for an extra $50 a month. A contingency fee, he named it."

"N0!" Nate was appalled.

"I plan to sell lease shares to cover that overhead," sighed Calvin. Although silver workings were no more sure-fire than a coon hunt, camp people would sooner take a chance on mine futures than buy eats. Calvin had an enviable reputation in the game. Folks would gamble on him, even on a year's lease.

That was sooner, Calvin thought miserably, wiping the mud from the pick end of his mattock and setting it aside. *This is later*. Nearly nine months later, when folks were no longer so eager to take a flyer on him. Monthly, he struggled to meet his contingency. He'd found little color, and a share of Pearly was plunged from one dollar to less than a ten-cent piece. He could scarcely hold his head up around camp. He'd sooner stay buried in this cellar-hole and dig.

Sutton had stopped by often of late to mark his progress. And Cal knew to stomp his pride. In the main, he tormented him about the apex-sideline question. The apex lunacy claimed that a man who owned a main vein of ore would then own every sideline branch of that ore, like the numbers of limbs on the trunk of a tree—ignoring the common practice of awarding a 300-by-1500-foot claim to any man with the sand to locate, stake, and work improvements on such a parcel. Should the apex proposition take hold, it could ruin a raft of small miners who'd struck good mineral on a thousand of sidelines. Not only in Aspen, but all across the West. Apex foolishness had been tested for centuries, from the gold mines of Silesia to the tin mines of Cornwall, and had hardly ever carried the day. Despite ill-advised new Colorado and Nevada statute establishing the primacy of the apex, public sentiment was so against the notion that around the great Comstock and Leadville works, jury after jury ignored statute and ruled for the sideliners.

Now here it was again, a Hydra whose heads would not stay lopped off.

Over the past two years, Sutton's and Gabe Tacker's attorneys had initiated enough apex-versus-sideline lawsuits to paper the halls of Congress. They'd finally prevailed on Judge Theodore Percy of Denver's high court to hear the question again this fall. Judges, unlike juries, were apt to favor the apex. If Percy ruled in favor of Sutton and Tacker, who controlled most of the apex claims on Aspen, Smuggler, Highlands and Ashcroft peaks, they would own a monopoly across Aspen's four principal mountains and two mine districts. Moreover, if the matter lingered much longer at law, the sideline boys would run out of money and forbearance. Big Gabe Tacker owned an ample supply of both.

Only this morning, on his way to climb up over the hump into Leadville, Sutton had ridden that gelding of his, a nervy black single-footer he called Arsenic, to the Pearly and caught Calvin outside the shafthouse. Calvin's teeth grated at sight of the slick mouth and arctic eyes. Silky as a puma, Sutton wheeled around the adit. The gelding was so close Cal could count the old spur gouges where the black's hair had grown in white.

"I'm on my way over the divide. I thought you'd want to hear, Krueger, that the apex hearing has been rescheduled for the thirtieth day of August."

Calvin's heart skidded in his chest. That hearing had been slated for mid-October. Now the villains were tampering with the court calendar.

Sutton's tone was imperious. "When Percy decides in our favor, your wrong-minded friends will be sitting high and dry on claims they've worked for nought."

"We have right on our side," bristled Cal.

"We have the law on ours," sniffed Sutton. He sat up on his sixteen-hand mount, looked down on Cal and fired a parting shot. "You may as well lay aside that pick, Krueger. Enjoy the holiday. When the matter is settled our way, your work will be finished here. The Pearly is a sideline claim. Lease or no lease, she'll revert to me."

If Cal had felt low before, he now felt so down he could have been in his grave. In place of three more months, he'd have something less than eight weeks to locate color. He'd tried to put a good face on matters for his dear wife, who did not suspect the half of it. He'd not only wagered their savings, he'd taken out a mortgage on their cabin and city lot. *A mortgage is like the poor*, he thought dejectedly. *It is always with you.*

"On the other hand," said Sutton, smiling a very small smile, "I'll be much obliged if you keep opening new drifts for me. Just don't blow yourself to smithereens."

Then he'd raked arsenic's flanks and headed up the pass.

####

CHAPTER TWO

MRS. GARRETT SUTTON

On the evening of the third of July, 1885, Emma Sutton leaned against her eiderdown pillows, and with a familiar sense of mourning, harked back to the passing of the judge.

When her father traveled, there had been a hole in Emma that could not be filled. Not with the droning condolences of church elders. Not with wringing hands nor weeping buckets into the void. Nate Phipps had been out of reach, wintering on the far side of the San Juans. Polly had ululated and chopped off tufts of course jet hair. Finally, wailed dry, she'd turned to stone—her stolid grief more unnerving than her howling. Emma, fainthearted and dazed, had stumbled as directionless as a locoed horse.

Garrett Sutton had moved unerringly into the void, making many treacherous journeys across the Great Divide on the Carson Bros. Stage or astride his high-stepping black. He'd forded the Arkansas in heavy spate, maneuvered the narrow, sawtooth heights of the Sawatch Range, boarded the D&RG Line at Granite Station and arrived in Denver picking cinders from his fastidious linen. Eventually Emma, numb and heart-sore, had taken to trudging in his wake, a marionette pulled by the slightest tug of a string. Garrett, ten years older, seemed to own the sense her pa valued. He sat a horse well, leaned down to whisper fetchingly in her ear. He escorted her to church services and to chaste afternoon teas. In time, she found herself looking forward to his visits like a welcome opiate after an amputation. He had taken the edge from her pain.

Though the memory was hurtful, Emma thought back on the passions this man had once aroused. After a surfeit of grief, she'd suddenly been consumed with a frenzy to return to life. When at last Garrett came to her bed to cover her, she'd felt as unhinged as her mare Harriet being bred. In high fever, she'd paid Polly Panakarpo's disapproval little mind. The Ute woman muttered darkly, "Mistah Billy Goat *bad.* You hear me talk?"

"I hear you talk, chickey, chickey," she'd answered, making a rude Indian sign.

24

Tonight, shivering like a horse shaking the wet from its coat, she lay in her bed and forced more memories to the front of her mind. A year to the day after the judge's passing—which some in Presbyterian circles thought unduly hasty—Emma had changed out of her mourning dress to say her marriage vows. Her mind had not been on stitching "Bless This House" samplers, nor on setting bread to rise. Her thoughts were of climbing under the bed covers with the man who held her in thrall, her blood running hot as water at the boil.

Later, when Polly kept up her hen-pecking, Emma grew provoked. "Quit, you black savage! Quit your bicker and get out the trunks. We're bound for the Roaring Fork Valley over the Great Divide!"

As they jounced and rattled aboard the spring-rigged, cream-and-red-painted Carson Bros. coach, the exultant bride had felt the familiar blood rush that in the old circuit days signaled new country and fresh ventures. With snowy peaks and granite massifs growing nearer, the air as icy as the black-running creeks, the smell of spruce and fir as tangy as a balsam pillow, they'd climbed torturously behind successive teams from way station to way station, the driver cursing mightily, then leaning down from his seat to make his apologies to the ladies. They'd sidestepped boulders big as steam engines, crept along shelf ledge so narrow they dared not thrust an elbow out the coach windows. Struggling up and over what the driver called "the hump," they skirted valleys so far below that grazing sheep appeared the size of mites. Fourteen-thousand-foot peaks, like the gnarled and creased knuckles of upraised fists, wrote their names across the sky. Though Emma's backside was as sore as a bunion, her head buzzed with excitement. The air grew thinner and a maiden lady smelling of naphtha gasped and pitched over in a swoon, the snowy egret on her hat nearly jabbing the new Mrs. Sutton in the eye.

Alighting at last from the coach at the Aspen stage station, Emma unlimbered board-stiff legs, stumbled to the nearest horse trough, and dashed her face with cold water. Then she smoothed the intricate pleatings of her pink and white linen redingote over its matching dress and the latest S-shaped corset from Paris—worn in an effort to surprise and please Garrett. She climbed up onto the boardwalk for a good look. Hooding her eyes against the late afternoon sun, she spied a very different vista from home. Denver City sat with its back to the foothills, facing out on high prairie that stretched paper-flat, swept by unremitting wind. Aspen nestled deep and lofty in the heartland of the Rockies, in an 8,000-foot-high parkland with mountains rising out of its decks like the sails of a great schooner.

The station master, following her gaze, spoke beside her, "Park reaches forty miles down-valley—to the banks of the Grand River. We say 'down-valley' because she loses 3,000 feet in altitude. 'Spect you might's well say 'up-valley,' since she goes north and west."

"Prettiest town setting you'll ever see," he added.

Streets had been laid out wide, he explained, to allow for steadily increasing commerce. "Come a mid-May blackberry winter, you'll be hard-pressed to cross Cooper Street. Forty feet of spring mud, bogged-down mules and carts."

The station master was a short, stout man with button-bright eyes and a yen for gossip. "Name's Hines. Billy B. Hines. Seen by the manifest you're the new Mrs. Garrett Sutton. Hear you was once Little Emma Kershaw."

Emma nodded and smiled abstractedly, drinking in the ramshackle camp. Mountains on two sides were half stripped of trees. Prospect holes, shafthouses, stacked timber, and stamp mills abounded. Shacks, tents, and lean-to's squatted elbow to elbow, heaped helter-skelter. Cabins were roofed with unplaned boards, often in wackily differing lengths, looking only half thought out.

"Tell me, Mr. Hines, with all this fine space, how come folks to build so close?"

"Aw, they got some fool notion they want to winter snug. Dern idjits don't give a thought to fire. One bucket of hot ashes thrown on a back stoop, one overheated stove, and a whole dern row'll go up." Mr. Hines placed a pinch firmly behind his lower lip. "These here shacks is one hundred percent green wood—bleed sap all summer, curl up like dried beefsteak in winter—but they burn, all right."

Steam dollies, sampling works, and hoists hissed and threw off clouds of sulphurous yellow smoke. From somewhere on the mountainside rose the snarling of a sawmill. Draymen shouted orders. Donkeys brayed. Roosters quarreled over whose turn it was to crow.

Just then a giant powder explosion rocked the camp, startling Emma so her stylish silk bonnet, anchored by a lone hatpin, flew askew. Billy Hines plucked a shiny nickel-plated railroad watch from his vest pocket and eyed it importantly. "Four o'clock shift change," he announced. "Setting off charges before the swing-shift muckers come on duty."

Emma knew something of silver operations, though in her youth she had experienced mostly gold excavation. She had almost forgotten a mine camp's thrilling bustle. She sensed that the judge had been right. She could have found her proper home.

A young mine nipper, his face black with powder, a worn, formless hat in hand, came rushing up. "M-m-mister Sutton'll b-be along, Missus. The b-basta—er, he's h-h-holed—er, held up…You—you stay here!" The nipper, his sharp little face pinched with worry, gulped, turned and scooted back up the mountain to the mine offices before Emma could blurt out a how-de-do or hand him a few coins.

Avoiding the deep ruts worn by carriage wheels in past wet, she strode across Cooper Street to the boardwalk on the other side. Within minutes she was calling, "Why, hidey, yourself, Josh Peterman! Good to see you! Land, if it isn't Tom Bigelow." And she shook a big, warm, splintery hand, her clasp as firm as Bigelow's.

Popping her head in the open doorway of a gunshop, she cried, "Jacob Levy, you sly rascal." Jake was a longtime prospect partner of Uncle Nate Phipps. "You've gone and got you a fine-looking wife. Or a mighty handsome store clerk, one!" Plump, shiny-faced Bertha Levy beamed, wiped inky fingers on a rag, and was introduced by her proud husband. "Got us three fine sons, Little Emma," he called after her out the door. "Have you to supper soon as you'll come!"

Some of the gathering men could not restrain themselves. They threw burly arms around her as if she were a long-lost child.

When Garrett Sutton finally wheeled up in a splashy black and red landau, he was not pleased to find his entrance superseded. His bride stood in the center of an unseemly crowd, the men stretching to call greetings and shout out shared recollections. Garrett, his face drawn in disapproving lines, was reminded of a tawdry traveling show. But if he was out of sorts, Emma herself was tickled. She was to be more thankful than she knew for old friends in new country.

Coming back to the present with a start, Emma stretched firm-thewed legs across the plump feather mattress, her skin dappled with leaf shades cast by the rising moon. She noted that the tick and mosquito bites around her boot lines, contracted while hoeing cabbage heads in the garden and tracking buckskin up Hunter Creek, hardly showed. She'd been dousing with witch hazel so she wouldn't anger the bites with her scratching and get Garrett's dander up.

She thought wearily of how, a mere two years ago, she had fled mosquitoes, dutifully trussed herself in hurty whalebone corsets, pinned her hair down tight. She'd soon learned that her insignificant bosom and careless coiffures—tendrils of rebellious hair escaping her hair bun—did not suit her husband. Nor did he approve her lean look. A string-bean body and good head were not the style. The style was short and plump and soft-minded. Emma was weedy and rope-muscled and strong-willed.

Though no corset laces were about to choke off her wind, nor any iron-willed husband curb her spirit, Garrett had, she thought, damn well tried.

Gradually she had come to see her husband as the flim-flammer he was. It was adversity that had laid him bare.

In the late autumn of their wedding year, when the aspen leaves had turned to doubloon gold, the scrub oak a flaming orange, and the wooly bear caterpillars had grown broad black bands, her husband had stormed and paced their parlor, his face magenta with fury. "That bookkeeper the stockholders sent out from Cincinnati is undervaluing the accounts! I'll have the man horsewhipped!" His anger was so irrational that Emma, having taken in talk around camp, judged the silver had either played out—or in some mines, never appeared at all.

Then, in January, a warm chinook wind blew down from the Wyoming territory. There was the drip and trickle of unseasonable thaw. The ensuing instability undercut a massive cornice of snow up-mountain by Tourtelotte Park. The loosed avalanche tore down the steeps with the force of a giant battering ram, the mines' trouble whistles shrieked and the bell atop the Durant Street fire tower clanged, more spine-chilling than the screams of a cougar in the night.

"It's the Hallelujah!" bellowed Garrett's foreman Bull Mudgett, pounding at their front entryway. "The Hallelujah Mine's slid!"

The wet, heavy snow had carried away half the Hallelujah shafthouse, burying four men at the bottom of the shaft, trapping others in tunnels and cross-drifts. Every able-bodied man in town—aided by numbers of women—rushed headlong to Aspen Mountain with picks and shovels and even dug barehanded until their knuckles were skin-stripped to the bone. They were too late for the four trapped in the shaft cage. The young Welshman Olwen Davies lived, but his arm was so shattered that Doc Alderfer could do nothing but fuse it in a permanent, claw-like grip.

Emma carried baskets of provender to the grieving families. Garrett, concerned only for his mine's destruction, scoffed at her concern for his people's welfare.

"They know the risks when they elect to go underground," he'd sniffed. She had tucked her personal bank drafts in the baskets, telling the wives and mothers with their sorrowing, hope-fled Welsh and Cornish faces, that the money was a small consolation from her husband. Though they recognized the lie, they felt too kindly toward the missus to tongue-lash her man.

Within weeks, both the Columbine's and the Pearly Everlasting's output were so poor that Garrett let the Pearly out on leasehold. At this, her husband's dark inner core displaced any tenderness he might have owned. The man who had heretofore been a lynchpin of his community now imagined a foe in every smiling face. Never a coward, he became a shameless bully. Though he remained the picture of gentility, he harbored not an ounce of pity. At length it dawned on Emma that he no longer loved her—if indeed he had ever cared for her at all. Garrett, it appeared, had needed the judge's bequests for his misbegotten mines. Her heart scalded, she faced the truth. She had been well and truly duped. She took to mouthing the words aloud, not shrinking from them. Furiously blacking the stove or oiling harness, she repeated in ringing tones, "I've been duped! Hoodwinked!" Polly stood by in graven silence, her face shamed for her missus.

From the start, Garrett had considered his headstrong young wife little more than a vexatious child. It was beyond him how the daughter of a noted jurist, with a not inconsiderable dowry, came to vault onto a horse like a wild Indian, shoot, skin, and butcher game and pack it in from the wilderness, work like an indentured servant, cuss like a bullwhacker, or care so little for bonnets and beads. Or why she should be partial to a grizzled squaw-woman who glared at him like he was a pile of pig leavings. When they wed, Garrett had planned to deal with Emma in short order. Yet the more he determined to shape his wife to his liking, the more she stiffened against him. As he lost his grip on his mine operations, he had more need than ever to rule his household. Emma plagued him like a bur under a saddle, and he carped about every little nitpick: her management of their meals, their household accounts, his collars wilting for want of starch.

Emma, in her turn, was in a limbo of the self. She had not been reared hateful. Nor, God knew, with peacock sensibilities. Though it went against every law of dutiful matrimony, it was not in her to bear continued abuse. The judge had taught her to be a fighter.

Polly was a constant sticking point. Garrett ranted across the nickle-plated Otis Leander parlor stove, "I will not have that savage underfoot! And I am fed up with your goddamed jibbering!"

Emma, hands planted on hips, declared, "This so-called savage has saved my skin more times than I can count." Her eyes sparked like lantern flares.

"What's more," she'd added defiantly, "I favor jabbering a little Ute."

Some months past, at the Sunday dinner table, Garrett had eyed their venison roast, his handsome face twisted with disdain. Emma had shot the buckskin high above Maroon Lake. Quartered the animal, cut poles for a travois, and ridden down-mountain through the streets to Bullion Row as bloodied as a red savage. Almost as unseemly, the squaw had stuffed the roast with sage and field plums—outlandish fare to a man raised on plain boiled beef brisket. With one swat, the outraged Garrett had sent her mother's best Moss Rose serving platter to the carpet, the venison haunch flying, succulent juices coursing down the dining entry's tasseled velvet portieres, over the wrinkled nose of the pug dog Chester asleep on his old muslin cushion in a corner, and across the long, crisp white apron of the quaking hired girl, Bridget O'Reilly.

"This meat tastes like pig swill!" he'd blustered. "It's a wonder to me why you insist on hunting down meat, why we have that dirty Indian in our scullery—or why you cannot serve a proper beef roast and conduct dignified dinners like other households." He glowered at the squaw, at the Irish hired girl's bristling carroty hair, at the scowling three-legged pug dog and at a dingy white cat named Sneffels suckling a large, mewling litter under the black walnut sideboard. To Garrett's eyes, this higgledy-piggledy domestic scene was the final indignity in a litany of outrages.

Eyeing him levelly, Emma inquired, "Proper? Dignified? With broken crockery and tobacco chaws besmirching our floors and furnishings?"

"'A man's duty,'" Garrett quoted haughtily, "is not to work around the house. It is to make work for others."

Emma snorted. He'd more than once called her attention to that hogwash in a sanctimonious *Proper Housekeeping* tract by a British fop named Silas Eastlake.

One week ago as they'd prepared to attend church services, her husband had looked her over, his mouth turned down in a querulous apostrophe, and sniffed, "A lady should have skin like English porcelain. You, Emma, have been prancing under the sun 'til you're freckled as a hen egg." He wished a wife of his to look suitably wan, to mince like a peahen—a proper contretemps to his own stately progress. Emma would never in her life boast lily-white skin. Nor was it in her to mince. She strode.

This morning, before heading to Leadville to pay attention to more silver mines and lewd women, the last words her husband spoke were, "I will be back when you have climbed down from that outlandish July Fourth wagon."

She had consented, albeit grudgingly, to appear as "Liberty" in the Appalachia Society's July Fourth parade tableau. But only after Mrs. Ollie Davidson insisted, "You're the only woman tall enough to play the part, Emma." The society also knew they could count on her not to swoon. Garrett, readying himself to depart, had looked so pained that it struck Emma he seemed wistful.

"I don't know why I expect you to keep up appearances, Emma. You have never in your life cared a fucking fig for them. Look at you now," he'd said resignedly, fastening his silver-chased Remington in its scabbard on Arsenic's saddle. "Grass stains on your skirts and horseshit all over your boots."

For an instant, Emma almost pitied him. He had had such high hopes for enterprises that failed him. He had wished for a wife with a hundred graces it was not in her to provide. More from habit than fervor, she said, "Garrett, we live in a mine camp. Every woman in Aspen has shit on her boots."

Emma rolled over on her pillows, weary of being testier than a rusted bedspring. Sometimes she wished that she had not found her husband out. More than anything, with all her being, she wished the unspeakable had never happened.

####

CHAPTER THREE

LUTE KELLOGG

Deep in the Pearly, Cal Krueger felt his sand return. Only a minute before, he had come close to reaching for the bellrope from the windlass. When he gave a good tug, young Lute Kellogg, topside in the shivery mountain evening, would stumble from his bearskin covering, likely bung a knee. The boy had had another growth spurt, and his long legs tangled like a cat's cradle. Lute would cuss a little. Then rouse Gracious the mule, start the winch, and haul his employer up in the deepening dark.

Only lately had Cal reverted to mule and boy power. The engines that ordinarily drove the hoists in the Pearly's main shafthouse required a full head of steam, cords of firewood, an extra work force, and cash money he no longer owned. *Dumb animals and shirttail boys—that is how low I have fallen*, he thought gloomily.

Early in the fall of the year, Lute, who odd-jobbed for the Widow Wickersham and a few prosperous whore women, had caught Cal outside the rough-chinked cabin that served as the First Presbyterian Church. "Mr. Krueger, sir, my name is Luther Kellogg, and I'm lookin' to find real work—man's work. I ain't—I'm not—cut out to errand for a passel of women. Even a fine widow woman like Miz Wickersham."

The boy's lanky frame, his strawberry roan hair and fair skin set him apart from the usual run of stocky, dark-complected Cornishmen, Slovaks, and Italians. For a youngster alone in the world, he owned a straightforward gaze. "And sixteen is too old to be a no-account mine nipper," he'd added in a rush. "I'm right handy with stock—and I'll work for bottom wages any time you need an extra hand." There was pleading in his eyes as he stood there in the outgrown shirt he'd pressed himself, streaks from the sadiron marking the front.

Cal had taken a shine to the boy. He had invited him to his supper table, introduced him to the works of R.W. Emerson and Samuel T. Coleridge across platters of Vinnie's fried ham and potato fritters, and put him on as often as funds permitted, which had been little of late. Lute Kellogg still fetched and carried for the widow and the whore girls.

Last night at supper, Vinnie had piled Cal's and Lute's plates with chicken potpie, pieces of plump white meat steaming in the pale, bubbling gravy, and said, "I know all seven days of the week is the same to you, Cal, even the Sabbath. But July the Fourth is not your ordinary day. I won't have you blasting nor mucking a minute of it—nor working young Lute neither. The boy has little enough time for frolic."

"It's a good thing," said Cal. "At the rate he's springing up, he won't be an easy keeper."

"I don't mind the work, missus, honest I don't," Lute had protested. He'd eyed Vinnie Krueger with devotion. Her brown hair dappled with grey was homey-like, her big dark eyes filled with kindness. She touched everything around her with a sort of magic. Cedar waxwings, their sulphur-yellow plumage gleaming, held congregations in her yard. So did flocks of grosbeaks, their rosy breasts flashes of sunrise against winter snow. In summer, her sweet peas sprang up like rainbows untethered, unmatched anywhere in camp. And, as he had told his friend Scooper Hurd, "She makes the best damned potlikker I've et—ate—in my whole life." If he could stick his hand in a poke and pick out a mother, she would be just like the missus, right down to the hair-bun on her neck and the work knots on her knuckles.

Cal surveyed the charges the crew had set in the headwall, ready for him to fire as he left. He was not only employing sprats and mules, but also old-style black powder. The new giant powder, called dynamite, was safer. But it cost dear. And its fumes were worse than a dead mole in a cistern. His air was close as it was. This far corner was thick and smoky from the shale oil in the rock. The smoke, together with the cloying smell of wet timber and his fatigue, caused him a turn of dizziness. He leaned against the drift's cold edges and shook his head to clear it. He regreted that he had fallen behind in his ventilating, although installing air pipes took anxious time from the digging. He laid aside his mattock, its heavy oaken stock worn from his relentless grip, its pick-end and adz-end gleaming sharp in the yellow candlelight. Not only had he loaded a last tramcar, he had picked almost a half-foot from this side section. The drift ceiling, at five and a half feet, was not high enough for him to stand erect. The cruel bent of his back caused an ache that numbed him to the roof of his mouth. Yet Cal Krueger's resolve, like his legs, held firm. With the lease payment over him like a noose, he could not let the tunneling be.

An unexpected spate of loose dirt struck him sharply from above. There was a deep groan, as if the earth were giving birth. With the cost of timber ever in mind, Cal knew that he had been spare with the shoring. Spare, but ample, he reassured himself uneasily as another harsh groan followed on the first. He ran his calloused hand up and down the main drift support, certain it had not shifted. With a sudden start, he recalled that Lute was no longer topside. Cal had raised a message in the cage some time back, "Lute, go home. Leave Gracious in the thills with the tickler attached. I will hoist myself."

It was chancy having nothing but a lop-eared mule on the big hoist-cable whim above. But Gracious was steady in the traces. Lute had earned a reprieve. Tomorrow, for a blessed change, the lad would be shed of dawn-to-dark choring. No one in his right mind would order up a lick of work on the most hell-for-leather holiday of the year. Come July Fourth, Aspen let down her hair like a wanton woman. Camp wives squandered hard-saved coins on sprigged yard goods for fresh aprons and slat bonnets. Men layered deep with half-a-year's grease and woodsmoke appeared at wash houses and were soaped to a froth. Out-at-the-heels prospectors bought new red flannel shirts so stiff they stood of their own accord. "And I'm as addlepated as the next," Cal grunted aloud. He had declared a double holiday—as well be hanged for a sheep as a goat. "No swing shift this evening, boys. You'll need a good rest before the festivities tomorrow," he'd ordained as if he were John Jacob Astor presiding behind an opulent walnut-wood desk. *There was nothing so incongruous*, he thought, *as the largesse of a man living on the smell of an oily rag.*

He cocked an ear at the timbers, still moaning as if they carried the weight of the world, and rubbed impatiently at the sweat salt blurring his sight. There were pitfalls worse than a battlefield's in a mine drift. One miner in four got himself killed or maimed. Cal had held many a life in his own able hands. He'd been a skilled engineer amid topside machinery in other men's works, his eyes glued to gauges that measured air purity and pressure, ears fine-tuned to the codes of whistles that signaled, "Lower the hoist!" "Raise the cage!" And those that blew, "Man down!" or shrieked "Trouble!" He had averted more than his share of disasters and owned an enviable safety record. Men in the mines had come to count on him.

Now here he was, back underground. Not for the first time he wondered if he might be growing heedless of his own safety. Of late he could scarcely get shut of dreaming. He pictured the look of delicate glacier lilies on the high trail to Triangle Pass, visioned shift workers winding down Ajax Hill of an autumn evening, their headlamps a girdle of stars wrapping the mountain, recollected the great bull elk he'd surprised in Mountain Boy Gulch, his rack so heavy he had looked the weary king with a heavy crown.

Cal Krueger's mind did not run to the commonplace. He had taught a little school, was partial to debate, could argue politics, iambic pentameter, or military maneuver, even in a pinch, theosophy. He was fond of talking a little Plato with Deke Burdine, that well-schooled companion who kept the White Elephant Saloon. And now and again he attended meetings of the Shakespeare Society, although that was before the Pearly got him in her grip. He savored simple texts from Thomas Carlyle, rolling them around like a mellow cheroot. "Work alone is noble...a life of ease is not for any man..." Emerson suited him too. "Sloth, like rust, consumes faster than labor wears—while the used key is always bright."

"It would not hurt you to remember a pretty verse or two," teased Vinnie at intervals. "Something with love and fair maidens to it."

Of late, with the specter of ruin pressing in, he had taken to speaking to his own listening self, to companions lost in the war, lost in Indian country, lost in the digs. No one knew better, unless it was Vinnie, the hazards of such woolgathering. Her final warning about the holiday echoed in his head. "And it don't mean, Calvin, that you are to work in that hole like a body possessed to make up for the time lost at the festivities."

She had placed a worn hand on his shoulder. "I fear you'll go slack, Cal, let your mind boggle. Move into a stope before all your charges has let loose—that I'll have me a forty dollar funeral to arrange down to Willard Arey's." The faint tremor of her fingers indicated the terrible grief that would follow.

"Tarnation!" Cal muttered aloud. His thinking sidelined, he couldn't recall if Needle and Pete placed seven—or eight—of those charges. Black powder used live blast caps, which were volatile. If a forgotten charge was struck with so much as a nut pick, Vinnie need not bother with Willard Arey's Burial Parlor & Fine Furnishings. His grave would be the Pearly Mine.

Drift water seeped through, damping his boots. The smell of wet timber was strong, the taint of the morning blasting heavy, the cordite in the corner still thick as phlegm in a clogged throat. The stuff made his grave blue eyes water, causing small rivulets to wind down cheeks black as creek bottom.

"I thank the Lord that Nate is due in tonight," he breathed as he again swung the pick in a rhythm as familiar as the beat of his heart. "He'll get air moving double-quick." *In more ways than one*, was his thought. Despite his gloom, Cal chuckled. Nate liked to talk a man's ears off after he'd wandered the hills a spell. He'd be bursting with tales from other camps, news from far sides of the hump.

Cal had not seen his old companion for three months, since the late-April day he had snowshoed around the Raggeds from the Tincup country and waded through spring runoff into the Clarendon dining room. "Hear that lease hasn't taken hold yet," he'd remarked to Cal, who'd reached an arm and pulled out a pressed oakwood chair.

"Not so's you'd notice, Nathaniel."

When Nate had tucked his knees under the table and his napkin in at the neck, Cal went on, "The work is near seven months gone. We are one hundred feet from the main shaft and two levels down and have laced that dig with stopes and crosscuts. I have not struck enough good grade to silver-plate a teapot."

As Nate reached to hook the strap of his old Needle gun over the knob of the sideboard mirror, Cal raised his coffee to his lips." I am belly-deep to a tall horse, my friend." He lowered the cup. "I had no business taking on this affair. Silver mining has outgrown me. A man can no longer be sure about the ground below or mine law above—who owns what, whose rights are safeguarded. It is a rich man's game. A game for Garrett Suttons with silk hats, clean fingernails, and carpetbags of cash money."

Nate had never seen his old partner so low. "Just keep your mind's eye on that lode of silver down there. Good ore can run scared and she can run deep. Takes all a man's tricks to pin her."

"You're a fine one to chirp, Nate Phipps. You are not down under, digging your way to timbuctoo."

"That is because I have the sense I was born with. I like traipsing the hills, but I ain't married to the silver under the covers."

Nate hailed the wait girl. "Say, Persis, I will have me the usual. And some of Mrs. McClaren's scones with chokecherry preserves—that is, if she ain't quit canning and cooking and took to the stage to sing and dance."

The idea of her employer, that gnarled bundle of sticks and kindling, performing onstage caused the waitress to throw her apron over her head and hen-trot to the kitchen in a fit of cackling.

Tucking his napkin end inside his shirt buttons, Nate asked, "Are you digging this roadway single-handed, or have you got you assistance with the work?"

"Two on faith and one on shares. Vinnie is boarding Needle and Young Frank in exchange for shiftwork. Pete Beard is working on faith and about to live on charity."

"Cal, I have long entertained a secret hankering for your wife. For Vinnie's sake, I plan on coming to your aid."

"Let us hope you have found a gold-toothed, ore-busting tycoon who wishes to buy me out for ten thousand in cash money."

"Nosiree-bob," Nate said complacently. "I, myself, aim to help dig."

Cal groaned. "Nathaniel, that is on a level with helping me button up my pants. I can manage the job better on my own."

Persis plunked down a platter of steaming scones and poured coffee so oily it glistened like a slick. Nate dug contentedly into a tin plate swimming with eggs and mush, employing a hot scone for dippy bread. "You know that I can scarcely abide going underground, Cal. But with you near the end of your tether, it is a horse of another color. That Ajax incline will try a man," he added between bites. "But the Pearly owns more than idle promise, and I'll dig with you 'til we find her."

"I envy your faith, you old pole-picker."

Nate finished downing his fried ham and carefully wiped his mustache. He was finicky about his appearance.

When Aggie McClaren herself triumphantly produced a bowl of small red strawberries. Cal said, "Thunder, Nate. I have not seen a strawberry since last summer. Aggie must be sweet on you."

"Yep," said Nate complacently. "Soon as she's a wider woman, I got first call on her." He beamed conspiratorially at the Scotswoman who owned the hotel.

Agnes Mary McClaren had suffered a siege of mountain fever years before. She had nearly died of it, though she went back to nursing others before she was steady on her feet. The fever had left her yellow and hairless. Yet what her countless admirers mainly noticed was two kindly, intelligent eyes, never mind the long nose between. "Go on with yer blether, mon," she scolded as she wielded the crumb scraper and tidied the table, her face pleasured under the cambric bonnet she never removed.

Nate ate the strawberries one at a time, covered with cream and dipped in a painted china sugar bowl. Then he paused to blow on the coffee he'd saucered to cool. "I am committed to prospect with Moose Barrows in Eagle country come full thaw. But when I get back for the Independence Day doings, I'll crawl down under and scratch like a scalded cat. And I will do her on trust."

Cal's throat swelled with feeling. There was no beat of a friend like Nate. He planned to have him serve at his funeral. He could even sing, if he was of a mind. Nate loved singing more than taking in mountain air, though his voice was enough to make a congregation's hair fall out.

"Got any shareholders can swing a pick 'til I get back here?"

"Nate, you know Ward Moyer's huckstering." The camp's leading mine broker had sold Pearly shares to Grandma Tecoucic, Sister Coon, and half the lewd women on the Row.

"When it comes to selling a bill of goods," said Cal, "he can't hold a candle to Sutton. That silky deceiver is no doubt laughing up one sleeve and down the other, him with my last red cent and me with nothing but mud and tailings."

"Now, Calvin, you are about over the dog. It'll be a pure picnic sliding down the tail."

Cal reached for his round tin lunch box on a ledge of shelf rock. The pork and sauerkraut in the top half were gone, the coffee in the bottom ice cold. He took a sip, hefted his mattock, and calculated that the new right angle into the mountain seemed likeliest for fresh digging. Using the broad end of his pick, he gentled away loose rock, his touch as delicate as a woman picking lint for bandages.

I will just start a cut this direction. Then I will call it a day, he promised himself.

As his mattock raised and lowered, the pick nicked an untouched sidewall. "Sounds hollow," he muttered. He tested the wall more deliberately. Paused, concerned. "Doesn't make sense for dead air that direction."

He could not have struck a Columbine stope. That dig was two hundred feet to the east. He swung his pick end cautiously. The sound was the thunk of a fist on an empty cask. Moving uneasily, he pried at the footwall gangue. As he did, the rock gave way with the explosive pop of a cork bursting from an empty vinegar bottle. In the blackness, he sensed sudden airless space.

Could be a spring, he thought apprehensively. Miners lived in fear of flooding. Worse, a gas pocket. No miner lit a thoughtless match where flammable gas might lurk, and all miners chewed plug in place of smoking cigars. He sniffed, wary as a bird dog. Detecting no fetid odors, he struck a sulphur match. He waited, touched the flame to a long wood splinter, lit it, and sheltered the wick of a big number seven candle. With the flame probing like a palsied finger, he leaned guardedly around the jagged opening.

Squeezing his upper body partway through, he thrust out the candle, its light trembling for want of air, and peered inside.

Cal Krueger gasped. Before him rose what miners call a bridal chamber, a vast space shimmering like Ali Baba's treasure cave. In the candlelight, silver winked from every wall. Bands of ruby silver and strands of wire silver refracted and danced in the flame. In its usual state Aspen silver lurked mostly unseen in galena and agentite, often black as pitch, waiting for the cyanide process that would release its inner glory. Here he had struck what geologists call a vug, a cache of ore untarnished by oxygenated atmosphere. Ore to outshine the Arctic lights.

"Allmachtiger Gott!" whispered Cal.

The enormity of his discovery struck him like the ague. His legs wobbled. His stomach moved off-center. His head spun. Calvin Krueger, man of discipline, could not instruct his own body. Slowly his head cleared and suddenly, chillingly, he knew this was a strike men would kill for. His mind accepted that he'd located a bonanza to spark stampedes, incite gunfights, and ignite warfare.

Sinking to his knees, he put his bowed head in big, rough hands. "Lord God," he prayed, "I swear I never asked for this. I never did."

So thunderstruck that he'd momentarily lost touch with his good sense, Cal was only dimly aware of a deep, ominous grumbling, then of the panicked squeal of rats. Just as it came to him that, in opening the vug, he could have undercut a bearing wall, a great sucking of air hurled him from his knees. There was the harsh, brutal crack of rock tearing asunder. Too late, he struggled to run. When the tidal wave of stone and dirt crashed around him, he swam, leadenly driving arms and legs in a powerful current. Then the mountain engulfed him.

####

CHAPTER FOUR

BRIDGET O'REILLY

As the moon moved beyond her window, Emma reached for a lucifer match and emery paper to light her bedside lamp. When the wick flared up, she peered grudgingly at the carved steeple clock that tocked as monotonously and intrusively as a metronome, brassily shutting out the sweet-warbling nightbirds and peeper singsong coming from the Hallam Lakes. This whole overdone Bullion Row manor, built by Garrett without a by-your-leave from her, had the musty aura of a funeral establishment. Even in the knife-cutting cold of an Aspen winter, she threw wide the sashes to let in draughts of fresh air. Worshipper of moonlight and sunflowers, Emma Sutton was no more suited to the confines of her overbearing house than to her parlous marriage.

She dropped her book and leaned back in the only furnishing she cherished: the delicate federal bed from her Bostonian great-grandmother. Its glistening cherrywood and dainty fluted posts were as out of place amid the deep-carved black walnut guestroom suite as a thoroughbred in a corral of plow horses. Emma had been born in this bed. *Expect I'll die in it too*, she mused wistfully.

From the foot of Pratt Mountain came the triumphant yip-yipping of coyotes over a kill. Down at the bottom of the yard, Harriet Tubman whickered softly. In the spring, at the end of a hard winter, when the dreary, rag-gray snow of a mountain May-time at last ran away into the mud and thickets of mountain mahogany put forth soft green shoots by the creekbeds, Emma whistled Harriet out of her stall and brushed vigorously at her shaggy winter coat. Later, the rough coat shed, the mare shone like chocolate simmering in a candy kettle. The fine Huntley & Craig sidesaddle Garrett had pointedly bought Emma hung unused in the barn. When she rode, she threw on her old herding saddle, hitched the front of her skirts back through her legs, tucked them up into her waistband behind, jumped aboard Harriet, and galloped astride along the creek trails to escape house and husband. She was enraptured by skies blue as harebells. She caught her breath at hundreds of dark eyes peering from the pearly trunks of aspen groves. She breathed deep the first hot sun smells on burgeoning buffalo grass. She reveled in the cool balm of spruce needle beds where she dismounted to lie on her back, survey the sweep of sky, and ignore dropping ticks.

Only of late had her zest for the mountains flagged. Desperately, she fought to separate her feelings from her life. To hold her head high, not get down in the mouth.

Aspen, eager for entertainment, imported amateur harpists and down-at-the-heels minstrel shows. Even suffragettes were given a courteous reception. More often, camp people created their own entertainment. Emma, always in demand, took on as many theatrical roles as she could handle, crying out her chagrin and pain on makeshift stages. Harking back to last winter's role as Willa, the deserted wife in *My Silent Journey*, she was dismayed to feel an uninvited tear tracing raggedly down her cheek. She kicked aside the stone hot water bottle at her feet, threw back the bed covers and jumped up to lean from her window and yell into the night, "Oh, I will not die here like a poisoned rat in a hole!" She shook her fist at the mighty hump to the east, the Great Divide. "Mr.Congreve will have none of it! Nor will I!"

Bridget O'Reilly had drawn the heavy damask portieres tight. As usual, Emma had tied them back, letting the lace undercurtains flutter like moths in the cold night breeze. Her sudden histrionics awoke the dog Chester, who staggered up wide-eyed, then circled, and settled back on his sleeping pillow. Polly snatched open the door, gave Emma a careful once-over, muttered under her breath, and closed it again. The dramatics further rattled a hootie owl, which rose from a lower limb of a side-yard cottonwood tree with agitated cries. In her room behind the kitchen pantry, Bridgie O'Reilly heard the missus shout and the owl call. Snatching up an oil lamp and the hems of her flannelette nightgown, her heart pounding in her plump bosom, she scrambled up the back stairs. Hopping around the squaw that was hunkered by the door, she rushed inside, set down the lamp, crossed herself, and hurried to the window, scolding, "An owl in the night is turrible luck, Mum. T'is meaning someone's t' die."

Emma refrained from pointing out that somewhere, someone was always about to die. Bridgie yanked at the portieres. "And you'll be ketchin' yer own death. There be mi-asmas in the air will steal yer good health away." The girl's earnest, pink-freckled face was flushed with alarm. Her round little body quivered. Emma pictured the burnt orange hair, released from its mop cap, bristling like porcupine quills. She quelled a grin, absent-mindedly scratched a mosquito bite, and set to unwinding her bound-up hair, pins dropping in cadence with falling stars in the July sky. "Damn foolishness, girl. And don't go pulling those curtains again. Doc Alderfer says fresh air is salubrious. Look at the Indians."

"Jaysus and Mary, Mum, look if it please you. T'is scarin' me to my grave, they are."

The county Kerry girl, though widowed, was but eighteen and unworldly. She considered Indians in a class with banshees and skirted skittishly around Polly Panakarpo. Bridgie gave thanks the squaw guarded the doorway since that fearful night the mister had savaged her missus. But she still crossed herself and muttered feverish incantations against Injun ha'nt. *Small wonder*, she thought primly, the Utes were called the Black Ones by the Cheyennes and Araps. The Ute woman's face was as dark as old scalp leather. One blacksnake eye never blinked. The other had turned the color of sour buttermilk. Bridgie's friend Mavis Beachey insisted that Polly had got the blind eye hexing milk cows and frightening tiresome children. People in this camp had no use for Chinese or red hostiles. They tolerated the squaw because of Miss Emma.

Every Sunday morning, to the Irisher's unmitigated terror, Polly rose from the kitchen floor where she mended tack while the stovepot bubbled with pot likker. She harnessed the Suttons' pair of prancy sorrels and drove Bridgie at breakneck speed to early Mass. Garishly attired in high beaded moccasins—of all the tribes, the Utes turned out the finest beadwork—buckskin leggings, and a store-bought calico overdress cinched with an old cavalry belt, which held her long fletching knife and throwing hatchet, she grinned and raced through the streets. Bridgie, upright in serviceable black serge, gripped the carriage side and her rosary and prayed to Ste. Agathe to preserve her. (Following Mass, Bullion Row and Hopkins Street churchgoers on foot knew enough to keep to the ditches.)

While on her knees on the rough-hewn boards of St. Mary's Church, Bridgie worked her beads feverishly for the missus. Though the woman could be a trial, Bridgie cherished her like her own. No idle twit, Emma taught Bridgie her letters, tied on an apron and piled into the steamy business of soap and jelly-making. She was a follower of the M. Oliver Hughes Home Formulary, employing its receipts for making butter coloring and stove blacking—her splotched hands forever causing the mister another fit of spleen. She beat the daylights out of carpets on their clotheslines, scrubbed the horse stalls, attacked weeds in her flowerbed "like Jesus," declared the

Widow Wickersham next door, "casting out the Philistines."

In Bridgie's mind, the dirt was done by these godforsaken mine camps: roosting places for women in hats big as bald eagles, for hard-faced females in pants toting guns and turning men off their mine claims, for whore girls packing pocket pistols. Even their next-door, the Widow Wickersham, was no better than she should be. Bridgie was aware of precisely which nights, and at what hour, Mr. G.B. Tacker's fancy cabriolet rolled quietly into the widow's back stableyard. Yet the missus chattered with the widow over their fence like she was as good as anybody.

In these faraway mountains, without an upright man to rein her in, Miss Emma thought and spoke as she pleased. In all her days Bridgie had never known of "quality" to blaspheme so. Nor had she heard of other proper ladies reading so much rubbish: honey-dipped verse, tracts on the vote for the female. Only last week, as was the missus' habit, she'd finished her morning chores, settled Bridgie and Polly at the big oak kitchen table, rustled her newspaper, and proceeded to read aloud from that Dunaway woman's column to "broaden your outlook, my dears."

"Abigail Dunaway says here that one-half of American women are little dolls," she'd read in her clear voice. She'd paused for a moment to peruse the next sentence, then her sides shaking, managed to finish, "the rest are drudges—and we are all fools."

At that, she had pounded the table, hooting and choking so that Polly had to tilt her upside down while Bridgie thumped her on the back.

When she'd caught her breath, the missus had sputtered to Bridgie, "Now don't you be lighting candles and counting beads for me, you scamp. I'll not soon wear a straitjacket, nor will I require eye spectacles. And my mind is not unsettled from too much reading." A broad grin belied her stern tone.

Bridgie had been shocked at the downward slide of the Sutton marriage. One wintry afternoon, so cold that, even in the direct rays of the late-day sun, the icicles hanging from their mansard roof did not lose a single drop of water, two sideliners appeared at the door, their faces wind-raw, hands on guns, expressions reaper-grim, demanding to see the mister. With him away in Denver City, Miss Emma had insisted they come in, sit, and warm themselves by the parlor coal fire. Though the missus attended temperance meetings, she knew when to pour a man a drink. After serving up double jiggers of Kentucky red whiskey, she assured the men she wished to be of assistance.

"We got grievances, ma'am," said the old sourdough known as Thistle Joe.

"Then I will hear them," she said. So they told her.

"H'it was that squinty-eyed Bull Mudgett," said peppery little Joe Flynn. Him and Denver Bob Bisbee."

"Shot our pard dead over to Leadville when he caught Mudgett with a pegged deck."

Emma was appalled. "But Mr. Mudgett is my husband's head man!"

"The shitheel's—pardon, ma'am—more'n Sutton's foreman…"

"Does your husband's work, clean or dirty. Stole our sideline papers off'n poor Fred's warm body and moved in on our digs…"

White-faced, Emma heard the men out—as did Bridgie, her ear to the folding parlor doors. That night Bridgie had to choke down three glasses of baking soda mix to quell her dyspepsia. The missus retired hugging her bones as if they might jump from her skin.

When Bull Mudgett himself appeared at their door, Bridgie skedaddled. Miss Emma could not, though the foreman gave no sign that her glares discomfited him. He addressed her with every civility. But he was a powerfully-put-together brute who somehow insinuated himself into their narrow storm entry until Emma was so crowded she found herself bent back like a half-pulled bow. She could feel his sour, heavy breath and count the overlarge pores on his skewed nose. His bear-greased mustache ends bristled near enough to cut her face. When he looked her all over and grinned, she felt as dirty as if he'd interfered with her.

She'd stormed at Garrett, "If that damned alley dog comes to this house and backs me into a corner again, I'll take the buggy whip to him!"

The mister had eyed her as if she were demented. "You have not told me of one outrage or wrong-doing, woman."

Emma had opened—then closed—her mouth. She had learned to be right still, to bide her time.

Bridgie heard of the Drama Society encounter through the Mavis Beachey trap lines. At their meeting, the missus had asked the weepy-eyed wife of the bookkeeper for the Columbine works why she and her husband were leaving Aspen. The woman had turned on her to hiss, "The mister fired Henry for refusing to falsify production figures to show those Cincinnati investors."

Then, not a month later, the whole camp learned of Sutton's questionable mine takeover which ruined Abijah Scowcroft and set his wife Mamie to fashioning millinery for their living.

At last Emma Sutton had had enough. That night, she'd refused to jump into bed at her husband's beckoning. Bridgie had been about to knock, the heated bricks and stone bottles for the bed in a basket on her arm. At the angry exchange coming from within, she came to a halt.

"It is a wife's duty to obey her husband, madam," the mister had shouted.

"And a man's to honor his life's companion." The missus could still her tongue no longer. "You may have bamboozled senators and a few dam fool, old churchwomen—but the good working people of this camp despise you." Her voice icy as a frozen cirque, she looked at him straight. "Honor does not enter into your thinking, Garrett. You besmirch my good name."

"I am a man of affairs, doing what business I must," he'd snapped, drawing himself to his full height. Emma surveyed this man she'd once considered comely. His dark eyes no longer seemed soulful—only muddied. The mouth she'd thought generous was sharp as a card cheat's. Their ill-considered marriage was as much on her head as his, she knew. Marrying a man with good looks was like eating a songbird for its bright plumage. The bird was apt to have a very bad taste.

"Business is buying and selling and turning an honest profit," she'd seethed. "Your business is monkey business. You would steal anything not red-hot or nailed down."

"Do not think I'd miss your so-called favors," he'd sneered. "Of late, I'd as soon prod a coal skuttle for all I feel of womanly charm."

"That inconvenience will not continue, Garrett, for I'll not enter your bed again."

Her husband retorted, "Nor will you refuse me again, madam."

"To the contrary. You have abused my spirit and misused my money for the last time. I have finally got me some of that mule sense Pa was concerned about. I've exchanged wires with his old law firm. They will be serving you with a writ of replevin over the misappropriation of my rightful inheritance. In particular, for your ill-advised purchase of the Columbine and Pearly Everlasting Mines."

Bridgie stood rooted to the hallway floor. As the mister's footsteps pounded toward the bedroom door, she shrank behind the back stair corner. Then the mister had turned, stalked across the room to a large mother-of-pearl letter, and shouted, "Very well then. As you are so all-fired close with your favors—and your goddamned fucking money—I will sign over the Pearly and the two of you can go to hell together!"

In the silence, Bridgie crept to the keyhole. At the big rococo corner desk, the mister had pulled out the original Pearly claim papers, his steel pen, and bottle of India ink and begun endorsing paper over to his wife in a furious scrawl. "The Columbine is mine, and I will fight you for her 'til you're whipped. But the Pearly will be in your name—there can be no misappropriation to it."

The missus had had the look of a rabbit in a snare. Pacing the bedroom, she'd wrestled an emotion new to her: fear. A lone woman without loving relations or resources was, she knew, cornered. Small wonder that wives at the mercy of tyrants turned to the hurdy-gurdy halls as their only escape.

Whirling, the missus declared, "I *have* it! I will join a traveling troupe— 'Mrs. Garrett Sutton: Elocutionary selections...Juggling...Pistol Shot *Extraordinaire!*'"

Later, Emma wondered miserably if malice aforethought had caused her to utter the only words guaranteed to make Garrett snap. He had sprung at her with a terrible cry, moving so swiftly that he'd knocked her half-senseless. Had she been alert, she would have larruped him back. When he ripped aside her silk peignoir, she'd cried out once, then lain mute as a corpse as he drove his post with all the force of a hard-headed core-driller, sticking with his work until he planted the hated seed that grew in her now.

Bridgie had tumbled down the back stairs, out through the kitchen and across the shadowy backyard to the barn, where Polly was forking hay. "Jaysus God, come quick!" she gasped. "H-he's...the Mm-m-mister is...oh Mother Mary, help the missus!" Polly threw aside her hayfork and ran. When they reached the upper bedroom, the mister, adjusting his clothes, his face dark as soot, thrust them aside as if pushing loose brush and briars from his path.

Polly went to Emma, gathered her in her arms, and began chanting a gutteral sing-song tune. She stopped only to order Bridgie to put the big teakettle on to boil, to fetch her parfleche of ointments and herbs.

Since that awful night, the iron-faced squaw kept vigil, her blanket roll by her missy's guestroom door. Nor did the mister venture near. Should he try, he knew he could entertain a knife in his belly.

Though Emma's face was occasionally tinged with its old merriment, the last of her innocence had fled. Bridgie suspected she would nevermore trust in a man's blandishments or his word. There was a hard edge to the missus' gaze that had never been there before.

####

CHAPTER FIVE

NATHANIEL PHIPPS

Step lively, Miss Lind," Nate Phipps urged the burro. "Tomorrow's the holiday. Got to leg it into camp on the double." He had fried up the last of his flour and sidemeat, and with the Fourth almost on him, had no time for shooting or plucking a fool hen. Cal Krueger might swear Nate could travel three days on a soda cracker and creek water—*but*, thought the prospector, *only in a hard pinch.*

Short rations were only half Nate's care. In larger measure, he was troubled over Cal digging himself deeper into that mine hole. "Move on out now," he urged the jenny.

In the blazing white light of mid-afternoon, his burro flicked rabbit ears and picked a deliberate path across the northeast saddle of Taylor Pass, her dainty hooves click-clicking over the jagged scree. Hundreds of like cuts, their fields of barbed avalanche rock stretching to the sky, sawtoothed these middle Rocky Mountains. Nate and Miss Lind had crisscrossed them all, through country too high, too rugged, and too far distant for cattlemen or ranchers. They had climbed the year-round glacier ice of the Italian peaks, stood atop the Cimarrons with blue lightning crackling from their hair, looked down from the Never Summer Mountains into the bleak, wintry tundra of North Park. They had trod the two-mile-high South Park grasslands where mountains of buffalo bones rested amid arrows from Ute and Arapaho hunts and battles. Up here next to the clouds was Yutah land, still wild and raw. No matter the day or month, Nate had the same sense of lunar landscape, felt forbidden wind from ancient peoples.

From his Ute wives, Nate had learned the songs carried on the winds; from his Quaker mother, joy in clouds and constellations. He had long since ceased talking plain, dropped his 'thees' and 'thous.' He spoke mountain talk and the language of the Uncompahgre Utes. Though pacific by nature, he carried an old army Needle gun and was a tolerable shot. The notion would have saddened his ma, nor had she approved his boisterous singing—it was not the quiet Quaker way.

During his boyhood, they'd had a small spread at the foot of Lookout Mountain where the Widow Phipps boarded travelers. When a band of renegade Comanches raped her to her death down by the water trough, she never uttered a sound. Two days later, a party of Utes found seven-year-old Nate in the root cellar where she'd hidden him. Instead of selling him into slavery with the Navajos, they'd carried him back to the Gunnison country to raise amid Yutah song and laughter.

Cresting the pass, Nate raised his voice in the high, thin air. "Oh, as I went out one noonin', to breathe the mountain air," he roared, "lolly tu dum, tu dum…" He'd been told it was a blessing he did not perform in a church choir, where his noise would be confined by rafters and assault the delicate ears of women and children. Alone in the hills, he brayed of mansions in the sky, shining fields, forested peaks. He celebrated the flight of eagles, hallelujahed over carpets of wildflowers billowing like quilts across the laps of high meadows: scarlet penstamen, topaz glacier lilies, little blue elephant ears, ivory columbine as elegant as fine ladies' slippers.

Even bellowing at eleven thousand feet did not shorten Nate's wind. He had moved past the St. Elmo camp and along the Taylor River at a steady, ground-chewing pace. His straight-backed Indian glide began with his feet, clad in tough, spongy buffalo-hide moccasins in tune with the earth underfoot. The Yutah in him had no truck with heavy hobnail boots.

Bouquets of pearly everlasting bobbed from Jenny's canvas panyards, one a gift for Aggie McClaren, the other for Little Emma Sutton. The tiny white blooms would be welcome pretties for their parlors.

"I'm a notion not to board at Old Lady Cooper's," he said conversationally to Jenny. "Them boys at her table root worse'n hogs at a trough. The racket from hawking and tooting wind keeps a man astir half the night. Ain't other boarding houses any better."

"In the bargain," he added by way of a clincher, "she is the biggest jawer in these hills. I'll admit I am a fair talker myself. But that woman can no more shut her mouth than a jaybird. Pesters about why a handsome ore-picker like me has not found a good widow woman to marry."

Nate could have told her. A man in the gold and silver camps got out of the habit of women. Unless it was his own dissertation he was hearing, Nate liked peace. Unless it was him singing hymns, he preferred quiet. The Lord had granted him more than his portion. He had long since thrown in the towel on finding a white woman to laugh and roll in the gramma grass in the way of a plump, loving squaw. What's more, he felt he was most often in the right, and he was inclined to be bossy about it. He had no need of a thin-lipped, starchy-necked camp woman to out-boss him.

Off to the south he noted a cloudbank as big as a range of mountains. Lightning flashed from its underbelly. "Moving east," he muttered. "H'it'll miss us." He passed from windswept talus into up-thrusting fingers of spruce, fir, and lodgepole pine; black timber marching in ramrod-straight regiments up the mountainsides, the plush evergreen broken only by alluvial fans of aspen, trash trees which sprang up in pale green arcs in the paths of bygone avalanches.

Below him in the busy Ashcroft camp near the head of the Castle Creek drainage, Nate spied Stump Clancy shoeing behind his livery, hopping on one foot, his wooden leg propped against a corral post.

"That you, Phipps?"

"It's me sure enough, Stump."

"Can't hardly recognize you under all them whiskers. You're hairier than a Christly whistle pig."

"Mean to sit in a barber chair about dark," called Nate.

"Well, have Burkhardt douse you with plenty of powder and perfume."

"How is that?"

"Them whores on the Row gets choosy over the holiday. Hardly roll over 'less it's for a goddam banker or fancy drummer." Stump cackled joyously at his own humor.

Nate grinned and waved, about to hurry on down-valley to Cal's dig. But he was a born talker and temptation got him in her grip. He turned down the footpath to the livery. "Going into Aspen for the celebration, Stump?"

"Wouldn't miss it."

"You could do with a barbering yourself." Stump, a bandy-legged Scots-Irishman with a half-penny nose and three remaining teeth, owned a beard as full-grown as Nate's.

"Least I don't look like no fucking warlock."

Nate had had a look at himself back in the charcoal waters of Taylor Lake. Thick hair curled like vines over his flannel collar. Matted beard and mustaches covered his face almost to his hat. What little skin showed was blackened by nights spent over pitchpine fires. On the trail, Nate did not fiddle with grooming.

"Neither of us is a sight for starved eyes. Ever tried taking off those whiskers of your'n?"

"Nope. Need 'em to keep me warm. Need 'em to keep me warm."

In winter, Ashcroft was closed in by heavy drifts. Stump swore he'd watched his piss freeze before it struck ground. Even now, in July, the surrounding peaks were bundt cakes with icings of snow drizzled over their tops.

"Sides, say us homely types fare better in face hair. I mind Shoat Yanket when he got shed of chin whiskers and sideburns to cure that advanced case of head lice."

"Always thought Shoat a fair-looking specimen. Shiftier than a snake, but fair-looking."

"Till they shaved him down. With his carbuncle pockmarks and a mouthful of rotted teeth, he turned up a sorry-lookin' sight. Ugly as that puny polecat Fess Felcher."

"Say poor looks soured both men. Started running with Bull Mudgett and Denver Bob Bisbee. How *are* them two sorry articles?"

"Been jumping more claims."

"No!"

"Sick animals. Stepping up their sneak attacks for Sutton. Layin' dirty hands on every apex outcrop they can." Stump smacked the horse he'd been shoeing on the rump, chased him off, and leaned against the fence. "Say the Denver magistrate is about ready to hear the apex-sideline arguments."

"That matter has been hanging fire since creation."

"Well, she is finally going to law. End of next month."

"The apex don't stand a chance."

"No telling. Could be close." Stump leaned over to lose a stream of chaw juice. "By hook or crook, Tacker and Sutton aim to get their fuckin' injunctions. Shut down every sideline in Pitkin county. The Pearly first."

Nate didn't know whether to feel more heartsick over the claim-jumping or the court threat. "Did those jumpers turn the trick?" he asked.

"They did not. The shitheads forgot to reckon with the Major. When D.K heard one of the Swedes' claims was jumped, he sprinted straight fer the dig, got out of his coat, and walked into the hole where Bull Mudgett stood guard. Wrenched the gun out of Mudgett's hand and throwed it up on the bank."

Stump ruminated over his plug a moment. "Say his eyes was colder'n a block of ice. Caught hold of Bull, jammed him up against the dig wall, and ordered, 'Move on out of here, you pig-eyed son-of-a-bitch, or I will beat you to death where you stand.'"

"Deke Burdine ain't one to curse, Stump."

"He did this day. And Bull Mudgett don't care for no fight without odds. Moved like his ass was afire."

"I'll warrant he did." Nate shuddered at the picture of Deke in a killing fury. "That's one saved for our side."

"Deke is still hot under the collar about what happened to Young Frank Parker."

Both men, silent, harked back to the Parker boy. Late in the fall of last year he'd tried to dig alone, with no partner, down by the Conundrum hot springs. Frank was a worker, but he was also a squirt with a sight to learn. He'd left his location to buy powder and beans in camp. While he was about his business, Mudgett's men jumped his claim. When they threw down on him, he'd fought with the spit of a tomcat. Nate found the unconscious boy and packed him into Dan Alderfer's surgery, where Doc had said in a bitter tone, "He'd been better off to let it go. His jaw is busted, two, maybe three places. They've bit off half of that right ear, and one eye is rocky in the socket." He paused to wash up his tools. "I'll piece him together, but he may turn out cockeyed."

Vinnie Krueger had taken the boy home to heal. She worried about his state of mind more than his pieced-together face, fearing he'd be soured for life.

Nate's concerns grew. "Any word of Cal Krueger's leasehold?"

"His luck ain't changed. All bad," grunted Stump. "Got me a few shares of Pearly. If Krueger would strike him some color it would soften my hard winter."

"Well sir, I am on my way to help him dig."

Stump was shocked. "Not on Independence Day!"

"You know Cal Krueger. He works for the joy of toil."

"Bore me for the simples, Phipps, but I don't see no damn joy in swingin' a pick with the itch of a beard full of chiggers—and a glory show of fireworks overhead."

Nate turned to go, his mind in a turmoil. Aspen might have four church houses, two theaters, a roller rink, and fifteen saloons, but civilization had not yet fully taken hold. Silver had a way of making men forget the precepts their mothers taught them. Though Nate had a sociable side, dog-eat-dog dispute made him skittish as a hog on ice. Nor was he easy about working under wet rock and shaft timbers. Plenty like Cal might be smitten with mining, but Nate considered it a mean job for moles, not men.

"Best make camp before dark," said Nate, turning to go. He must still cover some eleven miles and more than two thousand downward feet into the Aspen streets. With a wave he headed out, polepick riding easy on one arm, Needle gun on the other. He'd made up his mind to have his own room at

Aggie McClaren's hotel. Aggie made up her beds with sheets, which she washed after nearly every boarder, tucking sweet-smelling sage and cinnamon under the blanket. He even fancied her dour Scots wit. Aggie had lived long enough to understand humoring a man instead of bossing him.

####

CHAPTER SIX

INDEPENDENCE EVE—TRAPPED

Cal felt so helpless he could have shed a river of tears—if his eyelids would only lift. Weighed down under rock and dirt, his head big as a pumpkin, he felt carved in stone. Not even Sisyphus could have born a heavier load.

Panic rose like vomit in his throat. His heart hammered. In a thin, inner voice, he reminded himself, *If you puke, Calvin, you'll choke on your own bile.* He was breathing. That was something. The weight that encased him had to be more gravel than silt. Caught under wet mud, he'd be a dead man. He had no notion if only one drift was caved—or the whole of the mine. If the collapse was massive, it could take days to reach him. Longer than he could last. He didn't know the time of day, or night, or even the day of the week. He willed his mind to quit yammering and go quiet. Then, slow as a windmill in a whispery breeze, he flexed his arm muscles. They seemed to move a shade. Maybe, just maybe, he might not be buried deep.

Time passed....He drifted....He could have dozed. Except for regular, minuscule movement in his limbs, he was still.

Sometime late in the night, he awoke to find himself wrenching an arm from the rubble. After a while, the other. He came quickly to his senses, scraping gravel from his face. He was shocked at the harsh noise of his breathing, as raspy as if he had run full-tilt up a hard hill. He paused to rest a minute, then whispered a thankful prayer and began working his legs free. At length he was loose. He quelled an urge to whoop and as suddenly was downcast again. Raising up, he'd cracked his head on the top of the drift. Groping shakily on his belly, he felt his way back and forth. Then, lying flat beside a facing of dry rock, he reached deep for the sulphur matches in his pocket safe. Stilling the tremor of his hands, he counted out six of the precious matches, separated one, and refastened the safe lid on the others. Then he returned the match case meticulously to the depths of his trousers. Igniting match on stone, he squinted hastily around at jumbled rock. He was in a cubby hole a few feet high and perhaps four feet wide. In this tight corner, he was scarcely more free than before.

As the match sputtered out, his cage was again as black as the insides of a bull buffalo. He finally understood why Nate so feared going blind. At that, a blind man could feel the warmth of the sun on his skin, the touch of a breeze on his cheek. Here there was nothing but dank. *Mein Gott In Himmel,* he prayed dispiritedly. *You can't expect me to dig my way free of this?* He lay back, stretching his legs, colder than a church house on a weekday morning.

Don't act foolish, he chided himself. Someone would be along. If this was still the third of July, and if Nate reached camp before dark, he'd soon search him out in the shafthouse. Then his heart sank. Nate could get more side-tracked than a foot peddler. His friend took an uncommon interest in what made fellow creatures tick. He knew a power of things: how to assay mineral in the field, that snow geese mate for life, that a compass does not point toward the North Pole, that foxes are downright dumb, that lightning often strikes in the same place—and that pigs are fine swimmers. He'd had Vinnie show him how to cut lard into flour and roll out a pie crust as flaky as her own. He'd pestered Cal to dissect the writings of Thomas Carlyle. He'd kept after Deke Burdine to teach him to shoot close—though even Nate's sharp eyes would never be a match for the major's. Deke had once made money creasing mustangs, a trick that required dead-sure aim. He placed a shot through the neck close enough to the spinal cord to stun the animal without killing it, and while the creature lay still, slipped a halter over its head. Then he broke it for riding. He'd only once lost a horse, and even the feistiest studs came dancing up when he whistled.

Cal groaned. It would be no surprise if Nate stopped to help Aggie McClaren black her stove—or to watch Mamie Scowcroft fashion millinery.

Cal's thoughts turned to Vinnie. Lord! He himself had sent the men home, had said he'd bed down in the shafthouse. Vinnie'd have no cause for worry—not before breakfast.

Scarcely glancing Nate's way, a bobcat crossed to water in Castle Creek by the Conundrum confluence. This year's snowmelt had been heavy. The creek still boiled with muddy runoff. After years of wandering these uplands, he knew them to be a great sopping sponge never wrung out, the boggy ground beneath the summits no place for a dry camp.

Suddenly he shouted, "Oh, the Spanish Main, she's dark and deep, a landsman's not at home there…" On the rocky steeps in the growing twilight, a family of bighorns stood startled by the echoes of Nate's song.

"Good thing it's sheep and not bears," he muttered to Jenny. That she-bear up on Sopris had streaked along the trail, her sides rolling up and down, had treed him so fast that he'd dropped his skillet in a cleft of rock. He had to fry his fatback on a shovel blade 'til he could get to camp for a new pan. Today, he'd be a goner. He felt the tightening of heel cords on uphill pulls, the ache of knees on the downward. Often he rubbed crude oil from mine seeps into painful joints.

"Count your gifts, Nate," Cal counseled. "We are surrounded by young pups with legs like pistons and eyes like chicken hawks. There's no better way for us oldsters to end our days than doing a young man's work."

In all Cal's years underground, he'd never known such total darkness. Ignoramuses could natter on about keeping your wits in a cave-in, but no man could know a full measure of terror until he lay in this same black dark. The cold had seeped in. His teeth rattled, and he shivered like a dog crapping bones. He wondered miserably if it was near breakfast time when Vinnie would miss him during grace. He might be unmindful of a prayer meeting, but he wasn't a man to miss the blessing before a meal. And Needle Newsome, eager to shovel in his grub, would be acutely aware of Cal's absence.

With all his being, he longed for a few swallows of coffee to take away the dry. Never mind that Pete Beard swore coffee was the broth of the devil. The first time Cal had heard Pete's astonishing point of view, he and the boys had been sitting around their fire back in '79, on their initial expedition over the hump.

"Thet coffee'll kill a man," Pete had declared as Cal refilled his cup from a big bent-up pot on the coals.

The other boys looked at Pete askance.

"I once taken twenty cups a day—when I could get it," Pete explained. He sat cross-legged, his sawgrass hair sticking out from a rusty black hat, the brim chewed for its salt by porcupines. "Then, one morning up the Arkansas, I'd just emptied the pot when I seen red flashes before my eyes."

"Could have been one of those sudden lightning storms, Pete."

"The day was clear as glass—except for them red flashes and blue flares. Like devil dancers, they was." Pete shuddered at the memory. "Suffered the godamn flashes 'til I moved me and the girls onto a ranch and drank all the milk I could hold."

"I swear." Needle's neck apple bobbed agitatedly. "How come you thought it was the coffee done it?"

"Cuz I kicked thet coffeepot in the crick, and I ain't seen snakes from that day to this."

Cal chortled at the memory of Pete's coffee attacks. He let his aching arms fall to his sides, and harked back to the '79 trek when he and Pete, Nate Phipps, Needle Newsome, Jake Levy, and Deke Burdine, along with Willard Arey, were the first permanent party over the divide. They had pulled up stakes in Leadville, crossed their homemade sledges over the hump at night when the moon was at the full and the snow rock-hard, worked their way down Hunter Creek, marked their locations and built the first cabins in this camp—and they'd done it with the Utes on a spree and half the forests "spontaneous-combusted." That expedition had needed coffee by the gallon just to quiet their nerves.

These mountains were a strong place, their strength as daunting as the bitter taste of cold iron. Founding a town in the heart of them was a thing to make a man proud. He and the boys had not only dug Aspen's first prospect holes, they had stayed to throw up a church and Aspen's first sawmill. And, after a spell, a school. He doubted anyone would erect monuments over their graves, but prospering had done them a sight more good than eulogizing. When Vinnie arrived in the spring, she'd breathed, "Oh, Cal, I never saw skies so blue. The ground's good, the sun warm. I can put my lilac slips to sprout. Let's come to rest."

This had been their seventh camp in a score of years, and Cal, to his own surprise, had been as ready to light as Vinnie. Venturers claimed there was no bankrupt life couldn't be set straight by heading off down the road. After countless miles of roadwork, he'd found peace at last. The Roaring Fork Valley was far more high-toned than Leadville—that sink of sin where a man must walk the center of the street or be whacked on the head for his pocket watch. By now Aspen boasted a fair portion of women, both domestic and sporting. Also children, dogs, hogs, horses, cats, and Sunday school teachers. With no railroad as yet, the place didn't draw your fly-by-nighters. Among eighty thousand western mine districts, Aspen was one of the few known as a clean camp. It boasted a going temperance union, literary and relief societies, a theatric troupe, a roller rink, a boating club, and only two or three killings a year.

Cal grew aware that his air was none too good, his breath wheezy in his ears, his tongue turned to flannel. His head and the leg that carried the grapeshot pounded like a bad tooth. He felt the same bone-deep ache he had experienced more than twenty years past, after manning his sixteen-bore guns for three head-splitting hours near Acquia Creek, in the war that started him down the road to this sorry pass. He'd crept home from battles to find his two small boys taken by the diphtheria, his farm gone to seed, and Vinnie in bed at the preacher woman's house. His heartache then had been a good deal worse than his headache now.

With no voice nor mettle for the old song, "Planting in the springtime, Reaping in the fall," he and Vinnie had sold what was left and over-landed to the Kansas Territory. He'd brought only his books. Like Prospero, his books were his dukedom.

By and by the ore fever in the mine camps around Cherry Creek had seized and held him, easing his grief, and luring him deeper into Rocky Mountain mineral country. Even so, these many years later, the memory of his young manhood turned to trash and his boys to ashes, still caused him to wake trembling in the night. He had thought nothing could ever flatten him that low again. Not even a busted mine.

In the darkness, he felt a sense of shock at how little he'd considered his new-found riches. All these long months, he'd been propelled by visions of Vinnie in rustly silk dresses, Vinnie on plush turkey carpets, Vinnie driving a stylish barouche. Suddenly he saw those visions as the chimera they were. He was only fooling himself about pretties for Vinnie. The harsh truth was he'd been driven by lust. Oh, he'd been faithful to his marital vows, had never once taken a squaw or a whore. His brand of lust was wanderlust, the siren that sang to him as a boy, that called him off to war, called him West into the mountains, down in the mines. Cal Krueger hungered after the unknown. It was the seeking that intoxicated him, more than the finding. In the mines, he was as enthralled as a schoolboy exploring a new cave. The world down here was as spellbinding to a miner as new seas to a sailor. These mighty Elk Mountains were geologic crazy quilts, full of uplifts and fracture lines that sheltered veins and pools of precious metals forged in bygone volcanic heat. There were always fresh puzzles to stretch a man's wits and dangers to test his pluck.

Despite his appetite for hidden treasure, Calvin counted himself a decent man. He would pay a fellow what he owed him—and add something for good measure. He could hold onto a confidence for a lifetime. His friends called on him in all weathers. He believed in a Divine Providence.

While his thoughts wandered, Calvin dug with big, blunt fingers toward what he judged was the main tunnel. Though his muscles cramped, and loose dirt kept refilling his hairbreadth tunneling, he felt solaced for the effort. *This may take me half of creation*, he thought. *But at least I am not lying here waiting for my redeemer to receive me*. A kind of peace settled over him. It would be hard on Vinnie to be left behind. But if it was his time, he reckoned he was ready.

Nate skirted the carter's trail where bull-whackers, jack trains, and men afoot and on horseback jostled their way through holiday crowds bound for town. The clank and jingle of harness, creaking of wheels, and snorting of dray and pack animals was as noisy as Denver City traffic. At this rate, the countryside would soon be knee-deep in shit. He moved along a high, thin ledge of shelf rock above, detouring past the Highland Peak tipple, where banks of raw mine tailings piled at the tipple's sides, bleached in the last rays of a fading sun. He regretted seeing the place rotted and splayed, a sure sign the Spence boys had gone bust. He had located that strike, along with many digs dotting Castle Creek. After placing his discovery stakes with the name of the claim, his own name and the date, he'd written a brief physical description of the three hundred by fifteen-hundred-foot parcel, listing landmarks, then registered it at the shack that served as the Pitkin County courthouse. When he was blessed, he sold out to a willing mine operator for cash money. Sometimes he'd go shares, gambling on a digger's grit—as he'd done with Young Frank Parker on the Conundrum claim.

Climbing around a cutbank and fording the creek at a shallow crossing, Nate and Jenny Lind struck the town trail by the Silver Queen Hill where Aspen Mountain dropped her skirts abruptly into the streets of town. He planned to deliver Miss Lind to Rob Skinner's Elkhorn Livery for boarding. Others might let their burros loose to scavenge and chew clothes off housewives' lines, but his always had fresh feed and a clean stall. He prayed Pie Burkhardt would not have a long waiting line at his bathhouse. Ordinarily, mountain men averaged maybe six good washes a year. But July third was a banner washday. Burkhardt claimed the drain dirt outside his place before the holiday was enough to dam the Yampa River.

From here Nate could see the first flickering of coal oil lamps. In the distance, the sharp snapping of firecrackers mingled with scattered gunfire. He was near enough so the camp noise struck him hard. It always did. Along with the crash and hiss of dollies and hoists, he even imagined he could hear the pounding presses of the *Aspen Daily Times*. One of these days he planned to go in there and watch the boys set type, though he doubted he'd make a printer. Too blamed noisy.

Below him, the Roaring Fork River twisted through town with its burden of effluvia: wood shavings, dead skunks, old dogs. Trout venturing into camp had long since turned belly up or swam downstream for their lives. If they made it to the confluence with the Grand River at the hot springs, they could turn south into the mighty Grand Canyon and head on out to the California sea.

The smells assaulted him too: the stink of outhouse holes dug shallow, of smoky beer-soaked saloons, of hogs turned loose to root in the streets. Aspen was not yet big enough or persnickety enough to outlaw pig-keeping. Where no women were in residence, backyards filled with trash, bones, bottles, cans, discarded mineral retorts, and mine gear. While men shoveled ore, bottlefly-infested manure piled up in corrals and streets.

Yet touches of wives and daughters were beginning to show. Vinnie Krueger had instructed Pete Beard's girls how to rake manure into flower beds and plant potatoes in hills. Emma Sutton's and the Widow Wickersham's gardens were a summer glory. Doc Alderfer had cussed out the city fathers 'til they'd hired Reuben Hurd to collect the offal around hitching posts and act as town scavenger. Drunk, Reuben kicked and cussed every bloated carcass and foraging hog in his path. Sober, he kept the streets and walkways half-clean. A few grass lawns had been planted, with a sheep or two to keep them in trim. Water ditches coursed along streets shaded with young cottonwoods.

At Aspen's great height and far distance, none of the niceties came easy. Every stick of furnishings, every roll of carpet, must be pushed, pulled, and windlassed over near-impassable peaks and canyons. Small wonder the *Aspen Daily Times* touted each small home as a witness to courage and conviction.

He peered at the prospect before him. All places in the world have their moment, a time when the angle of repose and the lighting are most flattering, when they're at their most resplendent. This instant of dusk was Aspen's finest hour. Few warts showed, the town looked a picture. The moon, just shy of full, had risen through the twilight as the fading sun pulled a rosy curtain across the plum-purple sky. Cotton from cottonwood trees floated like feathery summer snow. Heady scents of honeysuckle and rambling roses drifted up and over the meaner smells. The red rocks of Pratt Mountain opposite Aspen Mountain had the gleam of copper kitchenware in the bittersweet, dying light. To the east, up Independence Pass toward the hump, traces of snow glittered in luminous aspenglow.

Grateful to reach haven, Nate turned in the direction of Rob Skinner's livery. His beard itched. His stomach rumbled. He'd settle Jenny, then catch Pie Burkhardt before he locked up his tubs and store soap, come clean as a whistle, finish supper with a double slab of Aggie McClaren's Montgomery pie, and bed down in shameless ease. Cal Krueger had waited this long. One more night would not be the death of him.

####

CHAPTER SEVEN

INDEPENDENCE DAY

Promptly at dawn on July the Fourth, Aspen exploded. In the stated opinion of one old-timer, the salvos of giant powder were "wuss'n the fuckin' guns at Chickamauga."

When the cannonading finally ceased, the silence was as overwhelming as the noise. All of the camp's thumping, pounding machinery was shut down.

In the eerie, unaccustomed stillness, Bridgie O'Reilly, feeling spooked, served the missus her breakfast toast with mayapple jam and sassafras tea. Then she turned her mind to m'lady's toilette. If she did not pay her mind, the woman absent-mindedly forgot an important layer. One by one, Bridgie assisted her into bloomers, cotton hosiery, silk over-pantalettes, underslip, chemise, french boned corset and corset cover. Over this firm foundation, she then slipped a delicate lavender and green madras organdy morning gown with smooth-fitting basque and elaborately draped overdress. Although bustles were back, the missus flatly refused to wear a contraption that interfered with her "seat."

Bridgie sat her mistress on her dressing stool, meticulously arranging her skirts so the starch would hold, then removed the lid from the painted china hair receiver, draped a clean linen towel over the going-to-town dress and set to work on a tangle of hair. Since the missus would have no part of a nightcap, her silver-handled hairbrush with bristles fine as silk was useless for the job. Instead, Bridgie wielded a stiff-bristled curry brush from the horse stalls. *Ah well*, thought the Irish girl, a dollop of pride mixed with exasperation, *here is a woman with no need of the switches and transformations worn by ladies in other grand houses.*

While she yanked and curried, her lips pursed, the missus, her eyes watering from scalp pain, kept up her talk. "I am sick and tired of that pettifogger Judge Silas Duckworth! When Mr. G.B. Tacker orders 'Jump!' the man squeaks, 'Downwind or the other way?'"

Anchoring herself with both hands to her dressing table as Bridgie brushed harder, she stormed, "When women have the vote that pack of

Republican thieves will hear plenty from us! To think they're still fobbing off their damnable apex schemes on the unwitting public!"

Bridgie understood little of these diatribes. She knew about the apex battle, but considered it a man's affair, no business of hers.

"Trying to bamboozle honest miners out of hard-won digs!" Emma snorted, then as suddenly smothered an urge to giggle. She knew very well that Bridgie closed her eyes and pictured her cantering through Congress, whipping ogres out of office with her riding crop, settling sideliners on high-backed thrones at the head of marble halls. She was also aware that her tangled hair, slapdash dress, and sharp tongue caused the Irisher vexation. When she thought about it, she supposed that sharing her vigorous views— on the law and so-called justice, on women's rights and men's wrongs—with a pipsqueak Mick and an aged Indian was no better than calling down an empty canyon. All the same, it was better than talking to herself like a crazy person. *It's a damned good thing the O'Reilly is fond of me*, thought Emma merrily. *If she weren't, she'd have Doc Alderfer examining me for bumps on the noggin.*

Emma was in fine fettle. Shortly the footracers would assemble at their marks on Cooper Street. Out by the racetrack, the camp's fastest horses, groomed sleek as sea otters, would backstep and curvette, ready to run. Over by the Hallam Lakes, crushed berries awaited ice cream churns and sarsaparilla chilled in iced buckets. This was the celebratory Fourth. She was young. She could not stay down in her mouth for long.

Bridgie, triumphant at last, swept a gleaming swathe of hair across one wrist, deftly twisting and pinning until she'd achieved a stylish French knot. "Sure and 'twould look fine with a touch of bangs, Mum, and a few neck curls I could frizz with the hot tongs."

"I could never sit still for it, girl. I'd be blistered from scalp to chin." Emma glanced in the big black walnut-framed vanity mirror, started and reached to touch Bridgie's red, cracked hands. "Why Bridget O'Reilly! Your skin is as scoured as tree bark."

Bridgie tucked her hands under her apron, "T'is a family curse, Mum. My hide's so tender I've but to brush against a pat of butter...."

"Don't flummox me, girl," said Emma. She turned over the scarred hand. "What on earth caused this obscene blistering? Out with it now!"

Bridgie, mortified, whispered, "Pardon, Mum, I expect it be's the scrub board, what with the mister's company and all them extra bed linens."

"Goddamit!"

Bridgie drew in a sharp breath, wishing for the hundredth time that the missus would not curse like a common bogtrotter.

"That settles it! From now on we send all the laundry to Sister Coon."

"Oh, but we can't never. The mister would take on turrible at the expense!"

"Let him." Emma's face darkened. "There's worse in store for the blasted penny pincher. Before long, there'll be a carload of work for Sister—infant nappies and such."

"Oh! Oh!" gasped Bridgie. Unable to restrain herself, she flung her arms around the missus. "Thank the gracious Savior," she breathed. Bridgie belonged to the school that considered a precious babe the answer to any ills of a troubled marriage.

Emma patted the bristly red hair and sighed. "I wish I were filled with your thanksgiving, Bridgie girl. The truth is, I'm more of a mind to jump off the Silver Queen Hill."

Though Bridgie missed Emma's exact point, she was nevertheless horrified. "Surely you can't be jumping…nor running…nor riding in that parade, neither. Not in yer, er…condition, Mum."

"Nonsense. Mrs. Ollie Davidson is right as usual. I have the constitution of a draft horse. I won't swoon. I won't get wet-sweated. And I won't suffer the vapors. Furthermore," she finished, "I'll have none of your counting beads or lighting candles, lass. The Lord and I will tussle over my predicament between us."

Scooper Hurd jiggled the reins, swearing through his teeth at the fat dun mare breaking wind as she ambled up-valley from the Miller Ranch. The stars were winking out, the moon gone down in a grey and pale violet dawn. The holiday promised fair. "Dern nag," muttered Scoop. "Just because you pull fer the Doc, you think you can move in your own good time. Never saw the beat." He longed to jump over the dash of the slow-moving buggy and give Dolly a swift kick. Then he felt shame. Dolly might be a leisurely mare, but she carried the Doc in all weathers, forded swollen streams cool as a trout. Even a driving March snow hardly slowed her.

Scoop, so-called because he helped his pap scoop dead carcasses from the Aspen streets, often accompanied Doc on night calls, loosed Dolly's girth, slipped her from her thills and suspenders, gave her a watering and the feed bag, and later drove the exhausted man home to bed. This night, Scoop had caught little more than catnaps. Some months back, Bessie Miller, pigtailed and saucy in school, had gotten a bun in her oven and married that shiftless son-of-a-bitch Fess Felcher, who ran with Mudgett's gang. Last night, before she could get the bun out, she'd bitten off three wood spoons and nearly shredded a kitchen spurtle. When she commenced shrieking and howling for her Lord Christ Jesus like she was being burned at an Apache stake, Scoop had been so unnerved he'd stuffed himself with the green sarvisberries dangling by the Miller porch. Now his belly griped him, and he was due to race in the junior footraces this morning. The boys' sprint prize was a gold piece, a two-and-a-halver.

"Whoooeee, have me and Lute got plans fer that money," he whistled over his weariness. He barked at Dolly, "Giddyap, godammit!"

"What is it, sonny?" Dan Alderfer raised his long chin from his chest as instantly awake as he had been sound asleep, though his voice was thick.

"Aw, dangit, Doc, I didn't mean to wake you. Sun's comin' up—and I got to be at the starting line on time."

"Hand me the old bag's reins. We'll see if we can't shake some fat off her belly."

At the touch of the Doc's big, bony hands, the sound of his rough voice, Dolly stepped out as smart as a blooded trotter.

"Jesus, Doc, lookit her go!"

"All of us, boy, have juices only waiting to be stirred," he said, giving Scoop a big, bawdy wink.

The man was smart as Solomon, and of late Scoop had considered asking his ideas about courting Svea Hoaglund. Svea's hair was goldenrod yellow and her milkers soft as pillows. It was beyond Scoop why any man would want to bed a chicken-breasted ranch girl like Bessie when he could hope to lay his head on the soft white pillows of Svea Hoaglund.

In the creek-misted half-light at the foot of Buttermilk Mountain, Titus Pomeroy finished harnessing his knobby white cart horse to the family gig. He and Annie were getting an early start into camp so they'd have a good streetside seat for the parade. His wife waited on the seat, picnic packed in her pie basket, skirts and petticoats starched, red face shining under the new bonnet Tite had ordered special from Mamie Scowcroft's Millinery. He'd bought the hat with part of the ten dollars Mayor McDade used to persuade him to lend his big Suffolk Punch horses to the parade.

"Pretty as a picture," Titus muttered. "Like them mitts you tatted." Tite was a big-bellied, powerful man, not much for talk. Annie smiled at her hands, lump-knuckled, heavy-veined, folded in her lap. All the fine crocheting in the world could not hide years of milking, cutting, and baling buffalo grass with a sheath knife in hard times.

Noting a small grimace as her husband lifted the heavy leather hames, she said, "Tite, I know that shoulder pains. Why must you be so set on harnessing when I can handle Elmer good as you?"

"Won't have you rumpling your best dress," he'd said determinedly. "Want camp folks pointing out Mrs.Titus Pomeroy. Owns them fine Suffolks."

The massive horses, Gertrude and Irmgard, Tite's most prized possessions, were to be the centerpieces of the parade. He'd gentled the animals across Cottonwood Pass like Hannibal crossing elephants over the Alps, hacking out a trail so their great 1,600-pound bodies could squeeze through. Tite treated all his animals as overgrown children who didn't know their own strength—which was how he'd misjudged the temper of his Brown Swiss bull. Though the bull was small, he'd thrown him into a stanchion. Tite's dislocated shoulder had sprung back, but it was so aggravated he could hardly milk.

"I pray Rob Skinner can hold those girls in check," worried Annie. It was the worst luck that Tite's arm was so bad he could not drive his own haywagon carrying the Liberty belle tableau.

"Only man ever broke a pair of elk to harness." Tite adjusted the blinders on the cart horse. "Reckon he'll handle Gert and Irmie. Never mind cherry bombs and gunfire."

"Land!" breathed Annie. "Won't it be a rouser of a holiday?"

Vinnie Krueger felt her kitchen, already small, had shrunk. *Could be the smells*, she thought. Rising above the usual kitcheny odors of cinnamon, vanilla, newly baked bread, and freshly roasted coffee beans was a powerful mix of damp wool, gunpowder, and armpit sweat. Nothing brought home to her than this man's world like the smells.

She was entertaining an overflow crowd. Lute and Young Frank and Needle sat at their usual places, knives and forks at the ready. Pete Beard had risen for the morning shift out of pure habit and, his four girls still abed, had dropped by. Soon he'd return to his own place to help Tacy, his eldest, pigtail her sisters' heads for the parade. Even now he was explaining to Needle the niceties of the French-braid over a straight three-ply plait.

"Pete, you are something," said Young Frank as Vinnie prepared to dish out pan-fried grits, "the way you are training up them little women."

"Some days I wonder," sighed the untidy Pete, "which of us is the bear on the chain." After seeing that his girls were neat as pins, he then neglected his own beard and hair. He was a lean, powerful man, as unkempt as the *Voyaguers* who'd once roved this mountain wilderness. "I'm out of the wind, that's all that matters," he'd say. In Pete's Nebraska sodbuster days, the wind howled, coursed, and shrieked until it blew his wife Beulah's mind away. Pete guessed she'd been searching for it when she walked out in a bitter Norther and was lost in the deep-drifted snow. After that, he disliked nothing in this world so much as wide open spaces—and the wind. He had packed his girls and a Mexican hand named Olvera into the high country to live. There he'd found a home down in the mines, where he felt sheltered. Underground, there was seldom a mild breeze.

Willard Arey's funeral parlor was closed for the holiday, and the proprietor had arrived on full alert at the Krueger's kitchen door. "Morning, Lavinia dear. You've done the trick again —fried up a fine mess of scrapple. I smelled it through the back window of my establishment."

"Come in, you rascal." She'd smiled at Willard's imaginative smeller, cooking up those crosstown smells. Vinnie's windows would not be open, nor her breakfast smells let loose, until the sun was fully up.

"It's paunhaus. With a fresh tub of molasses. Come in, sit."

By the light of coal oil lamps flickering against tin wall reflectors, Vinnie shaved salt off a block to sprinkle over sizzling side meat and eggs. Then she added another eggshell to clear the coffee in her big blue enamel pot. From the corner of her eye, she saw Pete searching, his cheek abulge. More at home in a saloon than a woman's kitchen, he'd forgotten to get shed of his tobacco.

"There's no spitter in here, Pete. Just open that door and shoot your chaw out the back. Aim high and right, and you'll miss my sweet pea bed."

Willard Arey shifted his own cud, gave Vinnie a grateful look, and stumped after Pete to the door. Vinnie, along with most camp women, favored the anti-tobacco league. But she didn't preach it. Nothing riled Willard more than a woman who preached. His wife Arbella was no doubt rocking away in their Philadelphia parlor, her mouth creaking in concert with her caned rocker. He had never once acted to suit that woman, and when he lit out for the West, she'd had one of her frothing-at-the-mouth fits. It had been seven years since he'd laid eyes on her, more than five since she quit mailing him home-baked sermons about other men with only one leg who were handy garden-hoers and ample providers and attended five church services a week.

Hah, he thought. Wouldn't Arbella be fit to be tied if she could see the spiffy gold-lettered sign over his Cooper Street storefront. "Arey's Mortuary & Fine Furnishings, Willard M. Arey, Prop." He'd wager he was the most prosperous one-legged son-of-a-bitch west of the Arkansas River. On the other hand, he didn't care to have the woman taken it in her head to make the trip out to the state of Colorado to see his situation with her own eyes.

"There's coffee on the stove, boys," said Vinnie. "Pete, I know you're partial to buttermilk. There's aplenty in the springhouse, if you'd care to fill this pitcher." Seeing Young Frank's yearning looks at the rhubarb pies cooling on top of the big pine wall safe, she added, "And all of you help yourself to the pie plant pies." She'd baked them for the church supper at the lakes. Never mind. She could roll out more crust in a jiffy.

As Vinnie dished up slices of paunhaus and passed platters of eggs, Willard tucked a hard-used bandanna under his chin. "I do not know why I bother to inquire, Lavinia, but where is that bullheaded husband of yours?"

Vinnie shook her head. "You know Cal. He wraps up that Pearly like she was an infant put down for a nap. He was expecting Nate last night, and they like to jabber a spell. If it's late, he beds down in the shafthouse. He'll be along."

She looked up at the sound of boots on the porch scraper. Through the window, she spied Major Burdine hanging a brace of geese from a log rafter. When he came in the door, he ducked his head. Their lintel was cut for a smaller breed of man.

"If you can abide the smell, Lavinia, I'd let those birds hang a few days. I'll be over to clean them the middle of the week." Though long removed from the South, Deke Burdine's voice held shades of limpid wisteria.

Vinnie smiled at the man's considerate ways. She could not remember a time when she'd thought of a thing she needed that the major did not think of it first. "I thank you and that plate's ready for you, " she said. Her partiality to Deke was in part a bow to Cal's deep affection for his friend. She herself found the major's masculinity in some wise overpowering. And his moods could be unpredictable. At times he was silent, almost removed. At others, chock-full of Virginia charm and wit. He was one of the rare men in a rough camp who removed his hat in her presence and rose to his feet when she entered a room. Yet under the graceful polish and the easy drawl he was as steely as an anvil. If a thing struck him wrong, the sparks flew. He sometimes put her in mind of a wildcat she'd startled down by her henhouse, though his eyes were not yellow, they were cool and grey as a winter sea. One of them was bullet-scarred at the corner where the smile lines fanned out white in his sun-darkened face.

Deke eased long legs over the bench beside Lute. "Morning, son. You and I seldom sit down at table together. With no soiled doves cooing over you, this is indeed a pleasure."

The praise gave Lute an exalted feeling. He thought Major Burdine the most heroic figure he'd ever hope to know. Though plenty of camp folk wasted little affection on Johnnie Rebs, most admired the major. Word had gotten around, how he'd run away from that Virginia Military Academy, a man-size boy of fourteen on a "borrowed" horse, had fought where it was warmest, had stood at Salem when the 45th Virginia mustered out, him a seventeen-year-old officer with an old man's eyes. Lute sat a horse well, but he suspected he would never be half-hoof and half-hock like his idol. Even so, it was his fondest dream to own a fine mount and silky mustache in the very same style as the major's.

As the men pitched into Vinnie's breakfast, everyone helped himself to seconds and thirds from the big ironstone platters in the center of the table, even Willard's chatter slowed. Needle finished thirds and looked so longing that Vinnie said, "Needle, my hens is laying like it was Easter. If you don't clean up those eggs, they'll be cold and not fit to eat."

Needle grinned bashfully and ducked his gristly neck. He had got in the habit of silence after years of meals with dog-tired miners in packed boarding houses where long-winded gabbers got the short end of supper. Eating at Lavinia Krueger's table, where a man did not have to swallow his food whole for fear of missing seconds, was Needle's notion of died-and-gone-to-heaven.

Young Frank started to wipe his mouth on his coat sleeve, thought better of it and said, "We sure do thank you for the pie, Missus. Nobody in this world makes a finer pie-plant pie."

Vinnie beamed and patted him on a disfigured cheek. He had been near killed over that Conundrum claim, and him scarce twenty-one. The age her Jim would have been had he lived. She thanked her Lord that she no longer needed to fret over Frank's peace of mind—not since he'd taken up with that Irish parlormaid over at the Sutton place. The sainted girl cared not a whit about his lop ear or quilt-stitched cheek. Young Frank Parker's better nature was fast resurfacing.

Pete's booming voice interrupted Vinnie's thoughts. "Still planning on that Peacemaker of mine to start the races this morning, Willard?"

"No gun I ever knowed of is a Peacemaker," grouched Willard. Since the war, he'd had no truck with firearms. "Pistol, rifle, shotgun, the lot is all trouble-makers."

Pete ignored the grousing. "Did you have Jake boil her like I instructed? She needed the gum loosened; the action ain't been freed in a good while."

"I give her to Jake day before…"

A rolling wash basin clattered on the porch slats and Nate Phipps burst through the back door, whooping, "Merry Christmas, boys!"

He shook hands and clapped backs all around, then hugged Vinnie so hard she blushed.

"Have I missed the feed trough? I've downed so much jerky and beans they have backed up on me, though I did have me some prime pickled buffalo tongue over at old Miss Mann's place by Mosquito Pass. Thank you, Major. I know I look good. Had me a full bath and I am wearing a new suit of clothes—though I dern near ruined the press in my coat over at Rob Skinner's lots."

Nate beamed at Vinnie and dug into the breakfast she'd put before him, talking as he chewed. "Got up early to check on Miss Lind's oats and found Skinner in a bad way. He'd grown a boil bigger'n a peach pit on his ass end—pardon me, Lavinia—and it came to a head while he slept. Had to lance it for him, send word to Squaw Polly to mix up a poultice. He's in considerable pain. Won't set for a week."

Young Frank Parker sat open-mouthed, marveling at the way the prospector could talk non-stop without taking a visible breath or choking on his food.

"That reminds me, Deke. Skinner is in a hard corner with his poxed hinder. He is looking for you to drive that pair of hard-mouthed, high-strung pair of greys for Old Man Tacker this noon. Skinner's already in a world of hurt over what to tell Tite Pomeroy about not handling his prize Suffolks in the parade. Tite wouldn't promise the use of them big mares 'til Skinner swore on a stack of bibles he'd be on the reins. What we need in this camp is less barristers—and about two hundred more jockeys and horse handlers…"

Nate surveyed the men at table, awaiting agreeable nods. "Say," he asked, "where is Calvin?"

"You mean you ain't seen him?" blurted Pete, startled.

"No, I have not. After my barbering last night, I got settled on one of

Aggie's good beds and had me a fine night's slumber. Then, come sunup, I was pressed into surgical service." Nate cut himself a large wedge of pie, carefully scooping up the escaped juices. "You're a true godsend, Lavinia Krueger. With no fruit or greens in my belly, I was close to turning costive."

Suddenly aware of the frozen faces around him, he said, "Now don't tell me Cal is late for his holiday breakfast. If he is working that mine hole I will blister his hide."

The sun had popped up from behind Smuggler Mountain. The kitchen was growing warm. Yet there was a sudden, palpable chill. With studied care, Pete put down his saucer of coffee. Young Frank ceased chewing and, with an audible gulp, swallowed his last bite. Needle snapped shut the clasp knife he'd opened to pare the troublesome corn protruding from the hole he'd opened atop his boot. Deke rose from the bench, reached for his shotgun in the corner, and said, "Lavinia, we thank you for the splendid spread. Now if you will kindly excuse us, I believe Luther and I will just check on that bullheaded husband and his mine workings."

Pete said, "I'll walk you over. It's on the way to my place."

Lute and Needle were out of their seats, followed by Young Frank and Willard. Even Nate took one longing look at his plate and abandoned his eating. In the blink of an eye, the small kitchen was as empty as it had been full. Her eyes fearful, her breath shallow, Vinnie Krueger found herself staring out the window, her apron twisting in her hands.

####

CHAPTER EIGHT

THE SEARCH

A round nine o'clock that morning all Aspen knew the Pearly had caved. Children were shushed and ordered to "Set still, or Pa will knock you spraddle-legged." Women rushed to Vinnie Krueger's side. Men raced through the streets to the mountain, where they bunched up around the Pearly adit like sheep in a storm.

Deke Burdine and Nate Phipps barred the adit and shafthouse entrances, reassuring the crowds 'til their voices threatened to give out. "That's the whole story, boys. It's just the one drift," called Deke over the crowd noise. "She's only a small slide, Abner. Yessir, in a side drift," said Nate. "No, she did not strike the main shaft."

Someone shouted, "How's Calvin?"

"Once we located him, he picked up faster than a old maid at the altar," announced Nate. "The boys will soon have him out from under..."

"We're here to help dig," bellowed a man at the rear of the crush.

"Thank you, Sam. We thank you kindly." Deke turned to the clamor of others. "Cal is grateful—and he'll soon tell you that himself, Rudy. Appreciate the offer, Josh, you know, but three men can shovel at one time. There's not much headroom."

Nate and Deke exuded a confidence they only half-felt. Cal was not out of the woods—or the slide either. Only four of the seven charges set the night before had been located. It was slow, cautious digging behind the probe man.

With the holiday beckoning, the volunteers, like guests at a cancelled wedding, began awkwardly drifting away.

"Land!" Nate mopped his forehead when they had departed. "I feared a stampede."

"It's a blessing the foot races are about to start," muttered Deke. "If this was the only show in town, we'd be sold out of tickets."

It had been approaching good light when Cal's friends hurried uneasily to the Pearly shafthouse. Needle had announced, "That bunk ain't been slept in.

He tole me he was going to bed down here. Don't see his ledgers on the desk."

Nate said worriedly, "Could be he's up and at it again…. Tarnation! "

Lute came flying in the door. "Gracious is in the tread, the oat bucket's empty and the hoist ain't been raised!"

Their apprehension growing, the men hustled to the whim. Lute was the first to point out the heavy cage pull, broken and dangling in the way of a useless arm. The others stared mutely.

"Damn it all to hell," Pete whispered.

With firm authority, Deke broke the stunned silence. "Lute, run get that heavy rope in the machine room. You're the lightest and the spryest. Think you can slide down, splice new rope on the cage hoist?"

"Yessir, Major. There's fair purchase on the sides of the shaft. I've climbed down for the lark."

"First, look for the trouble. Then for signs of Cal. Then see to splicing rope, rigging a new hoist…Frank, we'll need as many lanterns, lamps, and candles as you can tote. Needle, you and Pete get on this rope with me and we'll lower Lute hand over hand. Strap on a head lamp, son, and your knife and pop this whistle in your mouth. Blow two when you need us to halt. Once will do when you want to be raised."

As the men lowered the boy, Nate whispered, "Lord God. Oh dear Lord, don't let Calvin be kilt."

Quick as a whipstitch, Lute located the slide. When he shouted into the bank of rubble, he was answered by a muffled, far-off voice. His throat choked up and Lute had to make two starts before he was able to call loud, "We're coming, Mister Cal! Hold on! You're saved!"

Shortly, Needle and Pete and Nate roped themselves down, raced for the cave in, and, working an air-pipe like an auger, got it shoved through.

"About time you boys got here." Cal's voice was hollow-sounding as if at the far end of a dry wash.

"H'it's a good thing this weren't a full-bore avalanche," boomed Pete. "Your pards like to think of the Pearly as your salvation—not your death."

Cal Krueger may have been trapped and his voice muffled, but as Nate remarked later, his mouth had been plenty free. He'd croaked, "I'd take it kindly if you'd quit your jawing and dig me out of this."

"Why," said the startled Needle, "he sounds cantankerous."

"How is your air?" called Pete.

"On the stale side."

"We have the bellows, we'll pump in more fresh. And we're digging to

72

beat the band." "The boys from the Lady Day gave us the loan of their new widowmaker, case we hit hard rock!" bellowed Pete. "That'll be the ruckus you'll hear."

The new pneumatic air drills were noisy as Gatling guns, threw off great, hissing clouds of deadly rock dust, and—if there was friable rock—might even create more slide. The widowmaker would be a last-ditch choice, though it was faster than greased lightning.

"How much space you got in there, Cal?"

"About the size of Willard's number three coffin—too cramped for my liking," said Cal crossly.

"This may take a spell, partner. We must conduct close inspection for loose charges. Have yourself a rest."

Cal groaned. Might as well lie on a hornet's nest, every nerve and sinew tensed, waiting for a charge to be nicked and blow them across the hump.

Shortly Nate announced between heaves of his shovel, "I'll be leaving in a bit, Cal. Going topside to line us up relief teams."

"Don't you dast!!" Cal's roar came through the pipe. "Now just you hold on there, Nate. Stick your ear on this tube and mind me. Is everyone heedful?"

"We're listening."

"Who is out there with you?"

"Your most devoted companions…Pete, Young Frank, Lute, Needle. The rest of us—Willard, Deke, and Jake Levy—is working upstairs."

"Nathaniel," Cal licked cracked lips, "I have struck it rich."

Nate did not pause in his shoveling. "Says he has struck it rich. Struck by a rock to the belfry is more likely."

"That is," rasped Cal, "if the whole affair has not collapsed on us. Nate, I have located that mother load you promised. A bridal chamber of pure silver. You have never seen the beat."

"I swear!" Needle was shocked.

Nate's tone remained nonchalant. "Well, my friend, first things first. After we have you freed, we'll see to this find of yours."

"Don't you let any outsiders down here," Cal warned hoarsely. "Keep the news quiet. I know that is a tall order for a yapper like you, Nate Phipps. But you mind me now." Cal, worn to a frazzle, lay back against the rubble. Going up against a strike leak was as fruitless as holding back flood waters. The entire camp would soon be engulfed in talk. But a find of these proportions would require a world of planning. If they could only stem the deluge a short spell.

The first sign of the rescue party to greet Calvin was the light from Nate's two candle lamps. Then, blurred through the light, Nate's blackened face. Since there was not room for a shake, Nate clasped his friend's near hand and squeezed. "Good to see you, pard."

Cal was too choked up to do more than grip his friend in return.

"Anything broke?"

"Only my lunch pail."

Nate turned his head to direct the others. "Got him. Take hold of my shinbones and pull, boys."

They snaked Cal out over the top of the slide and half-carried him from the drift to the main tunnel, where they put him on his feet and pinched him good for damage. Cal took them all in, his grin so wide it nearly split his face.

Young Frank mopped at a freshet of tears. "I ain't had anyone this glad to see me since I went home to Ma."

"Wasn't hardly buried," Nate said huskily. "Not enough dirt on him for a good-size garden patch."

Calvin looked shakily around, taking the measure of the slide. "You're right, by cracky. Hardly bigger than an outsize load of coal." He digested this fact, his grin growing wider. As a general thing, Calvin did not smile over often. Yet, like a jack-o-lantern in a window, he kept beaming. Now that he was out from under, his mind was giddily re-accommodating itself to the bonanza beyond the dirt.

"My friends," he said, "we are sitting on enough silver to make tea services for every fete from here to Buckingham Palace." To everyone's amazement, Cal even capered a little, though the effort staggered him and he had to sit. "The Pearly has gone from sinkhole to glory hole. Wait 'til you see her. The biggest humdinger this side of the Comstock."

Holding a lantern close to peer in Cal's red-rimmed eyes, Nate said, "This mine will hold. The first order is to hoist you topside and see you to your bed."

"You'll do no such a thing." Cal's voice was firm. "This is the most glorious happening of my born days, and I don't plan to miss a minute. Needle, if you'll hand me that water piggin, I'll wet my whistle. Rest a minute...Luther, would you hightail it over to the place, let Vinnie know what's afoot. Alert Deke to keep a close watch above. What day is this? What is the hour?"

Everyone began to talk at once. "It's a shade past ten in the morning of July Fourth...year of our Lord eighteen and...Deke is topside reinforcing the cage hoist. Thing must have snapped when the slide struck the tickler. Every mother's son in this camp offered to dig for you, you old turnip. "Not only the mother's sons, neither," said Young Frank. "Some of the sons-of-bitches offered too."

Cal took them in. "First I want each and every one of you to see the prospect before us. Next, we'll try keeping this occurrence under wraps. Then—and this is a powerful favor I ask, on the holiday—we should pitch in to get this drift shored so she won't cave again. We can nevermore bury that bonanza."

"I swear, Cal," said Nate wonderingly, "if a slide will not slow you, I wonder would a typhoon?"

The men wriggled cautiously, one by one, over fallen rock to the vug. Like a curtain gone up on a stage, the slide had opened the chamber to full view. Nate and Pete, the first in, got to their feet, set their candles, had a good hard look, and were struck dumb.. By candlelight, the lode was as luminous as the Northern Lights. Greens and blues and pinks glimmered from sprays and ribbands of silver. Nate, who savored the forms and colors of flowers and clouds, had never thought to see such a sight below ground..

The other boys were struck by varying degrees of stunned reverence and, in Frank's case, religious conversion.

"I' God, I never seed the beat!" Pete Beard had removed his battered black hat and held it over his heart. "Well, I will be dipped in shit…mother in heaven…Landamercy…Looks to be thousands a shift." Needle's voice cracked on him.

"That is what she will mean," whispered Pete. "A goddam million or more in ninety days!"

The spell broken, the men seized and pounded Calvin. His hands were pumped so hard that he feared for his shoulder joints.

"Hellfire! You must have struck her soon after we left the shaft last evening," said Young Frank, wishing with all his heart that he had been by Cal's side at the great discovery.

"That was about the way of it. Moved past the headwall. Thought to test a new sidecut. Felt dead air and there she sat. Silver fit for Mrs. Astor's stomachers, just as she lies."

"Well sir, Cal…" Pete took a deep breath. "All this is mighty fine. But Nate's talking sense. This here golconda ain't about to run off on us. And your system has had a pounding. If you come down sick, where would we be?"

Cal balked, insisting his system had never been stronger.

"Use your noggin," Nate scolded. "A played-out captain is no use to his crew. We'll tend to your silver. You got over the dog. We can slide down the tail."

"We'll rough-timber and muck her out."

"By late afternoon, she'll be tidy as a preacher's front parlor."

"We'll report to you over at the place about five."

The men were so fevered by the strike that Independence Day was left far in its wake. They teamed up to hoist Cal to the surface, smuggle him down the back road to home, cart timber from storage chambers, shore the vug opening, and clear the drift.

Cal, at last aware of his rancid reek and crippling exhaustion, dropped on his bed and said raggedly to Pete and Needle, "I'll not soon forget this, my friends."

####

CHAPTER NINE

THE RACES

At the foot of the steep downhill pitch below the Pearly Mine, throngs of men, children, housewives, and whores swarmed over the rutted edges of Durant Avenue. Adding to the hubbub were loose burros, cats, dogs, and a number of irritable old hens scratching for feed. Ranchers had stripped the last cow and harnessed the team for town. Faro bankers boxed the cards and covered their tables for the day. Storekeepers pulled down green oiled-canvas shades and hung out "Shut" signs. Town women slopped the pigs, washed at the pump, and tied on fresh-starched bonnets. Men slicked their hair with moist hands from the water dipper and hurried to the race course.

Pins-and-needles anticipation over the foot contests were sharpened by a rumored cave-in at the Pearly. A cave in—fatal or not—set a camp on edge. When the clanging of the firebell reverberated, hearts pounded. Women grew faint. Children dove under beds. Men stood frozen, not a few swallowing chaws before springing into action. Even the chickens grew agitated, zigzagging in berserk circles underfoot.

In the morning's rising heat, the air shimmered like fumes from a kerosene can. The sun was turned up full, blinding anyone looking toward the cleft where Independence Pass cut through the Sawatch Range. Townspeople were hugely relieved that rescue teams were not needed in the Pearly. What the hell was Cal Krueger doing down there, anyway? A man needn't be such a bear for work. Those with sense were content to lean back in the sun, pull on their busthead, and relish the day. Camp people loved nothing more than an open-air contest—horse, foot, wagon, or drill.

Near the fire tower, men shifted chaws from cheek to cheek and held spur-of-the-moment spitting matches, although everyone stayed clear of a particular patch on the uphill side of the avenue. The patch marked the spot where Miss Eppa Strait had fallen to her death not a month past. Eppa and two maiden friends had been escorted by Boots Buckstraw to the top of the fifty-five foot fire tower to take in the view. Boots was courting Eppa, who was no beauty, but a cook renowned for her chocolate layer cakes. Undersheriff

Apostle Thatcher, unaware of visitors above, had roused himself from immersion in Matthew 4:35 and rung the clangorous firebell to mark the noon hour. The shock of the clapper immediately beside Eppa caused her to lose her footing and plunge to her death.

"Left a widowed mother and two baby brothers," mourned Boots, "and me." Boots was said to be grieving still. Marriageable women remained scarce in these hills. Apostle, who in some way felt responsible, had had a considerable sinking spell, though he'd found strength in prayer.

Undersheriff Thatcher was no hand with a gun, but he was in heavy demand for ceremonials. He'd come to this role late in the summer while sharing a jail cell for the night with Hog Tooth Haynes—in for inciting a fatal fight at the Chloride Saloon. Thatcher had overslept in the top bunk and Sheriff Dirty Harwood, after packing up Hog Tooth to transport him to the Canon City House of Corrections to cut stone, had inadvertently locked his assistant in the jailhouse. For seventy-six hours Newt Thatcher had no solace but a pitcher of dead water and a copy of the *New Testament*. He finished off the water and committed an astounding amount of scripture to memory. He'd then become a devout student of the Word and was interviewed at length by the *Aspen Daily Times*.

Other than the site of Eppa's passing, the street was packed with crowds afoot, in rigs and in spring wagons. Women sat placid and worn in home-stitched calico, their skirts shiny with fresh stiffening, their hands yellow from dipping snuff. Scattered like hothouse flowers among mullein were Bullion Row women in upholstered bustles and the latest plumed, pancake hats, their faces plump and pleasantly unlined. The smell of lemon verbena and bay rum hung in the air. The smell of sour washrags hung heavier.

The best seats on the street were held down by the bench boys. These old roosters—out-to-pasture prospectors, miners, cowhands—gathered daily on the telegraph office bench to await wires bearing news of disaster and to yearn for a hair-splitting dogfight. On the side, they sold mail order shares in played-out silver mines to suckers in the East. In the street, small boys scuffled and fought, and along with the loose burros, were a trial to hose men trying to lay dust that rose in blinding blankets to mix with the flies. One wiry little devil, Amos Blackwell, threw a lighted cracker into a grocer's pickle barrel, was roundly cuffed and sent home roaring with indignation.

Jake Levy, squinting beneath the shade of a raised hand at the race start line, said irritably to Willard Arey, "Now why in thunder do you suppose we're to run with the sun in our eyes?"

"Seems fittin' everyone runs toward them whores on the Row. " Willard shifted the big starter pistol to his other hand, his chaw to the other cheek. "Been chasin' poon, most of us, since we was boys."

Jake gazed past the false fronts of a smithy, two greengrocers, the offices of the *Aspen Daily Times*, of his own Watchmaker & Gunsmith, Jake Levy, Prop., the White Elephant Saloon, and Dunbar & Black, attorneys-at-law. "Now that you mention it, most of us have run aplenty—from the law…creditors…bad news…and our thirst." He smiled wryly. "Might's well have a little nooky at the finish."

The two men had been shouldered firmly out of the shafthouse by Deke. "Go on with the race," ordered the major. Later, Deke was to thank his stars for that felicitous foresight. If Willard had been apprized of Calvin's bonanza, lions and tigers could not have stilled his tongue. He'd have chattered and pranced like an organ grinder monkey.

Willard's mind was blessedly elsewhere. "Just don't pull up too fast by them girls' shacks," he cautioned Jake. "Their slats is so loose they'd blow over in a stiff breeze."

"Hear tell not all those girls are black-hearted."

"Little Annie and Lily Lorena is good souls. Don't see them leanin' out their windows and doors—makin' impudent remarks to every miner changin' shifts."

Jake thought of his well-cushioned wife whispering into their pillow. "Bertha says that when Governor Pitkin rode by, Jamestown Jess and Hard-Edge Em pulled back their curtains and their dress fronts, knockers big as bed pillows."

"Thet pair of good-for-nothings hang their tits out like wash on a line. And they'll swaller a three-dollar bottle of sourmash at one sitting. Hardened in sin." Knowing Jake had never set foot in a crib, he added reflectively, "On your other hand, others bed their callers, offer hot coffee or a bowl of stew to make things homey-like. I've called on that Lily Lorena a time or two. She's sickly, but she has a housewife's heart."

"If I was colorblind," Willard added, "believe I'd give nigger Frankie a whirl. Boys who know their post-hole work swear she's the best fence-builder this side of Sacramento. Then again, if I was the Count of Monte Carlo…" Willard's longing thoughts had turned to the fancy establishment across the hump in Leadville. "Say a girl in Miz Catton's Hospitality House comes high. Twenty dollars or so."

"Noooooo," Jake whistled.

"A fact." Willard, though long yearning to set his post in refined surroundings, could not endure the thought of parting with that kind of money.

"No doubt some of that'll go toward paint. Not on the girls—on the house."

Everyone in the mountains knew of Miss California Catton's startling establishment, which sat like a prize white hen on a Leadville hill. Fresh-painted once a year, the house was a landmark in a class with the presidential White House. As a general rule, all mine camp buildings were a weathered brown, the shade depending on how green the wood. The Clarendon Hotel, rebuilt last year after a fire was still the yellow ochre of fresh-sawn spruce. To men burrowing for silver, paint was nothing but folderol.

Willard's voice grew dreamy. "I wonder if a fella could maybe mosey into Miz Catton's and set his post without running up a big supper bill?"

"Now why would you ever want to miss the Hospitality House's famous Rocky Mountain oysters?"

"I would not—if someone else was standin' the bill. I ain't made of money like Gabe Tacker and them big city nobs. Men in full suits of clothes and clean shirts five days out of seven."

Jake restrained a smile. Every man in Aspen knew Willard was so close with a dime that he chased off half his help.

"It ain't only my store clothes. It's this store-bought leg. One look, and that Catton woman might show me the back door." Willard would despise the indignity of being strong-armed out a whorehouse exit.

Jake looked fondly at his long-time companion. Twenty years had passed since Willard gave up that leg in the Fredericksburg fight. After a bucket of Reb grapeshot took it off, Jake and Calvin had felt low about leaving the leg on the field. They'd had a heated argument over whether to gather it up and carry it off with its former owner—or leave it be.

Willard had roused from his stupor to yell, "Forget the goddamed leg! It'll be reunited with me in the hereafter!"

Because they'd stayed behind to rig a tourniquet and a stretcher, they were the only men in their gunnery squad to make it home. Willard never failed to remind them it was his leg had saved their necks.

The racers had lined up. Jake's toe was on his mark. "Stop jawing, Willard. You are waving that gun around like a buggy whip."

"Until Cal is dug out," Willard muttered, "I hardly know which way to turn."

"His delivery is in good hands. Now quit jittering before you shoot your other leg off."

Willard fired the pistol and started the race without slaughtering what chickens the coyotes had missed. Jake, despite the grey salting his hair, won his heat. So did Young Frank Parker, pride of the Durant Hose Company, the fastest runner on the Western slope. With a raft of cash money wagered on him, and an uproar if he'd scratched, he'd been dispatched from the Pearly for his race. Though Bull Mudgett kicked dust in his face, he did not let blind hate for a man cloud his euphoria. He felt as portentous as a federal office-holder. He was the first man above-ground and into the crowds bearing direct knowledge of the greatest strike since Virginia City. His head was filled with sentiments and proposals. After they had the mine buttoned down against Sutton, he planned to ask for Bridget O'Reilly's hand in marriage.

Scooper Hurd's legs bunched and unbunched as he said, "Jesus Christ, Lute. Son of a bitch. After I couldn't find you, I thought you took by a bear." His friend stood covered in mine dirt, not even slicked up for the holiday.

"I'm sorry as can be, Scoop. Who'd ever know Mr. Cal would be caught in a cave-in?"

The major had sent Lute packing to the Durant Avenue course. "Mustn't miss your friend's big race. I'll be along directly to drive old Gabe's team." When he arrived, he'd whispered the thunderous strike news to Willard. Though sworn to secrecy, the undertaker puffed up like a Spanish grandee. Deke didn't begrudge him his moment. Over the past year, the miserly merchant had unclasped his purse to buy many a share in his friend's venture. Now, in his head, he was consorting with legislators, having his likeness painted in oil, and conducting commerce with Leadville's Hospitality House in clean white shirts. In addition, he was directing Calvin's finances, investing his profits, planning his future. Aloud, he instructed Deke, "H'it'll be a handy thing, you driving Tacker's team, getting in the good graces of Rob Skinner. We'll need every jack and mule in the man's livery."

Scoop shivered and clutched his middle. "I s-sure wisht you was running with me, Lute…"

"Wish I was too."

"God's sake, Lute, they're lining us up. I hate to say it, but I have the bellyache, and I am near scared shitless."

"I would be too, Scoop. Don't think it's not natural."

Scoop's face had turned chalky. "I—I ain't even certain about the shitless. Truth is, I feel the scours comin' on." Swallowing hard, he stepped shakily to the fresh streak of lime in the street.

Minutes later, through the buzzing in his ears, he heard Lute's faraway shouts. "You won, Scoop! Won by a country mile!"

Scooper managed to creak, "I—I'll see you back at the shack...gotta get...off the s-street. Hellfire! Musta shat a p-pint of them green berries!"

In the offices of Dunbar & Black, dead on the finish line, G.B. Tacker sat in the only stuffed chair, his bulk threatening to explode the filling. The stifling front room, its windows battened down against dust, teemed with men armed with flyswatters. Suddenly Gabe's big lumpy body began to shake. He sputtered, "Th-that boy, the one who just won the k-kiddies' race. Damned if he didn't mess himself."

After uneasy pauses (Gabe Tacker laughed seldom and he never laughed lightly), three bank directors, an insurance broker, and two officials from the Indian office joined tentatively in the guffawing. They put Deke in mind of minstrel show ninnies. Like a restive horse, Major Burdine moved his big body against the inner office doorframe, scratching his back.

Tacker, meanwhile, wiped streaming eyes with an outsize kerchief, then honked his nose in it. Fanning himself with a palmetto fan, he ordered, "Andy, send a five-dollar piece out to the race official, tell him to add it to the boy's purse. Ran a helluva race."

Gabe Tacker felt expansive. He liked being a fat frog in a small pond. He'd wearied of shark fights in the oceanic East, he was content with the game here in the high country. The Aspen camp in particular, where he was pleasured by the toothsome Widow Wickersham. Oh, he could live without that mean stage ride over the hump from Granite, rattling over fallen rock on a sky-high pig trail, inching over blasted boulders where nothing stood between him and a five-hundred-foot-plunge to an unpleasant end. Then again, he'd endured Arizona territory rides where a team of wild, unbroken horses was hitched to a stage, had their blindfolds torn off and were driven like wild animals twelve miles to the next station. The maddened, exhausted beasts arrived in Tucson lathered white and half the passengers staggered into the lone barber's to have their heads bandaged.

Big Gabe wasn't so old he didn't relish a dash of hot sauce in his stew— risky mountains or dauncy women. This afternoon he'd breeze through the expected niceties at the lakes, shower the church ladies with compliments, then adjourn to the widow's, she of the sweetly rounded stomach and bouncing buttocks. There was a woman to light a man's fire. Delightedly, his pale oystery eyes watering, he felt his sausage swelling beneath his fawn-colored suit. Gabe Tacker did not give a hoot in hell who saw him with his wiener at attention in mid-morning. Man his age, it was something to brag on.

Derned old stud, thought Deke, leaning harder into the doorframe. He redirected his thoughts to Tacker's pair of greys. They were a matched set, fresh-broke, tender-mouthed. Rob Skinner had said gratefully, "I God, Major, you're the only man in camp I'd trust with that team. Parade hullabaloo ain't no place fer unpredictable animals. Hate like thunder askin' you to drive—but I've had to put Toby on the parade wagon and Macky here at the livery." He'd repositioned a worn cretonne pillow under his behind. "Gabe Tacker must have his show. A wonder he don't carry trumpets and motherfuckin' chariots."

The hostler took a deep pull on his whiskey, sniffed the manure-scented air. "If I can ever haul you out of a tight corner..." At which point Deke had concluded a satisfying bargain for all of the upcoming Pearly freighting.

The livery man had been too preoccupied with his throbbing bum to inquire into Deke's sudden heavy commerce. "You wouldn't want to buy me out?" was all he asked, misery in every line of his weather-honed face. "I would not mind traveling out to my sister's place to soak in that there California sea water."

Deke glanced around the hot, fly-infested room. In one way, he was tickled to be dead-center in the enemy camp. Keeping his ears open at close quarters got his blood up, reminded him of the old cavalry days. On the other hand, had he seen the beauty in the organdy dress sooner, he might have bolted. He narrowed his eyes, trying to locate the violet and green plaid parasol through a grime-laden window. There, she had swept off her straw boater and was waving it in sweeping circles to cheer a racer. It was the young Sutton woman. A sight to see. He'd often spied her from a distance—now and again entering a store, riding the creek trails like a hoyden in a man's hat. In a camp where he was a saloon keeper and she a mine owner's wife, they had not had occasion to take tea or exchange words.

A woman who loved saddles more than carriages was out of the ordinary. So was a white woman attended by a squaw packing a Bowie knife and a Ute throwing axe. If he had not spent so many nights in card rooms and days keeping an eye on whiskeyed men, he might have sighted more of that rough-riding filly. Now he was trapped again, committed to drive to Delmonico's for a heavy midday meal neither he nor Tacker needed. Deke Burdine was not a philandering man. To his surprise, he found himself thinking, *I'd like to trifle with that handful.*

Arrived at the restaurant, Tacker beckoned him to his table at the window. "Come sit by me, young fellow. I appreciate your style." Soon they were discussing the merits of a saddlemaker who'd just relocated to Aspen from Leadville. Deke had to admit Tacker owned winning ways. There was little mention of the Pearly. A small slide. No one maimed or killed. And the mine was one of Sutton's played-out holes. Most of the talk was the same old talk of cards and horses and loose women. If strike news had hit, there would have been talk of nothing but strike.

The parade, to start in half-an-hour, would wind its way down Main Street, move south on Monarch, east on Cooper, then north on Galena, past Delmonico's eatery. "And," said Gabe, as he spooned up the last of a piping hot clam bisque with a big liver-spotted hand, "if the affair goes on schedule, about the time we get to our strawberry shortcake, the entire shebang should be heat-prostrated or skunk-drunk. Ought to be some kind of hell break loose, right about this block." He slurped his bisque noisily, his digestion greatly enhanced by the thought of calamity to come.

\####

CHAPTER TEN

THE PARADE

Like parades in all times and places, this one was tangled in the forming and late in the starting. Balancing herself against evergreen-draped ropes strung on stakes around a big, ungainly ranch flatwagon, Emma felt oddly removed from the commotion. Men of the hose companies and fraternal lodges scattered helter-skelter, drinking from foaming buckets of beer. The Knights of Pythias molted feathers from ancient headgear and refused to form up or close ranks. Two hell-raising bachelors from the Red Star Hose outfit tamped black powder into the tail cavity of an anvil, inserted a fuse, turned a second anvil upside down on the first, and lighted the spitter. With a ponderous *whoooooooommmmm* the anvil lifted into the air, missing by a hair the stuffed chickadee on Mrs. Titus Pomeroy's new hat. An ordinarily sedate, buttoned-up store clerk beat on a dishpan, and a cur dog with firecrackers tied to its tail flew howling in circles. So did Mayor McDade, his ragged whiskers in wet strings. Cherry bombs blew, pans racketed, the fire tower bell tolled, steam whistles shrieked, cats yowled, men chased boys, and boys taunted girls. Rancher Tite Pomeroy's Suffolks, their great heads plumed and rosetted, shuffled restlessly from foot to foot, fetlocks growing dusty and disheveled, harness leather creaking.

Over at the Elkhorn Livery, Skinner lay miserably on a bench on his belly. Squaw Polly, summoned by Nate, had peeled down his pants and applied a foul-smelling poultice. She growled, "Stay on stummick" and ordered him not to pull up his filthy pants. He'd had a notion to give her a whack upside the head. He was already in a world of hurt, breaking his word to Pomeroy, sending that cork-puller Toby Flanagan out with Tite's prize horseflesh. "Mind you stick to them reins—and your pledge," he'd snapped at his hostler. "One nip, and I'll deliver your Popish scalp to the hostiles."

Toby sat on the wagon seat sullenly picking his nose. He'd planned on a day of carousing with Jim McPhee and Johnny Callahan. It was the worst luck that Skinner come down poxed. His mood was not lightened by Jim and Johnny punching each other slyly, tormenting Toby about escorting women through the streets. He snarled bitterly at the team when, at another pistol shot, they backed, shuddered, backed again. "Goddam you, stand right still— or ye'll feel this whip on yer flanks!"

Though Emma did not approve of Flanagan's way with horses, the heat made her too lackluster to scold. Her loose hair, hanging halfway down her back, felt as cumbersome as a fur cape. She had never appeared in public in such disarray. When Bridgie had suggested confining her tangled mane in a snood, Professor Palazzi, dancing master and tableau director, had sniffed haughtily, "What sort of Liberty would wear her crowning glory in a fishwife's hairnet, madam!"

"Dammit," she muttered half-aloud, "I'm melting away like a tub of hot butter."

Draping her flimsy skirts over an arm, she slipped under the ropes and off the wagon. "I'll hold the girls, Mr. Flanagan. Have a drop of beer with your friends. It could be the middle of next week before the mayor achieves order."

"Why I thankee, Miz Sutton." Toby doffed his derby and handed her thick, leaden reins. He clambered down, calling back, "You're sartain ye can handle them brutes? They ain't no saddle fillies, those ones."

Emma bridled. "I rode a horse on my pa's knee before you knew a muzzle from a pastern, sir. Now scoot!"

Toby scat. Emma stood crooning to the edgy animals until they grew quiet in the traces, the whites of their eyes no longer flashing. Leaning her head against a massive chest, she harked back to jousting and fair maidens. These were the horses of chivalry, bred to carry knights in heavy armor. In her mind's eye she pictured a Tudor castleyard, bright pennants in midday English sun, men with courtly manners carrying a ladylove's kerchief into the contest.

"'In peace, love tunes the shepherd's reed…in war, he mounts the warrior's steed.'" The remembered verse softened her face. At such times, caught in a tender moment, Emma stole men's breaths away.

A young voice invaded her reverie. "Pardon, Missus. I'd be pleased to lend a hand." Tacy Beard, one of the Liberty Belle attendants, leaned over the wagon ropes in her garish blue robe. Gwyneth Davies and Svea Hoaglund were gowned in headcheese cloth dyed the same unfortunate blue, the other girls in red. Emma, in white, wondered fleetingly if they weren't debasing the American flag. Ah well, at a distance, the girls were a picture—Gwyneth with her dark eyes and curls, Svea tall and flaxen-haired. And at least cheese-cloth was cool. Tacy smiled shyly and climbed down to join Emma. "Tis not fittin' for fair Liberty to be dirtied up to her crown."

"I thank you kindly, Tacy girl...I warrant I should have stayed on the professor's chalk mark. But I feared Flanagan would fly the coop."

"He might, the drunken Mick!"

Later, someone located a bullhorn and Mayor McDade's voice rose shrilly over the din. "Mount up and line up! We will proceed in ten minutes exact!"

Toby returned brimming with beer, Texas low john, and effusive thanks. As he assisted the ladies up on the wagon, Tacy noted Mrs. Sutton's troubled face, worried a bit over what Pa called her own forward manner, hesitated, then leaned close to the lady's ear. "Have you heard about your mister's Pearly Mine, ma'am?"

Emma was puzzled. "I've had no news of it."

Tacy gulped again. "Tis said," she whispered, "they have made a great strike there. Say this camp has never seen the like."

Emma, shocked, found her mark on the wagon bed. As her tableau led off the parade, she stood rooted on the spot.

Like some unwieldy prehistoric creature, the procession began to move haltingly toward the center of Aspen. Behind Liberty and her Belles stepped the Hook & Ladder boys, the foot-racers, a half-dozen Sunday school classes, the G.A.R. veterans of Winfield Scott Post #49, the youngsters of the juvenile hose company, the Woman's Relief Corps, prominent members of the Appalachia and Shakespeare societies, the waitresses from the Clarendon Hotel, and members of the Masons, Knights of Pythias, Oddfellows, Eagles, Moose, and Elks, all in a loose patchwork of uniforms and formations. Within a few blocks, they had achieved a semblance of order, the oompah beat of the Hamtown Band helping the marchers to step in tempo. The parade, like all parades, had found a life of its own.

Emma, stunned by Tacy Beard's news, scarcely heard the beat of the band. Erect on an overturned chicken crate behind the wagon seat, she held her plaster of Paris torch high and stared blindly at Aspen Mountain. A strike in the Pearly! Did this mean her mine stock could pay? Might it mean escape from Garrett? The mine was out on lease to Mr. Calvin Krueger. She knew something of the man from the Shakespeare Society, though he had not been in attendance of late. Her recollection was of a taciturn Pennsylvanian whom Uncle Nate counted a friend—and a superior mine operator. Would a decent man, a man who esteemed the bard, have the sand to outdistance her husband? If there was indeed a strike, there would be war. She thought of the rough customers who reported to Garrett, men with mouths and eyes hard as owls. Despite the hot sun, she shivered. By now she'd heard that contemptible Mudgett named a card cheat, claim jumper, killer. Few men had ever caused her fright. But when Mudgett looked at her with hooded eyes, a wintry chill coursed through her. Counting the ways her husband, or Mudgett, might cause grief, her head hummed as if filled with bees.

When the marchers came within earshot of the Clarendon, scattered calls broke through the muddle in Emma's mind.

"Sure 'nuff, R.C., that there is Little Emma."

"Hidey, little Emma!"

"Damn!" she muttered, "That pesky child will plague me 'til the end of my days." Then she summoned a cheery smile and a wave to cover the ungracious thought.

Aggie McClaren, eager to catch sight of the band, clutched her fresh bonnet and leaned out over the hotel boardwalk. She'd just returned from Doc Alderfer's infirmary, where the Blackwell boy lay stuporous with laudanum. He'd mangled himself with a homemade cracker. Two fingers showed signs of putrefying, and Doc figured they'd have to come off. She'd looked forward to the parade and the afternoon balloon ascension like a schoolgirl. But with the imp gone from a little mannie's eyes, her spirits were no longer so blithe.

As the German Hamtowners duck-walked, horns blaring, toward the hotel, Aggie called indignantly to Nate Phipps, "Will ya look at those uniforms, mon? All that money down the spout, and the half o' them not brushed nor pressed!"

Nate thought the band very spruce-looking. Aggie's indignant glare had alighted on the single exception: butcher Herman Klausmeyer, marching with his top buttons open and a pigsticker belted to his untidy middle. Aggie had little use for the Beck & Bishop meat-cutter. He shorted her on weight and left too much fat on his chops. She had stated clearly, "I'll na' have m' donation goin' on the back of that pear-shaped Kraut!"

Had she been able to read Klausmeyer's mind, her resolve would have hardened. Moaning inwardly, the butcher stumbled in and out of step. *Verdammter,* he swore. If the talk was true—and all his shares of Pearly stock gone…Then his pace quickened. A notion had begun to form in his head.

Nate, mesmerized by the Hamtowners, felt the guilt of a small boy lollygagging on the road to school. He was en route to Jake's gun shop to help oil and sight guns. This time tomorrow, Calvin would have posted round-the-clock guard shifts at the mine. By now strike news was seeping out, sand through a sieve. But Nathaniel was bent on waving to his girl Emma—and he meant to decipher how the man on the tuba mustered the wind for his job. "The boys look muckle fine, woman!" he called above blaring trombones. The new tuba, blazing brassily in the sun, blew deep, sepulchral notes that thrilled him to his vitals. He'd have a good look at Miss Emma and the full-of-wind tuba player—and then he'd be off to Jake's.

There was a shout from the edge of the crowd. "Whooooooooeee! Will you look at thet beauty aholdin' the torch!"

"Watch yer tone, Malachi. Thet there is Little Emma."

"You don't say!"

"Course nowadays she's a growed-up Mrs. Garrett Sutton."

"I swear! Thet son-of-a-bitch owns half the silver in camp—and a half-nekkid wife in the bargain!"

"Best shet your trap, Malachi. Thet's not nekkid. Thet there is a angel costume."

"Well, if she be a angel, may I be took straight to heaven!" bellowed Malachi.

The angel, teetering precariously on a rutted curve, cursed silently. Her torch was far heavier than the professor had led her to expect. *It isn't plaster-of-Paris*, she thought grouchily. *It's cast iron.* A pine knot burned on top, adding distressful warmth to the blistering day. She managed to shift the torch to her opposite hand and grasp the flat wagon's rope where evergreen boughs bled sticky sap on the decorative bunting. Hot air blew, sweeping her hair in damp tangles about her face and sending her flimsy skirts well above her ankles. *Why didn't I have Bridgie sew sash weights in the hems*, she wondered. Garrett had probably been right about her making a shameless display—and she could scarcely endure Garrett being right about a single thing.

By now there were fewer delays for fights and children playing "toad-on-a-rock" in the streets. Even so, sweat trickled down her face, causing itches she could not scratch. She set her jaw and hung on.

Tacy Beard moved out of her tableau position. She was concerned for Mrs. Sutton. The woman's face had lost color and her robes were drenched. She could be sunstruck.

Then, almost to the block and the minute, the disaster Gabe Tacker had jovially prophesied came to be. Shoat Yankel, taken by drink and twisted patriotic fervor, tightened the bucking strap on his bewildered mare, and firing his Winchester, bolted crazily out of Delmonico's alleyway to conduct a Wild West holdup of the parade. Gertie and Irmie, blinkered and amiable, were caught unaware. Shocked by the sun-fishing horse and crackling gunfire directly in their path, they reared, their massive weight unbalancing the wagon. Two liberty belles flew into the street. Toby Flanagan, befuddled by drink, followed. The big Suffolks, released from restraint, opted to flee this noisome hell. In perfect tandem, they broke into a gallop and headed for home.

As the parade approached, Deke turned gratefully from the heavy midday meal. He was bored with talk of women and faro, of apexes and sidelines, talk he heard every day and night of his life. He could hear the band through the restaurant's poorly-caulked windows, could see the big, heavy-headed chestnut draft horses pulling a tableau which appeared to feature a statue, holding aloft a torch. Then he recognized Mrs. Sutton. Excusing himself, Deke pushed his way to the door.

By the time he reached the walkway, Shoat had ridden, the accident was done, women screamed and the runaways hurtled toward the Main Street intersection.

"Help me, girls!" cried Emma as Tacy and the remaining belles flailed amid a tangle of legs, arms, and robes in the careening wagon. Her voice muffled in a mouthful of bunting, she cried, "Push! Push me up!" Amid bouncing and jolting, the girls managed to hoist her toward the front. Clutching the seat, she gasped, "Watch the corner at Main and Galena! The wagon will tilt! Grab a stake! Hold on!"

The Suffolks took the corner at a full run. The wagon canted at a crazy angle to the earth and, after an interminable moment in mid-air, righted itself. Iron wheel rims screeched. The crash jarred the camp from mountain to mountain. Titus Pomeroy, seated with Annie by the armory, rose to his feet with a wordless cry as his team blew past like a funnel cloud. Tacy Beard's horrified sisters watched as Tacy flew by, white as a haunt. Every eye on the parade route focused on the heedless flight of Tite Pomeroy's team.

Horses, flatwagon, and liberty belles pounded along Main Street, potholes kicking them into the air, clouds of dust rising like fallout from explosives. Emma searched frantically for knights in armor, men a-horseback—until it came to her that everyone had tethered animals in quiet side streets or corrals. Parade routes were no place for skittish horseflesh. A blur of faces as featureless as cabbages rushed past, expressions frozen in disbelief. People by the side of the street scattered like ptarmigan. A few men braced themselves and leaped for skipping reins, although a man on foot would have been trashed along, a leaf in a flood.

Emma, well up on the wagon seat, tried again and again to catch a rein flying tantalizingly out of reach. Now and again, the cumbersome leather struck a hoof or rock and flew high in her direction, bedeviling her with its nearness. Her mind was a stew of calculations. Polly's grandson Iacono had instructed her, years before, "Stick with runaway, Em. Sticking safer than jumping."

She'd stick. But how to halt these crazed animals? Their mighty heads bucketing, they thundered out Main, north and west toward King's Butte, a high, knife-edged ridge of maroon rock cut off from the main body of West Aspen Mountain by a long-gone glacier. Dead ahead, over Castle and Maroon Creeks' orange and magenta gulches carved deep by slashing snowmelt, lay two crude toll bridges. She felt certain the team would stay with the main trace which bore right, past the camp racetrack, down the steep Slaughterhouse Hill to the banks of the Roaring Fork, where Beck & Bishop butchered the store's beef, pigs, and sheep. If they held on for the turn and the headlong run, they'd eventually strike the Slaughterhouse Bridge—a bridge the exact width of this broad-bedded wagon. They'd be kites hurled in a cyclone.

When the horses hurtled aslant onto the Slaughterhouse track, there was a shriek of protesting wood, and the hind wheels skidded until the tugs finally snapped them straight. The jerk made Emma's neck pop. Now she had a little time. There was only one answer, and Emma made up her mind to it. *Lord God*, she prayed, *let me do the right. I promise I will no more harbor harsh thoughts or unkind words. Just let me do the right.* Then, her voice shrill, she turned to shout to Tracy and Svea, "I propose to jump on Gertie's back—the mare on the left. I'll need help!"

She bunched her skirts high above her long silk and lace pantalettes and swung her soggy hair from her eyes. The girls' faces were grim as they twisted her trailing costume into a semblance of rope.

"Good work! Now hold tight!" she called over the cacophony of hooves, harness, wagon and wheel rims as she rose to a half-crouch. "Keep a grip. Steady…"

The girls were camp-bred, reared with accidents and disaster. They stiffened, doing as Emma directed.

"Let me out slowly. That's the ticket! I'll shout 'GO!' You let loose…I'll jump."

She swallowed, took in a deep breath, flexed her legs and shouted, "Reeeeady…GO!"

She pushed off and leaped out, landing aslant and well back on the big chestnut haunches, hitting the heavy, jouncing, brass-studded trace carriers, back straps, and tugs so jarringly that the pain jolted her to her teeth. She scrabbled for a firm grip on the harness straps, gaining a surer hold. Her body heaving with Gertie's back, her ribs on fire, she stared down through a reddish-brown haze at the manure-splashed doubletree clattering like a crazy thing beneath the horses' bellies. Steadier now, she turned blinking from clouds of grainy dust, getting her bearings.

Roadside tangles of wild raspberry brambles, chokecherry bushes, and sagebrush streamed past in a blur of dirtied green. They were approaching the steep, where the trail headed sharply downward. She was taken aback that even with her long limbs she could not reach the horse collar nor the hames. She inched forward, her silk-clad legs sliding treacherously. Finally, her breath a whine, she grasped the heavy horse collar, pulled hard and groped for the left safe, the loop which threaded the check rein. With all her strength, she caught hold of the rein and pulled.

She raised her head from Gertie's wet, slithery back and called to the horses in her strong voice, "Hooooooo. Ho-Aaah…Hoo, there!"

She pulled and called until her head swam and the ache in her arms brought tears to her eyes. In her mind's ear, she heard the splintering of wood, the clang of mangled iron at the bridge. Then, faint as a shrug, her unremitting tug began to cant Gertie's head. The big mare tossed her mane, lowered her chin. Her stride broken, she appeared to come from a trance. Slowing, the mare pulled her harness-mate off-balance beside her. The team's galloping became a half-trot. They stumbled and blew and stumbled again. Hearing the rush of the Roaring Fork, they sensed pasture and drinking water. And came at last to a halt by the bridge, limping from the strain to quivering legs.

Except for the tumble of water, there was little sound. Still snorting and blowing, the horses worked their way to the bank, munching clover and wild mustard. They reached the water and began sucking in big, noisy drafts. Svea climbed shakily from the wagon to catch up reins and keep the animals from drinking 'til they foundered. Her voice unsteady, she whispered Swedish endearments to the staggered team. Emma lay spent, spread-eagled across Gertie's back.

Tacy Beard cried from the wagon bed, "You done it, Miz Sutton! We're saved!"

Leaning against a wagon stake, Gwyneth Davies began to sob convulsively. Svea hollered, "Quit that! Quit or I'll slap you silly!" She herself stood gripping reins, her knees turned to mush, and doubted she could haul her arm back, let alone smack poor Gwyneth. Della Butler, a thin girl with overlarge eyes, lay quiet in the wagon. She'd fainted at Main and Monarch Streets.

"You've done wonderful, ma'am!" Tacy's black eyes shone with relief as she reached up to give Emma a hand.

Emma felt drained away, her will sucked out. At length she unclenched her hands from the hames and slid weakly down Gertie's soaking wet side.

Tacy's voice was a shocked undertone. "Land, Missus! You've gone and stuck yourself!" Faint pink stickiness spread through cheesecloth, the stain growing. "Quick now! On the grass with her."

The girls eased Emma to the ground, smoothing aside tangled hair. "If you'll pardon ma'am, I'd best have a look." Tacy's tone was stern.

"I—I am not hurt. But my, I do feel poor." Emma was surprised that she, never sickly, should be so light-headed.

Tacy ripped off a piece of robe and dipped it in the Roaring Fork to dampen Emma's brow. Then, gently, she said, "I need ask, Mrs. Sutton. Were you in a family way?"

Emma shuddered, an involuntary movement. "That I was…"

Tacy's voice was stricken. "I'm powerful sorry, ma'am. I believe now it is gone from you…"

Emma turned her head into hot, sweet-smelling clover, her face buried in blossoms. Bees hovered. She murmured, "Oh Father in Heaven, thank you! I do thank you!"

From Delmonico's, Deke had raced to the Elkhorn faster than any foot racer timed that morning. He'd leaped on the first bridled horse in the feedlots, a big, rough-gaited roan called Cassius for his Roman nose. Old Cass wouldn't do for cutting or barrel-racing, but when Deke took a hastily-cut switch to him, he broke into a heavy lope, doing his startled best as the major lathered him to the ears.

From a distance, to his horror, he saw Mrs. Sutton catapult from the wagon. When he pulled the heaving Cass to a halt by the river, she was lying in the grass, her eyes closed, the girls bathing her forehead and patting her hands. She looked as spent as a pup in a rainstorm. His face was so filled with concern that Tacy Beard touched him lightly on the arm. "She was not thrown, sir."

Svea had recovered her usual booming voice. "She saved us, she did. Jumped right on that monster horse and pulled her up short."

Deke shook out a linen handkerchief and gently wiped away grime. Mrs. Sutton's skin was greenish under her dusting of sun speckles. True to her promise, she had not swooned. But she now began bucking like a horse with the heaves. Swept by nausea, she grew white from the cramping in her loins. She knew that someone held her, heard gentling words. Then she turned her head—and vomited all over the front of Deke Burdine's ruffled shirt, sateen vest, and fancy frock coat.

Between gasps, she managed to sputter, "H-hell and d-damn, my m-mouth feels like a slop pot…"

In all his years, Deke had never heard any woman but a whore to curse. A moment passed before a faint smile lifted the corners of his mouth. Here, he'd decided, was no woman to trifle with.

####

CHAPTER ELEVEN

THE LAKES

The Thins won their ballgame against the Fats, five to three. Attendance was light. In face of mine rumors and runaways, baseball seemed intolerably tame.

"The horse races are cancelled!" announced Mayor McDade from the armory steps. Town officials agreed. There'd been about enough horse racing for one day.

Intent as an army of ants, Aspen town folk moved on the Hallam Lakes for the afternoon's speeches, contests, and eats. Talk of a strike at the Pearly eddied, slowed, ran stronger. Many said no, it was only a small slide. A big strike was so rare that few gave the idea much credence. Just the same, scalps felt prickly and there was the on-edge air of folks forted up against Indian attack.

On a grandstand of raw timber draped in red, white, and blue bunting and fresh-cut pine boughs, Judge Silas Duckworth prepared to hold forth center stage.

"Will you look at that old fox?" said Nate to Willard with grudging admiration. "He has surrounded himself with liberty belles."

"Well, h'it's a welcome change from the usual compliment of pot-bellied politicians," said Willard. "Now if we could just drum that warty mayor off of there—he's spoiling my view."

The two men, Calvin's top talkers, had been sent to the lakes to begin signing on tram crews.

Judge Duckworth, who prided himself on an ear tuned to the electorate, had re-tooled his all-purpose speech from "this glorious nation" to "our wondrous womanhood." The judge's privately held point of view was that talk of female suffrage was a pile of horseshit. After hearing that Stanton woman orate on women's rights, he would have liked to give her five or six licks with a good stout staub. However, as a prominent statesman, he dare not risk a single impending vote. Colorado, it was feared, would soon award women the ballot. He might suffer bitter rue in his heart, but he'd climb on that bandwagon with a smile on his face.

Poised in his finest declamatory posture, one hand tucked in his waistcoat, speaking without benefit of bullhorn, the judge shoved off in full voice, "One hundred and eight years ago, this babe of a nation cut the umbilicus tying it to a unnatural mother…"

Sixty-seven minutes later, the judge moved croakingly into his last-word-roundup. "And so, in the greeeeaat tradition of distinguished women through history, in the footsteps of our gentlest patriots—the intrepid Molly Pitcher…the gallant Dolly Madison…the invincible…" His Sunday clawhammer coat damped through, the judge leaned over to his wife to hiss, "Sarey, what the hell was the name of that niggra, the one that run across the ice?"

Raring back, he roared, "And of the valorous Harriet…Beecher…Stowe, let us give a eighteen-gun salute to Aspen's own proud daughter, that gloooooorious personification of Liberty who, singlehanded, saved the lives of seven," the Judge had miscounted his numbers again, "of our finest flowers of young womanhood: MRS. GARRETT SUTTON!!!!"

Boys whistled. Men cheered. Willard Arey muttered, "Damn windbag." The clamorous ovation set quakie leaves trembling far up Aspen Mountain. Over on Bullion Row, out of earshot, Emma Sutton rested in her bed. Had she heard the judge's overwrought panegyric, she might have swooned at last.

By mid-afternoon, strike talk had risen to a crescendo. Men gathered in clutches, buzzing behind hands into waiting ears. Many hoofed it up to the Pearly shafthouse, where they found Deke Burdine and Jake Levy—genial but close-mouthed—packing guns. Here at the lake, one of the ablest miners in camp, a slab-sided Slovenian named Mike Medjeric, was the center of a sizeable gathering. Mike, a young Samson who could whip any four men at a go and load a tramcar fast as a dishpan, was the first known to have hired on at the Pearly. "Can't give particulars," he said laconically. "Willard Arey and Nate Phipps are here hiring help. Put me on starting with the night shift tomorrow. Double wages."

Eight dollars a shift was so unheard of that men were stunned. The Bohunks and the Dagos in the soft coal mines down around Trinidad did not make that in six months—although everyone knew Aspen's hard rock boys were a superior grade of digger.

"The Pearly has surely hit a streak," declared Cowpie Burkhardt, as respected a newsmonger as the *Daily Times*. "Double wages is gilt-edged insurance against high-grading."

Men nodded agreement. A well-paid miner in a rich dig was not one to smuggle paydirt into the lining of a coat or between the soles of his boots. One of the bench boys muttered, "Course that piss-ant Sutton holds the opposing view. The fool thinks a half-starved trammer outworks a well-fed one."

Everyone marked time, waiting for an end to the judge's long-winded introductions of committee heads and acknowledgments of visiting dignitaries. The high points of the afternoon would be the core-drilling contest and the balloon ascension.

At length Apostle Thatcher, with the aid of a megaphone and ten brisk rolls from the Hamtown drummers, readied onlookers for the drilling contest—an affair to make even strike news pale.

Aggie McClaren trembled on tenterhooks beside the rough platform where a six-foot block of Gunnison granite had been hoisted by four mules and eight men. Its upper surface, dressed flat, glistened like a polished headstone. Aggie peeked at the hard, unforgiving rock and quaked. Beside her, Nate shook his head. Drilling was an enterprise he'd not care to try his hand at.

"Hand core-drilling," bellowed Thatcher into his horn, "is the highest art form in these hills. She is a exhibition of crackerjack skill…of manly endurance…and of your true grit!" By way of introduction, he held up a handful of drills, wicked-looking as Cheyenne war arrows.

The drillers' weapons were heavy sledges and sharp drilling steels. In a mine, two men required as much as half a day to drill a thirty-inch core to hold a powder charge. In today's contest, top teams, by turns pounding the sledge and turning the steels, striking more than seventy blows a minute, would drill farther than that in the allotted quarter-hour. The Cornish team of Olwen Davies and Sell Williams, Aspen's finest, had reached something over thirty-eight inches the summer before Olwen lost the use of his arm in the Hallelujah Mine avalanche. Olwen still prized his set of steels, worth more than a blooded horse. His portrait hung on a number of saloon walls lined with tintypes of dashing drillers, their steels on display like braces of prize pistols.

Spectators, packed fifty-deep around the drilling ring, jammed the grassy sward sloping up from the lakes and boys leaned down from perches in trees. At Thatcher's signal, an eerie silence fell. The Buckskin Joe team of D.J. Newbury and Cousin Jack Cowan stepped up on the rock and were greeted with a rousing ovation. Cowan was well over six feet tall, his partner less than five-and-a-half. Though ill-matched, both were hard-muscled and fit for the job. Newbury grasped the starter steel, a twelve-inch, octagonal rod sharpened to a plain chisel tip with a slight flare as insurance against "fitchering," or slippage. Fresh drills in graduated lengths waited on the slab. When a bit grew dull, the drill man would reach for a longer, sharper one.

With Thatcher booming out the cadence, Cousin Jack began to pound, the kneeling Newbury to turn the drill. It was pound and turn, pound and turn, with Apostle's voice, deep as Moses on the mount, counting out the beat. At measured intervals the men changed places, the steel man turning the drill steadily so as not to fitcher, his partner striking full force behind the eight-pound sledge. The chance that the drill would slip, the awful hammer come down on the drill man's arm, hung heavy in the air. The hushed crowd, drawn by the danger as well as the artistry, might have been at a hanging. Now and then Aggie hid her eyes in her starched apron. Even Nathaniel was half-sick with worry.

Some here had seen last summer's Leadville contest when the rhythmic beat had faltered, then halted, then the audience groaned a terrible groan. The driller'd been struck! As the horrified Leadville sledgeman paused, his partner had looked up and howled, "Come down, boy!" Down came the sledge. Women wept. Though the drill man's hand turned crimson, he held on. When it was his turn to rise and wield the hammer, the injured arm looked as if he'd been butchering sheep. Water from the hose used to flush out the drill cuttings ran thick with blood. At every stroke of the hammer, it sloshed up and spattered spectators like spilled red wine. Though the grievously injured man had sagged lower after every blow, he never quit 'til the timer signaled fifteen minutes—when he fell in a deep faint. They said the platform was like a slaughtering block. The Leadville affair was in every mind as Thatcher called, "Strike! Turn! Strike! Turn!"

When a few nervy boys elbowed their way into the hush, hawking fudge and dippers of lemonade, irate onlookers sent them packing. There were no more interruptions until near the end of the cadence. Then, echoing Thatcher's, "Strike!" a new voice, a different voice, howled, "Strike!" Down the hill loped Denver Bob Bisbee, his voice a roar, "Strike! She's struck! H'it's the Pearly!"

Not far from Aggie and Nate, Bull Mudgett grinned his vulpine grin, his mustaches bristling like hog whiskers. On the platform, the swift pounding ceased. Some, fearing the steel man's hand was indeed struck, moaned aloud. People milled in circles, confused as cattle in a storm. The Buckskin Joe team stood as if wakened from a dream, their perfect timing sundered.

Willard muttered to Nate, "Hell, there goes the last horse out of the barn."

"It's Mudgett's and Bisbee's turn to drill," said Nathaniel. "I'd wager they pulled that stunt to throw the Buckskin boys off their beat."

"Well, they done it, the sorry pieces of dogshit," said Willard balefully.

Nate was enraged. "It isn't right. It's not only their claim-jumping and killing. Now this. It ain't right." He squared his shoulders. "You can bet your bottom dollar they'll torment Calvin over that silver."

The two companions glared hotly. The Buckskin drillers tried fruitlessly to get back into their swing. The audience was in a dither, the contest as dismembered as the parade before it.

Then, in a crowning catastrophe, the big yellow and red balloon sprang a leak, and the afternoon ascension was cancelled. Aggie McClaren was so dismayed that she sat right down on the grass. Finally, the men of the church guild left off their gossiping about Bob Bisbee's ancestry and erected the sawhorses and picnic table planks. Covered with bright quilts and jars of wildflowers, the tables looked fresh as May Day. The drilling debacle faded, all eyes turned toward the food. No spread in a year outshone Aspen's Fourth of July picnic supper. Women's cherished cut-glass bowls awaited the mixing of strawberry shrub. Mammoth ironstone platters held lean cuts of beef and venison. Loaves of fresh-baked bread and dishes of piccalilli and coleslaw stood covered with damp rags against flies. Prize chokecherry jellies shimmered like jewels in cut glass dishes. Pungent odors of homemade sausage and headcheese beckoned, along with tureens of Welsh meat pasties and shoofly pies in pie baskets. Strapping boys got busy on the ice cream churns, the ice retrieved from layers of sawdust where it had been stored since being cut from the ice pond last winter.

At four-thirty in the afternoon, Mrs. Ollie Davidson opened the picnic for business. Appetites were not only whetted to a fine edge, but she was sick and tired of hearing Emma Sutton and those silly tableau girls lionized.

Soon her arm moved non-stop from potato salad platters to plates, a whirligig in a stiff breeze. The mouths of the women in the Anti-Profanity league flapped at the same speed. They had about finished discussing Vinnie Krueger, who'd delivered four rhubarb pies, helped with serving and excused herself early.

"Now that she is rich as Mrs. Midas, she no doubt considers herself our better," sniffed Florence Dunbar.

"Oh pshaw," said Sadie Sears. "Lavinia has not got a uppity bone in her body."

"We'll soon know about that, won't we?" said Mrs. Ollie Davidson, her ear bent toward the cursing balloon pilots at the lake edge.

"I near broke my back," howled the one they called Bud, "seein' to that fartin' bag of wind!"

"You seen to it all right. Them rips was never patched proper!"

"H'it was that cunt Carlita. She din't sew them seams with heavy fish line like I directed."

"The only directing you done was tellin' her which hole to stick your puny pricker in."

Bud looked low. "We not only ain't made one ascension, we are out our balloon—and all our mother-fuckin' pay."

The League ladies within hearing of the balloon boys were a tough-skinned bunch. They'd buried infants and children, wintered in tents, fed flour to horses to see them through blizzards. They tended poultry and pigs, canned, scrubbed, split kindling, shingled roofs, bore the living, dressed the dead and hauled water and wood and coal without a flap. Yet the pilots' profanity was so voluble it had them fluttering like robins put out of their nests by cowbirds.

Bert and Bud Hoople, to their despair, had polished off the last of their Taos Lightning.

"I God, Bert, I thought you was bringin' plenty of likker," wailed Bud.

"I ain't your goddamed pack mule, buster!" exploded Bert.

"Well, move your sorry ass over to the supper table," grumbled Bud, backing off. "Fill up on free food…Line yer pockets while you're about it."

Glaring first at the balloonists, then at Rosie Klausmeyer, Lena Davidson snapped, "Rose, stop that fanning yourself and take over this ladle for me."

Rosie, who looked up to Lena Davidson like she was a saint, quailed at the sharp words. Lena, bent on giving that balloon trash what-for, had no time for Rosie's frail feelings. The League ladies knew that Mrs. Ollie Davidson's buttonhole mouth could sting worse than a peach switch. They watched, faint of heart, as she sailed down to the lake edge. Though they could not hear her words, they could just well imagine. Then to their shock, they saw Lena's stout back stiffen, heard one of the pilots roar, "Aw, go fuck a goat, lady!"

As the redoubtable Lena stomped off to locate Sheriff Harwood, the pilots marched on the picnic tables. Grudgingly, the churchwomen served them supper.

Willard and Nate carried baskets to tote delectables to those at the mine. In the food line, they encountered a wan-looking Rob Skinner. The liveryman had hiked up his filthy pants, washed his neck at the pump, changed into a half-clean shirt and made his way gingerly to the lakes. By all rights, he should be face-down on his pallet at the Elkhorn barn. But he'd had a belly full of boardinghouse grits and thin gravy. If he must crawl on all fours, he didn't plan to miss the finest feed of the summer.

"Howdy, Skinner," said Willard. "Hear you had a pustule the size of a geyser."

"Feared I was a goner."

"Good thing Nate here laid the knife to you."

"The pain was intolerable. If Phipps had not happened along, I could've shot myself."

"An ill wind befalls us all—but not without good. Understand the Pearly has engaged your full quotient of stock. At $1.50 a head, prosperity has hit your corner."

"I've heard like talk before from men about to go bust."

"This time you may be pleasantly surprised."

"It will be the first surprise of my life that was not the unpleasant variety."

"As the treasurer on that Pearly proposition, Skinner, I will see you are paid in full and on time. $1.50 per diem for every head in your yards."

"Word is," said Skinner with care, "that Cal Krueger is rolling in silver like a horse in deep pasture—to the tune of thousands a ton." Skinner removed his hat and scratched his head. "The life of a liveryman is chancy. I could lose half my mules to the epizootic. And flatland stock must be rested weeks before bein' worked at eight thousand feet…"

"Is that a fact?"

"Coaxing one wrong-headed mule fifty-odd miles over the hump, with the damfool itching to break a leg ever inch of the way, is no easy matter."

"Nor is the lot of a one-legged mortician carting perishable merchandise over that same hump during the sudden sleet storms of September."

"A liveryman's portion is dependent on a gaggle of dumb animals. Half mine is ordinarily threatenin' to check out. If it ain't the Monday morning sickness, it is the three-day heaves."

"None of that cuts ice with a man in the business of burial."

"I will require financing to buy fresh stock at the Denver auction next week. I expect the Pearly could afford $2.00 a day."

"The agreed-upon price was $1.50. That is the sum you shook on, Skinner."

"I had no notion I was dealing with persons of great wealth."

"There is no wealth to it. It is a matter of honor."

"I cannot fill feedbags with honor. Feedbags takes oats, and oats is high; they've gone to ten cents a pound. I'll need at least $1.75."

Willard gave the man his hardest look. "One of these days, Skinner, you will pass over. All you will need is forgiveness, a preacher—and me. If you have not stood by your word, I will see to it you're buried bare. In a undressed box. With no headstone…so no man will know where you lie."

"Them's harsh words, you shitty old skinflint."

"We can no doubt see our way clear to an advance for fresh stock at the auctions. But the cartage fee will stand: $1.50 a head, and there is an end of it."

"I will allow you to hoodwink me, Arey, so that I may take my plate under thet shade tree and eat my supper in peace," groaned Skinner.

Nate rolled his eyes skyward. Calvin, he could see, would be in the hands of a fiduciary expert.

####

CHAPTER TWELVE

THE KITCHEN CABINET

Though Vinnie Krueger saw a good many men every day of her life, the current convocation of males lounging over her sinkboard, pie cupboard, and chairs—and not a one eating—left her a little breathless. She was having trouble with her breath as it was, what with Cal's thunderclap about the silver. She pumped water for coffee, wondering what on earth she would do with a fancy kitchen on Bullion Row or with the catalogue dresses Cal took on about. She was delighted with his good fortune, but notions of two-foot bustles and Oriental carpets unsettled her. She'd started Aspen life in a sideframe lean-to with a green elkhide for a door. She was content with her cozy cabin and her next-doors here on Spring Street. Besides, she knew very well that Calvin dug for his own reasons. Pride, mostly wanting to prove right, to win through to buried treasure. Every man in this camp had it in his head to find buried treasure.

Well, Calvin had found his, and it was about to turn their lives upside down and around a bend, to an unfamiliar place she could not picture. Mr. Sutton was a hard man. He'd have his mine back if he must summon an army for the job. As for Calvin and these turkey-cocks in her kitchen, they were no better than small boys spoiling for a fight. Soon there'd be trouble no one could take back.

"Calvin, I'd best see to the chicks before slap dark." She hung her apron on a nail and started for the back door.

"Did you set out the cheese for Olwen's coffee?" Cal asked.

"I did, Cal."

"Shut that door good behind you."

"I will, Cal."

"If Lavinia don't suit you," sniffed Willard, "I'll marry her myself." He considered Calvin had done nothing special to deserve his jewel of a wife. She not only made better scrapple than a reading Dutchman, she remained a fine-looking woman.

Calvin flushed. He hadn't meant to issue orders like a gunnery officer. "'Fraid I'm strung tighter'n piano wire, boys."

"Well then, when Nathaniel arrives he can sing, you can play, and we'll have us a musicale," announced Willard.

"I personally would prefer a solo from Olwen," said Pete dryly. Olwen Davies owned a baritone so beautiful that Pete grew weak-kneed when Olwen's voice soared.

"I don't have my mandolin," said Young Frank anxiously. He had somehow lost the thread and missed the leg-pull. Like many youngsters, his mind did not yet run to the finer points of humor.

Cal Krueger looked around with affection. The hard edges on these men covered an almost womanly tenderness. The fellowship in a silver dig was very like that of a battle zone. Call them together and miners collected like wolves (or maybe, as Vinnie suggested, laughing hyenas). It wasn't men riding easy atop horses who had blown open impassible mountains, scaled sky-high peaks, carved paths for the railroads to follow. Let a cow-man or sheep-man get down out of his saddle, and he could scarcely gimp his way to the nearest saloon. It was rambling men, the prospectors, and the blasters and the trammers—not the cowboys and not the soddies—who had explored and settled the steeps of the San Juans, the crags of the Sawatch, the snows of the Sierras. A good million of diggers with their pole-picks and black powder— uncommon men like those in this room—were bringing the western high country to heel. A score of years from now, in mine districts from Aspen to Park City to Grass Valley, men would sit of an evening harking back to silver and gold skirmishes in the same way they recollected war stories. Some would no doubt recount the discovery of Cal Krueger's glory hole.

Laughter brought Calvin from his reverie. Deke was describing his ride to the would-be rescue of Mrs. Sutton on a "hundred-proof, kiln-dried, officially notarized plug. It's a blessing the lady's grit saved those girls. I was useless as a pump on a dry well."

"I'd have paid to see it," chuckled Jake.

As Deke removed a stove cover by its lifter and scattered his cheroot ashes on the fire, Young Frank squirmed in his chair. He felt jumpy as a belled cat about speaking out to these older men. Major Burdine could look at a fellow like he'd as soon cut your throat as tolerate interference. Finally Frank's fervent hope that he'd escape to embrace Bridget O'Reilly got the upper hand. His voice cracking, he said, "I'd be mighty obliged if we could get this meeting over with."

"I' God, Frank, you put me in mind of my little sister Essie," said Pete. "Used to roust us out afore dawn so she could make the beds and get it over with." His face softened in recollection. "Come picnic weather, she'd have us eating two hours before mealtime so she could clean up and get it over with."

"Don't recall you mentioning no sister," said Frank.

"Died of the pleurisy six summers ago," said Pete. "Went ahead and got it over with."

While Frank puzzled over Pete's sister, the older men choked down their hilarity. The boy kept forgetting that Pete was a heavy josher.

On that note, Calvin looked searchingly around. "Boys, you know why we're met this evening. We not only have a good-size Eldorado on our hands, we are beset by the exigencies of time. Though my lease has more than ninety days to run, the apex question may come to court in less than sixty. I am in a thicket of thistles and I'll need a power of help." He pushed back his chair and reached for two burlap sacks lying against the stove leg. "Jake badgered Gus Ackerman into opening up shop and running some ore samples through his potions." Cal pulled out chunks of ore. "Gus says she's even richer than we figured—at the least, eight-hundred ounces of pure grade to a quarter ton. At best, a good thousand or more." His voice nearly failed him. "This is no ordinary proposition before us."

"Lord Almighty," breathed Willard, "if Nathaniel Phipps ain't been proved right again. The U.S. Treasury should hire the man to scout for their Philadelphia mint."

"Never saw the beat, not ore fresh from the ground," marveled Deke, rolling a length of shimmery wire silver in strong fingers. "And ripe for picking by Sutton & Company."

The jumble of voices lowered. Deke had brought them to the dark heart of the matter.

Calvin turned up the lamp wick. "D.K. sees things as I do. Until my lease runs out, Sutton will fight to keep this lode underground. There'll be a battle—and it'll be hard-fought."

"He wouldn't dast break a lease," declared Willard irately. "Them leases is iron-clad."

Jake Levy scratched his chin through his whiskers. "Sutton is not ignorant. He knows the law."

Calvin's expression was grave. "Sutton knows the law—but he does not respect it. He'll call out attorneys and bully boys, muddy the waters, make mischief—or a sight worse." His blue eyes darkened. "The Pearly will prove

105

no light matter, and I'll not think less of a man with family who decides not to chance a fight."

"I'll throw in with you, Calvin," said Pete.

"I'm in fer the haul, pardner," said Willard, quickly echoed by the others.

"I thank you, boys." Calvin paused. Cleared his throat. Though he had not shed a tear since the gravesides of his sons, there was a suspicious mist in his eyes. "For an enterprise of this magnitude Vinnie and I propose granting each of you equal shares in the whole with the two of us."

"I God, Cal, that's almighty generous."

"No, it is not. That skunk Sutton will have his cut. Twenty percent is the owner's major strike standard. We ourselves voted it into law. In addition, Ward Moyer has sold a slew of quarter-shares to plenty who won't work a lick. Still, there should be ample so we can all take up residence on some easier street." Calvin rose to stoke the stove fire against the deepening chill. "I further propose to help bankroll the sideline lawyers, see if we can't settle that question our way."

There were murmurs of approval all around.

"Some of you will need to captain a squad, some will pitch in and dig, others stand guard. You'll earn your shares. Emptying that vug, with Sutton's crew on us like wet hornets, will be a mean job of work."

"We have a small edge," said Young Frank. "Sutton is over to Leadville." He'd had this straight from Bridgie in church. "Won't be back 'til tomorrow at the earliest."

"You mean to say he missed Little Emma's finest performance?" Nate Phipps, relieved of guard duty, had let himself in the door. "That woman's a seven-day wonder!"

"It irks him when his missus performs in public," said Frank. A sly gleam flickered in his eye. "And I'd just be tickled to irk him some more. If Calvin will give me the loan of that Sharps, I'll hold the bastard off at the pass."

"You'll carry a weapon shortly, Frank. Jake here, and Nate, are already lining up Sharps and Henrys, a few Remingtons, about to fit them with tang sights. We'll all need to go armed."

"Though it pains me to see it," sighed Calvin.

For the first time, Willard looked glum. "Any man throws down on me, I dive for the nearest horse trough."

"We ain't got the law on our side, not if we're talking Dirty Harwood," declared a gruff Pete. Sheriff Dick "Dirty" Harwood was known as the slowest gun in the West, as well as a toady of Sutton's.

"Newt Thatcher will stand in our camp," said Willard, "though he is not armed with much but the good book. Then again, prayer could serve us better than iron. We can't hold off no army of hundreds—not without the good Lord's assistance."

"Been keeping my ears open," said Nate. "The strike news is all over this camp like a wet blanket."

"Still only talk," said Willard. "No one is dead sure about particulars."

"Willard, every last particular sifts through walls, blows on the wind, travels like brushfire." Calvin's tone was matter-of-fact. "The speed of speculation has been calculated at twice the speed of light. I'll wager Sutton, over the hump, has heard every little particular about Gus Ackerman's assay."

Willard licked the point of the pencil he'd brought from behind his ear. "All the more reason to get straight to business."

"I'd like to call on Willard to be our treasurer," said Calvin. "Nate to act as senior agent. Olwen as shift boss. Deke to supervise packing and freighting and guard detail."

"I volunteered for that duty," said Deke with a deprecatory chuckle. "I'm counting on you brave hearts to spare me the dark netherworld."

Deke Burdine had been marked by a hard burying over in Leadville. When he'd first arrived at the mines, his wartime experience with black powder put him in demand for delicate blasting jobs. He hadn't cared much about going underground, but the pay was high. He'd been planting fresh charges in a fresh stope in the Little Pittsburg Mine when he got into a soft bed of zeist and it caved on him. Calvin Krueger was the topman, the hoist engineer, on that dig. For thirty-six hours, defying the gloomy predictions of others, Cal had directed rescue crews, never leaving his task 'til they'd tunneled through to the pocket that held Deke, breathing the last of his air. The major had emerged from his rathole like a sulled-up possum, rank and frazzled, and startled to be alive. Cal had fed him water and whiskey, cradled him like a baby.

"Well, you derned Reb," he'd said, "missed shooting you at Fredericksburg. Had to dig you up if I ever wanted another crack at you."

Deke's feeble smile had been lost in his blackened face. He'd grunted, "They told me the South would rise. Whoever knew it would be from the fringes of hell."

Deke Burdine had never gone underground again.

Over the next hours, the men talked over suggestions for drovers, worked out shift crews, and agreed on guard duties. Storage sites were planned, hostlers and carpenters and blacksmiths approved, purchases of equipment formulated, and plans formed and firmed up. Later, as the summer night turned mountain cold, the men departed one by one, each with a profusion of duties in his head and a clap from Calvin on his back.

When the last man had slipped into the darkness, Vinnie appeared at the kitchen door, shawl pulled tight, her hair in a thick braid down her back.

"Set right still, Calvin. I'll fix you hot milk and whiskey or you'll not sleep a wink."

Cal's earlier jubilation was gone. He owned a rising sense of dread, a feeling that he had backed himself, Vinnie, and good men into a terrible corner. He pictured knife fights, bushwacking, and ambuscades. How could he have forgotten all the frights of war when he swore he never would?

With milk set to scald on the stove, Vinnie searched her husband's face, then reached out a work-worn hand. "Cal dear, try to remember the old words: 'What a friend we have in Jesus.'"

Calvin patted his wife distractedly. He and all these other veterans of Chancellorsville and Seven Pines, of scraps with the Kiowa and the Cheyenne, of mean-minded claim-jumping, knew good and well when there was a fight afoot, Jesus had no part in it. Why else were there so many bible-readers and church-goers lost across the years, lying dead in the ground before their time?

####

CHAPTER THIRTEEN

HERMAN KLAUSMEYER

In the shadowy Sutton parlor on Bullion Row, Bridgie made her way through a maze of ottomans, birdcages, statuary and rubber trees. Spittoons, china pug dogs, and stained glass pictorials cast ghostly shadows, causing Bridgie an involuntary shudder. "On me mother's grave," she murmured, crossing herself. Skirting her way through gimcrackery, she let out a yelp. She had stubbed her toe on the gewgaw the missus most despised: a large walnut cuspidor. Its hinged lid inlaid with jasper and agate, the latest in household fashions. The mister ignored this contraption of his own choosing, allowed his guests to spit where they pleased and himself came and went as he liked. Bridgie rubbed her toe, then hobbled to light the lamps. She would have liked the feel of Frank Parker's brick-hard shoulder under her head.

The afternoon had seen a steady procession of women bearing layer cakes, small girls carrying sugar cookies, little boys toting lemon sponge and vinegar pies. Even a few gentlemen had paid their respects, leaving their cards. The Reverend Campbell had called and bless him, the good Father Downey, though the missus was a heathen Presbytery. By and by, after the last caller, the missus had insisted she was in fine fettle and ordered Bridgie off to the picnic and fireworks. As if she'd ever leave! In any case, her Frank had sent a note by Mr. Hurd's boy Scooper. *"Dear Briget. I can't go to the picnick. We have found silver. Do not tell. I will rite soon. Your frend. Frank Parker."*

Easing her toe, she sat in a red plush chair and marveled at all that had transpired in a day. A babe come and gone. Silver found. Mrs. Sutton a sainted savior. The sight of her mistress, sturdy as an oak, lying limply abed in the midday sun had turned Bridgie's world wrongside out. Eyeing the deepening shadows, she decided to light every lamp in the parlor. The mister would not be home before tomorrow or the day after. He'd not be on hand to scold the expense.

Upstairs on her mother's feather mattress, Emma thanked her stars she had shepherded this bed over the mountains, cheering the carters as they lowered it down sixty-foot drops with big mules and choruses of cursing. A bed warm with hard-won memories was a comfort.

She had heard that the loss of a child was a time for spiritual rumination. She'd closed her eyes and looked solemn when the Reverend Campbell knelt in prayer. The truth was, she felt as giddy as a tumbleweed in a stiff wind. After a few teaspoons of Doc Alderfer's poppy concoction, she'd begun floating between the floor and the ceiling in the southeast corner of the room. From there she'd gazed down on herself lying against the pillows in her tucked batiste bedgown.

This is how I will look when I'm passed on and laid out, she'd thought pleasantly. She did not shy away from dying, although she'd never care to be bed-bound under Garrett's roof. When she voiced her concern to the doc, he'd promised she'd soon be right as rain.

All afternoon Polly had bristled in the hallway, scowling at every caller. Bridgie had tiptoed in and out, setting Emma's teeth on edge. Even Chester, ordinarily an amiable dog, bared his fangs at visitors from his corner cushion. By and by Emma had dispatched Polly across town with orders to locate Aggie McClaren—and Bridgie downstairs with a firm directive not to disturb her unless her bedbell rang or the house caught fire. She then scratched Chester good behind both ears and emptied all the doc's medicaments into the chamberpot. The dratted laudanum had rendered her simple-minded. She needed her wits about her.

If only she'd had one reliable report on the Pearly! None of her callers had heard more than wild rumor. Her next door, Leorah Wickersham, might have been helpful, but she had come and gone while Emma slept. The Reverend Campbell didn't even suspect there was a strike—small wonder the man was forever praying the Lord watch over him. If Father Downey knew, he wasn't saying. Uncle Nate Phipps had sent a bouquet of pearly everlasting and word that he'd be around the next day. Until Polly located Aggie, Emma needed to leash her impatience.

She planned to stash her Pearly stock with the McClarens in the hotel's big Hurley & Hutchins floor safe. She could then think clearly about how to cope with Garrett. His spleen at finding the mine paper worth a fortune—and gone—would be worse than a thunderclap. Though he'd not dare abuse her again, he'd curse and stomp and demand the return of the stock. She'd be obliged to set her jaw and bolt her door against the storm.

At the Hallam Lakes, butcher Herman Klausmeyer had fetched and carried as meekly as he knew how. The first minute he dared, he'd excused himself to Rosie and her friends. He did not mention his need to visit the Row. Herman had many needs, few of which Rosie satisfied. Worse, she commandeered his pay so that he was always short. *No man should have to suffer needs and shorts*, he thought aggravatedly.

Under his smiley, self-effacing facade, Herman Klausmeyer was about to fall to pieces. Some months back, a liquored-up old geezer had traded him a hundred-share pack of Pearly mine certificates for a meager grubstake. Herman had pocketed the paper behind his employer's back. Later that night, he'd wheedled the whore nigger Frankie into taking the stock in trade. Though the shares were hardly worth anything, they were gussied up with pretty seals and flowery handwriting. Nigger Frankie might not read, but she admired penmanship. She'd treated him to a prime ass-hauler for that packet of paper.

In the cool of the July evening, Herman sweated buckets, dribbles trickling down his legs into his boots. If half of what he heard was true, those Pearly shares could be worth hundreds. Whatever it took, he planned to have them back.

Rosie was grateful to see him leave. The man never knew how to say his goodbyes, lurking past his time, looking hangdog. Rosie was a great one for stories, and she did not consider Herman a suitable backdrop. She'd been telling the ladies about the Sykes gang up on Independence Pass, and she had Sadie Sears' rapt attention. Even Lena Davidson was listening.

"Well," she continued, "Herman and I got caught on the hump in some weather early in the fall of the year. A gullywasher, it was, turning to sleet. We was held up short of the Wellers' way station. Had no choice but to bunk in with the Sykeses."

"Goodness!" said Sadie. "Was it true, what they say about marryin' their own kin?"

"The old man admitted it. He was on his third wife, said the first two wore out givin' birth."

"That ain't no surprise, Rose. Most of us thins down after birthing."

"The point is, Sadie, he had three families from different sisters, and yes, all the children has took to marrying one another."

"No!"

"It's the Lord's truth. Old Sykes said they was so mixed up he didn't know which was which, but he guessed it didn't much matter."

"Whose cake batter?" barked Florence Dunbar, cupping both deaf ears.

"Brothers has married sisters, and they are not particular about who's half and who's whole, and some of the girls is cross-eyed and gabbles like geese."

"It ain't in the Bible," said Sadie firmly.

"Course it ain't," said Rosie. "I give him a good piece of my mind."

"Who's that behind?" cackled Florence in her voice like the Hamtown tuba.

Rosie wished that Florence would get a hearing horn and quit her infernal yelling. She took all the starch out of a person's best stories.

At the concession stand for boat rides, Pie Burkhardt checked his cashbox and re-counted his roll of tickets. It was just shy of dark and trade had fallen off. He'd sent Ollie Davidson to eat supper a while back, saying, "I ain't hungry, Ollie, had me two slices of berry pie earlier."

"Need two tickets for the boats, Burkhardt."

Pie looked up. Bull Mudgett towered there, the Hoaglund girl beside him. Runaway celebrity must have gone to the ninny's head. Pie doubted her pap would approve her keeping company with the likes of Mudgett. "It is not a good idea to be out rowing after dark," he grumbled. "Might not navigate your way home."

"That's my lookout. Yours is to sell me them tickets."

"You can pay me, Mudgett, but we don't give refunds, and I won't guarantee your money's worth at this hour. Take that near boat, the one with them yella oars."

Bull helped Svea over the gunwales. Juggling a dish of strawberry ice cream in one hand, she teetered, setting the boat to dipping and rocking. He wished she'd mind her step. Though he'd assured her he was a practiced oarsman, he'd only rowed one time before.

Svea was in a swivet. She was still a schoolgirl and her pap guarded her like a mastiff. She had never had a fellow buy her ice cream and boat rides, oh my! Tonight pap was up the mountain, having a word with the Pearly men about shift work. Before she knew it, Bull Mudgett had been at her side, handlebar mustaches on point, muscles bulging through his red-and-white-striped rugby shirt. Bull was so burly he made Svea feel dainty. She was a big girl, and not many made her feel delicate.

The day had been thick for Bull. He and Bob won the drilling contest all right, but he'd taken a terrible hazing about the Pearly. He'd wired Mr. Sutton every hour on the hour, but had not yet received a word of instruction. Fuckit, he'd decided, he might's well have his fun with the Hoaglund girl. He'd watched her on the grandstand, her eyes big and blue as morning glories, her boobies near bursting her dress. At the picnic, when he brushed against her, for a wonder she wasn't trussed like a roasting chicken in stays and bones. As he moved carefully to the oarlocks, Svea rearranged herself, setting the boat to rocking again.

"Watch yourself, girl!" he snarled. "Set right still and stop yer jiggling." Subdued, Svea sat.

After rowing in half circles, Bull finally got the hang of things and zigzagged toward an arm of the lake he knew, full of rushes, with deep grass on the bank. When he pulled in, it was full dusk. Leaning on the oars, he bent toward Svea. "Give us a kiss, there's a girl," he coaxed.

Svea had only ever kissed Nils Soderstrom, an unschooled peck at a box social. She wasn't practiced, but she was willing to learn. Bull pulled her to him with care, minding the boat. He kissed her on the mouth, on the neck and on her thick-braided hair, his kisses growing rougher as his blood warmed. Then he covered her with his hands as well as his mouth.

This, thought Svea worriedly, *was a far piece from Nils Soderstrom, who was a shy, fumblesome boy.* Bull was a grown man, bigger than her pap. Thoughts of Pap made her uneasy.

"We best go in now," she said as Bull's hands pulled at her dress. "Quit that, Bull."

"Aw, Svea, all I want is to love you." He bent her hurtfully over the side of the boat.

"Listen here, Bull Mudgett. Loving is a sight more than kisses, and Pap says I'm too young." Eyes wide, she grappled with him.

"Goddamit, girl, stop that!"

With a garter-snake wriggle, Svea doubled out from under, giving him a shove. Off-balance, his arms flailing, he tilted into the water, sending a family of ducks squawking from their nest in the reeds. The lake was only chest-deep, but Bull was mired in mud, the bottom sucking at his boots like swamp gum. Floundering to the surface, he reached for the boat, ready to give that girl a cuffing she'd not soon forget. When he squeezed the water from his eyes, he discovered her halfway to shore, pulling the oars with the finesse of a single-sculler.

"Damn the luck!" he howled.

If he'd wished to wade out of the lake unremarked, he was in for more disappointment. The commotion of ducks and a pair of Canada geese was noisier than the Tower of Babel. As he stumbled on hands and knees up the bank, his boots sloshed like a water wagon in hot weather.

"Is that poultry thieves in them bulrushes?" inquired Bert the balloonist in a loud, disrespectful tone.

His brother Bud belched and said, "'Pears to be a haberdasher wearing a fancy city shirt."

"Not to me he don't. I like my dress shirts well starched and ironed dry."

"That's about enough," said Bull bitterly. "Your sass don't go down with me. Hand over that fucking blanket before my teeth rattle out of my head."

"Is swim instruction usual in this camp?" Bud belched again, smirked ,and handed him a filthy saddle blanket.

"No more'n flight lessons," snarled Mudgett.

Bull squatted on the grass warming himself, taking in the enormous deflated balloon. He lowered his voice. "Listen here, will that broke-down hoop skirt of your'n go up in the air, or do you use her for a damn dust rag?"

Bert was wrathy at the insult. "She'll fly all right, once she has a few small repairs."

The germ of an idea was growing in Bull's head. "Can them repairs be made in these parts?"

"Takes a seamstress and ready cash is all."

"You boys engaged for the next few weeks?"

The Hooples eyed each other. "Ain't got a job of work 'til the Fort Bent Fair mid-August."

"The name's Mudgett. If you two keep your lips buttoned, I could have a proposition right here in this camp."

"We're listenin'."

"Not now you ain't. I got to change out of these wet things before I take the quincy." Bull's teeth chattered. "Reckon you're flat busted..."

The Hooples stared at the ground.

"You can put up at Old Lady Robinson's boarding house. Tell her I'm footing the bill. She's on Hopkins, the big grey shack with the side porch, third from the end after Galena, directly above Swedetown." Mention of Swedetown reminded him of that yellow-haired square head. He'd show that Swede cockteaser a thing or two. She'd learn more than kissing, and the lesson would be painful. Bull felt a flush of satisfaction at the prospect. "Got any whiskey on you, Mudgett?"

Bull pulled out his pocket tickler and threw it. "Drink up, boys. You'll need a sight of Dutch courage before we're through."

Freed at last of fetching, Herman Klausmeyer dogtrotted from the lakes around the lower reaches of Bullion Row. Though he'd sworn to himself he wouldn't, he could not resist one quick circle of the Widow Wickersham's house. In her side yard, he gentled aside two honeysuckle bushes to peer through the window of her first-floor bedroom. There she sat, her knockers peeking from a shiny dressing-gown as she caressed the hand of the big man lying on her pretty bed. When she leaned over to place a kiss on his forehead, he stroked one of those handsome titties like he was stroking a velvety cat. Herman nearly wept. His fondest dream was to have a taste of the curvaceous widow. A whole meal, even. Only his deep concern over his mine stock wrenched him from the sight of her, allowed him to turn away and head for the Hopkins Street footbridge, then toward the mountain on Mill Street, avoiding the lighted saloons where men spilled onto front boardwalks.

Though he was grateful he hadn't had to fabricate an improbable committee meeting of the Sons of the Black Forest, he still poured rancid sweat. Rosie was adept at sniffing the smell of Herman's agitation. With her mind on her tattle, she hadn't nosed around like a dog after a bone. When he finally puffed onto Durant, he saw to his dismay a line of waiting men outside Frankie's door. *Dumkopf!* he thought. How could he forget the heavy trade on a holiday?

Inside her shack, Frankie was filled with thanksgiving. The line outside was the longest of the year. If she could keep her boiler stoked, she might make enough in one night to provide food and fixings for the balance of the summer.

Herman cut into the alleyway behind the row of cribs, deftly sidestepping a dead dog buzzing with flies. He could have found his way blindfolded, he knew this stretch so well. If he must, he'd wait in the rickety privy, though it needed a dose of quicklime to stifle the stink. Creeping around the side of the crib where he was out of sight of the line of customers, he again peeped through a window. The glass was poor and things inside wavered. But he could make out Frankie's trunk against the wall by the stove where her rocker sat. On another wall was the sink, its pump handle standing at attention in a salute.

Over on the far wall stood a table with two chairs. And on the rough slatwork wall above...*Ach!* he moaned, it was gone! The scroll from the front of the stock packet had been nailed there—and it was gone! Herman's heart fell so hard he swore he heard the thunk. Then he got a grip. The mine shares had to be somewhere inside. Frankie had been too pleased with the paper to lose sight of it. He leaned closer to peer through the wavery window into the near corner. She was on the bed, her strong, dark legs glistening against a man's body white as sleet. They were jumping to beat the band, the man's pants around his ankles, his boots still on.

Herman liked peeping, which made him feel manly and all-seeing in the dark. His eyes grew bright as a fever patient's, his stomach and the inside of his head turned soft and wooly. At last, as the fireworks down at the lakes exploded, so did Herman Klausmeyer. His groans were stifled against the side of Frankie's crib.

####

CHAPTER FOURTEEN

DEKE BURDINE

Deke Burdine rode the streets of Aspen savoring the night smells and the moonlight. In the South, the world was often blurred and misty. Here, the air was so sharp it possessed the cut of a razor. When the moon moved over, stars glittered brighter than pendants on a chandelier. He'd grown so accustomed to the cold and the clarity he doubted he could ever again feel at home in the warm, clinging lowlands of the South..

Buford, his stylish bay stallion with the long switch tail, ambled along, splashing through ditchside irrigation water, snorting and snuffling his approval of the crisp evening. In the daylight, the bay, anticipating a good canter, tossed his head and pranced. At night their rides were more leisurely. Deke leaned over to stroke the horse's strong neck. Buford was thick-barreled, long-legged, hardy enough to carry his big rider fast and far. Deke had given a high price for him in Denver City.

"Fordy, my friend, this is a new one for us: calling on a lady by the light of the moon." By all rights, he should be petered out. But he'd had himself a wash, a change of clothes in his room in the back of the bar, and felt fresh as dew in the night air. He'd left the Elephant packed with men well-fed at the lakes, their barroom babble at an all-time high. Deliberation over the Pearly had been played through until it was worn down. It had then been replaced by a lively discourse on the Scriptures.

"Say, Apostle, what does the good book foretell about Cal Krueger's prospects?"

The undersheriff did not fumble for words. "'Be sober, be vigilant, because your adversary the devil walketh about, seeking whom he may devour,' Peter 5:8."

"Pity the devil didn't devour Toby Flanagan," called Stump Clancy from the far end of the room where he was bucking the tiger at a scarred faro table.

"Toby or Shoat Yankel, one."

"Tite Pomeroy's set on whipping the shit out of both."

"Ain't but two camp men meaner'n Shoat. Most men works their way up to it. Shoat was born mean."

Apostle frowned and intoned, "'Let not the sun go down upon your wrath,' say the Ephesians."

The roomful of men had turned from their cards and drink. Many had had strict bible rearing, and the Scriptures brought bygones to mind. The clink, clink, clink of the roulette wheel slowed until it sounded like the tick, tick, tick of a shelf clock in the stillness. The piano player spun his stool toward Apostle. Men seemed lost in thought, recalling Bible passages, formulating questions.

"Newt, have the disciples words for that fine circus acrobat Little Emma?"

"'She wears a crown of glory that fadeth not away:' Peter 5:4."

"I mind hearing that girl recite 'The Maid With the Golden Hair' back in Central City," said an old meat-hunter by the name of Shotgun Hayes. "Not ashamed to own I was in tears."

"My, she could thump the walls with them soldiers and battles," said Stump. "Coulda outgunned 'em too. Seen her hit a turkey in the eye at three hundred feet."

Deke listened with interest to the old hands' memories of Little Emma until Apostle's voice rang out like a circuit preacher's. "'The foolish things confound the wise...Drink you no longer water,'" he cried, "'but use a little wine for thy stomach's sake!'"

Shotgun yelled, "Christ's sake, stand the sher'f a drink so he don't dry up and blow off down valley!"

Deke had departed shaking his head, the merits of Matthew, Luke, and John Barleycorn in his ears. Thatcher was too pontifical for his own taste, but the man was more popular as entertainment than any six banjo players.

"So 'the foolish things confound the wise,'" he murmured to Fordy. "Makes sense." Ore fever was a foolishness that tangled men's thinking— that and whiskey. He'd watched many a sensible man go to hell over the craziness of whiskey and ore.

Deke pondered Calvin's improbable strike. He was pleased for his friend, although it would be a gift not tidily packaged nor easily opened. The bonanza would no doubt alter his own fortunes. He himself owned considerable Pearly stock. Maybe he'd sell off the saloon. It was not his natural line of work. But that was not the reason for his elated feeling; he did not hunger after silver or gold. What stirred his blood was challenge. Life without challenge slowed to a crawl, the days so alike they lost color and splash. With the strike, there was such challenge in the air that he could hear the crackle, imagine flashes of green and blue. His grin showed white in the moonlight.

Buford nickered in answer to another horse and Deke looked up to see Axel Nillson lowering an arc lamp at the corner of Hopkins and Mill. "Evening, Nillson," he called cheerily.

Axel was just reaching up to lower the light pulley and only nodded his way. Horace, his old gelding, was so in the habit of the street lamp route that he walked the course with no prompting, knew every lamp location, and backed the exact distance from each pole so his rider could reach the pulley without a stretch. No challenge there. That was the way Axel liked it. He was a man who dined quietly on habit.

Deke caught a faint whiff of lilacs blooming late in a shaded corner out of the heat. The sweet scent mingled with that of the pale pink and white stock in the bouquet in front of his saddle pommel. "If my mama could see me with a nosegay in hand," he chortled, amused at the picture he must make.

Deke's memories of his boyhood were clouded. The Widow Wickersham, an Alabaman, was his only reminder of Southern ladies soft as down, their speech a blanc mange of syrupy, smooth-sliding words. Western women spoke their minds in loud, plain voices. Sometimes, hearing the widow, he captured a faint, remembered picture of his mother, presiding at a table of fine linen; though the linen he recalled was frayed at the edges—like his folks. The war had killed them as surely as if they had fallen in battle. They were so long gone that it was like they had been buried under the weight of time. He felt he had been alone most all his life. Although he knew a good many men, and counted a handful as friends, he and the widow were Rebs among Yanks, a peculiarity in a peculiar land. Yet here in this place, he was as close to his own kind as he could hope to come. The West was home to wanderers, men who disdained roots, who picked up and moved on to the next prospect.

Geography had little to do with Deke's uniqueness. He had always been apart, even as a boy. He skirted the ruts traveled by others; some of him stood back, disdaining those who walked the easy path. Nor had it been his way to stay in a finished place, laboring for bare existence. He liked ventures, and he throve on the double-dare.

It had been a spell since he'd embarked on his last venture, leaving Leadville for the Roaring Fork Indian country at the end of the seventies. In Leadville, mineral discoveries had drawn swarms of main-chancers to what

Eastern newspapers called, "an awful spectacle of low vice." At length, when Leadville drunkenness and fighting had tuned up to a roar, Nate Phipps and Cal Krueger had convened a meeting.

"We've got to find clean ground to light on," said Nate. "There's no good left to this camp."

"The soiled doves outnumber Vinnie ten to one," said Cal.

"I vote we try our luck across the hump," said Nate. "From what I've seen, the mineral formations there is about the same as Leadville's."

"They's just the one drawback," said Pete Beard. "That country is deeded to the Utes."

"Not if you look close at the treaty. Chief Ouray signed away everything east of the 108th meridian. That gives us a good ten, twelve miles of prospect ground."

"Too close for comfort." Willard's tone was firm. "I have not met Chief Ouray, but unless he is a ninety-year-old with spent arrowheads in both knees, he could no doubt outrun me, dry ground or wet. I barely squeezed through one war. I ain't hankering after another."

"The Utes are mean, hard fighters, but they don't ordinarily carve and cut enemies like their Apache kin," said Nathaniel.

"I say we take our chances," said Calvin. "There is no law in Leadville. In the Roaring Fork country, we can write our own statutes, see that they stick."

"We will need your rifle arm across the hump, D.K," he'd added. "Keep running faro banks and refereeing fights in this hellhole, and you won't live out your ninth life."

Deke, who'd gone from blaster to barkeep, could not resist the call of new country. For the first few years after the group migrated, he had traveled the treacherous hump, talking up Aspen's prospects, guiding parties to the new enterprise.

The White Elephant Saloon had been Nate's and Calvin's idea.

"A going camp needs a high-toned drinking parlor where lonesome bachelors can gather," Calvin said one night around their campfire. "We figure you're the man with the presence for the job."

"You know I ain't partial to hard whiskey, major." Nate chewed thoughtfully on a piece of spruce gum. "But miners' lives without women leave them prickly. Barrooms are social clubs, like. Your mine man will have his gab and his drink. Might's well have it from a man who'll hold his respect—a sure shot and a boon companion of the Earp gang to boot."

"Just don't invite them Earps to settle out our way," pleaded Willard.

After the ruckus down in Tombstone, Wyatt Earp and John Holliday had shaken off the cactus spines of Arizona territory and now called Colorado home. Doc Holliday was a lunger, his breathing troubled, the clear air to his liking.

"Wyatt has settled down," said Deke.

"Bounty hunting," sniffed Willard, "ain't my idea of settled."

"Least he does it stylish. Goes after a man with papers on him in a fancy barouche, his lady friend in tow," said Nate. Wyatt's woman was a feisty little spitfire who wore hats with big birds roosting on them and took to the hunt as eager as her man.

"I God, it's a disgrace," snorted Willard. "Them two spin around in their patent leather carriage like they was Mr. and Mrs. Astor."

"Guess Wyatt may be half-tamed. Doc ain't," drawled Needle.

"That mean son-of-a-bitch would as soon pull a knife on you as deal the cards," said Pete. "Heard he's gunnin' fer Billy Watling at the Far East Saloon this minute."

"Why is it that people get shot either inside, coming out of, or going into saloons," sighed Willard. "Nobody ever does the deed on a church lawn or the courthouse steps."

"It's only saloons that are open all night," said Deke. "Plenty of time for men to drink and turn mean. You take Doc. With that cough he can hardly sleep more than a half-hour at a stretch. And his legs won't stand. If he must sit, he'd as soon have congenial company to sit with."

Needle shook his head. He slept like the blessed every night of his life.

"The man's down to one hundred and twenty pounds," Deke said with concern. "His consumption has him thinned to a blade."

"It's his conscience, not his consumption," insisted Willard, who did not share Deke's compassion for the sickly Southerner. "He's thinking about accounts at the heavenly gates for all them he mortified and shot."

Calvin and the boys had helped Deke throw up his first dirt-floored, mud-and-sticks drinking establishment. Before Deke could count the time, the place had grown by four large rooms and more or less elegant improvements. Today the White Elephant was the most prosperous saloon in Aspen. Only the Solid Muldoon and Joe Garrity's approached it in the matter of clientele. Deke thought it a fine irony that he, who liked the company of his own thoughts, should have become a saloon man, consigned to listen to men weep into their whiskey, mourn lost loves, and failed chances. It must be his penance, he thought, that he be confined in a gaseous tavern with gaggles of orestruck, homesick geese.

When he could no longer abide the incessant fuss over water, land, whores, claims, and cards—or the fetid smells of the unwashed—he reached for solitude, searching it out like a feast. During the deep snows of winter, he strapped on Swedish snowshoes and climbed away from the reek of stale beer and wet tobacco. Snatching an hour or two of a summer afternoon, he raced Fordy up Hunter Creek to test his gun arm on a distant badger. Sometimes he camped in clean mountain air a few days. He and Nate had laid out and cut the secondary, gut-twisting Half Moon Trail over the divide. Used only by the hearty—or as Willard claimed, "the foolhardy"—it was a sure short cut through the Williams Range to Leadville. Deke liked the steep, dark, pine-scented silence away from the main track. He was among the few who troubled to keep the deadfall and spruce swamp cleared.

Some nights he went to Calvin's and Lavinia's for supper, carrying fresh gamebirds or sweets from Julius Berg's confectionary. Vinnie mothered Calvin's "batching" friends—they were in want of it, most of them. But though Deke enjoyed bandying ideas with Calvin, he did not need small repairs or buttons sewed on. He shied away from closeness, never suspecting that his starchiness flustered Calvin's wife so that she fumbled with the pins in her hair bun.

Now and again, in the Krueger's warm kitchen, Deke thought fleetingly of marriage. He had never lain with a good woman—or even, for that matter, held a lengthy conversation with one. Though he owned a touch of the poet, he'd got out of the habit of thinking about love or refined talk. He dulled his need with a satisfying gallop, or stopped off in Leadville, where a brown-eyed Hospitality House girl named Hettie quoted from the *Rubaiyat* and took off the worst of his edge.

Often he stretched out in high meadows, watching red-tailed hawks catching up and down drafts off rust-red cliffs. Summertime clouds, tufts of cotton caught in a bright blue bowl of sky, took on the shape of animals, of flowers, and fragments of dreams. He'd never thought of himself as a romancer. Yet here he was, riding through the night to call on a woman he scarcely knew, a married woman, a woman with a sword-sharp tongue a world away from the dulcet, honeyed creatures of the South.

####

CHAPTER FIFTEEN

THE MOUNTAIN

At the Sutton place, Deke ground-tied Fordy, dropping his reins by the front walkway. It was now going on eight o'clock, and Mrs. Sutton would no doubt be dulled with a dose of doc's poppy.

Yet the overblown cottage was as lit up as an opera house. He would speak with whoever was at hand and leave the bouquet he'd borrowed from five or six different gardens. All the slips and cuttings tenderly transported by housewives in slots of raw potatoes had born riotously flowering offspring. Mrs. Dunbar and Mrs. Davidson, among others, prided themselves on their prolific zinnias and cosmos, their showy dahlias, and geraniums.

Bridgie O'Reilly, feeling peevish, slid aside the walnut wood parlor doors and answered the pull on the door ringer. She unbent a little when she saw the major, the one had carried the missus into the house after the runaway.

"You may as well step inside," she said, "although the missus ain't receiving."

"Mrs. O'Reilly, I believe? We met briefly this afternoon. My apologies. The hour is late, and you're worn out with callers."

Bridgie touched a hand to her hair, flustered in the presence of fine manners.

"I won't linger, but I wished to inquire after Mrs. Sutton's health and leave her fresh posies."

His smile was lovely. She had not seen his smile earlier. "She'll be thanking you, I'm sure, sir."

"I have enclosed a brief note for her, if you would be so…"

The upstairs bell pull rang sharply.

"Pardon, sir. It's the missus needs me." Bridgie scurried from the parlor.

In a few minutes the girl flew back down the stairs, her look disapproving as she again slid back the parlor doors.

"She wants you should visit a minute, Major Burdine."

Deke mounted the stairs wondering, for the first time in years, what on earth he might have to say to a lady. Propped up on her pillows, Emma considered the reverse of that question. She had heard the major was a war hero of the Confederacy, knew he'd pioneered the Aspen digs with Uncle Nate and Mr. Krueger. Both Doc Alderfer and Aggie McClaren held him up as a superior saloon man.

"'Tis a mystery why camp people look on saloon keepers in a class with bishops," Aggie had sniffed, "though the major is one a' the few worthy of th' regard."

Down at the bridge, Emma had felt so ill that she remembered little of the man who'd carried her home. She pictured him as spindle-shanked, dignified and graying, something like that old miscreant, General Lee.

Emma was concerned that Polly had not yet returned. *Surely the major will have word of the Pearly*, she thought anxiously. She was so humbled by her trembly legs and weak condition that she could have chewed the bedclothes. But then she'd been humbled plenty of late. She was growing accustomed to humble pie.

"Good evening, sir," she said. Though startled that he was neither aging nor spindly, she continued, "I will not apologize for my dishabille, Major. I judge you have encountered women lying abed before."

"I hardly thought to…er—" To his surprise, Deke was nonplused in the face of a proper woman in a ruffled bedgown lying against lace-edged pillows. He had last seen her as sick-looking as a wet cat. Now she was bathed and curried, her bright coloring—green eyes against tawny skin and sun-streaked hair—as luminous as day-shine.

"If those flowers are for me, I thank you. And I thank you, Major Burdine, for lugging me to my house today."

A glint of amusement flickered across Deke's face. She spoke her mind like a true westerner all right, though her voice was as throaty as a night bird's.

"Well, I…." Deke, looming above the bed, felt distinctly ill at ease. With a swift motion, he pulled over a tasseled side chair and sat so he could look into her face.

"Mrs. Sutton, you are a most remarkable woman." He hesitated. "But that is no reason for me to turn tongue-tied…" He searched her face. "Men are awarded medals for what you did today. You, madam, are truly heroic—and I kiss your hand."

Emma was taken aback when he did just that.

She had heard more high-flown language in one day than she had heard out of Reverend Campbell in a month of Sundays. Such talk recalled Garrett when he was courting, and it did not sit well. Nor was she impressed with this man who towered, his legs thick with saddle muscles, his grey gaze direct, his hat off his head. *Just one more rake, sure of his charm with women,* she thought jadedly.

"Major," she said, withdrawing her hand and looking coolly into his eyes, "I have had rumors that you are part of the strike team at the Pearly. I have few places to turn, and I would thank you kindly for any information you could give me."

Deke's look turned wary, his voice faintly distant. "Information of what order, Mrs. Sutton?"

She knew she should be more beguiling, but she could not summon the wiles for it. She turned her head away.

"My dear lady," he said, "I hardly need tell you that Calvin Krueger and his friends have no reason to trust your husband or his people."

"Nor do I, Major, I assure you."

Deke looked unconvinced.

"Nor is this my husband's bed I lie in," she blurted, her voice turned harsh. Immediately, she could have bitten her tongue. The blamed dope must have made her daft in the head, to share such a confidence with a stranger. And a *man.* Then again, she thought with an inward half-chuckle, she *had* puked all over the gentleman's dress shirt and frock coat. Furthermore, he had carried her home like a sack of oats. Like it or not, they shared an intimacy.

Coloring slightly, she amended, "This bed belonged to my benighted mother, God rest her. I sleep here alone, sir, for I am Mr. Sutton's sworn foe."

Though Doc Alderfer had assured Deke in low, awkward tones that Mrs. Sutton had lost a child—and that the loss appeared to gladden her—Deke was nonetheless dumfounded at the venom in her voice. He had never heard a married woman to speak so ill of her husband. Her eyes hard as iced needles, she looked at her speechless visitor. "I pray, sir, that the rumors I hear are true, and that Mr. Krueger will pull every last ounce of silver out of the Pearly before Garrett may lift a hand to stop him"

"It is what we hope for," he said evenly.

"When you do, the owner's share in the Pearly will come to me, not to my husband."

Deke looked more startled than before.

"The mine was purchased with my money, and she is in my name. But only because my husband thought me an imbecile and the mine worthless—and I threatened to take him to law."

"Good heavens," breathed Deke.

Emma stared levelly at him, then went on, her voice sagging slightly, "Major, I have learned something of men since my days of innocence."

Deke quelled a smile. He judged Mrs. Sutton barely grown to womanhood.

"I will never again put my trust in any man, young or old." She looked pensively into the reflection of a glass-globed wall lamp. "'One half of American women are little dolls…the rest of us are drudges…and we are all fools,'" she said, her voice infinitely sad.

Deke Burdine had the sudden sense that this was a woman he'd wait for. If he must, a good long spell.

"But I have not inquired after your health!" he sputtered, abashed at forgetting his manners.

"When Doc stops doping me with this damn—er, dern—poppy, I will be right as rain."

"No sprains or broken bones?"

"Land, no. Not a horse has bested me yet."

Making up his mind to it, he stood. "Mrs. Sutton, the Pearly strike assays more than nine hundred ounces to the quarter ton, premium quality, from one thousand to four thousand dollars a carload. We are hiring double and triple shifts and hope to remove ninety tons of ore every twenty-four hours between now and the 21st day of September. The find looks to be worth a good million or two—more than all the mines in this camp have yet removed in a year."

"Glory be!"

"We feel certain your husband will fight for it, as will Calvin Krueger. We will take every measure in our power to see that Garrett Sutton does not deter us."

Emma's eyes were wide at the figures. Then, abruptly, they narrowed. "Do not underestimate this man, Major. I have reason to know he is hounded by ill fortune and unwise investments. He is more dangerous than a threatened she-bear with a cub. In my view, he will fight for control of the silver, as he will battle me for control of the stock. He will fight, uphill or down, until he is done for. He will never stop. Never stop, I promise you, short of destroying those who corner him."

She turned her head to gaze into his eyes. "I will pray for you, sir. You hold my fate in your hands. It appears only silver will set me free."

Up on Aspen Mountain, not more than one hundred yards from the Pearly, Lute Kellogg and Scooper Hurd huddled under the chin of the Silver Queen

Peak, which lay face up to the heavens, looking God directly in the eye. Clutching buckbrush and scrub oak, they had clambered along the steep lower face of the mountain—along the hems of the queen's flowing garments—'til they were out of earshot of the shafthouse. In any case, the crowds, disgruntled with Pearly crews as tight-mouthed as #4 beaver traps, had mostly left off loitering and cut for bed. From their outcrop they looked down on the Clarendon Hotel and up the Durant Street Row, where flickering oil lamps gave the line of cribs the look of lamplit gingerbread huts. Bundled against the night cold that typically followed feverishly hot days, the boys sat under a canopy of moonlight. Lute felt blessed relief that the skeeters had thinned down, their breeding season about past. It was beyond him why his tender skin drew mosquitoes like flypaper, while Scoop, who was dark-complected, never got bitten. Seated in cozy companionship, they dug into a roasted chicken pilfered from Delmonico's open pantry sill. Running their legs off on Pearly errands, they'd missed the town ladies' picnic supper.

"Hell, Lute, we gotta eat. The supper places is closed, and they'd broom us out of the bars." Scoop retrieved a pint bottle of 16-to-1 from his jacket pocket, pulled the cork with his teeth, and had a swallow. "Spect the drinking is wors'n thievin'."

Lute tried a cautious sip. "Miz Wickersham and Mrs. Krueger won't tolerate me drinking hard likker. Won't have me acting like that good-for-nothing drunk, Jamestown Jess."

"The doc neither. Hard drink provokes him. It ain't as if we plan on doing it regular. This here is our first honest-to-god toot." Scoop held his three gold pieces up to the moonlight. "Gold in the hand and silver in the Pearly. Whoooooeeee!"

Lute wiped his mouth on his frayed corduroy jacket. "I start on double wages tomorrow, Scoop. Man's wages. The major has put me in charge of my own ore wagon. I'm to carry a pistol in the bargain."

Lute had long pined to pack a pistol. Men in Leadville and Fairplay bristled with knives and guns. In some way a fellow looked important wearing armament. Today he had summoned the grit to ask the major, "You think I might carry a piece, sir?"

"Reckon we're all forced to it, boy. You're a fine shot with a rifle, no reason you won't have respect for a sidearm."

Lute could scarcely believe so much bounteous fortune. With important work afoot, he might earn a real stake, enough to buy his own horse and maybe a used saddle. Enough even for his own small cabin. Silver was a marvel. A fellow with silver in his pocket had the world at his feet.

"I been thinkin' about this here prize money." Scoop hugged his thin knees, his sharp-edged young face pinched in thought. "Have a notion we should buy us a tumble with that Little Annie whore, her or nigger Frankie." Scoop dared not mention his secret yearning for Svea Hoaglund. He thought of Svea up on a pedestal, a shining star to be worshipped from afar.

At talk of whores, Lute's heart had dropped, his elation of a moment ago pricked like a bubble. He felt the first acrid taste of torment in the back of his throat. He and Scoop had been boon companions since early in the winter, and the single thing Lute had not got around to confiding was that he knew about tumbling a whore. Oh, Scoop knew he'd worked among the cribs since he was a boy. After his ma took sick in Leadville, she had traveled so fast that it seemed she was here one minute and gone the next. The Leadville whores had admired Mary Kellogg, who was never snippy about sewing for other working women. When she went under, they were the only ones who cared to see her buried, or to look after her orphaned boy.

He had been raised uneven. When business was good, the girls petted him like a china-faced doll. In lean times, they washed his shirts in a lye tray. Sometimes, as he grew older, he was the one who put beans on the table. At ten, he was big for his age, and a crippled farrier named Dick Tibbs began teaching him to shoe. Lute had a natural feel for horses and mules, and by the time he was fourteen he could shoulder a horse with a hard lean and doctor the meanest split hoof. He could cold-shoe or hot-shoe and could gentle down rough mounts, break them to halter or harness.

Miss California Catton, madam at the Hospitality House, had singled him out. A sharp-nosed businesswoman, she'd prized his honesty, his knack with horses and with numbers. She addressed him by his given name of Luther, made a point of him learning his letters, corrected his grammar and taught him behavior. She watched him like a chicken-hawk, and her girls were under stern instruction to let him be. He hadn't learned about sporting around the Hospitality House. And he never brought up the matter with Scoop because—well, because it was ticklish.

"Hear that Frankie builds a fire so hot she has you haulin' ashes for a week," said Scoop eagerly. Lute's heart plunged down around his knees.

He'd followed old Dick Tibbs to Aspen, only to have Dick up and die on him in the diphtheria epidemic. After that he'd taken up choring for Miz Wickersham and Mr. Krueger. Both warned him to keep clear of the Row. But the crib girls hardly had anyone to do for them. Some were sickly, and

Lute didn't care to turn his back on sisters who'd once taken him in. So he fetched and carried, and the girls insisted on giving him a whole half-dollar sometimes, they were so grateful.

One day late in the summer, niggra Frankie had beckoned him into her shack after he toted her a heavy load of grub in his wagon. She had invited him to sit, promising a good stew on the back of her stove. The stew smelled so appetizing that he had a wash in the basin and pulled right up to the table. He liked Frankie. She was a big girl with a hearty, rib-shaking laugh and with a handsome patrician nose, more Indian than nigra. And she sang to make the angels take wing.

When they'd finished sopping the gravy with dippy bread, Frankie looked him in the eye and asked, "You ever done it, sonny? Ever laid with a woman?"

Up to that very minute he had not begun thinking of himself as a man. Not a sporting man, anyway. He was old enough, nearing sixteen at the time. But over the years he had seen so much of half-dressed women that the female form did not over-excite him. A naked bosom was about the same to him as the sight of a cow's udder.

Taken aback by Frankie's direct question, he'd lowered his gaze. "N-no," he said, "I ain't. Haven't."

Frankie had led him to the bed and crooned to him, "You're sure a pretty boy. Ain't all used up, and you're cleaner and nicer than most." She'd gentled down his pants, still crooning, and took his bean in her big hands. Before he could think of any good reasons why not, she straddled him and, singing and praising the Lord, tumbled him good. When they were done, he hardly knew which way to turn. Then she sat back and, big as he was, pulled him onto her lap. Rocking him like a small boy, she purred, "Did I pleasure you, sonny? I wanted to pleasure you, you is so sweet and nice. You's a good boy." He was too astonished to say a word as she rocked him and hummed "Jacob's Ladder" in her deep, tuneful voice. He knew he should be out of that shack like a shot. But after awhile the feeling was so warm that he could not bring himself to get up and go.

All through the winter he stopped by Frankie's for a stew and a tumble and a rock. As there were no cats in Oro City, where Frankie last hailed from— at an altitude of over 10,000 feet a cat was said to take fits and die—he'd given her a grey kitten. He had pried the kitty out of Cat Calhoun, an old sourdough with jittery eyes, his neck and hands cross-hatched with deep, dirt-caked creases. All summer Cat prowled around camp with a gunny sack gathering stray kittens, which he took back to his shed to fatten and, when winter snowed him in by his prospect hole, cooked for eats. Lute had terrible dreams about cats crying, and it drove him half-crazy. When he had a bit of spare change, he bought kitties off Old Man Calhoun and found them homes as mousers.

Lute and Frankie, both orphaned, talked of hard days. Frankie, starved for talk and cuddling her kitty, told him about sporting. "Plenty of girls is born restless. They likes new men like some men likes new towns. Or they bad, they hanker foh the raw edge. Some is plain dumb. Think men folks all gonna fall in love with them and marry up." Frankie whooped at the very idea.

"I took to sportin' 'cause I'm a big girl, and I likes to eat. It ain't no easy row. Mos' mens is 'bout the same as a dawg in heat."

She put the kitten in Lute's lap, and her hand firm on the knife, peeled more potatoes and wild onions for her ever-simmering stew. "It be's better than washtubs. When a customer uses me hard, I know how to fight him off. And I got money put by. Sister Coon keeps it fer me. Some day I'm gonna head home to Kaintuck, see if I still has kin."

"What kind of kin you expect you'll find?"

"Been gone so long I ain't sartain. Ain't never had no solid fella neither. Won't let no man beat me or cuss me like a cur dog. 'Spect you and Sister be the onliest family I has in this world," she finished shyly. Then she laughed her broad belly laugh, and she stroked his hair back from his forehead like she was his mammy. "I be your kin, boy, you and kitty-cat be mine."

After he and Scoop took up as friends, he had started to feel shame. He was sick with worry that Scoop—or Miz Wickersham—would hear about him lying with a Row woman. Worse, rocking in her rocker. He could just picture what kind of hell there'd be to pay. On the other hand, Frankie was a born story-teller, her tales full of the frolics and follies of men. Nor had he ever had a soul to rock him or to sing to him—he liked that part every bit as much as the tumbling.

By and by it was the major who broke him of his Frankie habit. The major bought him a used Winchester 44-49 rifle with an extra rear sight, taught him the care of the gun, and began carrying him off for gallops and target-shooting up Pratt Mountain or out on the Flats. He had a way of clapping Lute on the back like a regular companion, laughing that rumbly chuckle of his. He also owned a hard stare that made a body turn soupy inside. Lute hated to think of that stare turned on him if the major learned he was sporting with a dark-skinned Row woman.

At last he had quit Frankie's shack. He felt terrible about it, but he could not go there forever. He kept thinking he would say goodbye proper-like, but he knew it would be too hard, that he was apt to cry and act the fool. Time after time, he put it off. When he ran across Frankie on the street, she smiled uncertainly, her big dark eyes so sorrowful that he felt torn apart inside. Frankie was the nearest thing to a sweetheart or a mother he had known—at least until Mrs. Krueger began to win a similar place in his affections.

Scoop's voice chimed in on his gloom. "Heard Frankie is a first-rate banger. On the other hand, I seen that son-of-a-bitch Herman Klausmeyer lyin' in the sarvisberry bushes outside her crib. Don't know as I'd care to slide around on a wet floor after that turd's slopped her up."

God in heaven, prayed Lute silently, feeling sick. *What will I ever do?*

Scoop nattered on. "Say, you don't suppose Klausmeyer could be that Peeper Tom folks been complainin' about? Old Lady Davidson's set to mount a posse after the sick bastard. Her curtains was cracked, and he caught her in her naked shift. The Peeper musta run like hellfire at *that* sight!"

Lute hardly heard Scoop's chatter. He'd fastened his eyes on the Durant Avenue parlor lamps like he was looking into a campfire. If he stared hard enough, he thought miserably, he might get a clear picture of where to turn next.

####

CHAPTER SIXTEEN

THE ROW

Herman Klausmeyer wriggled around Frankie's crib on his belly, looked up and down the now empty street, then brushed himself off and tapped on the back door.

"Oh, h'it's you, Mistuh Kraut," the girl said sleepily.

"Yah, Frankie."

Her eyes were heavy with fatigue, and she smelled swampy, her body glistening under a loose, shabby wrapper. "Had me a sight of trade tonight, Mistuh Kraut. Think you could come back tomorry?"

"Now, Frankie baby," he said, pushing his way through the door, "you know I hurt bad when I need to peel my sausage."

"Ah, shee-it, I's weary."

Though sweet-talk was not his way, Herman's voice was wheedling. Somehow he had to sweet-talk this whore. She might not read, but that didn't make her a dummy. Even now, he could not be certain one of her customers hadn't spilled the strike beans. He struggled to keep his voice even. "Tell you what, girl. Let's us just set a spell. I haff a bottle here in my pocket, and we vill haff us a good drink."

As Frankie watched dejectedly, he went to the lopsided shelf by her sink and got down two old china cups. With drinks poured on the table, Frankie had little choice but to sit. She pulled her wrapper tight and sipped dispiritedly of her whiskey.

"Thatta girl. This here's first-rate Mexican Hat." He leaned over to top off her drink.

"What you want of me?"

"Well now, I haff a little business proposition for you. Remember them pretty mine certyficates I give you not a month ago?"

"Yessuh." She had grown watchful.

"I need them papers back—and I am prepared to go high. Five dollars." He held open his hand, showing her the cash money.

"Hain't got 'em."

132

"What the hell do you mean, 'you ain't got em'?"

"What I said. Traded 'em to Jess up the Row for that new red dress in my trunk. I ain't handed 'em over, but we has made the trade and I already wore the dress."

"Where is the paper already?" Herman asked, barely controlling his rage.

Frankie eyed him more guardedly than before, wishing she'd had the wit to lie, though lying was not part of her nature.

"I don't know that it's any of your say-so, Mistuh. I done promised Jess..."

"*Verdammter* whore, don't you sass me!" Herman roared. Yanking his pigsticker from his belt, he brandished it so it glistened in the low, smoky light of the battered oil lamp on the table. He kept it honed to a good edge with wood ash. "Hand me them certyficates or I will stick you like I stick a pig," he cried, his voice rising to a stifled howl.

The big girl felt weariness wash through her. Mr. Herman Klausmeyer gave her the heebie-jeebies, him with his white, meaty hands and hoggish little eyes. Deep in her bones she just knew the Kraut was about to prove a sight more trouble than any blind-drunk cowhand or drover. Worn to the bone or no, she decided, *I ain't gonna let no fat, mean white man lay a knife to me.* Willing herself to whatever scrap was at hand, she prayed, *Lord Jesus, help me. This ain't no time to give in to the wearies, Jesus.* Reaching behind her, she clutched the stove poker.

"Don' think you gonna scare me with yo pigsticker, Mistuh Kraut. I ain' handin' over no pieces a paper that belong to Jess. Promised 'em to her. Now you git."

The Kraut's eyes were not right. They were so filled with fury she wondered if he could see her plain. He put her in mind of an alley dog she had watched snarling and frothing white at the mouth as Mr. Hurd took aim and shot it. Before she could complete her thought, her adversary swung at her with the big knife. Instinctively, she parried the stroke with her poker.

In an instant they were circling like two wrestlers. When he struck again—and missed—his lunge carried him so near that they grappled. Wondering dazedly how this misery could be happening just as she was blessing a fine day, she wrenched her mind from scattershot recollections of seeing young Lute at the parade. As they caromed off the walls of the crib, Klausmeyer striking and Frankie fending off blows, she grew certain she was in a terrible tight corner. This was an ugly customer, dead-set on having that paper—or her life.

With her oil lamp making grotesque, leaping shadows on the walls and ceiling, they wrestled and closed, Frankie frantically seeking some means of escape. After what seemed an eternity of fight, her arms ached, her chest pained, her breath hissed, and she could have shed dry tears. Though she was larger, the girl and the man were of equal strength. They tangled nose to nose, falling to the floor and struggling back up, the reeking smell of each heavy in the other's nostrils. Frankie had been used hard in the last hours, and she feared she would soon give out. Her throat was clogged with dread. She would have to get in a good lick, and get it in soon, though she was terrified of doing real harm. Men were reluctant to hang a woman, but a nigger girl who killed a white man would hang, whether she acted to defend herself or not. Neither did a whore have the same rights as other folks—man or woman, black or white.

Her worries about inflicting serious damage put her at one more disadvantage. She felt the warm blood where her shoulder had been cut. Though it had hardly nicked her, the pigsticker sliced sharper than a buffalo skinning knife. Her desperate feeling grew as strong as the smell of her blood.

With one of his powerful blows, the Kraut swept the lamp from the table. The lighted coal oil spilled across the floor, and the talc-cry boards began to feed small fires. At length she forced the Kraut's knife hand across his chest, where it struck his opposing arm so that he spurted blood to mix with hers. With a howl, he spit in her face. Frankie sprang away, leaping onto a crooked-legged chair. From there, she swung her poker with all her might. The chair wobbled. She missed. Her own force—and the wobbly chair—caused her to lose her grip so that the poker flew from her grasp.

Flinging aside his pigsticker, the man grabbed the poker and swung with both arms, hitting Frankie in the ribs so that she uttered a primeval groan. She felt herself falling and she grew puzzled, the way she felt when she attempted to cipher sums. Then her head struck the protruding pump handle, and the sound was of a muskmelon being cracked.

Frankie lay still. It was all up with her as the flames reached out for her wrapper.

Gagging in the gathering smoke, the butcher stumbled to the trunk where she kept her meager belongings. Sniveling over his damaged arm pouring blood, he tore through petticoats and tintypes, baubles, shoes and a crimson dress until he located the packet of mine stock. Without a glance at the lifeless body on the floor, he fled the shack barely ahead of the fire, Frankie's terrorized cat on his heels.

An owl hooted mournfully as Lute, his mind in a muddle, stared at Frankie's oil lamp, the third from the end of the Row. Only gradually did an off-key note register in his head. The flame was not steady like the others; it was growing taller and wider, coming and going. He must be addled with worry to make his eyesight quaver so.

"Scoop," he said carefully, "look yonder. There's something not right about those shacks. There, down the Row, it's a flickering like."

Scoop had had a good deal more to drink than Lute. His vision was blurred. But he closed in on where his friend pointed and squinted his eyes. "Don't look like no lamp light to me. H'it looks like…looks like…"

"Damn! It is…it's a *fire!*"

Amid a welter of chicken legs, bottles, blankets, and gear, the boys leaped down the mountainside. They skidded and stumbled onto Deane Street, then galloped at top speed toward the Row. There was nothing so feared in the camps as fire. Aspen had not yet arrived as a metropolis, had not erected fireproof brick and stone building blocks. The town was a dry-wood tinder box.

"*Fire!*" both boys yelled, their voices cracking.

"Fire! Fire on the Row! FIRE!" they hollered as they streaked past the Durant Hook & Ladder, headed for the blazing crib. When they pulled up, Frankie's back door was open, flames eating around the frame like it was watermelon rind. Throwing his jacket over his head, Lute bowled straight inside, aiming blindly through black smoke for the sink and its bucket of water. He tripped, then sprawled over something on the floor: Frankie, asleep or sick. Staggering to his feet, he grabbed an arm and tugged at the dead weight of the big girl. Scoop was soon on the other side to help. Eyes streaming, they pulled her out into the weeds away from the flames.

"Oh God," cried Lute, cradling her head. "Feel here. She's bad hurt." Under his hand, the side of her head felt mushy as a stove-in squash. Gathering her in his arms, he knew in a minute that he was too late. By the light of the fire, Frankie looked old, her life gone away. He put his head down on her warm bosom and wept.

Recovering from a stormy fit of gagging and choking, Scoop stuttered, "I' God, Lute, h'it's only a sporting woman."

"No it isn't, Scoop. It's Frankie." The tears on Lute's cheeks were hotter than the flames, his heart so hurt that he thought he could never endure the pain. By this time they were in the midst of gathering bucket brigades, crowds of men pouring out of saloons and boarding houses, shouting and shoving and hauling water to fight the fire before it spread. Young Frank Parker, at last on his way to call on Bridgie, found himself cheek by jowl with Angus McClaren, passing water buckets from a nearby cistern.

Angus howled at Buckets Smith, always first at a fire, "Where are the hose boys with the water wagon, the filthy shitheels?" The Clarendon had burned to the ground not two years past and had only just been rebuilt. Aggie could not endure the torment of another holocaust.

In the midst of bedlam, the whore going by the name of Jamestown Jess, shrieking like an insane person, tried to claw her way past the men nearest the crib door. "My Pearly stock is in there! Git me my stock! Save the goddam trunk! It holds my Pearly stock Frankie traded me!"

"Quit your racket, woman," ordered Buckets. "Ain't nobody going in that bonfire. Stop it now!"

Scoop attempted clumsily to shield Lute's unaccountable grief from the crowds. Then he realized that no one was paying any mind to a thing but the fire and Jess's caterwauling.

"Well," he muttered awkwardly, "looks like she was in a helluva tussle. Leastways she went out with a fight." He was so mortified at Lute taking on over a black sporting girl that he hardly knew what to say. "Grabbed this knife off the floor," he said, "and lookit, they's blood on the knife—and on me too."

Lute kept right on weeping, the tears leaking out of his eyes and zigzagging down his face. Frankie's cat rubbed against his leg, arching its back and purring.

"Hell, Lute," said Scoop, feeling low and at a loss, "this should be the most hallelujah day of our whole life. How come I got this bad feeling—like everything is just turnin' to shit?"

####

CHAPTER SEVENTEEN

THE WIDOW WICKERSHAM

Gabe Tacker belched explosively and bit off the end of his cigar. " Damn, Leorah, you sure know the way to a man's gizzard!" Caressing the widow's partridge-plump hand resting on the Belgian lace tablecloth, he said in his deep bass, "and his cock too. About the time I get my dinner settled, my flag'll be flying at top mast."

"That elk steak was fresh as they come, Gabe. Ellsworth Hayes bagged him yesterday morning, up by Tourtelotte Park." Leorah Wickersham was no spring chicken, but her voice was as honeyed as a young girl's.

"A man could die happy in this house," he grunted as his caresses moved up the bare white arm.

Leorah gazed at him fondly. She considered him an imposing man, in a class with President Cleveland. To her surprise, she'd found the comparison irked him.

"Man's a fool Democrat," he'd barked. "Worthless as that port director Chester Arthur!" Gabe belonged to Gabe, and did not care to look like a living soul but himself. Indeed, aside from flowing yellow-gray sideburns, a bushy mustache, and a portly stomach, he bore no more resemblance to either president than to the Ute Chief Ouray. With his immense red neck and fleshy nose, as intricately veined as a chunk of quartz pyrite, Gabe was not a particularly pretty sight. But like many powerful men, he exuded an aura which women, not least the widow, found irresistible. And he was as hot-blooded as he was high-powered. On her feather-filled ticking, under the comforters, he'd warmed juices she'd thought no more than dried-up dregs. Warmed them 'til they'd stirred and flowed like sap in a warming woodland. Gabe, in his turn, declared he'd never known a woman as full of sap as Orey.

Feeling her face grow hot, Leorah pushed herself out of the fan-backed chair at her mahogany dining table to glance at her reflection in the gilt-framed mirror over her credenza. She adjusted the stylish chignon holding her chestnut hair, pleased with the satiny shoulders and deep cleavage peeping from a custard-colored ninon and lace dress cut recklessly low. She knew she was a striking woman. She knew too that, if not for Gabe, she would have withered away in her widow's weeds, old before her time.

Harold Wickersham, mine superintendent, had carted her to this godforsaken end of the trail and then, following a dinner of braised pork roast, chitling gravy and candied yams, clawed at his chest, heaved up his dinner, and died in her lap. He'd left her in moderate circumstance—and unhappily alone. When Major Burdine came to call—like most Southerners of their class, they lay claim to kissing cousins—her heart had leaped high in her throat. But despite her coquettish ways and masterful cookery, he was a younger man who saw her as no more than a neighborly fellow Confederate.

Tired of being snowed in, isolated, without lively companionship, she'd begun packing boxes and trunks for the long trek back to Alabama. At the time, it was court week on the Pitkin County calendar and Aggie McClaren had implored, "I beg of ye,' Leorah, the hotel's full to overflowing. Gabe Tacker's not a man to share a bed—and roaring like a mad bear. If you'll rent him your lovely upstairs room, I'll bless ye' to the high heavens."

Gabe had materialized imposingly in her front parlor, flung aside his beaver-lined cape, looked her up and down and announced, "Well, well. I thought I was to meet a landlady. And look here—I have found pure treasure."

She'd hastened to fix him a warmed-over supper, listened raptly as he talked of high finance, Washington gossip, and Western adventures. She had answered his penetrating questions about her own condition and much later that night found herself following meekly as he led the way to her bedroom just off the front parlor.

"My, oh my!" he crowed as she let down her long chestnut hair, her gown, and her shift.

Gabe Tacker never set foot in the widow's upstairs. And Leorah Wickersham shortly unpacked. Gabe was a passionate man and a generous one. She became his unofficial hostess, kept in style, her life a cornucopia of luxuries. In addition to a Peking jade hair receiver set and modish bonnets, a jasper and diamond ring and silk undergarments ordered from Paris, Gabe presented her with a clever little ivory-handled Remington pocket pistol for her bedside table when she complained of a peeping tom at her bedroom window.

"I can't always be with you, Orey. Will you have the sand to use it?" he asked, looking her square in the eye.

"I assure you, my dear."

Seeing her indignation, he figured she would at that.

No invitation was more prized by local bigwigs than dinner and an evening of poker at the widow's. She knew the wives talked and she cared not a whit. Her furnishings were the finest, her wine cellar richly stocked, her table lavishly set, her bed properly warmed. She was secure in Gabe's hunger for her. She knew he made many more trips into the mountains than his affairs demanded.

In his turn, when scratch got in Gabe's pants he liked not only a plush woman for cushioning but also a woman with fire in her belly. In addition, he desired a companion with a head on her shoulders. He could mull over his business quandaries, ask for her views on investments. She not only lighted his fires, she oiled the cogs of his thinking.

"Why wiggle between a lady's legs if you can't get her to say a sensible word?" was his view. "Might's well use the nearest sheep or goat."

Gabe opened the silver box by his plate and removed a large, hand-rolled Havana cigar, which he clipped with chased silver nippers. He produced a smaller, slimmer cheroot for Orey. When she'd placed it daintily between her lips, he leaned close to light it, fondling her arm once again. They'd lingered, settling the supper on which Gabe had appropriately heaped compliments, not only for the elk, but for the saltwater tang of the littleneck clams, the lightness of the whipped potato soufflé, and the delicacy of a raspberry mousse served with one of her springy coconut layer cakes. He leaned back in his high-backed chair, blowing a series of perfect smoke rings. He began telling her of plans for the railroads to come in, measuring her upthrust breasts with his eyes. Though he could already feel his tongue moving hungrily over her large nipples, he reached instead for his glass of claret, tasting the anticipation along with his wine. He pictured the emergence of that fine full figure only half-suspicioned under cover of shimmies and bustles, of laces and stays. Naked, she was as plump and succulent as a young squab. His eyes grew heavy with desire.

"Ah begs pardon, ma'am. Powerful sorry." Orey's niggra houseman, Suppertime, was aghast at intruding. He could smell the lust in this room from down by the back alley. Spotted black and white as an Appaloosa pony, Suppertime had once traveled with Phineas T. Barnum's circus as "the calico man." He'd known the smell of lust all his life.

Though the widow felt the same deep affection for Suppertime as she did for her pug dog Teeny, she was visibly annoyed.

"Fella say he hafta see Mr. Tacker. Say it God Almighty important."

Behind Suppertime hovered a big, sullen brute in a wet rugby shirt. Beyond the big fellow was Gabe's Aspen attorney, Harry Dunbar.

Gabe rose reluctantly to his feet. "Now what in hellfire can be this pressing when I've barely got down my dinner?" As Harry had warned Bull, interference with the tycoon's mealtimes—or bedtimes either—made him crosser than a bull elk in rut.

Mudgett himself was in an ugly frame of mind. To avoid being shanghaied into fighting the Durant Avenue fire, he'd had to stable his horse and slink around town afoot searching for Tacker. He'd detoured down Hopkins Street and plunged across the Roaring Fork at its most turbulent, his second cold-water dousing in one night—and he was an alley cat who hated getting his whiskers wet. He'd finally roused an ill-tempered Dunbar from sleep.

"Gabe's over to the widow's," said Harry. "Hates like thunder to be interrupted when he's with her. Hell, I'll go with you. He might shoot you in your pecker. Doubt he'd gun down his lawyer."

Bull was in no mood to have a gun pointed at his crotch. His hand was on his own Schofield .45. Harry shoved Suppertime aside, nodded briefly at the widow, and leaned close to Tacker's ear.

"Sutton's shift-jobber at the Columbine, you say? Oh very well. Come in, come in. But be quick about it." Gabe appeared more truculent than murderous as he stood in the archway between dining room and parlor, framed in ivory damask hangings.

Bull, gape-mouthed, was nearly overcome by his surroundings. Mrs. Robinson's boardinghouse stank of old ham hocks and rancid grease. Its furnishings were spur-gouged, paint-peeled, and splintery. He could not avert his eyes from the gleaming tables, the artful flower arrangements, the thick carpets and pretty paintings, to say nothing of the curvaceous, pink-cheeked widow herself.

"What is it, speak up, dammit, speak up!"

Bull eyed Mrs. Wickersham skeptically.

"You can talk, Mister. It's only one tight-lipped lady, her husband's ghost, and two first-class shysters here."

"Well, er, it's about the Pearly, Mr. Tacker. The Pearly Everlasting Mine. Word's all over that they have hit the biggest silver lode in the Rockies. It is worth thousands, they say. Sutton's office already has wireless inquiries from Manitou Springs."

"Bully for the Pearly," said Big Gabe, his gaze narrowing.

"The hell of it is, that holding ain't in Mr. Sutton's hands right now—h'it's Cal Krueger has it under lease."

"Oh shit..."

Late in the afternoon, Gabe had heard that the Pearly'd struck some order of paydirt. He'd thought this slightly ludicrous on a holiday. Should it prove valid, however, he'd soon have the money that upstart Sutton owed him. At one time he'd admired the younger man's voracious ambition, his get-up-and-go. Then the mine operator's enterprises began to sour, and the fellow himself to lose his touch. If there was indeed a strike of major dimensions, Gabe suspected he'd need to take a hand in the affair.

"Who's this Cal Krueger?" he barked.

"Pesky sideliner. Sold the Keystone awhile back. His lease on the Pearly has near three months to run."

"Son of a bitch!" Gabe rarely cursed in Orey's presence. Now he dropped her hand and sank onto the arm of a nearby chair. "The Columbine and the Pearly are the two I told that fool not to let out of his hands. Greedy pig must have gone rooting after ready cash."

Harry spoke up. "Happened when you instructed no one was to extend Sutton another cent of credit, Gabe. You were putting on the squeeze to diddle him out of his Aspen bank holding."

"Why wasn't I told?" snapped Gabe.

Harry appeared dazed. "That Pearly wasn't worth a weak fart," he said. "Never thought the leasehold worth mentioning."

Gabe glared at his attorney. Then he beckoned Mudgett to a seat. "Well now—Mudgett, is it?"

"Yes sir, Mr. Tacker."

"Just how did you come up with your figures? In the thousands, you say?"

"You know what they claim about smoke," said Bull, his eyes darting to Mrs. Wickersham's creamy bosom daringly half-bared in the lamplight. He could scarcely credit this as the primly buttoned-up-tight-in-black-silk widow he saw old Suppertime driving to church on Sundays. "Well, my boys know the mines, and they're poking everywhere. There's smoke enough for a six-alarm fire. When we tried to pin Gus Ackerman on assays, he turned us out at gunpoint. Armed guards is by the Pearly shafthouse. Krueger's hiring the camp's top trammers—at double wages. By our estimates, this has gotta be one helluva find." Suddenly conscious of his scruffy appearance, Bull hastily yanked his derby hat from his head and tucked it under his arm. He added unctuously, "Thought by rights you should know, sir."

Gabe sat stroking his chin, his lower lip moving in and out, his oyster eyes hooded in thought. "Harry, did you and Andy do any of the paper work on that lease? Think you could locate loopholes?"

"It was Embert Oakes drew it up, Gabe. Sutton held out for his price, but Krueger insisted on his own lawyer."

"Sutton best file adverse claims. Then we'll see if we can't get Judge Duckworth to issue an injunction."

"I'll get right on it," said Harry, starting for the door.

Gabe held up a hand. "No use spoiling the set of that outstanding holiday picnic. Bright and early in the morning will do the trick, Harry. Bright and early."

Leorah Wickersham had absorbed this exchange like a soft mute sponge. *Aha!* she thought, it *is* true then, every speculative word she'd heard at the lakes. The Presbyterians had done it! They had got the upper hand of the Apex crowd! Despite her premiere interest in lining her own pockets, in her heart of hearts Orey was with the sideliners. She cared for Big Gabe Tacker. He was hard, and he sometimes had a mean mouth, but he treated her like a queen. By the same token, she owed a debt she could never repay to Aggie McClaren and Lavinia Krueger. When the mountain ague struck last winter, she had been hard hit. Out of her head with fever, and with no family to care for her, she could have died in the night. Doc Alderfer had spoken to Aggie, who appeared at her door laden with linens, food supplies and medicaments, sent Suppertime packing, and proceeded to wear a path between her bed and the kitchen stove, nursing the widow back to the living. After a few sleepless nights of damping high fevers, wrapping Orey in cold wet sheets, boiling beeplant for tea, and spoonfeeding her barley broth for strength, the exhausted Scotswoman called on Lavinia Krueger, who spelled her so that Leorah was never alone. Though neither woman had known her well, and surely were aware of her questionable repute, they'd tended her as lovingly as if she were blood kin. Since they judged Emma Sutton too young and dauncy for hard nursing, Emma was consigned to making kettles of soups and broths and collecting linens for washing while Bridgie scrubbed down the widow's house.

When Gabe returned from an extended business trip to San Francisco, it was to find the widow badly shaken but recovering. Knowing him impatient with weakness, Leorah had employed the rouge pot and managed her brightest smile, glossing over her near-brush with the sweet-bye-and-bye. In this man's world, it was women who, in the hard pinches, looked after one another. She prayed the Pearly would make Lavinia Krueger rich as Mrs. Cornelius Vanderbilt. Gabe Tacker had more than plenty. Furthermore, Orey owned a bundle in the Pearly leasehold herself. She'd bought a good number of shares by way of lending the Kruegers a hand. She might just realize enough to install the new electrical lighting, already in several dozen Aspen business firms. She'd also admired a pair of dappled carriage horses at the Denver stock barns. Already she was totting up sums in her head.

"As for that cock pheasant Sutton, why ain't he here to report on his own mischief?" growled Gabe to the men.

Harry's tone was caustic. "He could be sitting up with that wife of his so she won't bleed to death from all the medals they pinned on her."

"Nope," said Mudgett. "He's in Leadville. Taking in the celebration over there."

"What's the problem?" snorted Gabe. "The fireworks in his home camp aren't fancy enough for him?"

####

CHAPTER EIGHTEEN

MINNIE MULQUEEN

Minnie Mulqueen breathed deep to quiet the fluttering in her breast. It was nine o'clock in the dress circle of the Silver City Theater on Grand Avenue in Leadville, the most exhilarating boom town in all the West. Mr. Eddie Foy had left the audience howling and foot-stomping. He was followed onstage by six bespangled chorus ladies dancing a new version of the fandango to the accompaniment of a full orchestra in boiled shirts and black silk ties. The famed San Francisco chanteuse, Mamselle Jeannie Marceau had in her turn, brought down the house. Mr. Sutton and a number of overweight senators were throwing gold eagles at the feet of Mamselle like they were five-cent chaws. Minnie yearned to jump on the stage apron and gather in a few for herself. What she couldn't do with those gold pieces!

This was what Minnie had dreamed of back in Maryland. This was the life she was born for. She didn't feel a single pang over Patrick, her husband who knew no better than mucking in mine mud, who never exhibited an ounce of up-and-at-'em. Not her. Her fat pink lips, brightened by biting on a piece of red ribbon, fixed themselves in a moue. Ever since she took the job writing out messages at the wireless office on the Avenue, a world of men had stopped by her door. She peeked again at her small pouter pigeon chest in the darling pink crepe de chine gown Mr. Sutton had insisted on buying her.

"This is Leadville, honey lamb," he'd said reassuringly, "not Hagerstown. If you are to accompany me to the theater you must look 'de mode.' Believe me when I say the gift of a fancy dress is no different in Leadville than a box of Argenty chocolates back in Maryland. Out here, we spend real money on pretty trifles."

Minnie knew very well there was a world of difference. In Hagerstown, no lady would tolerate the shocking proffer of a dress. But this was Leadville, two thousand miles removed from her cousins and aunties and Father Sweeney, a place where fortunes were made in a day and spent overnight. She was caught up in the frenzy, a frail flower in a firestorm. Each week, swept deeper into the rush of events, she forgot a little more of her catechism, of her ma's repeated warnings about hellfire and damnation.

"More champagne, my dear?" asked Mr. Sutton, leaning against her to pour. Minnie dimpled and narrowed her blue eyes, making them sparkle amid small, crinkly laugh lines the way she'd practiced in her hand mirror. Though she would not have believed it, her posturings, spoiled little mouth and darting eyes made her look like a plump, willful capon. "Oh, Mr. Sutton," she breathed, "I shouldn't and you know it."

She thought it very clever that she had been surreptitiously tilting her glass so that most of her wine spilled onto the carpeted floor. She could not afford to lose her head, though she shivered at the nearness of a man so pretty and so polished. A man who smelled of fine talcum, wore a silver-encased diamond on one of his long white fingers, and had an aloof look in his eye. She had never been touched by a man without rings of mine dirt under his nails, and she sensed that she soon would be. With a sidelong glance at the cool, handsome profile, she thought, *I'll be a match for him.* Minnie Mulqueen knew men thought her luscious. She planned to use her good looks while she owned the chance. Patrick could keep his mine dirt. She was going to have her fill from the plate of mine-town riches, and then go back for seconds and thirds.

Just as Mr. Sutton placed the bottle of sparkling wine back in its bucket of ice, she looked up to see old Tinker from the telegraph office making his way down the smoky center aisle. He approached her wretchedly. "I didn't know what to do, Miss Minnie. Swear I didn't. This is the eighth wire that come in for Mr. Sutton, and they sound mighty important." He thrust out a handful of telegrams.

Minnie felt a tremor of fear—so many of the wires she delivered meant death or disaster. She watched anxiously while Mr. Sutton tore open his messages, his face darkening as he read. He fished for money for Tinker, scribbled a reply, gave curt orders and grasped Minnie's arm in a steely grip. "We are leaving," he said.

This was not one of her many well-rehearsed scenarios. She stumbled after him as he stalked out of the theater. Still in his grip, she followed as he plowed his way through jostling crowds into the lobby of the Tabor Grand Hotel. When she paused in confusion among great chinoiserie urns stuffed with incongruous potted palms, he gripped her arm harder and pulled her up the wide staircase behind him. In his suite of rooms, he eyed her so strangely that she felt a chill very like the foreboding over an unexpected telegram. When she started to speak, he put those long white fingers across her mouth and shrugged out of his tailcoat. Though she tried to wriggle away, he put the fingers in her dress front and ripped the pretty pink bodice away. *Oh, oh,* she thought. It had cost so dear, that dress. For the first time Minnie felt real alarm. Nothing was happening as she had foreseen. She wasn't even certain how she'd been maneuvered into this hotel room. It came to her that it would be useless to cry out. The street noises were louder at this hour than at midday. Masses of men on the avenue below poured in and out of saloons and dance halls. Freight wagons and Concord coaches clattered past, jouncing from street ruts into deep potholes. Women shrieked and floor managers bellowed. Orchestras and pianos and hand organs played a jangle of conflicting tunes. Hers would be a lost voice in a noisome wilderness.

Then an outsized linen handkerchief was stuffed in her mouth. She could not utter so much as a squeak. Minnie Mulqueen ceased thinking about street sounds or wasted gowns. She did not think of anything except being tormented and terrified and fighting for air. What she had daydreamed as a grand stage performance that carried her off on the wings of love became instead an act of savagery. A steel bludgeon pounded her in a bitter, persistent flogging, until she leaked as if she'd been sieved with a knife. At last, when her muffled cries were the mewings of an iron-trapped animal, the refined Mr. Sutton stood up and wordlessly adjusted his clothes. He looked coldly at the huddled, shaking creature on the floor, then strode away into the other room.

Minnie clutched the remnants of dress about her and in some way stumbled to the door. She did not wish to be anywhere in sight of Mr. Sutton when he reappeared. She half fell into the hallway outside, where she huddled against a wall to summon her strength. The place between her legs was abraded and bleeding, the wet that ran there scalded raw flesh. Minnie expected she was lucky to be alive. She had been a fool, thinking herself a match for such a man. As she crept along the hallway, Minnie knew, under all her pain and ignominy, that she had learned a hard lesson. Unlike Father Sweeney's or Ma's bland instruction, this was a remonstrance branded on her with a red-hot iron.

Early in the morning of the Fifth of July, Emma was awakened by the chittering of squirrels, the chattering of house finches, a sharp crackle of paper, and the ache of her bruised body. She groaned, then groggily groped for the thick packet Polly had tucked under her pillow in the night. The Indian had returned late to report that Aggie McClaren was beyond reach. She was assisting Doc with a grim amputation of fingers before the blood poisoning lost Amos Blackwell his hand. Worse, the fire bell had been in earnest. A roaring blaze threatened the entire Durant Street Row. Half the camp, led by Angus McClaren, was on the water line. Polly had looked bleak, her face twisted in a distraught grimace.

Emma had clasped the squaw's two hands in hers. "Hellfire. I was counting on the McClaren's hotel safe. It's the only one not in a bank or the assayer's or Garrett's offices." If she hadn't been so befuddled, she could have entrusted the major with delivering her stock to the hotel.

"This is a fine kettle of cod," she said, half to herself. Her father's law firm had not yet overturned the power of the court that she, in her naiveté, had assigned Garrett. She muttered gutturally in Ute, "If that devil gets his hands on these shares, he'll sign them over to himself and have his mine back...not his mine...mine..." She'd been so played out that she tangled in her own words. "Never mind, my friend...you and I...we'll stash the stock...in the morning...the stage will not be in 'til after..." Polly's hands slipped from hers as Emma slipped away into sleep.

This morning she felt as if she'd been backed over by an ore wagon. Creaking like an aged tree being felled, she turned to bury her face in the pillow. She so seldom ailed that the state of her body dismayed her. *Just when I need all my faculties, I'm a crippled crone.* Then she heard the jingle and squawk of horse tack, the low sound of men's voices down by the stable—and her door burst open.

"Missy, missy!" Polly's voice was a low growl. "Mr. Sutton come. Mister here! Quick! Give paper!"

With Emma's head whirling, her mind asking, *Why? How?...* Polly snatched up the heavy, string-tied bundles of stock and vanished from the room. In another few minutes the sound of heavy boots on the stair echoed the pounding of Emma's heartbeat, the door flew open, and Garrett was in the room in mud-soaked riding clothes, glowering, his Remington in one hand, a driller's sledge in the other.

Oh my God, thought Emma, *he is going to beat me to death.* Then, behind him in the hallway, Polly appeared, her face more ominous than Garrett's, her long fletching knife in one hand, her throwing axe in the other. Beyond Polly huddled Bridgie, quaking but determined, wielding a silver butter knife.

Emma stared at Garrett as if he were an apparition. "How did you..." she began, her voice thick with sleep and laudanum..

"Surprise you, my dear? I was so eager to see you that I rode the Half-Moon Trail. Pleasant evening for a moonlight ride."

"Garrett, I…"

"Let us not waste each other's time—or words. Where is the Pearly stock, Emma?"

A resolute note firmed her voice. "I do not have it."

"That was not my question, Emma. I asked where it is."

"I do not know," she said, truthfully.

"By Christ, I'll…"

Emma had seen Garrett disdainful. She had seen him incensed…indignant…provoked. He stood before her now with his face undressed, naked hate laid bare in the morning light. From somewhere inside him, like molten magma simmering below ground until it finally boiled up and blew, had risen a rage more terrible than any she had ever witnessed. For the first time in her young life, she was terrified. Then, as her husband turned to slam the door and close them in together, a skin of ice settled over her. She noted that he did not let out an animal howl when he found Polly barring his way, her squat, twisted body immoveable as a bristlecone pine. Bridgie, appalled but game, cried, "Oh please, sir, the missus is hurt. She was throwed from the parade wagon. She was…she lost…" The high, shrill voice wound down and broke off.

"Hold your peace, Bridgie girl." Emma sat up on the side of the bed. She wished to face Garrett head-on, but her legs were so unresponsive she could scarce gain command of them. "Garrett," she said with care, "it will do you no good to rant and storm. I have handed over the stock for safekeeping. It cannot be had—by me, or by you." The lie came out so slick that she wondered at herself. Was she to spend her life dissembling, as dishonest as the man who shook with impotent fury before her? Her legs still unsure, she rose to her feet.

Garrett glared wildly at his wife, at the glowering Ute with her knife at-the-ready, and at the shaken Irish girl. From the corner of the bedroom, Chester showed his teeth and snarled. Her husband looked so murderous that Emma thought for a moment he might do for all four of them.

Then, without another word, he grasped his rifle by the barrel, and using the brass-edged walnut wood stock like a club, began smashing Emma's delicate cherry bed. He laid about him with the gunstock until the remnants of lower bedposts were the pale pink, jagged shards of sickly bone. Emma cringed once but no more. Her face grey as an old snowbank, she leaned against Polly as Garrett threw aside his gun and set to work on the headboard with the sledge, pounding it into the same raw splinters. When he had reduced the bed to ruin, he gave her one final, searing look, pushed his way past Polly and Bridgie, and blew out of the house, leaving desolation in his wake.

####

BOOK TWO

CHAPTER NINETEEN

UNDERGROUND

"IRE IN THE HOLE!" shouted Pete Beard.

"Fire in the hole!" he called again, his voice deep and rough as he applied lighted spitter fuses to the last of the rattails dangling from the vug wall. Pete was one of Aspen's ablest blasters. Before touching a match to his fuses, he'd used a long, slender copper spoon, unsusceptible to sparks, to painstakingly probe the twenty-one charges inserted in the core holes of the facewall. The holes had been drilled in a pattern of three triangles, each holding charges—in the center, in edger holes at the top and both sides and in a "lifter" hole at the bottom. Every core sprouted a Bickford safety fuse, or rattail, a charge of powder surrounded by twisted strands of jute wrapped with a layer of twine and then re-wrapped with waterproof tape.

Needle Newsome crouched by Pete's side. They worked as deftly as a team of jugglers, Needle handing over lighted spitters, Pete igniting charges until the tips of his fingers were seared.

"FIRE IN THE HOLE!" Pete bellowed a last time.

"FIRE IN THE HOLE!" echoed Needle as they sprinted half-crouched through the passageway leading from the glory hole. They picked up speed around the breast of the main tunnel, where they could straighten and stretch out their legs. Making two half-turns, they came to a heavily post-and-cap-timbered side cut where Young Frank, Aaron, and three other crewmen hunkered down.

"Fire in the hole!" reverberated from the throats of men sheltered snugly in the back of crosscuts, from the new Lavinia tunnel being excavated toward the front of the mountain, from the shafthouse above.

Nothing in these parts approached the half-thrill, half-chill of a big mine blow. Every man, woman, and child in camp was tingly aware that deadly forces were in play; forces which only the skill of seasoned blasters could harness without murdering half the men on the job.

Today's explosion would be a full-fledged tiger. For three weeks, Calvin's crews had picked silver like hazelnuts from a shell. They'd brought

153

out forty-odd tons of ore per shift—without a single round of blasting. Gus Ackerman figured the paydirt was already between $200,000 and $400,000, figures so staggering they seemed a chimera that could vanish into a passing thunderhead.

Most of the Pearly camp had not had enough sleep to put in a teaspoon moon. Every man on the job felt he could live on sand, that there'd be sleep aplenty when this affair was done.

"I'll sleep when we've put enough by to get you your teaching certificates," Pete promised Tacy, the shining star in his firmament of girls.

"Luther can sleep when he's growed," declared Willard. "The boy's got a head for figures. I need him awake." Lute was learning to keep ledgers under the curmudgeon's finicky tutelage.

"I'll rest when I get to my grave," Calvin assured an exasperated Vinnie. "I'll have all the hereafter to rest, Lavinia."

The digging to date had been easy as licking frosting from a cake. Now they needed a better notion of the extent of the deposit, of how much more manpower to throw into the affair. The ordinary expectation of an end-of-shift blow was to extend a working tunnel another few feet. Today, employing extra charges, they hoped for a more far-reaching result. Blasting was a prickly business. Too much powder could weaken drift walls, even concuss a mountain. Although dynamite could be molded or sliced slick as a banana and was more reliable in close confines, its ugly fumes made some men sicker than goats on a surfeit of trash. Cal had again reverted to black powder.

The men in the near side-cut finished plugging cotton batting in their ears, sat back against the gangue-wall timbering, put their heads between their knees, and wrapped their arms around themselves in tight compact packages. When the first explosion came, it slammed through them like a mammoth dose of black pepper. The *Vrooooooommmmm* of sequential charges rocked not only the mine and the mountain, but every street in Aspen. To a greenhorn, such detonation could've heralded the onset of Armageddon. To seasoned camp people, heavy blasting meant going mines, and going mines signaled prosperity. They complained, but their complaints were genial.

Over on Bleeker Street, Mrs. Ollie Davidson wiped the laundry bluing from her hands and grumbled, "First my wash gets rained on, then the blamed blasting shakes down the clothes poles."

In Swedetown on the bluff over the river flats, the floor lifted beneath Svea Hoaglund's feet, and she juggled one of the family's three china plates from hand to hand. She peered out the kitchen window at the pastured cow Lisalotte and muttered good-naturedly, "It's a wonder her milk don't sour."

Herman Klausmeyer wiped bloodied hands on his butcher's apron and ogled Mrs. Florence Dunbar over the Beck & Bishop meat counter, hoping she'd shriek, jump off her high horse and out of her starched house dress. Deaf to the thunderous clamor, she did not budge.

In his surgery, Dan Alderfer was so intent on sewing up a miner's newly-bobbed nose that he never dropped a stitch. Rich Case was the latest in a streak of men shy part of a nose because they'd tucked a blast cap in their pockets with their loose tobacco, forgot the cap, stuffed the lot in a pipe, and lit up.

"It beats me, Case," rasped the doc, "how any man could be this Christ Almighty forgetful. It's a wonder you didn't light up in your lap and blow off your pecker."

When the concussion hit the bench boys, Rheumanalor Wilson shifted his cud and remarked, "That one had a whang to it."

Only in the Sutton kitchen was there unreasoning displeasure. Garrett looked up from a jumble of papers and dishes on the big oak kitchen table and cursed, his words a poisonous stream. Bull Mudgett, digging into a can of pears, thought of his boss as stripped down, his furies exposed like the hot coals of a raked fire.

"Won't be long now," Bull muttered into the pears. "They'll find out what blasting is, by God!"

Garrett did not answer. Before him, in the *Aspen Daily News*, like acid eating into his brain, were the latest reports of Pearly production. The smallest details of the workings, every incidental anecdote about the crewmen were daily fodder for the front page.

Counting off the final blast, townspeople breathed easier. A damp, unexploded charge meant that some poor Godforsaken galoot must go in there and pry with a pick to retrieve powder and cap: a mean job which could end with the miner blown to pieces like so much stew beef.

The crew in the cul-de-sac nearest the cathedral felt almighty suctionings of air, sensed the shifting of tons of rock, submitted to the bombarding of loose stones and dirt which burst from behind timbers. At length, Young Frank looked up and remarked light-heartedly, "I' God, Beard, if this hill bounces any higher, you'll have to tighten them pigtails." It was a matter of pride for the men to carry on jocular conversation in the midst of discordant destruction.

Pete grinned and pulled at his braided beard. "Beard's my name, and I reckon my beard's my mark." When Calvin's bonanza was struck, he'd been overdue for a barbering. Now, with no time for Pie Burkhardt's powders and pomatums, he had Tacy plait his flowing whiskers so they wouldn't interfere with his work.

Aaron said, "Least he don't have to wash his goddam whiskers every night. When Beulah was alive, she made him launder all the hairs on his head, clear hisself of 'baccy juice before she'd let him in their bed." Aaron waxed indignant. "Waren't nothing more than cold water and yellow lye soap give Pete the jaundice that time."

As the moment for the second triangle of explosions neared, Aaron kept up his grousing. "'Pears to me we're owed extry hazard pay fer this amount of uproar."

The other men looked at him askance. "Eight dollars a shift and shares of the profits ain't enough for you?" asked one young Croat incredulously.

Pete, mortified, said, "Aaron has had a better offer from the King of Prussia. He will sail on a packet next week to take over the mines of Silesia." Giving Aaron a disgusted look, he tightened back into his shipwreck tuck.

When the last explosion had vented its power, Calvin rose from his own blasting tuck in the shafthouse above, turned to Nate, and shouted over the rainstorm crashing around them, "That dose ought to plumb the depths!"

The downpour was one of many that tore briefly and violently through the mountains on summer afternoons. As the sky turned from fading blue to leaden gray to ominous black, lightning ricocheted in jagged blades from the underbellies of thunderclouds. The gullywasher hit hard. Driving rainwater slashed through roof holes and streaked in runnels down wood slats. In full voice, the thunder above repeated the eruptions below.

"Weather moved in fast," Nate shouted back, his face streaming water. "Wonder if them balloon pilots got down before she struck."

The Taos pilots, their balloon patched, had been taking their machine for trial runs almost every forenoon. Though Aggie McClaren continued rushing out of doors to watch, shading eyes filled with wonder, and the bench boys marked the balloon's daily progress, folks were mainly inured to the sight.

Nate could hardly credit how Calvin managed to be so many places in one day; swinging a mattock in the vug, monitoring the pressure in the steam boilers, ordering timbering here, stope scaffolding there, and supervising the crew working on the new lower-level Lavinia Tunnel, which would exit the side of the mountain directly above Deane Street. That is that adit would allow them to dump ore into chutes, where it would pour into hoppers and thence into lines of ore wagons beneath. With the Lavinia punched through the hillside, tram tracks installed, they could bypass loading ore in cages and lifting it arduously to the surface.

Two-way tram-car traffic already moved at a smart clip, the iron turntables for the cars shoved through more than thirty yards deeper, hinnies pulling the heavy ore cars to save the men.

Most often, Calvin presided over the shafthouse where a new steam engine powered two skips which sped smartly up and down the widened main shaft. No detail was too minute for Calvin's attention. He'd even reassigned Gracious, the Krueger family mule. Relieved of mine work and affecting a rummy walk and occasional spells of the vapors, the animal was now on ore wagon duty. "Animal thinks it's starring in a opera troupe," sniffed Willard.

One of the few matters Calvin had not gotten around to was laying a good roof on the shafthouse. They'd nailed sheets of oiled cloth over the most yawning holes, though heavy rain gusts frequently tore them away. As Nate hunched his way through the downpour to re-plug a gushing leak, Cal said, "The roof will have to serve 'til the boys aren't so hard-pressed."

Willard, who'd carefully finished counting off charges and now climbed out from under the weather-peeled shafthouse desk, had to shout to make himself heard over the storm. "Dern! H'it's raining sheet metal! Twixt weather and powder," he yelled, "we'll all be deef as posts."

Calvin peered out at the sky. "She's fairing off to the west."

Willard ignored the weather prediction. "Calvin," he hollered, "I want you to listen here. Our overhead is running too blamed high." He shifted on his crutch, huddled under a rubber sheet, and referred to his papers. "This ain't the goddamed Homestake. What with shift crews, timberers, hidemen, freighters and the like, we got us fifty-odd on the payroll." Calvin dealt not only with machinery and logistics, but with a steady procession of petitioners. Had it been up to Willard, all would have been sent packing. "And you're paying top wages--$30 a month for crippled-up guards and green-as-grass young'uns. You know very well who I got in mind," he shouted with the aggrieved air of a man who's bitten down on a sore tooth.

"I know it, Willard," Calvin shouted back. "Scoop Hurd is Luther's friend, and he means business. Stump Clancy was in need of work. I figured he'd serve for duty at the Hopkins Street lots." Deke and Nate had contracted for a number of vacant town lots where ore was being stockpiled. The local smelter—only recently blown in—despite operating full-tilt, could process less than a hundred tons of ore a day. Using the standard coking process, the smelter reduced the ore to a concentrate called matte, containing the base metals of lead, silver, and a smattering of gold. The slag was discarded, and the resulting matte was a rich essence, easier and cheaper to transport than bulk ore. With the heavy output of the Pearly added to that of other mines, the load was too much for the groaning furnace. Daily, their ore piled higher in the lots waiting to be jack-trained and wagoned across the hump to Leadville's and Denver's giant smelters. A sizeable portion of the Pearly lode would lie under open skies for time to come.

Deke had ore wagons moving up and down between mine and lots as smooth as trains shunted onto sidings in Denver's Larimer Street yards. But until Aspen's three wheelwrights turned out more new wheels, the staggered wagons must be augmented by old-style jack trains loaded with ore packed in green elk hides. Some days the major felt as if he were in a battle on five fronts. He was making do with even less sleep than the others.

Willard eyed a patch of blue sky. Calvin was right about the weather at least. The torrential rain was slowing as fast as it had quickened. In the soft after-shower, he could hear himself think. He felt a nagging sense of futility. It was little use arguing with Calvin about the profligacy of extending his good fortune to half this camp. The man's final pronouncement was always the same: "Vinnie and I might's well share the wealth. We can only spend so much in one lifetime, my friend."

"Right now, Calvin, you are sharing wealth that ain't reached your pockets."

"I expect we are," said Calvin mildly. "Isn't it always the way with the mine game?"

Willard's angst-ridden thoughts were on the tons of ore straining hastily reinforced cribbing on the mountainside, more tons being offloaded behind even more hastily erected fencing in town. Those ore piles still had to get to market, be processed and sold—and at a good price. What's more, every last ounce must first be packed over the hump; the most treacherous, most vulnerable-to-skulduggery, highest traveled mountain pass in all of North America.

#####

CHAPTER TWENTY

MAROON CREEK

Out in the Maroon Creek Valley close by the Sterner Gulch Trail, Emma reined Harriet to a halt and counted off the distant *thruummpp* of explosions. At the last charge, she too exhaled in relief. "That's done": she breathed, stroking Harriet's wet mane as she turned to beckon to Lute, riding behind her on a borrowed horse.

Trailing Lute, heads tucked low to shelter from the rain, were Polly on her paint, Chester, swift as a kit fox on three legs; and a tight-mouthed old sourdough named Cappie, dried-up as a stale crust of bread, assigned by the major as Emma's full-time watchdog.

"Lute, if you don't mind, we'll turn back on the other side," she said over her shoulder.

"I don't mind, ma'am, I surely don't," said Lute with relief.

Emma whistled for Chester and with an easy heel thrust, urged Harriet down the mud-slick bank toward the creek branch which led past dripping aspen stands and thence to the big open mesa between Castle and Maroon Creeks. The sudden storm had trumpeted up the valley, noisy as a herd of elephants, blotting out the sun and sending rain down sharp as mine picks. Then it settled into hard, swift sheets that left Emma damp and chilled.

Doc Alderfer had been appalled when she threatened to hang herself from one of Aggie's gaslights if she wasn't cut loose from the hotel. "It's not fitting," he growled, "to miscarry a child and go out prancing on horseback in public."

"Well now, I swore Bridget, Gwynnie, Svea, and Tacy to secrecy. Not another soul knows I lost a babe—not unless you've been blabbing to your customers," she said sassily.

The doc, accustomed to lady patients who must be delicately examined through five layers of protective clothing, actually turned red at Emma's unflinching talk. Though he admired Mrs. Sutton's pluck, he'd warned, "You won't be your old self for another few weeks, Missy."

Wiping and stacking dishes in the hotel kitchen, cleaning smoky lamp globes, dusting chifferobes, and washing down porch chairs had not eroded her need to saddle up and ride out. "I will keep it at a slow walk," she promised, "though that mare will think I've lost my wits." Their usual habit was to gallop through high grass down past the Hog Pastures, jump the white water of the Frying Pan, and lope along the Castle and Maroon Creek Trails. In the bloom of summer, the hooves of Harriet crushed penstemon and pearly everlasting as a pestle pounds sweet spices.

Even a slow walk in the open air was better than stifling, fly-ridden hotel rooms with Bridget and Polly sniffing at her heels. She knew the major had ordered them to stick like thistle burrs. Neither had a knack for dissembling and were as open with their concerns as biddie hens with peeps. She might be freed of Garrett's constrictions, but she was still caged.

Tommyrot, she thought. Garrett would not dare harm her in full view of the Aspen camp. Why, she had not so much as laid eyes on him since she had quit that hated house. After Bridgie had flown across town to report the bed-busting to the McClarens, Uncle Nate and the major had found her slumped in a chair, staring bleakly at her shattered pride and joy.

Nate took in the demolished bed, drew a sharp breath and whistled, "Thunderation!"

Deke muttered something unintelligible through his teeth, then said, "Mrs. Sutton, you must leave this place at once."

"He's right, Emma honey. The women can pack your trunks."

Still stunned, Emma had allowed her personal things to be gathered and herself to be bundled into a crocheted wrapper. The major, preparing to lift her in his arms once again, said lightly, "When you need a hansom cab, ma'am, just send a boy for the Burdine Express." He smiled, rays of white crinkle lines fanning out through the bronzed skin around his eyes. She'd attempted a wan smile of her own. "For an old married woman, sir, I am spending a deal of time being toted about by a stranger."

"But I presume to think of myself as a friend," he protested. "And as a friend, I take the liberty of meddling in your affairs, madam. Do you have any notion what provoked this outrage?"

"It was the stock, of course," she said. "The Pearly stock...as you know, major, the Pearly is in my name. But that is not the whole of it. Mr. Sutton currently has power of the court over my affairs, and he is bound to have that paper back. He no doubt plans to alter the signatures and repossess the mine. Should he not succeed in foiling Mr. Krueger's extraction of the silver, he would then, as owner, still reap twenty percent of the leaseholder's discoveries."

"Well I'll be blamed!" exclaimed Nate. "This here is a cow of another complexion."

"In addition to pestering Calvin at his work," mused Deke, "he must retrieve the Pearly paper from his wife." He looked at Emma so searchingly that she paled. "Your husband can be a rough customer, ma'am." His concerns were plain as the face on a clock. If a man's wife were deceased, that man would come into all of her possessions.

"You have the shares in a place of safekeeping?"

Emma looked hard at her hands and a startling sound escaped her: a giggle. Followed by others. At last she laughed so lustily that she had to wrap her arms around her battered middle to ease the hurt. "It—it...oh my stars...Polly hid it...in the one...container she knew he'd...never touch." Despite her discomfort, her eyes were merry as a schoolgirl's. "In the...in that...that god-rotted solarium!" Though the laughter continued to make her wince, she could not help herself. It tumbled out, catching Deke and Nate like a downstream torrent. In the parlor, where she showed them the ludicrous, hinge-lidded spittoon, both men roared along with her. Mopping teary eyes, Emma had finally felt at ease about quitting this hateful house.

The silver strike had brought a stampede of newshounds and fortune-seekers across the divide. Emma, grown stronger, was soon assisting the McClarens about the hotel. But amid boomtown hullabaloo, she sometimes felt forlorn. Now and again, listening to a customer carp about his bill, or the clamor of strangers choking the dining room entrance, she yearned for kin, an auntie maybe, someone to confide in.

Uncle Nate had sensed her low feeling. And, since she now owned a going silver mine, he took it upon himself to educate her. On his way to and from the Pearly, he often stopped by with ore samples, some plain as paper, others so dazzling her head reeled. "Now this here black piece is stephanite," he'd explain. "She's brittle, and she ain't pretty, but she holds fine silver."

"Looks like a chunk of coal," said Emma irreverently.

"H'it's a far cry from coal, young lady; mind you don't pitch it in a handy stove. Now here we have polybasite," Nate would continue, handing her a piece of ore as red and lustrous as a roan's coat. "This one's mother to silver just as fine."

He instructed her in host rock which had taken on hues of citrus yellow, lapis blue, and nut brown. He gave her samples of wire silver, bar silver, and ruby silver taken from the Pearly. He taught her the many variations of more ordinary galena, spar, and argentite. "It's a lot on your plate—but you best learn the look and feel of every last silver-bearing ore," he lectured. "This here rock has made you a woman of means. You want to lift it in your hands, take its measure."

Emma looked at him with respect. "Why, it requires a learned man to decipher a mountain's geology. That's what you are, Uncle Nate, a regular professor."

"Aw honey," he said, regretting her sorrowful eyes, "I just know that once you get over the dog, it's a snap to slide down the tail."

Emma entertained a number of callers. Tacy Beard, working part-time at the hotel, dropped by her room to wonder longingly if there'd ever be socials and cycling and skating at the rink again. Tacy was young, and time dragged unmercifully as she scrubbed floors and waited for life to beckon her on. The ladies of the Theatric and Shakespeare Societies came by on Sundays for a good gossip—and to seek Sutton grist for cranking in their mills. Aspen women were dogged and tough—a deal less strait-laced than settled-in-the-East women who'd never been to see the elephant. Above everything, they valued a neighborly hand. Garrett Sutton had never in his life merited a neighborly hand. Although some few looked down their noses at a wife who no longer sheltered under her husband's roof, plenty spoke right up to assure Emma she was not faulted for fleeing that fleecer.

The Reverend Campbell called, portly and puffed-up with piety. Although Emma suggested that the meek and the poor were in greater need of his ministrations than she, she took comfort in his habitual parting words: "May the Lord watch over me and thee while we are absent one from the other." She felt she must need watching over. Every man and his brother reminded her of it daily.

Dan Alderfer, racing through days and nights without end, looked in and pronounced her hale but for the painful ribs she'd parted from their moorings ("You've separated your costochondral junctions") when she hit Gertie's back. That and what he termed "the blues."

"Natural enough," he'd assured her, "after childbirth—or a child's death."

There was another visitor, more secretive. Wait-girl Persis Linkin confessed that it was Major Burdine left the nosegay of daisies by Emma's paperwork in the small hotel office. One morning there had been a rose, exquisitely carved from dark chocolate by Mr. Julius Berg in his confectionary. On another, a small clump of raw silver startlingly like a knight holding his shield aloft (she had been re-reading *Ivanhoe*). The major himself did not admit to it, although he called on her formally in the McClaren side-parlor to present her with a short-barreled Peacemaker .45. "You'd best carry a pistol when you leave the hotel, Mrs. Sutton. This will tuck into a pocket of your skirt. But never count on her at more than twenty feet."

Emma took the gun, not disputing his reasons. "I thank you, Major. I am a fair shot with a pistol, though I doubt I'd use one on any man."

"None of us ever hopes to fire on another being. But we endure parlous times."

"If we are indeed to be friends, Major," she'd said impetuously, "please call me Emma."

"I'd be honored, ma'am. My own friends address me as Deke."

"Is that your baptismal name, Major—er, Deke?"

"Well now, it is not," he admitted. "I would blush to have you know the truth. D.K. or Deke will serve. Perhaps when we come to know each other better…"

Despite all her earlier resolutions about no more trusting in any man, she had found she looked forward to the small surprises, to the deep, liquid sound of Deke's voice, for a glimpse of him riding by on his big bay horse or striding in and out of the hotel dining room. Many times in a day he crept unbidden into her mind's eye. She fretted that she might be as wicked as the biblical Jezebel. She was not yet wise enough to know that the failure of marriage vows and the loss of a child were bound to leave a woman with a grievous heart-hunger.

Above Highlands Peak, a double rainbow arced across the sky, and sure as a shot from a crossbow, spun its colors into Maroon Creek. A few clouds, rinsed out and hung up to dry, floated like feather comforters against the blue horizon. The riders' breaths hung before them in cold, condensed puffs. Past mid-summer, the rains brought more than a hint of arctic winter to come. Emma was not reveling in her outing. She was soaked to her shimmy, her ribs ached, her teeth chattered, and she felt feverish. She would be grateful to fall into her chair in Aggie's northwest corner room, gather Sneffels and Chester close for warmth. Looking back on her small entourage, she concluded sadly that it was heedless of her to monopolize hands badly needed in camp—not least her own. She'd not try this stunt again.

Her chill deepening, she gave Harriet her head down the rocky bank and across the churning creek. She called to Lute, "This was a mighty short excursion. I'd hoped to show you my favorite ride, up Sterner Gulch to the right."

"I'm pleased we're headed for the barn, ma'am," he called, adding hastily, "Not that this ride ain't—hasn't been fine. I liked hearing your adventures when you were Little Emma." It was true too. In particular, he liked the part where she'd been an infant napping on a summer porch when the Ute squaw spotted a renegade Arapaho creeping up on her cradle. The Utes despised all Araps, and Polly never paused to inquire into the buck's intentions. She'd tomahawked him at forty feet.

"Polly had to use Ma's bedding to haul off that Indian's body," Emma had recalled dryly. "Ma never did puzzle out where her Star of Jacob coverlet disappeared to."

Mrs. Sutton's tales were such a wonder they'd taken his mind off the sorrow that had settled on him since Frankie was laid to rest. When he'd insisted on helping to dig Frankie's grave, Reuben Hurd's jaw dropped. "Can't have it," he grumbled. "Ain't fittin', you diggin' no grave for a niggra whore woman." Lute could not explain that heaving shovels of dirt in a far corner of unhallowed ground in some way lightened his load. Mr. Hurd took another look at his stricken face, and glad of the help, let him dig.

Scoop, rallied from his initial shock, had proved his mettle. He'd shined the doc's Corning buggy and curried Dolly until her coat dazzled for the ride to the burial. Lute had sat in the buggy facing the rear, legs dangling, as the dismal road ran away from him like an outgoing tide. At the Evergreen graveside, when Reuben and Scoop lowered the rough wood box into wet red earth, he had looked up to find a regular gathering. A little apart, on the far side of the coffin hole, stood the girls from the Row. Congregated on his side were Young Frank Parker, Needle Newsome, Mr. Willard Arey, Mr. Pete and his girl Tacy, and Mrs. Krueger. Lute was stunned. *How did they ever think to come?* he wondered. No one had asked why he was grieving. Yet here they were, like home folks, standing by him in his sorrow.

"Calvin wanted you to know that he dare not depart the mine, Luther." Vinnie reached to touch his wet cheek. "But he sends his respects for your friend."

After the fire and the fallen girl's death, with Lute stony-faced at her kitchen table, Lavinia had made discreet inquiries. "It is not our place to ask the why's of Lute's heartache," she'd concluded to Calvin. "A orphan boy finds family where he can."

"I never thought to see you at a Row woman's burying," said Calvin stiffly.

"Why Cal Krueger, how can you forget Samuel? 'Yet doth he devise means that his banished be not expelled from him.'"

Calvin looked shamed, though he muttered, "Those women on the line are a hard lot."

"I won't hear such twaddle. This Frankie girl may have turned bad, but in some way she was good to Luther."

"There's folks will talk."

"Talk is cheap. I care nothing for it."

At the cemetery, Lute gulped, "But she was...Frankie was..."

"Remember Isaiah, son." Vinnie's voice was serene. Turning to the others, she said, "'Though your sins be as scarlet, they shall become white as snow.'"

At sight of the major riding up on Buford to sit with his broad-brimmed hat over his heart, with nothing of his hard look on him, Lute had to stuff his face in his fists to keep from falling to pieces. A girl from the Row named Lou sang Frankie's favorite hymn in a high, clear voice. "We are climbing Jacob's ladder...Soldiers of...the cross."

Standing under the shade of a young cottonwood tree was Sister Coon. No one knew her age, but her skin was as gray and wrinkled, her body as shapeless as an old rhino's. Mostly she was silent, her deep-lined face the repository of a thousand sorrows. Once she called out, her voice a wail, "Lift her up, Jesus! Carry her home!"

Scoop twanged mournfully on his Jew's harp, and again the tears coursed unbidden from Lute's eyes. He had never imagined he had so much water in him, water that kept pouring from some inner, endlessly gushing fountain. With Lute unable to speak, Lavinia led those assembled in prayer and said a few meaningful words over the grave.

Oh Frankie, Lute thought, *if you could only see your burying...It would make you proud. At least I didn't pass by on the other side*, he thought miserably. *I may have passed by when you were alive, when it counted for more. But not when you went under, which could count for a little something.*

He had located Frankie's gray cat, who now faced down the pack rats skulking around the Kruegers' chicken yard. Then he dickered with Mr. Arey for a prime piece of chestnut for a grave marker. The wood was like iron, the carving slow, and he had little time at the end of long days, but he was half finished with the inscription. It should weather good.

The doc's findings were that Frankie had been cut by a knife as honed as a razor. Her head was bashed in by something like a balpeen hammer. "Poor soul should not have died that hard." He had shaken his head, looking melancholy.

Lute Kellogg did not think so either. He and Scoop had quietly shown around the pigsticker Scoop found, had talked to Jamestown Jess and others on the Row.

"The hose boys got her trunk out," snarled Jess. "My dress was ruint and nobody seen hide nor hair of those Pearly shares. She was kilt fer them, surer'n hell. Only they weren't hers, they were mine. I traded fer 'em. Traded my best dress. The sher'f don't care. He could care less 'bout a nigger whore girl or who done fer her—though it had to be someone knew what was hid in her trunk." Jess's voice was bitter as alum. The boys suspicioned that with all the woman's vitriol, she was right. Lute meant to keep his ears open until someone got careless with talk. Barrel fever loosened men's tongues, and any time he passed a saloon, he listened close. Sooner or later he'd figure out who'd killed Frankie.

Splashing across Maroon Creek, Lute yearned for little more than to be back in Mr. Skinner's yards. He felt troubled riding out in the country smelling wet leaves and drooping wildflowers while the men on the job sweated peachseeds in town. He was needed to load wagons, patch harness, drive teams, pump bellows for the smiths and—the most unforgiving chore of all—make Mr. Arey's numbers come out to the penny in the ledger books.

On the other hand, this was no simple outing in the country. The major had warned, "I don't mind telling you, son, that Mrs. Sutton is at considerable risk. She herself will not face it. When it comes to peril, she is as unruly as a barn-sour horse. I figure that squaw is old, and so is Cappie, but they're both killers at heart. And with the four of you, numbers will count—too many witnesses, too many to shoot down." The major looked harried. "I can't get away. I'm depending on you to stick with her like mustard plaster. Keep your pistol unlimbered over your cantle. Don't loiter." The major had scared him so bad that he did not believe he could pass water. On the seldom used approach to Sterner Gulch, he had pictured gunmen bearing down from all sides. Here was a mighty poor-looking squad for holding off a determined attack. He was more grateful than he could say that the lady was calling it quits.

As their small party struck the trace leading from the Deane Ranch, something glistening wet up the gulch sidetrail caught Lute's eye. He looked back long enough to see fresh sunlight gleaming from a metallic streak snaking across a long level stretch. A stretch where a rider would let his horse out in a good canter.

Lute was uneasy. He would have been more uneasy to see the three sour-looking men, ugly-minded and wet, huddled in a thicket of dripping spruce up the gulch. Their eyes, grabby and darting as chickens, fastened on their tripwire as they ground their teeth and cursed when the Sutton woman's party veered off.

####

CHAPTER TWENTY-ONE

IACONO

Very early on the morning of the big blast, under cover of lingering night, Willard Arey had sat in the Krueger kitchen blowing on his coffee to cool it, lips pursed as he carped over the makeshift fencework around the stored Pearly ore. "A man could ease up to any lot, reach in, and palm enough silver to make him a flatware service for twelve," he grumbled, helping himself to a piece of Lavinia's hot corn bread. "Guards like Stump Clancy stops to jaw with anybody that wants to pass the time of day." The cornbread was hot and crumbs flew from the corners of his mouth as he talked.

"No fence constructed by man will hold a determined thief at bay." Deke sat with a box of 44-caliber rimfire bullets on the table before him. The flat-tipped rounds went "snick, snick," as he pushed them through the loading gate of Nat's gun. He had finished swabbing out the grooves and lands in the barrel with a wiping stick and patch and applying some of Jake's clear gun oil. The rifle was old but well-kept.

"However, Willard," he added, "the fence serves some purpose. Out of sight keeps a man's more temptatious feelings out of mind."

"It ain't only thievery." Concern etched deep in Needle's knobby face. "H'it's your weather." Wondering if it would be piggish to dish up more rhubarb sauce, he said, "Hate to see loose pay dirt blowed to the four winds."

"Well, Jake's downing timber like a regular north woodsman," said Calvin as he added more kindling and stirred up the stove fire. "Before long he'll have fences fit for a federal penitentiary."

Jake had proven a born lumberjack. His gangs were felling trees, his puffer engines and steam blades rough-sawing timber into planks across the face of every hill in view. Pete's tone was awed as he looked at him. "You've got us enough lumber to build a whole Parthenon—and you ain't even cutting aspen." Mountain men disdained aspen, a whorewood with a pretty face and rotten insides, not fit for building, barely serving for boiler wood. "When you're done, half this range'll be nekkid as a newborn."

Jake Levy looked uneasy. "Nate claims the Lord Jehovah fashioned trees to stand where they grow, to hold the earth at anchor. He may be right."

"You watch," Nate warned at intervals, "with the trees gone, won't be nothing to hold up the mountains. They'll let loose, slide down and swallow us up."

"Maybe," said Jake to the table with faint hope, "the aspens were put here to tie down the hills."

Calvin's corps of leaders had taken to gathering in his kitchen before daybreak. Though they conversed easily, this morning there was a galvanized air to the room. With the big blast set to go off, the first ore train ready to move on the hump in two days, everyone slept lighter and felt a sharper edge.

"I ain't easy about this ore trip, D.K."

Deke knew as well as Willard that a fixed route with a departure time that could hardly be kept secret would present a hundred possibilities for sabotage. His scouts had been patrolling the divide in search of hidden explosives, booby traps, and slide areas. Even so, there were enough cases of nerves in this room to populate a bughouse.

Though roadwork on the pass was ongoing, the Independence Trail was hardly fit for heavy freight. Boulders like massive building blocks caused creeks to breach their banks. Dense forest, mangled by snow and mudslides, clutched the sides of deep canyons. In places, the path was hacked out of sheer rock precipice. Sliderock tumbled onto the trailway from weather-shattered cliffs. No swamper worth his onions would try moving an eight-mule swing team over that tangled skein of mud and stone. Treachery aside, the jackstraw passage had become clogged with greenhorns, loose women, fortune-seekers, and fiddle-footed bunco artists, all headed for the new golconda in the Roaring Fork Valley. Freighters often found themselves backed up three or four miles. Willard swore they settled in and camped where they stalled.

"The skeeriest is, we ain't heard a squeak out of Sutton. It ain't like him." Willard chewed on a piece of cheese, worrying it along with his concerns.

"Not unless you count them pesky delays in coke shipments to the smelter…slides on the passes…guards that comes down sick," muttered Pete into his saucer of coffee.

To date, splintered wagon wheels and dynamited trailheads were nothing Deke couldn't handle. "It's mainly Mrs. Sutton concerns me," he said, his voice flat. "So long as she holds that mine stock, she is in harm's way."

"Sutton will find it hard to lay his hands on paper locked in the Clarendon's big Hurley safe," declared Jake. "That piece of furniture weighs more'n two tons."

"Even a Hurley can be blown…"

"And a good woman blown away," Calvin's unease echoed Deke's, "with Sutton shedding crocodile tears as he takes over his wife's estate."

The men at the table grew grim as a gathering of old Amishmen. Since Mrs. Sutton had moved into Aggie's hotel, she refused to act anything but safe as in church. In face of her grit, Nate and Deke felt helpless as plucked chickens. The plucked-chicken feeling made Deke low. There was no earthly way he could keep a close eye on his crews, on the dicey specimens crowding his bar, on the trail, and on a stubborn, rambunctious woman. Once more he pondered why he had ever yearned for challenge.

Calvin, steering the conversation down another road, said to Deke, "Appears you've got us prize transport in place, my friend."

Deke had hedged his bets, counting on pack animals for alacrity, ore wagons for heft. To this end, he had thirty-odd wagons with teams and a train of fifty jacks and forty mules at the ready.

Willard's tone was, for a change, respectful. "Hear you even have Shotgun toeing your line." To everyone's amazement, Ellsworth Hayes was not only sober as cold rain, but performing ably under pressure. He had riflemen bagging elk and deer as fast as they could draw a bead, fire, and bring their skinning knives into play. Stacks of green hides were immediately filled with ore, lashed on burros, and packed straight off to the lots. His hunters camped out in the hills. Before daylight, they stalked game as it went to water. At midday, they tracked the elk to where they lay up in dark timber. Shotgun's lone bellyache was of another nature. "I wisht them infernal balloon boys would move the hell away from my hunting ground," he'd griped to Deke.

"The elk don't care about the mine thumping, Ellsworth. Why would they mind a flying machine?"

"Your mine machinery noise is steady, and they've come to tolerate it. But thet balloon flits around, throws pecky shadows, and spooks the hell out'n the cows. Always at sunup, when they're movin' to drink and feed." Shotgun spewed a stream of tobacco from inside his dirty beard. Yellow-brown juice dribbled down his elk-hide shirt, already black with old blood and tallow. "The worst of it is the bitchin' ropes holding their ballast bags. They swing them boogers like pendulums. Expect a tweety bird to pop out and holler 'Cuckoo!'" Shotgun was so disgusted he nearly swallowed his chaw. "Much more of that ding-donging, and the herds'll all hightail it across the hump and hole up on La Plata Peak."

Willard meant to ask Deke to use a little hard-eyed persuasion on the Hoople brothers to skedaddle back where they came from. But that could wait. The mortician had further concerns. Though that pirate Gabe Tacker knew he'd be lynched if he shut down the town smelter, his bank officers had come up mysteriously shy of cash reserves—too short to advance monies for Pearly payrolls. Willard had had to dip into his, Nathaniel's, and Deke's deposits in Denver and St. Louis banks. The money had been a near thing. He'd rest easier when the first matte headed over the hump—easier still when the silver was bought and paid for at the Denver factor's.

In addition, Willard had had his heart set on selling Shotgun's game to local butchers. But Mrs. Sutton, seconded by Nate, had argued, "An ill-fed Indian is a troublesome Indian. We don't need Indian trouble in the eye of a silver hurricane." Thus Polly, two newly-arrived young squaws, and her grandson Iacono trailed Shotgun's hunters and were butchering elk and buckskin and jerk-drying it on poles in the sun. The Utes, penned on reservations, often waited months for permission to send hunting parties outside their lines. The Indian agent on the Southern Ute grounds was as crooked as a dog's hind leg. He denied his charges hunting privileges so they'd be cornered into trading for his putrid beef.

Deke and Nate were among the few who didn't hold with local mistrust of the Utes. Deke had outraged Emma by hiring young Iacono to work on Lute's team of packers and drovers. Mad as a wet hen, she'd stormed up to him on the street. "You can find other packers, Major. We need that boy to butcher."

Full of fury, eyes afire, she was such a splendid sight Deke thought it almost worth the price to get her dander up.

"He was being shamed," he said, not backing down. "Butchering is squaw's work. Worse, he was being wasted. That boy's a natural-born packer and drover—drives a jerkline or four lines from the seat like a seasoned hand—better than Lute, and Lute's one of my best men."

Looking into eyes turned Cimmerian dark, Deke, a little chagrined, added, "If I have to hunt game and jerk the meat myself, I'll feed your tribe, Emma. But I will do it in the fall, after our silver is in the bank. Besides, in this hot weather the game is out of condition—the meat tastes vile."

The thunder eased out of her face. Ruefully, she reminded herself that it was she who'd brought Iacono to Deke's attention. When the boy first rode his lean piebald pony up to the hotel, she'd pointed proudly, "That little

Indian taught me to ride bareback, with no bit, when he was a child. Best horsemen on the planet, those Utes," she'd said with proprietary pride.

"Looks too fat to manage more than a light trot," said Deke skeptically.

"He may be a tad plump, but he rides thin." Emma whistled through her teeth, a high-pitched, piercing sound that startled Buford so he shied. At her signal, Iacono's pony leaped forward, and the boy galloped down Mill Street in a hard lean onto Durant, swinging under his horse's belly, standing on her back, somersaulting over her like a circus rider. A crowd of bystanders gathered quickly around the bench boys, open-mouthed at the show. When the boy finally pulled to a halt in front of Emma, grinning cheerily, Deke was not the only one who applauded.

She should have hidden the boy away. She leaned back on one of the hotel hitching posts. "Is that a solemn promise, Major? You'll help feed the tribe?" she asked.

"A solemn promise."

Suddenly a whip cracked, and they looked up to see Lute jolt to a halt in the center of upper Mill Street. The whip snapped again, and Lute raised his voice. "Move, you derned, fiddle-headed mule!"

"Your top drover?" asked Emma impishly.

"That Gracious mule is the only stump in the boy's path of progress," said Deke dolefully. "If Gracious is on the hind wagon and wants to go, the whole operation moves. If Gracious decides to halt, every last load behind the mulehead stops dead."

Gracious had cramped the wagon, chewed his cud, and refused to budge. Lute was so exasperated he almost swore. In a wink, Iacono pulled up, jumped on Gracious' back, leaned over and bit the mule on the ear. The startled animal leaped like a jackrabbit and headed on down the hill. Iacono vaulted from the wagon, grinned bashfully, and called, "Mule try show him boss."

Lute was fascinated by the Indian's way of materializing out of thin air. One minute he wasn't there, the next he was. He longed to know how to turn that trick, though he expected it would not be possible with his gangly frame. Astride a horse he was at ease, afoot he tripped all over himself. As for Iacono, he was bewitched by Lute's big raw-boned body, strawberry hair, pink complexion, and startling adolescent voice changes. The two were forging a companionship, a fact which put Scooper Hurd's nose out of joint. He wondered irritably how Lute could be so interested in a lard-assed Injun.

"Good scalp," Iacono said his first morning on the job, eyeing Lute's thick, golden-red hair. "Habla Espagnol?" he asked.

"No...er, un poquito," said Lute, taken aback. This was his first occasion speaking directly with a hostile.

"Me Mericanz no good...You name?"

"Lute."

Iacono rolled the name around on his tongue, tossed back the course, black-as-tar hair which hung in thick braids to his waist, then repeated solemnly, "Lute."

"How 'bout yours? What do they call you?"

The boy grinned. "Iacono...I-ah-cone-noh."

Lute looked puzzled. "That's Ute talk?"

"Nope. I-tall-i-ann."

"H'it's Italian?" Lute felt so confused his eyes nearly crossed.

Iacono gazed placidly off at the peaks. "When...the people...pack...into reservation...agents no know...who is which...say Injuns," he paused to grin again, "all look same." He rolled his eyes back in his head incredulously and mulled over his explanation. "Give us names...same like Eye-tall-y-ann people off...big boat? Vote rolls? Place call New Yoka City. My name—I-a-cone-noh."

Lute scratched his head over the strange ways of governments.

"People call...Injun Ike."

Ike proved to be the best rider, driver, and packer Lute ever hoped to meet, and he considered himself first-rate.

Packing was an important art. On the upcoming ore train, camp supplies and vittles would be loaded in large panyards on mules, and there was a trick to it. The slightest imbalance to one side, and the whole boodle would take to sliding and end up under the mule's belly. Then a half-mile-long train would be delayed while the animal was unloaded and fastidiously re-packed. But a right-loaded mule, with plenty of solid corn mash laced with molasses for feed, could hustle three hundred pounds through close stands of trees up a dizzying mountain. It was also easier to snake burros or mules loaded with hidebound ore through jam-packed streets than to bully passageway for ore wagons. The big wagons with broad-based, six-foot wheels were often stalled in traffic. Deke and his lieutenants patrolled the lines, extricating teams and reasoning with surly street hogs. They never had to untangle the Indian.

With preparations for departure in high gear, Deke paused to look out Lavinia's kitchen window at the first streak of light edging the black vee that marked the pass. For a fleeting instant he pictured his and Buford's bygone gallops up Pratt Mountain, hawks soaring free, clouds drifting like dreams. He wished he might pause longer and ask Emma Sutton for her company.

Shaking himself back to the present, he packed up his gun-cleaning kit and rose to his feet, set to join the rising sun at Skinner's Livery. The night before, he had been about to check over the teeth and feet of five new braces of mules delivered to Skinner—mules came high, and he did not intend to pay for any long-in-the-tooth or sore-footed animals. "Nate," he'd called, "if you are not frozen to that spot, I could use a hand." Nate could size up a mule's teeth or a horse's feet as well as him, and the saloon's drinking crowd brought to mind bull shorthorns in rut.

"Deke, you ought to try this here electric."

"My system already gets its share of jolts, Nathaniel. I need you to check Skinner's new mules for me. This kettle of mine is set to boil up. I no longer know half my customers by name. Can't even guess who's worth saving in a fight."

Nate peered curiously past the double-swinging front doors through smoke layered deep as April fog. "Some of these jaspers don't appear your kind of trade, D.K."

The boardwalk outside had been even more rackety than the saloon, somewhere on the level of a full-bore cattle auction. Up and down Durant and Cooper Avenues, stump-speakers orated on the sin of avarice and the shame of indulgence. Drummers, operating out of old wagon beds, shouted the merits of the latest patented cure-alls for warts, carbuncles, Mexican beetle bite, bilious livers, and blighted pizzles. Electric shock machines operated full-tilt—patronized by incautious drunks and the ever-curious Nate Phipps.

Tearing himself from the show, Nate had picked his way through sidewalk crowds to Skinner's barns, puzzling over the omniscient allure of saloons and shysters. It baffled him that the bulk of miners, cowhands, and horse hockeys sought to lift their spirits and drown their sorrows in buckets of beer, bottles of busthead, and decks of marked cards. Nate Phipps had no sorrows. His life was full of wonder and he didn't hope to fuddle himself with whiskey or miss a moment of the joy. Humming an off-key chorus of "Yankee Doodle," he arrived at the lots to find the baffled Skinner noodling over a big black Ozark mule, the ugliest in his yards.

"Old Junus is festered with some kind of colic," said Rob worriedly. "Don't make sense. The hay and grain is dry, and we been rotating all the animals on fresh pasture."

Nate felt a twinge in his weather bone. As Skinner and his man Mackey began doctoring, he hurried back to the Clarendon to collect his blanket roll. He'd spend the night at the livery.

Just before that morning's big blow, Deke arrived at the yards, Scooper Hurd in tow, to find Skinner near dementia. Jacks and mules were strewn like pigs in the woods, the hostlers slack-jawed, Skinner himself dodging Junus's angry kicks. The big, parched, mad-as-a-hornet animal had been dosed and penned out of reach of water.

Deke took one long look around, removed his jacket, and rolled up his sleeves. "What is the trouble, and where do we start?"

"I' God, Major, you're a sight for tired eyes. More'n half my old-timers, near twenty head, is down with colic worse than the cholera. Get one dosed and another keels over. The new animals that just come in is sound. But my old reliables is on their way to hell in a breadbasket."

"How are you treating?"

"Cut off a plug of tobaccy 'bout as thick as your finger's long. Put it in a crock of cold water. Throw in four shovels of hot ashes—them's ashes Phipps is shoveling yonder."

Skinner stopped to curse Toby Flanagan, whose still-swollen face resembled a wormy cabbagehead. He was shy two front teeth and one eye remained at half-mast. Tite Pomeroy had boot-licked the living daylights out of him. "You shittin' sod-cutter, you've let the other fire go out!" He'd taken pity on the man, had hired him on again after his beating, which Toby had not taken well. Still mired in self-pity, he cut the tobacco plugs too big and let the fires die down.

Skinner turned back to Deke. "I let the mix set mebbe fifteen minutes and sort of simmer. Then drench the mule with a bottle this here size. The trick is, we can't let 'em near water for a good ten hours, no matter how they thrash and holler. Can't let 'em do a lick of work, neither. Not for a week at the inside."

"Set us a task," said Deke. "Scoop here is Doc Alderfer's stableman. He's apt, and he's willing."

"You shitepoke Hibernians! Quit yer standin' there with them damn jaws dropped!" yelled the exasperated liveryman. "Young feller," he directed Scoop, "would you leg it over to Beck & Bishop's, buy as many plugs of tobacco as they got to hand, charge it to my store account? Burdine, if you'll direct them useless peat-eaters in building more fires, stirring the ashes down, then drenching, Mackey and I will get back to shoring up corrals." He mopped his face with a handful of hay. "That Junus mule kicked in half a gate and got my elbow in the bargain."

Late in the day, with the last animal dosed, a rain and sweat-soaked Skinner sank gingerly onto his pillowed bench, his behind throbbing like the pulse of a frightened female, his elbow paining, too tired to bawl. Lute had raced in from his ride in the country some hours before. He and the Major, Nate, and Scoop, dropped beside Skinner.

"Boys," said the livery-owner downheartedly, "is this a biblical plague, or what?"

"More like a Mudgett epidemic." Short-handed as he was, Deke concluded he must now set a night-and-day watch on the Elkhorn.

"How do you figure them sorry excuses did the trick?" asked Nate.

Skinner rubbed his bad elbow and cringed. "It don't have to be arsenic. Hay that's a mite wet or moldy can raise ned. Soon's I work up the spunk, I'll go over my grain with a fine-tooth comb. I've sent word to Tite Pomeroy to haul me fresh feed." Skinner gulped down half a cup of cold coffee. "Meanwhile, I don't have to tell you the ore shipment is postponed."

"Damn that outfit! Damn them to hell!" Like all men unaccustomed to cursing, Deke swore slow and the oaths came out hard.

"A week might do her, if we're more'n lucky. But that ain't the worst of it. The worst is, the new flatland stock must be rested near a month before we work 'em at altitude. The three dozen head due in from Kansas City won't be worth a thin copper 'til mid-September."

Lute had been set to mention what he suspicioned was a tripwire on the Sterner Gulch ride. Looking at the major's troubled face, he decided it could wait.

Nate, relieved that Miss Lind was untouched, was busy analyzing the colic treatment in his head. "I wonder," he pondered aloud, "if a mule had two stomachs like a cow, and one of them was festered, could the animal get along on its backup stomach while the other was being doctored?"

Deke Burdine put his head in his hands and groaned.

That night, hereafter recalled as the night of the Big Blow, the entire camp appeared to collapse with a mixture of exhaustion and relief. The mule nurses were whipped, the blasters relieved that their work had gone well. Even the hucksters and gamblers, as if by unspoken consent, retired at a respectable hour. Deke and Nate had swallowed their bitter disappointment over the delayed ore shipment. "No sense fighting a bit that's set," said Nate. Calvin slept deep for the first time in a month.

Polly Panakarpo had not changed her own manner of sleeping. She still spread her blanket roll outside Emma's door. Hotel guests, startled at the sight of a snoring, cross-legged wild Indian in buckskin, beads and hatchet, gave her a wide berth.

In her room, Emma had unpinned her hair, had a quick wash at the pine washstand, dashed off her nightly prayer on her knees, and crawled shakily into bed. She was asleep before she could call up a single event of the day.

Hours later, with the last guest key dispersed, every door latched and locked, and the front desk shuttered, Polly's good eye shot open. Nothing moved but the eye. Her squat body was still as a headstone. She listened. The Clarendon was no fancy city hotel. Nate might think the place peaceful, but the muffled snoring and hacking and sleep-muttering of men sifted through thin-as-vellum walls like flour through a colander. It was not that. Polly's keen ears had detected a faint sound not at home here. Slowly the old woman uncoiled, rising up silent as a snake. Her worn fletching knife was between her teeth as her gnarled hands began feeling their way along the wall. She blinked her eye, getting her night sight. No oil lamps lit the hallways. Aggie was too fearful of fire. Nor did guests need grope their way blind to the eight-holer in the rear yard. Every room had its chamber pot with a delicately crocheted cover to still the clanking of china lid against china container. The back door to the outside privy was double-locked, and two of the major's men patrolled the grounds.

Polly inched her way down the hall into the front foyer and stopped, tingly alert. The noise commenced again, a small animal scratching. It came from the door to the office on the other side of the front desk. Hushed as a barn owl, Polly moved toward the out-of-place sound. The office door was ajar. She widened the opening a hairsbreadth. The only light came through the window from a low-hanging three-quarter moon.

In front of the big Hurley safe were two huddled men, their hands moving silently. The small sound that had alerted Polly had been the dull scratching of safety matches. There was a minuscule, blue-white flare as one took fire and Polly froze fast. She had wormed her way around the door, and should either of the men turn to look, he'd find her silhouetted it as if she'd been crucified there.

One of them whispered so low that the squaw could not catch the words. They appeared to be straightening coils of string or rope piled on the floor. Their rifles rested at their fingertips. In the small gleam of another match flare, she made out the familiar shapes of rattails. Still on knees and haunches, the men caught up their guns, held the rattail ends, and began inching backward in her direction.

She grasped her knife. Pulled back her arm. Threw. Then she ducked silently around the door. One of the men reached a hand for his neck, fell over on the fuses and lay still.

The other gasped in a startled voice, "Wha…?" and jumped to his feet.

At the moment when the upright man stood transfixed in momentary consternation, the Ute woman moved her weight onto her front foot and hurled the small tomahawk from her belt. The man made an ugly noise, "Ghhhaaaaa…" and doubled over. Gagging, he grasped his arm. Of a sudden, he grew wings and flew past the old Indian unseeing, making directly for a jimmied dining room window.

Polly went to the knife victim, turned him over and put her head to his chest, recoiling at his rank white man's smell. Hearing no heart pulse, she began gathering fuses, blasting caps, matches, and the abandoned rifle, using her long tunic as a catchall. It required two trips to Emma's room to shove all the detritus into the wardrobe. After checking up and down the hallway, she returned to the office a final time. When she satisfied herself everything was in order, that no one was abroad, she used a large roll of cotton batting, apparently intended by the intruders to muffle the sounds of explosion, to scour the blood from the plank floor. Then, with a gutteral sigh, she got between his legs and dragged him out of the office, down the hallway, and into Emma's room. She stopped at the side opposite Emma's soft purring, straightened the carcass, then rolled it under the bed.

In seconds, the Indian was back at her post by the door. Soon her snores rumbled down the empty hallway. The sound was of far-distant thunder.

####

CHAPTER TWENTY-TWO

THE CLARENDON

Emma looked up from her wash tubs to admire Harriet, gleaming like polished ore in the sun. She had given her a good wash with ditch water, rinsed her clean, stiff-brushed her mane and tail while the mare shivered her skin with pleasure.

She wiped her wet hands on her apron, then took it to the rivulets of sweat on her face. She scratched the mare's ear and surveyed the clamorous traffic across the corral fence. She could scarcely believe how Aspen had altered in a few swift weeks. News of the Pearly had flamed like foxfire at both coastlines, the contagion as unchecked as a pandemic. Men, boys, and not a few women, had piled over the hump from as faraway as St. Louis and San Francisco.

Crowds gathered in disordered lines at storefronts, telegraph and post office counters, hands outstretched for mail and money orders, for dried codfish and coffee beans, for cans of coal oil and sacks of sugar. Buckboards careened and saddle horses cantered the length of Cooper and Hyman Avenues. Jack and mule strings streamed down Mill Street with panyards of ore, up Galena with lengths of pipe, lumber, and cable. Men quarreled over space at hitching rails, and horse rentals rose to three dollars a day. Angus McClaren's cinnamon bear, Enrique, chained near the hotel entrance, was so dazed by the jangle of commerce that he no longer rose on hind legs to grumble at the pigs in the sty behind Dunbar & Black's Law Office.

Amid tumult and shouting, Emma was at last aware of Garrett's machinations. The attempt on the hotel safe, and the resultant killing, had horrified her. Deke and Nate, summoned by Polly in the dead hour before dawn, had reasoned with her as she stood shaking over the corpse in her bedroom. "Can't have Harwood locking Polly in his jail. Nothing would suit him finer than dispatching an old Ute woman to a U.S. prison." Deke had guided the agitated Emma gently to her chair. "Nor can we have the sheriff prying into our affairs."

"We'll bury this coyote so deep a panther couldn't sniff him out," said Nate with grim satisfaction. "Sutton'll be baffled—and mad as a wet cat. He can steep in his own bile."

The men had wrapped the body in canvas, heaved it into a waiting wagon and rolled off to a deep, untraveled coulee on the upper mesa west of town.

Emma knew Garrett would do more than steep and stew. He would wax more dangerous than before.

There were few occasions for her to leave the hotel grounds. The Literary and Shakespeare Societies had postponed weekly meetings, the social clubs cancelled all fetes. The September Firemen's Ball was in abeyance. When she walked to church accompanied by her small coterie, or scurried on a quick errand to the greengrocer's, she knew she was watched.

Foodstuffs of every sort were in short supply. Ranchers drove young beef to slaughter before it was fully fattened. The dearth of garden truck and wagons to truck it forced close-rationed boardinghouses, restaurants, hotels, and camp women to employ every ounce of their ingenuity. Most had put mid-season gardens in the ground and hoed pumpkins, squash, turnips, pole beans, carrots, and cabbage heads from morning 'til dusk. Each morning Tacy Beard led her sisters out by the racetrack and along the ditches to gather cow parsnip, wild celery, miner's lettuce, and rabbitguts. Polly showed the girls where to dig for wild onions and Indian potatoes and how to pry cat-o'-nine tails from the lakes—cat-o'-nine-tail meat was tasty in a stew. In a few weeks they'd fill lard buckets with wild raspberries, gather chokecherries and sarvisberries for wine and jam. What they needed, they'd keep. The rest they'd sell. Though miners and drovers considered nothing less than beans and fatback good for lining a man's belly and putting on muscle, they savored the variety of greens and sweets.

With the food shortages, Emma had had to back off drying Shotgun's game for the reservation people. This greatly mollified the women of the Ladies' Relief Society. Their men had been incensed at the notion of feeding wild Indians. "That meat is needed to feed the crowds right here," railed Lena Davidson's husband Ollie. "Never mind them brownbellies. They can locate their own meat—polecat, for all I care."

"If this pace holds," Aggie fretted, "Aspen will eat up its own strike profits. Flour is one dollar a pound and eggs are dear—a crack in an egg is a calamity kin ta' a crack in a mine timber. Annie Pomeroy and Vinnie Krueger are threatenin' their hens wi' a neck-wringing if they dinna lay faster."

The Times had tuned up its superlatives, announcing ever more details of the Pearly cars: the highest assays and tonnage per car, which trammer loaded the most tonnage per shift. Pearly crewmen were minor celebrities, their smallest utterances quoted in boldface print. At length, Deke marched thunderously on the editor and told the man he was inflaming the opposition to the point of high mischief—mayhap murder. Marcus Porterfield heard him out—and kept right on printing injudicious minutiae.

"'Tisn't that the major minds for himself," Aggie alerted Emma. "Word is that the news drives Mr. Sutton past his limit. The man's lunatic, ranting and laying about wi' threats. You stick to these grounds like plaster, lass."

Fully as inflammatory were headlines devoted to the upcoming apex-sideline court battle. "WE WILL NOT CONSORT WITH THE DEVIL!" ... "SIDELINE IS THE PEOPLE''S FRIEND!"... "THE APEXERS CAN GO TO JERUSALEM!"

Emma knew that, whatever the court decision, she herself would be embroiled in a snarl of lawsuits and injunctions. She looked forward to the legal imbroglio like a dose of salts.

"Never you mind, Emmy," Nate assured her. "Calvin is operating full-tilt to empty that lode of every ounce of silver before court convenes."

As the camp had changed, so had Emma. The recollected hate on Garrett's face, like a recurring bad dream, had grown in her mind to Brobdignagian proportions. She no longer obeyed her rapid-fire impulses. In place of being willful, she was watchful.

Still leaning on the fence, she pinned back wayward tendrils of hair. Disgustedly, she swatted at a clinging horsefly. As manure piled up, so did glistening clouds of blue-green bottleflies, of big black horseflies with stingers sharp as a snake's. Dan Alderfer had bellowed at the aldermen's meeting, "Boys, if you don't ordain charcoal in cisterns, and hire five more watermen to deliver fresh spring-water, and dig a few more good wells, and clean the shit out of the streets, we'll have us another epidemic. Cholera or typhoid. Diphtheria or the epizootic. Take your pick."

Plenty thought Doc's ideas entirely too newfangled. "Little dirt and a few flies never hurt no one," men muttered.

Aggie's efforts to maintain her own puritan standards were nearly flooring her. She was so unnerved by her perilously low supplies of yellow soap that Emma planned to manufacture soap late next week. She'd long since moved determinedly on Mr. Mac's province—the front desk and office—sweeping aside the Scotsman's protests. "You're boarding me on credit, Mr. Mac. I am no empty-head. I can keep books as well as any banker."

Although Mac had scowled and growled, he'd grown grateful for the spells of relief, for Emma's tidy figures and iron hand with expenses. What's more, she ate in the kitchen with the help. And when there was occasion to enter the dining room, decorously used the Ladies' Entrance and didn't overstep her bounds.

Emma no longer had leisure for noodling about the future. The present, a demanding taskmaster, was ever with her. She worked from sunup to sundown and often late into the evening. On this day, she and Bridgie had taken over the hotel laundry. The Irisher, newly betrothed to Young Frank Parker, flew about on feet so spirited they seemed not to touch the ground. With Garrett again off in Leadville, Bridgie had flown to the Bullion Row house to scare up additional clothespins. Emma prayed she would not take flight on wings of love and soar headfirst into the Hallam Lakes. Smiling to herself at the vision of a plump airborne O'Reilly, she turned back to the washtubs sitting on crude holders rigged from bent driller's steels. Wash water simmered over embers in rock-lined trenches and steamy smells of soap and starch rose on all sides. Though the scrubbing was a trial for her still-tender rib moorings, she welcomed hard work—a known remedy for befuddlement. On the one hand, she was happy to be freed of Garrett. On the other, she felt oddly displaced, like a newly orphaned child. Over the scrubboard, she knuckled down to mountains of dirty sheets. As her hands flew, so did her thoughts. What was it made men lust after power? Go mad with greed? How came a man to love—or hate—a woman? Her raveled thoughts and determined scrubbing were interrupted when Uncle Nate trotted into the washyard.

"On my way to the apothecary for smelling salts. One of the diggers is faint." He peered at the tubs, scowled at Emma's roughened hands and heated face. "We're at a sorry pass, Sister Coon havin' to watch her back so Emma Sutton don't swallow up her trade." As he leaned over to stir the coals under a tub and take another breath for scolding, Amos Blackwell tore around the corner, the indignant roars of Enrique the bear behind him.

"Amos! Mrs. McClaren will take a switch to you if you torment that bear again!"

The boy, his devilment undimmed by amputation, was already out of sight. Doc, chasing after him to change his filthy dressings, flopped against the Clarendon fence, reached to scratch Chester's chin, and mopped his own forehead. "It'll take a fifty-foot noose to lasoo that little lizard." Then he too frowned at the washtubs. "What have we here? Aggie's new hired girl? Dern it, woman…"

Emma had only just ceased being hostage to one scold. She didn't take kindly to men ordering her about. "Susan B. Anthony says, 'Woman must not depend on the protection of man, but must be taught to defend herself.'" She looked so indignant that Nate and the doc beat a retreat. Still irked, she hefted a pile of soapy sheets into rinse tubs and sloshed them hard with an outsized apple-butter paddle, used the hand-wringer to wring out most of the wet, piled them in clothes baskets, and carried them to the nearest clothesline. She was stuffing her apron pockets with pins and mulling over her supplies of hoarded cooking fat and wood ash for soap-making when the basket of wet linen was lifted from her hands.

"Which line shall I start with?" Deke Burdine stood in his shirt sleeves, looking businesslike. For a wonder, he wasn't ordering, he was asking. Her flushed face grew pinker. "I must look a sight…"

"Finest looking washerwoman I ever hope to see," he said and popping a clutch of pins in his mouth, proceeded to fasten sheets and pillowslips to the lines.

"But Major…er, Deke," she protested, "you have more important concerns. Laundry is woman's work."

"Poppycock! These lines are so high you can barely reach them."

"Mr. Mac had to string them out of reach of burros and dogs—Amos Blackwell's coon dog dirtied every last clean sheet earlier this week." Emma chuckled as she too set to work. "Aggie peppered him with a load from her Morris gun, and he lit out like a long-tailed comet."

"The laundry vigilantes ride again," grinned Deke around a mouthful of pins. "Only I have not seen *you* riding, my friend."

Now it was the major joining the chorus. "There's a surfeit of work," she said curtly, reaching for another sheet. She had no intention of inviting guards to escort her on outings. She would have felt shamed to strut Harriet through the streets like she was royalty attended by a retinue.

Deke pulled a pin from his mouth and looked at her searchingly. "This strike will pass, Emma, along with our troubles. And with them will go glorious summer days we can never recapture." He gazed at the Silver Queen atop Shadow Mountain. "If only I were free to accompany you up the creek trails…Maybe, after this first trip over the hump…" His voice was wishful as he bent to tackle another basket of wash.

Guessing her cranky mood, he pinned and talked, regaling her with light-hearted tales of Lute, Iacono, and Gracious the mule, who brayed like an army bugle at every approach to the Clarendon bear. Gracious had achieved mule

183

notoriety. Men told and retold the latest quirks of Gracious behavior as if the animal were a loony old lady.

"Gracious is about to have a change of scenery," he said. "We leave day after tomorrow, first thing Monday morning."

Emma dropped her arms, her look yearning. "My, how I would love to go up that trail. Oh Deke, do you think I might?" she asked in an eager rush. "I ride and shoot as well as a man, and I'd work my way."

Deke was taken aback. "My dear lady, not even Cattle Kate would ride shotgun on an ore run. You'd have this camp in an uproar."

Emma thought longingly of the onrushing Roaring Fork, of the deep, icy pools in the Devil's Punchbowl. She ached to lope through high grass by Stillwater, to water Harriet in Difficult Creek, to stretch out and splash her face in the cool, iron-tasting water of the grottos. Her eyes shone over visions of late-blooming larkspur and paintbrush, scarlet gilia and pink gentian.

Man and woman stood nearly finished with the last load of laundry, facing each other behind a field of sheets. Her face turned to his was filled with such longing that Deke clasped her chafed hands in his. "Oh, my dear, if you only knew how I long to ride by your side. To show you my secret picnic places...to..."

Emma looked into his eyes and her lips uncertain, raised her head near. Deke Burdine, officer and gentleman, could not hold himself in check. He folded her close, tilted her chin, and kissed her with all the pent-up passion and long loneliness that was in him. Then, after one deep, hungry look, he turned on his heel and strode away through the wet linens.

By four o'clock the next morning, Emma was wide awake, finished with her sleeping. At bedtime, on her knees for prayers, she had sent a good many mixed messages upward. She feared God's wrath for her dissolute ways. Yet try as she might, she did not feel the sinner. "Forgive me, Lord," she'd prayed, "for breaking my marriage vows and your commandments. Please do not consign me to burn in hell...and oh, I do thank you for sending the major my way." Now, as earlier, she could recall little but the feel of Deke's mouth on hers. What she had felt that day on her lips, her blood had carried to every part of her body. She had stood amid clotheslines clutching a wet sheet, her legs weak as washwater. Deke had been ardent—yet so gentle, as if she might shatter like thin, heirloom china.

"How could I not know about gentle?" she inquired aloud, her limbs trembly under the covers. There was a world of difference between the mindless cupidity she'd once felt with Garrett—and the sense of completeness she experienced now. She clasped her hands behind her head, picturing Deke's deep gray gaze and rare flashing smile, the scars by one eye she wished to trace and soothe with a finger. She felt joyful at every memory of the man—and the man's embrace.

Outside her window, other men, homeless men, slept, sprawled on the hotel veranda. Mr. Mac had barricaded her room with heavy flour barrels and packing crates so no one could gain entry. Polly had stationed Iacono at the barricade, where he slept light as a young puma in his blanket. In the distance, in this still part of the night, Emma heard the rumble of iron-rimmed wagon wheels and the clanking of milk cans. Svea Hoaglund. The girl was a worker. She rose before dawn to milk. Then she and her pop drove the milking, warm from the udder, to Aggie's kitchen.

Emma loved this time before daybreak, when the tumultuous mine camp world was quiet. There was something spiritual about it, like the hush of a church away from the bustle of Sunday congregations. Immersed in reverie, she lost a few moments before it came to her that the clanking of milk cans had ceased. That was an oddment. Svea and Pop Hoaglund had no other customers. They should be nearing the hotel kitchen. Emma sat up, instantly alert. No clanking. No wagon-rumbling. Only snuffling and snoring from the veranda. She jumped onto the cold floor and threw a skirt and shawl over her bedgown. She dragged a chair beneath the high upper window sash, unlatched the locked window, started to stretch a leg through, hesitated, jumped back down to snatch the Peacemaker from a drawer and shove it in her skirt pocket with a handful of bullets. Quick as a rabbit, she wriggled through the high, narrow opening. Her skirt snagged on a splinter and a crate creaked ominously. A hand reached up to steady her. Ike, crouched like a mountain cat. She whispered a few words of Ute, motioned him to follow. They crept down Mill Street in the early morning dark. In the distance, up Cooper Street to the east, a few saloons still spilled light and noise onto plank walkways. The moon had gone behind Aspen Mountain, and scattered stars were beginning to wink out in the pre-dawn sky. Moving barefoot along the splintery wood close on the sides of buildings, pistol drawn, she loaded the gun by feel as she worked her way toward where she'd last heard the wagon. At the Cooper Street alleyway this side of Hyman Avenue, the Hoaglund

horse stood in his traces, head lowered. From down the alley, she heard sounds of a struggle.

"Why you…you damned cat, you bite me again and…I'll shove this first down your fuckin' throat!" The voice, unsteady from exertion, was familiar. A choked half-scream mingled with course breathing and muffled cursing. Emma murmured to Ike, who sprinted around buildings to the far end of the alley as she sidled along the backside of Mulgrew's Mercantile. Even with backlighting from the Galena Street arc lamp, it was hard sorting out the to-do until she was nearly on top of them: two men wrestling with a big woman, one grabbing and hoisting her long skirts, trying to rut at her from behind while the other pinned her arms, both gasping profane orders.

"Pin her down tighter, for Christ's sake!"

"Sh-she's strong as…a…ox. Son of a bitch, she kneed me in the balls."

Emma took a firm stance, her gun pointed at the men. "And that is right where I'll shoot you, you damn devil. Square in the *cojones.*" She didn't shout. But her voice was hard and hot.

The startled men, their breath ragged, ceased their grappling and straightened to find themselves looking at the barrel of a pistol which glistened blue-black in the faint light. "Who—oo…what?"

"Up! Up high up with those hands. Never mind buttoning your pants, Bull Mudgett. A dead man won't fall out of that window. And don't reach for your gun. I'll shoot any hand not in the air."

"Why, Miz Sutton," Bull's voice was wheedling, "Bob and me was jest funnin'…"

Svea Hoaglund, panting, had stepped out of reach. Now she took a deep breath, hauled back and socked Bull Mudgett in the mid-section so hard his wind came out in an explosive *whooooomph!* She looked ruefully at her big fist. "Wish I…packed a better wallop," she gasped. "I'd like…to knock…his teeth down his filthy throat."

"We was just tryin' to steal a kiss," mumbled Bull sourly, resisting the need to rub his gut.

"It was…more than…a kiss you were after," Svea hissed. "My pop will kill you. You ain't got no call to…interfere with me, you sorry piece of trash!"

"Believe we'll just march these two over to the sheriff's lockup, Svea. Hands in the air now, both of you!"

At a sudden sly movement from Bob Bisbee, Emma fired, singing his pants leg so that it caught fire and began smoking.

"Keeeeeeeyrist! She winged me!" Denver Bob beat at the smoke, his pretty face twisted in pain and astonishment.

"Right where I aimed, mister. Go for that gun once more, and your pizzle won't ever make water or trouble again."

Motioning Svea to her side, she ordered. "Out to the cart. NOW, girl! "

"Aw, Miz Sutton, you don't mean this." Though Bull was in no rush to jump a woman who shot ready as a man, his eyes glinted meaner than a roused bulldog's.

"Try me, Mr. Mudgett. I'll get your hairy crotch, or I'll shoot you in the damned eye! Now start walking." She pointed.

Bull and Bob were shocked to their vitals by Mrs. Sutton's cold blasphemy. So shocked that they moved grudgingly down the passage smelling of manure, restaurant garbage, putrifying dead cat, and worse. As they backed, Denver Bob's raised right hand crept surreptitiously to his neck. He was working a small knife from under his collar when, with the call of a hootie owl, Iacono leaped from the roof above. The boy was only half the size of the man, but he was eely as a snake. "He got...knife, Em," he grunted, gouging Bob's eyes with his fingers 'til the man sank to his knees, yowling in pain. The boy then jumped Bull.

"Go, Em! I come!"

Grabbing Svea's hand, Emma raced lickety-split to the milk cart, jumped in, and whipped the startled old horse to the hotel. Iacono left off biting Mudgett's ear and sprinted after the women. All three scrambled inside the Clarendon kitchen and slammed the door, leaning back to ease their frayed breathing.

Polly had been waiting by the door, the hotel rifle in her hands. Amid an exchange of fevered Ute, Svea slumped into a chair at the big kitchen work table and willed herself to stop jittering. She stared unseeingly at hanks of drying peppers and mullein, of goldenseal and medicine tuft hanging in neat bundles from Aggie's rafters. Her voice dazed, she whispered, "That's twice now, Miz Sutton. Twice you saved my bacon. I surely do thank you, ma'am." She took a deep, shuddery breath. "If you had never come, it would have gone hard with me. Since I shoved that lowlife Mudgett in the lake he's been poison mean."

Emma struggled for composure. She was askance over what she'd just done. In turn, her incredulity made her so angry she could have chewed glass. She paced the floor, spun her pistol barrel, sighted down the gun. "Mine men may be rough," she seethed, "but they have always respected a good woman. What are we coming to if they hold no respect for a good woman—if she's no longer safe on our streets?" She put the safety on the pistol and let it fall to her side. "We'll report this to Sheriff Harwood at good light."

Svea looked harder at her hands, which had grown quiet in her lap. "Won't do no good, Missus. Pop already told the sheriff that Bull Mudgett's set on interfering with me. The skunk's been watching our house, following me, waiting for me by the post office and storefronts. Never says a word, just gives me hard looks." Her face was so overheated that a tear sizzled as it trickled down. "Never says a word. Not a word," she repeated despairingly. "Just eyes me. I ain't safe anywhere. That high sheriff only laughs. Says Pop is your regular over-protective father. Says he best marry me off."

"I only come out this morning," she went on, "because Pop has summer fever. There wasn't anyone else to send, and the milk would spoil. Started out at a fast clip, but that horse is old. He give out on me."

Emma recommenced striding the kitchen floor, scarcely aware of the stone bruise on one bare foot. "This is preposterous. Garrett Sutton has me pinned down in this hotel. His men have a girl like you afraid to ride the streets. We could be at war."

For once the cheery Iacono wasn't smiling. "Worst kind. Bad men got guns. Good Injuns—no guns."

Aggie and her sleepy-eyed kitchen help appeared in a sudden pack, the demands of ravenous men about to assail them like a windstorm. Beaming bashfully, Iacono bustled out to help Svea unload the big milk cans. Caught up in a frenzied press of coffee-making, biscuit-baking, and sidemeat frying, no one thought to ask about the peculiar pre-dawn gathering of Indians and whites around the hotel stove.

Lost in the to-do, Emma eased outside onto the porchway. Faint light was creeping up the hillsides. Clouds of pink and lavender chiffon slowly unfurled around the mountains' shoulders where they shrugged up against the sky. The morning, as delicate and feathery as a spring bouquet, held resplendent promise. Soon it would be full day, the sky achingly blue. Three small clouds, like puffs of dandelion gone to seed, drifted from behind the Silver Queen's nose and dissipated in the rosy half-light. Emma had a sudden vision of black-eyed Susans embroidering the gullies of Sterner Gulch. Suddenly she could not endure one more moment of noisome men and braying animals. She was fed up with being bullied and fearful. In an instant, all her hard-won lessons of self-restraint flew away, mindless as moths.

Bisbee and Mudgett, she knew, would be back at their boardinghouse, licking their wounds, certain she too was hunkered down. She hurried to her room, drew on boots, a hand-me-down pair of Pa's pants and his canvas jacket, snatched her oilskin from the wardrobe, tucked her hair under the old cow-driving hat, stuffed her oilskin in a deep pocket and headed down the hallway. She'd be long gone before a soul missed her. Her heart jumped with joy over Deke, and the titillation of playing truant filled her with childlike excitement. Polly was busy in the kitchen, Bridgie asleep until time for Mass. Even Iacono, ever watchful, did not see her leave.

#####

CHAPTER TWENTY-THREE

STERNER GULCH

As horse and rider trotted west on Cooper Street, Harriet tossed her head and blew plumes of steam into the misty, pastel-shaded morning. Already there was a sharp tang to the air. Here and there a harbinger clump of cottonwood or aspen leaves had turned the color of polished brass.

Street-hawkers and bunco men had taken refuge who knew where. Sunday mornings in a mine camp were inviolate, though few men employed them for prayer. Renegade Sabbatarians and miners lay in their bunks re-reading old letters, set clothes to soaking in tin tubs over low fires, drew heavy needles from housewives to mend pants and boots. Sunday was a time for housekeeping, tale-telling, and leisurely cork-pulling. All Aspen was still as a sheltered tarn. Emma wished she could command the mare to tiptoe. Not that she was thinking proper Sabbath thoughts herself, though she did feel a kind of reverence. Her head was full of Deke, of his man's touch, his man's smell. She longed only to be alone, where she could hug those feelings close.

She gauged the roiling water of Castle Creek and murmured, "No toll bridge for us, girl. Too many nosy nellies at toll bridges." Harriet snorted, bunched her muscles and took the creek with room to spare. Emma praised her, stroking her sleek neck. She cut across the Wozniak place to avoid what few horses or wagons might cross the mesa this early.

Tite and Annie Pomeroy made a regular outing of Sunday mornings. They hitched Elmer and drove into camp to treat themselves to one of Aggie's hefty breakfasts before church, Annie the rare wife dining away from her own kitchen. Tite's friends and acquaintances stopped by, sometimes just to hear a womanly voice, and Annie basked in the attention. She missed the next-doors they'd had in Ohio. A serving of gossip, even from rough-spoken men, was a welcome change from the loneliness that ringed a ranch.

On the town trail in, Tite noted the distant rider and groused, "Wozniak's got field hands out on a Sunday." He hated to think of any man outworking him. Annie shaded her eyes against the rising light. "Why, Tite, I believe it is Mrs. Sutton on that brown mare of hers."

"Don't look like no lady to me."

"Look again, you old goat. That's long yeller hair falling from under that man's hat."

"Rides good, don't she?"

Emma, feeling guilty, loped across the pasture without waving. Annie Pomeroy always urged her to stop in for a wedge of pie and a glass of cold cider when she rode their way. Leaning over, sometimes dismounting to open and close pasture gates, she crossed Maroon Creek and was on the far side of Buttermilk Ranch when a rider on an ungainly, sway-backed horse slow-trotted over the rise, his elbows rising and falling in the manner of an apprehensive chicken. He was such a sorry sight that she grinned as she hastily stuffed her hair back under her hat and leaned down to re-latch the final gate.

The rider, eyes darting, jounced past where the Buttermilk Trail curved close. Fess Felcher, hurrying into camp from his wife's family place, was in a sulky mood. He hadn't grown up a-horseback like most around here. He didn't take to ranching either, and here he was, stuck on a hell-and-gone ranch and riding a spring-haltered old plug. When he'd got Bessie in a family way, he'd been proud as punch at the good-natured ribbing, feeling it marked him a man. Now look—the baby had a snootful of colic, had turned last night's air blue with his shrieking. It was beyond Fess how any mite that small could make such an infernal racket. He'd come close to stuffing it under a pillow to shut its noise. Instead, he'd sat the night, pulling on his whiskey 'til his head was ready to crack.

With his wife and the brat finally at rest, he'd ridden out feeling like a wagonload of shit. Fess knew himself the youngest, puniest, and the most tormented of Bull Mudgett's crowd. Like many of this world's slow-thinking and unschooled, he felt frequently and unfairly abused. Why Mudgett had to call a meeting for Sunday was past his understanding. Then his spirits rose. He'd wager he was the only one to lay eyes on Mrs. Garrett Sutton, riding out bold as a nickel in men's clothes. He rehearsed his recital of this news. The woman had no sense of decency, he'd declare. By rights, she oughta be home dressing for services like a lady, he'd remark.

With a sigh of relief, Emma cut across the Buttermilk's irrigation ditch and turned up the Sterner Trail. She loved this ride. On a hot summer afternoon it was permeated with the sweet sad smell of damp needles and spongy mosses. Early in the morning, it caught and held the first rays of sun peeking around the edges of the Elk Range to come to rest and shine like coins on leaf-dappled ground. Yanking off her hat and letting out a *whheeeeeeeeeaw!!!* Emma galloped full out up the trail. Under the trees and along the gradually sloping stretch this side of Schoolhouse Rock, the horse tore, mixing clouds of pent-up steam with trail powder. At length they came to the sheltered clearing beyond the rock, a natural small amphitheater warmed by the sun and ringed with thick stands of red fir and blue spruce. Leaping from the saddle, she threw back her head and cried to the sky, "'It is too rash, too sudden, too like the lightning!'" Her voice trailed off as she hugged herself with her arms, then flopped back against a bank of sedge grass. There was plenty of time before she must return and dress for church. She tilted the old hat over her forehead, put her arms behind her head and commenced daydreaming.

As her body healed, so had her heart, this heart which had long ago left Garrett Sutton, if it had ever been his in the first place. Of a sudden, sealed with a kiss, that heart had found its rightful place. Her thoughts drifted over the look of Deke, the feel of Deke, the looks to come, the feelings to come. She pictured kisses and caresses—in fields of flowers, in a cabin, in a mountain ravine amid drifts of snow. Saw herself, to her surprise, in a tumble of laughing babies.

Smilingly she admitted aloud, "Aha! Jane Austen was on the mark! 'A lady's imagination is very rapid. It jumps from admiration to love. From love to matrimony. All in a moment…'"

Untethered, Harriet moved leisurely along the trail, munching wild grasses. Emma's face grew serene, her skin warmed under the embrace of the rising sun, her eyes fell shut.

In the dingy side parlor of Old Lady Robinson's boarding house, Bull and Denver Bob slumped amid a handful of men, boot-scarred doors pulled shut against interlopers.

Bert Hoople griped, "Ain't no call fer us to be penned in this fartin' room. Oughta have that machine up right now; early morning is the time we'll go."

Bud hootched around in his chair. "Today's the right air, quiet, but with good cross-gusts. Today's a better-than-middling day for a practice run."

Bull hadn't slept, his shirt was full of alley dirt and alley stink, and he felt meaner than a cornered bobcat. "You've pissed and moaned about them crosswinds 'til I've a mind to blow you a crosswind that'll knock your ass into the next valley."

"Now listen, Bull. Balloon ascension is not an exact science," whined Bert. "We ain't magicians, and we can't do her without help from the weather."

"Well, fer your sake the fucking weather best not hold you up 'til next month. No balloon weather, no pay."

"We got everythin' set. We've had three flights with a good wind off the pass. We have red sky in the evenings, ought to pull her off sometime this week."

"This week it better by God be."

Bert looked at Bud and shook his head. Nobody in these parts understood that a balloon was at the mercy of the elements. They could guide it up and down with their burner blasts of hot air. But when it came to the back and forth, they were as helpless as birds in a storm.

Stomping across the porch, Fess scraped half the mud from his boots on a rusty scraper, came into the parlor tracking the balance. He knew the boys had been following Mrs. Sutton, though he was unclear about their intentions. Now he was puffed up with importance. "Never guess who I just seen," he burst out.

"Madame Mustache, riding nekkid on a white horse." Shoat's voice was heavy with scorn. He was high-handed with Fess, whom he considered a fool.

"Nope. Mrs. Garrett Sutton. Riding out in man's pants, no better than a whore girl."

Bull and Bob straightened in their chairs. "Where?" they demanded in unison.

"Sterner Gulch way. Tryin' to hide under a man's hat, but I seed her, the baggage."

"Alone?" barked Bull.

"Bold as a brass ring." Fess was gratified with the stir he was causing.

Bob scrambled to his feet, his face truculent. He muttered, "I'll go. I owe that bitch a lick or two." He fingered his singed leg, swollen and stinging worse than a wasp bite.

"Mind you don't use your piece, Bob. Gunning down Little Emma would get a man strung from a tall tree."

"She shot me. She'd have shot you too." Bob's tone was bitter.

The others looked quizzical, trying to puzzle out this strange conversation.

"Women keep bellyaching about their rights," said Bull scathingly. "A man ain't got those same rights. Which means we can't have fingers pointing at the boss. It has to look accidental-like."

"I'll use the wire, don't worry."

"And keep in mind that bonus we been promised," muttered Bull half under his breath as Bob snatched up his rifle and headed for his horse. Spotting Fess's open mouth, Bull said grudgingly, "Good job of work, Fess. There'll be something in this fer you."

Polly knocked on Missy's hotel room door, eased it open, and discovered the bed empty. She peered up and down the halls, went back to the kitchen, and hurrying her pace, hustled out to the street, searching the verandas. She rushed back inside and pounded on a door down the hall. Bridgie, still fogged with sleep, was readying herself for early Mass.

"No see Missy?"

"'Tis barely light." Without a drop of hot tea in her, she was crabby as well as sleepy. "She's not abed?"

"She ain't."

"Likely graining that horse."

Polly rushed to the horse stalls around back. Harriet's stall yawned empty as a ghost-town barn. With a groan, she picked up her skirts and raced as fast as her squat legs would carry her back to Bridgie's room. "Missy gone! Horse gone! You run. Get Mrs. Lavinia, get Major, Mista Phipps." As Bridgie stood gape-mouthed, Polly raised her hand. "Move!" she yelled. "Scat! Missy get kilt!"

The unsettled Bridgie yanked on a shawl, sprinted out of the Clarendon and raced full-tilt toward Spring Street.

In Lavinia's kitchen, Young Frank, Deke, Nate, Needle and Willard sat at the breakfast table, hands folded, eyes cast down. "And we not only say *danke,* Lord, for the riches thou hast bestowed, but for the blessings we are about to receive," prayed Calvin. "Anyone have anything to add?"

"I have," announced Willard, looking upward. "Lord God, D.K. Burdine's ore train leaves tomorrow. Hold him and that silver of our's safe in your arms."

"Amen, God," said Nate.

"Amen," repeated Vinnie and the others.

Polly had never before set a moccasined foot in the hotel dining room. She now puffed into the big room, calling, "Mrs. Mac, Mrs. Mac, Missy Sutton and horse, they gone!" Aggie, exchanging the time of day with Titus and Annie pomeroy, held a hand to her mouth, her face as colorless as raw bread dough.

"Just saw her," said Tite, "riding across Wozniak's spread."

"No doubt on her way to Sterner's. She favors that ride," said Annie. "Is it bad news?"

"Only for the lass, if that husband or his men get their witches' claws in her," agonized Aggie.

Bridgie pounded on the Krueger's door and burst inside, a study in terror, her hair springing up in Medusa snakes. "She's gone!" cried the wild-eyed girl. "Sure and I know I promised to watch her good! But she rode out in the dark, before I ever knew it." Hiccupping with fright, she gasped, "Please find her, Major. Please find the missus before that divvil does for her."

Deke was on his feet, out the door and on Buford's back as Polly ran his way. In her agitation, she called out in Ute, then corrected herself. "She go Sterner's!" she cried. Pointing north and west, she shouted louder, "You go! Sterner Gulch!"

Deke laid Buford straight out, streaking down the dusty streets toward the west of town.

Emma wakened with a chill. The sun had warmed her. It wasn't that. The chill was not morning cold, it was uneasiness. She never should have slept. If she were going to run off like a scalded cat, the least she could do was watch her back. Peering warily around, gauging the hour from the sun, she pulled the Peacemaker from her pocket and loaded the empty chambers. She tucked the gun in the waistband of her serge skirt, hurriedly pinned up her tumbled hair, pulled her hat down hard, tightened the chin strap and whistled piercingly for Harriet, grazing on dandelions and comfrey. As she readied herself to ride, her face was in the crosshairs of a rifle down the hillside. The scope followed her as she moved, a fox stalking a rabbit. The finger on the half-trigger twitched, itching to pull. Emma shivered and bent to scrape a sharp stone from her boot sole, moving out of the rifle's scope. She thrust a foot in the stirrup and swung into the saddle. The scope lost, regained, then lost her again as she and the horse picked up speed amid the passing flash of tree branches. Approaching the straight stretch after Schoolhouse Rock, she put Harriet in a full-out canter. The mare's long stride almost missed the wire stretched across the trail. Then her hind leg struck it, and with a high-pitched whinny of pain, the horse hurtled through the air. Emma flew to one side, hit the ground, bounced, and lay still. Harriet, eyes rolling, whites showing, staggered to her feet and limped a few steps, head hanging, leg oozing blood.

Denver Bob scrambled out of a stand of sarvisberry bushes, tugged himself up the steep, and reached the fallen rider. Panting, he nudged her with his boot, then rolled her over on her back. His thin mouth curled downward. "Don't look so sassy now, do you, Missus?"

Blood ran from a cut by Mrs. Sutton's eye, mixing with trail dirt, streaking her face. He could not resist a swift kick to her ribs before he began searching the sides of the trail. At last he spied what he wanted: a good-sized chunk of jagged rock. Using his knife, he dug and tugged it out of its place in the ground. He employed the knife to scrape dirt enough to fill the hole, stopping twice to rub his singed leg and whimper. He picked up the heavy rock and cleaned it of damp dirt on the underside. Then he lugged it back and placed it in an experimental position near the woman's head. He sized up the look of things, took in a shuddery breath, and prepared to lift the rock high, to bring it down with all his force. "This won't hurt a bit, lady. One good bash and we're done." He raised the rock above his head, judging how best to strike. He'd gathered his forces for the decisive blow when approaching hoofbeats rocketed toward him.

"Son of a bitch!" He started to bring the rock down, hesitated, then with a grunt of disgust, threw it under a thicket of wild raspberries. He started to retrieve the wire, found it knotted too securely, slid down the steep bank, and took off through the trees to circle back to the creek. He had no feelings but bad for the high-handed woman who'd creased him with a bullet—but neither did he intend to be caught red-handed doing Mudgett's murdering business. Not when it concerned one of the best-known, best-liked citizens of this camp—a woman at that.

Deke had not spared himself or Buford, and he pulled up beside Emma as soaked with exertion as Fordy. He leapt down to feel for her pulse beat. He gathered her exultantly in his arms and smoothed the yellow harvest of hair away from one bloodied eye. He watched her face, coaxing her awake with soothing words.

At last Emma moaned. Looking aslant at Deke, she muttered, "My land, not again!"

Deke hugged her to him. "Yes, dear one, again."

"Oh Deke, I—I could not help myself. I felt so…hemmed in." She spoke hesitantly, the words furry in her mouth.

"I know. Hush now." Deke had scanned the trees and the trail, narrowing his gaze as he took in the telltale wire. "Those lily-livered cowards were lying in wait."

"But...I never saw a soul," she said groggily. "I've no notion what happened. Harriet! Is she all right?"

"Limping a speck. Hungry as a horse."

After looking to see Harriet safe, Emma felt of her puffed-up eye, winced at the hurt in her ribs. "Not a month past, I bragged that no horse had bested me yet."

"None has. You were caught in a Mudgett tripwire." Inwardly, Deke fumed that any man would stoop so low. Emma, seeing his anger flare, reached a hand to stroke his face. "Never mind the ribs, just hold me."

"I want never to let loose of you again."

They could have been the only two people in the wilderness. His anxiety and his fury damped, Deke felt suddenly boyish as a sixteen-year-old. He'd long ago memorized the look of Emma's strong wrists and hands, of a hairline softened by wisps of escaping half-curls, of the slender hollow at the back of her neck. Now, tracing each memory with a finger, caressing the downiness of neck and arms, he felt a sudden shining in his life. His heart pounded, he wanted to whoop and holler. "My love," he said, "I have waited for you...wanted you...wished for you my livelong days."

He had never thought to say such words to a woman. He could not fathom where they sprang from.

Emma did not answer except to pull his face toward her own. With his mouth exploring hers, they rolled joyously on a carpet of spruce needles. She cringed only once at the pain in her ribs, then turned playfully, half on top of him, to quiet the pounding of her blood. "Deke, my dear," she said, "if we are to know each other more...er...biblically, do you not think...now is the time..." She looked sidelong into his face, a wicked glint in her eye. Deke reached eagerly to kiss her again...

"To share with me your baptismal name?"

He looked doleful, his voice low. "Dalrymple...Dalrymple Knowles Burdine" He looked despairingly skyward. "And now I cannot embrace you without shame."

"It is a beautiful name," said Emma gently, "and I bless your dear mother for it...but I believe I am more at home with Deke. Deke my sweet, Deke my protector. Deke of mine." She smoothed his hair with her hand.

"I cannot believe that you care for me, Emma, that you are in my arms. You who are so generous, so full of gladness. You make me spring to life. I was only half alive before. Now I'm a bonfire, so lit up I could fire all the mountains."

They forgot they were on hard ground. They did not wait for a bed or a feather mattress. They reached and grasped and gasped and explored. They floated on clouds and were swept away in waves of dappled sunshine and summer breeze.

####

CHAPTER TWENTY-FOUR

BULLION ROW

Garrett opened the front door to Gabe Tacker and Tacker's lawyers with a curt greeting. He was in a vile mood, in no frame of mind to face a cantankerous Tacker. The mystery at the Clarendon had him at his wit's end. One of the safecrackers Mudgett hired had fled south with a half-severed arm and nary an explanation. "Acted possessed, like a haunt had got him," said Bull, perplexed. The other man was inexplicably missing. There'd been no reports of crime nor punishment—not in *The Times*, not at Harwood's hoosegow. Garrett could not countenance the notion of a man dissipating like chimney smoke. Ranting at Bull did no good—Mudgett was more confounded than he.

Nor was the tycoon's mood sunny. In place of his usual congenial self, he appeared tight-lipped and simmering. *At least*, thought Garrett, *the old geezer couldn't have heard about the bungled break-in*. Gabe could not tolerate bungling.

Though Tacker had long been partial to what he termed the younger man's "giddyap-and-go," of late he'd retaken his measure. A fellow with true sap took setbacks in his stride. Setbacks were part of any game. Sutton, however, treated every reversal as a personal affront—one to be avenged and punished. The fellow's outlook was no longer sensible.

Planted in the middle of the parlor, Gabe said, "For God's sake, can't we pull the drapings back? This room is fustier than a funeral parlor. And throw open the infernal windows. It's a prime summer day."

Although Garrett was vain about the collection of fine art in his front room, nothing had been dusted for weeks. He'd had difficulty locating help, and his new hired girl was a half-witted affliction. She'd lost all her teeth, her savings, and her virginity to a traveling dentist who persuaded her that a fine set of false teeth would be lifetime insurance against toothache. Her porcelain dentures were a poor fit, and the girl clacked as she talked. If she'd dust half as much as she clacked, his house might be fit for receiving. He had never before comprehended the many complications in the simple maintenance of a household.

As for open windows, the bird squawking in his front yard was a trial. Busybody Emma had set out enough suet and sunflower seeds to supply the cockatoos in a New Orleans cathouse. Finches bustled about in young cottonwoods, gabbling over their housekeeping. Magpies screeched deep within thick branches of spruce. Jays called raucously from tree to tree. Garrett said, "I reckoned we couldn't half-think with all the bird racket."

Gabe's voice was caustic. "Your thinker has not been exactly primed, even in dead silence." He had just returned from a trying week in Denver City. He was out of sorts over the multiplying sideliner arguments being pressed on Judge Percy—and with reports of heavy production in the Pearly. This entire Pearly to-do was threatening to get out of hand. He must employ all his faculties to remove thorns and thistles without unnecessary loss of blood.

"If you are implying that I have been idle..." Garrett began indignantly.

"Oh, you ain't been idle, sonny. You're not all wind—there's weather to it."

Despite his aversion to being addressed as "sonny," Garrett rose with a brittle half-smile from his high-backed plush chair. "You've heard about Skinner's colic epidemic, of course. In addition, we festered Pepperell's and Iselin's liveries. There are no stock reserves for miles. The ore shipment had to be postponed. The silver lies idle in the dumps."

Tacker appeared wary. "Might I ask how you turned that trick?"

"So no one could put a finger on it."

"How is that?"

"Mudgett's boys got every thick Mick on night duty likkered up. Then they damped down the hay—only a smidgeon—with quicklime. Not sufficient to detect, but enough to tear up the stomach of a good-sized mule."

"We will hope and pray no word of this gets around. You'd be railed out of town."

With brief nods at Andy Black and Harry Dunbar, who sat at attention on the big horsehair sofa, Gabe said, "What I ain't heard about is that mine stock, twenty-five percent of which I can lay claim to on the last promissory note you give me. Harry, how does that stock stand?"

"She was going for right around one dollar a share after they struck the vug. In a little over four weeks, that price has gone to twenty-five dollars. If the deposit holds, it is not beyond reason that she'll move into the hundreds."

"With thirty thousand shares outstanding, that could run total par value near three million—some $500,000 you'd owe me to date, Sutton. For that kind of money, I'll set in any man's parlor."

"Pie in the sky!" scoffed Garrett. "I'll believe it when I see the sales figures from the Denver factor." He struggled with a window sash until it creaked upward a few inches. "I'll have your stock for you in short order, and you can take that guarantee to the bank," he declared coolly over his shoulder.

Andy Black peered under his bushy brows at Tacker. "Plan to hold up the Clarendon and blow that big Hurly safe, Sutton?"

Garrett readjusted the window drapes. These men couldn't know of the hotel break-in. If that injured safecracker showed up, he'd shoot the damned bungler himself.

"No use shilly-shallying, sonny, we know you ain't got the stock to give." Tacker, regretting the surfeit of pan-fried onions he'd eaten with his ham hocks at Orey's, belched dyspeptically.

"How?"

"I got me spies all over these mountains. I got spies on the water wagons, in the graveyards, in the smithy's. In whore's beds and preacher's pulpits. But we'll come around to the matter of the stock…" Gabe had been looking over the Sutton parlor. Though a man's home was a more inconspicuous place for a meeting than the Adirondack Club, he wasn't at his best on women's ground—cathouses and the Widow Wickersham's excepted. "I will say it is a sin and a shame," he added, "allowing a feisty female to get the upper hand of you."

Garrett reddened and glared. Gabe went on, his tone more mollifying, "Even if you ain't got a woman in the kitchen, we could stomach a pot of coffee to oil the cogs of a dirty business."

Garrett stalked to the kitchen, stirred up the fire, pumped water and threw some used grounds in the pot, damning the hired girl as they spilled across the cold black stove.

When Gabe finally swallowed his coffee, it was with a sour grimace. He leaned forward in his chair, oyster-shell eyes fixed on a large, yellowish lithograph of *The Surrender at Yorktown*. "Harry, report to us on the Pearly's affairs."

Harry Dunbar cleared his throat, slicked down a seedy mustache, shrugged one shoulder (he had a tic there—a 200-pound soiled dove down in Georgetown had whomped him with a coal shovel in a dispute over her fee), hooked the stems of grease-spotted spectacles over his ears and pulled a pack of papers from his portfolio. "Report on the Pearly Everlasting operation. Date: August third, this year. Mr. Calvin Krueger, holding an allegedly valid leasehold on said mine through September 21, same year, now has some sixty-three men in his employ. His treasurer is Willard Arey, his transport and security officer, Major D.K. Burdine, his vice-president in charge of miscellaneous matters, Nathaniel Phipps." Harry paused to hawk loose phlegm into a rag from his pocket. "They have not got those titles—only the jobs."

Garrett snorted audibly. "That Phipps is nothing more than a chiseling silver-pecker." He despised Nate Phipps. He despised any man who outstripped him in a trade.

Harry Dunbar, scowling over the top of his smudged specs, said off-handedly, "And about the savviest prospector in these hills…" His shoulder jumping, he turned back to his report and continued. "They're still plumbing that bed of pure silver in what they call 'the Cathedral'. Heavy blasting did not open her as much as they hoped. Present working area only allows for three seven-man shifts around the clock." He paused. "I will amend that. Krueger is trying something different. He's using four shorter shifts of six hours, so the men can work with more vigor." Harry's voice was aggrieved. "Such practice will lead to no good," he sniffed. "It's known fact that a hungry hound hunts best."

"The so-called Cathedral is being enlarged with all possible speed so that more men can work her." At this, he nodded a brief acknowledgment in Sutton's direction. The man had an informer in the Pearly workings. One informer in a mine was worth a world of credit at the bank.

"Shorthanded or no, the workers are pulling out twenty thousand to fifty thousand in high-grade every twenty-four hours. Even allowing for downgrading of deeper deposits, the projected gross take through the balance of the lease could very well run two million or so." There was a fine sheen on Harry Dunbar's forehead.

Gabe now had his eye on a plaster of Paris muse who to his mind needed more meat on her bones. His lips puckered. "How did that proposition go with Ducky Duckworth?"

Harry pursed his lips in turn. "Not as we expected. He did not do his duty by you. We filed suit asking for half the strike ore and for a court-appointed receiver to manage the Pearly—at least 'til a circuit court judge could establish proper precedent." His look was one of disgust. "Their lease held." He moistened dry lips. "Ducky said if he issued a injunction and appointed a receiver, the men in this camp would tear him from his wife's arms and string him to a courthouse beam. 'I am hemmed in by unfriendly miners and irate womenfolk' was the way he put it."

"Offered him plenty?"

Harry Dunbar paled at remembrance of the amount. "He said money don't solace a dead man. Nor his widow neither."

Gabe snorted. "Forgets h'it'll say 'Judge' on his gravestone, courtesy of G. B. Tacker."

Garrett was apoplectic. "The apex supplying the Pearly lies dead center in the Columbine. Any way you examine it, that strike belongs to me!"

"Or to your wife, as we understand matters," said Gabe in an arid voice. Before Sutton could retort, he continued, "How about Krueger's overhead, Harry?"

"High. At the rate he's hiring, the wages he's paying, his payroll could run three thousand dollars a month."

Gabe whistled. "For a man in a slab cabin burdened with a mortgage, he is ladling out money like free spring water. How about shipping and smeltering?"

"If he don't go overboard, that could cost him a good twenty thousand over six weeks."

Gabe shook his big head. "Total overhead, near eight percent of his entire take. The man has no head for business."

"We have not found a loophole in the leasehold," interjected Andy Black, "but we're still combing."

"Expect they're in a hard pinch for cash money." Harry held his dirty specs up to the light. "We keep tightening the screws."

Andy Black's smile was pious. "Called in Krueger's mortgage on his cabin. Put the knee-twist on Tite Pomeroy, Ed Wozniak, and the other ranchers that owe the bank. They've had to triple hay and grain prices."

"Well, gentlemen, all this is small potatoes and few to a hill," grumbled Gabe. "That peppery Phipps is tighter than ticks on a yellow dog—and smart to boot. Owns him a passel of gilt-edged rail stock and gold bullion. My Denver man checked." Gabe reflected sourly into his coffee, "It is not ordinary, all this savvy. The fellow ain't usual." Every other prospector in his memory had blown his strike money and ended in the county poorhouse.

"He was brought up plain," explained Harry. "Quakers is close traders. They're smart—and they're mean with money. Say they'll sell guns to Comanches on a killing spree."

"Heard Phipps was a squaw man in the bargain," said Andy.

"The trouble with the little pipsqueak is, he don't drink. Nor gamble. Nor even whore."

"Many more of these holier-than-thou specimens, and we'll be erecting churches to hold 'em all," muttered Gabe. "Even the mortician Arey and that young saloon-keeper, Burdine, have considerable reserves of cash money put by." He'd been taken aback to learn that the big Southerner, a fine horseman and dinner companion, was not only a leader in the Pearly camp, but had recently purchased an Updyke piano of fine curly maple—taken apart, freighted over the hump in pieces and reassembled at the unheard-of cost of one thousand dollars. Even Leorah Wickersham owned nothing better than a small box organ.

He stiffened in his chair, put aside the bitter coffee. "But we are going at matters from the wrong angle. The Pearly has got her camp, and from what we've seen, they'll stick."

Not to a man they won't, thought Garrett smugly. He'd save that piece of grapeshot for later.

Gabe plucked a long cheroot from his vest pocket and bit off the end. "Understand, I'm not saying the colic siege at the livery ain't a good idea. Hold 'em up, slow 'em down, that's the ticket. But I'd be a deal happier to pin that silver underground. If not, and we aren't able to halt production sooner, when the apex decision goes our way, we'll have a cease-work order in hand, stop production cold, repossess all ore in the dumps."

Rolling his stogie contemplatively in stout fingers, he said, "In the meantime, sonny, I should think you'd concern yourself about that mine stock under your wife's thumb." Gabe tabled the unlit cigar and used a finger to explore his ear. "That woman of yours may or may not honor your debt to me. In the main, I have not found one solitary female reliable in these matters." Again he held up a hand to forestall argument. "Yes indeedy, it'd be best to have that stock in your keeping. But you must manage any such affair with delicacy. This camp is crawling with newsmen. From Frisco, from Chicago, from Cleveland. At the first sign of hanky-panky, they'll light on you like a thousand of brick."

Thinking of the news rabble, Andy sputtered, "There's not an empty bed in this town." He was as indignant as if they'd invaded his private rooms. "Say Old Lady Robinson is sleeping four to a mattress—and doubling her prices tomorrow."

At length Gabe lit a match to his cigar, leaned back, and blew three perfect smoke rings. When he did, Harry's shoulder became a jumping toad. To his mortification, it was nothing more than smoke had driven him from saloons and men's clubs. He blew his nose in his dirty rag, then furtively wiped his weeping eyes.

"Little Aspen, the silver queen of the hills, has lost her head," said Gabe, not wholly displeased. He had brought in greasers from Santa Fe to throw up four new flophouses, to be finished in a jiffy. He planned to charge four dollars a night, not including board. Gabe shunned no opportunity, however modest, to turn a dollar.

"Anything further to report, boys?"

Andy Black assumed his pious look. "Your wife, Sutton, will shortly be serving you with a bill of divorcement."

At this, Garrett was truly taken aback. "Good riddance!" he managed to sputter, though he was shocked that Emma had had the gall to go so far. "I planned to serve her myself."

"The papers, as filed by Davis, Daniels & Kershaw this past Thursday forenoon, claim you have abused her person, mishandled her finances—and demolished her property." Harry Dunbar's mustache quivered over prim lips.

Gabe eyed Garrett mockingly. "I don't reckon we dare hope for a reconciliation?"

Garrett opened, then closed his mouth, his face as sour as a man sucking lemons.

"Her grounds are 'harsh and unmannerly treatment'," continued Harry. "However, there is a downside to the hill. It will require time to examine the charges and process the papers. You'll remain her legal custodian until sometime in the fall."

Gabe said, "Perk up, sonny. With Percy eating from the apex trough, we'll outflank your missus in the halls of justice."

"I am ticketed on tomorrow's stage," he said. "In the meantime, I wanted you to be apprised of your situation, not sit around diddling yourself until I can get back to this front." Again he pulled on his cheroot. "Whatever it is you're up to, mind you be clever about it. There's no use to a man who ain't clever."

Bull Mudgett, Denver Bob Bisbee, Fess Felcher, and Shoat Yankel pulled by turns on a jug of mash at the bottom of the yard. Bob and Shoat threw knives at a stake in a game of goat-peg. Bull paced, his nerves still on the raw edge over the hotel or bungling. The Leadville man had run off leaving a dead pard behind. He didn't expect to hear from the muddle-headed fool again. But there was still no word of a body. The conundrum gave Bull the spooks, though he'd bet his bottom dollar that Burdine had something to do with the disappearance.

Every now and then Fess and Shoat glanced enviously at the big house. They had never once been invited inside. Sutton wouldn't hear of asking the likes of them to set foot amid his fancy furnishings. Restless as chained dogs, they alternated between gloating and discontent.

"How come we ain't seen any mule trains trottin' by?" crowed Shoat, a sly grin on his twisted face.

"Listen right smart. That there's mule retchin' you hear in the distance," smirked Fess, his little eyes darting. Fess had been laughed at his whole life, and it had turned him spiteful.

"Hate to think of a mule-size bellyache," said Denver Bob. "Them brutes must be as thinned down as that stork Needle Newsome."

"Say Burdine has got the most of them back on their feet—and under tight watch," said Shoat.

Bull's eyes narrowed. There'd be no more face-to-face encounters with Burdine. He planned to bushwhack the crafty son-of-a-bitch from the rear.

"Never did like worming a horse," said Fess. "Mules is worse."

Shoat hurled his knife so hard it yanked his wry neck. He still talked with his head cocked to one side. Tite Pomeroy had caught him whiskey-softened on the steps of the Chloride Saloon, had whipped him 'til his neck was as twisted as a Pennsylvania pretzel. He'd vowed to sink a knife in the rancher before summer was out. Fess didn't care to see it. Shoat was a violent man.

"A shame only one or two mules died on him. If more had checked out, we could leave these parts for a warmer winter." Denver Bob combed his hair and looked himself over in a jagged piece of glass propped above the stable wash basin.

"Bob, you can comb 'til your hair falls out. That Tacy Beard ain't ever gonna have you comin' around," Shoat said sourly.

"Who says?"

"Even with your pretty face, you don't stand a Chinaman's chance," Bull agreed. "Her pap's in the Pearly camp. You keep the wrong company. And you ain't that persuasive."

"Don't see you persuading that peppery Swede to your way of thinking, neither," muttered Bob in an injured tone.

Mudgett's eyes grew dark as an animal's. His mouth and mustaches twitched, his jaw tightened.

"Them Swedes is sure good-lookers," said Fess, thinking of his own scrawny wife.

"No damn Swede is the right size for my taste," said Shoat. "Got tits big as pork barrels. As soon whup a man as pleasure him." The truth was that Shoat didn't care about women. He'd never been known to pester one.

Bull wore his dangerous look—meaner than a tomcat on the stalk. "I got my ways with a square-headed cunt too big fer her britches," he said. "She's bucked me twice. She'll be sorry more'n two times, she will."

#####

CHAPTER TWENTY-FIVE

ORE TRAIN

The last down-valley drovers had pulled in late afternoon by sundown on Sunday. They'd grouped their high-sided freight wagons at the west end of Cooper Street, camp-firing, yarning, and bedding down as night moved in. A Cattle Creek drover named Elroy Mimser and his swamper son Tubby, hired by Deke to direct the out-of-town freighters, beat a theatric troupe all hollow. On the tight corner at Cooper and Third, their lead horses raced past what seemed an impossible point before wheeling into the turn, the swing team following at a slower lope, the wheelers at a measured trot in a narrowing arch. Mimser, his face intent, whistled a dozen directives, then hit his foot brake at the required instant. The wagon slammed to a dead stop, swaying mightily on its thorough-braces, the animals in perfect alignment. Stump Clancy's mouth had hung open in astonishment. Lute exhaled in admiration. He'd have sworn the whole shebang would crash headlong into the Hallelujah Mine supply building.

In the dim quarter-light, the following morning was as charged as a circus before the opening trumpets. "She's a sight to see," marveled Stump Clancy, who'd cut for bed early so he could rise in the Monday dark to wave off the ore train. The clangor was enough to drown the shrieks of a woman in distress. Handsaws buzzed, drovers shouted, hammers pounded, and axes thunked. Men whistled, horses whinnied and plunged, and mules brayed, shivered their skins, and switched their tails, shaking off flies. Riders tore to and fro prodding pack animals into line. Teamsters' curses blistered the air. Guards and meat hunters stood calmly tying rolled canvas coats into saddle latigos, coats they'd need against the cutting night cold on the hump. Throngs of Aspenites, unable to sleep, had turned out for the spectacle.

So many clouds of steam rose from piles of fresh manure that Nate remarked, "We're throwin' up enough steam to power a Whitcomb locomotive."

"Don't you wish." Willard's fervent desire was that Calvin's silver strike might finally draw the railroads their way. With profit to it, J. P. Hill or

Senator Moffitt would surely conjure up a rail-line to these mountainous parts.

Zedediah Johns, the town's most enterprising waterman, pulled his heavy barrel of spring water up and down the line behind a spavined old bullock left from a bygone westering. Though he'd found a number of parched customers willing to fork over a thin dime to swallow deep of cool water from the tin dipper hanging on his barrel, Willard was not among them. "Dammit, Zed, I won't tolerate highway robbery for water that's the Lord's gift to us all."

"I ain't peddlin' water," sniffed Zed. "I'm peddlin' convenience. You're more than welcome to stroll on up to the Ute spring and help yourself, Arey."

Calvin sipped a dipper of water and looked around with pride. "D.K. has put together some kind of outfit," he said, removing his hat to let the early breeze riffle his hair.

"Looks makeshift to me," grumbled Willard, his mouth so dry he couldn't spit.

"Willard, a big silver shipment is an affair for hard men and sharpshooters. Would you have them uniformed like British dragoons?"

"Huuuuumph. Children and Injuns. Cripples and wore-out old meat hunters."

"The finest riders and shots in this man's valley," said Nate, checking the cinch on a big red mule named Hazel. "Ellsworth ain't pretty, and he ain't young, but he's a dead sure shot. And that Ute boy can smell trouble like it was skunk juice. As for me, I may be slowed, but I am not wore to the nubbin."

Willard scowled at the prospector. "Well, there's *some* that looks like they're attending a damned social." Nate, as usual, played his own tune. He was decked out in his new suit of clothes, a starched shirt, a Piccadilly collar, and a modish beaver hat. Only his feet remained Indian. He ignored his friend, who'd grown crankier by the day. Nate liked feeling stylish now and again and considered this a full-dress occasion.

The bench boys, unwilling to miss the equivalent of a carnival leaving town, squatted beside a dying cookfire, their thick miners' and drovers' fingers with split nails and horny yellow callus so armored they held tin cups of steaming coffee that would have blistered ordinary hands. They braced the coffee with bust-head and downed it sucking in gaunt cheeks over sinking gums, at the same time reminding anyone who would listen of their own last cattle drives, of meaner horse thieves, more slippery Indians than any this outfit would ever see. They finally focused on Lute Kellogg. The youngster was respectful and didn't pass remarks about old coots full of hot air.

"I' God, Luther, that ore wagon's a load for a young feller. Must hold seven thousand pounds," said Rheumanalor Wilson.

"'Bout that," said Lute, trying not to puff up like a toad.

"Who's riding the seat with you?"

"Scooper Hurd, when he ever gets here."

"The hell! Ain't neither of you past sixteen."

"Huh!" snapped Henry Gant, "I mind when I drove ten mules pulling fifty thousand pounds on the Virginia City road. Just turned fifteen and weighed less than a medium-size stump."

"Most of it shit," snorted Spanish Joe.

"Age don't matter. It's knowing how to hoodoo a mule. Our boy Luther has the touch." Nale Wilson's tone was admiring. Lute beamed. Most mule drivers cussed out their animals' lights and livers, reaching for ever lower levels of profanity. Lute took another tack. He'd braked his team and helped Skinner settle a string behind him, walking the line, talking in silky "eeee-ha's," and "ooooh boys," stroking and nuzzling the brutes like restless babes. It was no light matter, softening up a hardheaded mule. It gave him a warm feeling to know his work was noticed.

"Train's gotten considerably bigger than you planned," said Calvin to Deke. "How long do you figure before you make first camp?"

"With bottlenecks and the uphill pull, we'll do well to get to that open pasturage on Lost Man, the other side of the grottos."

"If we hit the grottos late, the evening floods will be on us," said Nate. He and Jake were to act as trouble-shooters up and down the line—gandy dancers, they called them on the railroads.

"Notice all them tolls we pay don't cover no bridge over the Grottos," grumped Willard.

"Toll men prefer the easy crossings."

"We'll manage if she don't rain and mud up on us."

"Some of Ellsworth's boys packed timber for emergency bridging."

Apostle Thatcher, standing with the Pearly honchos, raised a hand in benediction, his voice sonorous. "All Aspen wishes you well, Major. Be of good courage."

"We'll do it, Thatcher."

Calvin reached to clasp Deke's hand. "May the good Lord keep you safe."

"H'it's the skulkin' of that peckerhead Sutton worries me," said Willard.

"He won't skulk within reach. Injun Ike can spot a man through a thick stand of timber like it was thin newsprint," Deke said reassuringly. His own look was stern as he turned to Calvin. "It would be more his style to break down the back door while I'm guarding the front. Keep a close watch on your mine, old hoss."

"We'll keep her double-locked and bolted." Calvin handed him a package of molasses cookies, his favorites. "Lavinia wishes you godspeed."

Deke tucked the cookies in his saddle bag, tipped a finger to his old cavalry hat, rose in his stirrups, waved the hat high in the air, and rode out toward Independence Pass. Cal saw him off wondering wistfully when they'd ever talk Tennyson again.

"This outfit looks like a dern minstrel show." Jake had trotted up to join Deke. "Never saw so many red shirts off a Monday washline."

Deke peered back at the procession. Red flannel shirts were common as tunnel coughs among miners, but this day it did seem even the freighters had broken out in a blaze of bright color. Even the animals appeared caparisoned. Skinner had laced red yarn as warnings in the tails and manes of his biters and kickers. Many a mule had kicked a cougar to death—and half-killed more than a few men. The precautionary ribbons, along with the shirts, gave the train a kind of dash. It looked to be flying regimental flags and guidons.

Standing on the small bluff above the Roaring Fork at the edge of camp, Emma too sent them prayers, resisting the urge to blow a kiss. Under her breath she whispered, "May the Lord watch over thee and me while we are absent one from the other." Her blackened eye and yellowing cheek bruises hidden behind a sturdy lodgepole pine, she yearned to run off the bluff down to the caravan and boldly embrace its leader in an unseemly display of affection. Though it made her heart hurt, she had insisted to Deke they not meet again—not until she was lawfully parted from Garrett. Her conscience had more watchdogs than she'd dreamed: the miners and prospectors who'd admired her as a girl, her Uncle Nate, that stern Scot Aggie McClaren, her father's observant eyes above, Polly's disapproving looks below. As for her own sense of right, it might be weak, but it had wobbled to its feet. She would not get off to the same unheedful, headstrong start with a fine man she admired as she had with the villain she'd married.

Despite her caution, she'd been seen. Deke raised his hat, placed it over his breast and bowed her way. Then he rode on, though he too longed to spin around and bolt up the bluff to her side.

"A fine horse and a handsome girl to speed you off to the wars," sighed Jake a little enviously. By now everyone suspected the major and Mrs. Sutton fancied each other. Jake himself felt nothing like an object of romance—nor of adventure over the hump. Grave and newly bespectacled, his shaggy black hair salted with grey, looking more professorial than combative, he rode the

Levy family gelding, a fat, amiable animal named Heinz.

"Work some of the grease off him," Bertha had said as she patted Heinz, then her husband, then the horse, who was a family pet. "He's eating us out of house and barn." Jake had smiled fondly and leaned over to hug his wife, almost as plump as Heinz.

Iacono, his blanket roll lean over his shoulder, rode silently by Deke's side, obsidian eyes everywhere. Over the past week the Ute boy had been one of those riding the trail from end to end, knew every boulder, every marker down to the last bent twig, knew it better than Deke himself. He too wore a new red flannel shirt, and over his braids a high-crowned black hat with no crease. He used no saddle, only a hide apishamore, his body one with his pony's. Though Deke had tactfully suggested he look as "white" as possible for the job, there was no escaping his aura of woodsmoke and wild creatures' dens. *A shame he can't daub on a mess of war paint,* Deke thought with amusement. Then again, it would never do to have him startle a trigger-happy drover and get laced with buckshot.

"Ike, take the point. Stay a good two miles ahead. If landmarks have been moved, if you see a suspicious change, ride back here like blazes."

With a wailing hawk's cry, the boy was off up the trail, eyes scanning the mighty lift of the Sawatch before him.

High on an escarpment, from a hidey-hole in a stand of Engelmann spruce, Bull and Denver Bob blearily watched the train wind its way below. After a long night's work, most of their bunch had headed for home. Shoat and Fess were on up the trail.

"Wasn't no need for us to rush the job," sniffed Bob. "That outfit is slower'n molasses in January."

Bull took out a nickel-plated watch and squinted in the shadows. "They might look to be moseying, but they're ahead of schedule."

Bob peered through the tang sight on his rifle. "I'd like to give the major a shot in his other eye. But for him, they'd be readin' sermons over that wildcat."

Though Bull too took in the major with loathing, he said evenly, "Don't get your dander up, Bob. And put the goddam gun away. That major is mine—when I get around to him." He turned his horse's head. Bob, with a last, sour, downward glance, followed.

The train moved east up the gradual incline along the valley floor. Soon the sun would be full in their faces, reflecting off granite walls and boulders studded with glinting quartz and mica. Even in the dawning, the mountains ahead appeared ominous. Unlike the softer maroon and peach tinted sandstone of the Elk Range to their rear, these Sawatches rose gray and black, their granite faces sharp-edged as scimitars. With hundreds of cuts and cliffs and intervening rises, the summits were far from view, although every man knew the way ahead loomed amid tangled deadfall, razor-sharp rockslide, roaring water, cruel ruts, and slashing ravines, rising up and up until it crossed over the chiseled backbone of America at the Continental Divide—the Hump. Nightmare ground for guarding a cumbersome, vulnerable ore train.

Here on the Stillwater stretch, where the Roaring Fork had no roar and beaver dams dotted the gentle, meandering stream course, their only blight was mosquitoes. Marshy reaches of willow and mountain mahogany harbored thick swarms of insects until the first hard frost, and the men slapped oil seep on faces and hands as they rode. Lute was so smudge-smeared that he looked like a minstrel in blackface. Only Jake, in his delight over the swooping and whistling of bluebirds and tanagers through the meadows, was oblivious to gnats and skeeters.

A third of the way back in the train, Nate bellowed his singular tuneless version of "Follow! Follow the gleammmmmmm." Every burro within earshot flipped its ears agitatedly, although not an animal slowed its pace or balked. "Mebbe Nate'll swallow a mouthful of bugs," said Shotgun hopefully.

Olvera, riding the chuckwagon seat, screwed up his face in scorn. "Is no musica," he growled. "Is donkey noise."

Nate ignored the rude commentary. Hazel, the stiff-gaited red mule, jarred his knees something fierce. Singing eased the ache. Soon he'd dismount and move on shank's mare—he still walked smarter than most animals could pull or carry.

At the rear of a cluster of ore wagons, Scooper and Lute rode the load pulled by Gracious and harness-mates. Lute handled three sets of lines, Scoop the fourth. When the major rode up to assess their rig, Lute assured him, "Don't you worry about the team of Kellogg and Hurd, sir. We can do her one-handed." Over the summer, the boy had put on man-size muscle and heft, and Deke surveyed him with pleasure. Even Scooper had added a little gristle and looked less like a wet water rat.

Ellsworth's boys were deployed the length of the train, some running jacks, all riding shotgun. Nate's Needle gun was at the ready in case of trouble at either end.

####

CHAPTER TWENTY-SIX

INDEPENDENCE PASS

W hat in blazes have you got on your face?" called Deke, interrupting Nate's tuneless rendition of "Old Dan Tucker."

"Sun spectacles. Bought 'em off Bill Jackson over in Sawpit. Saved him going snowblind last winter."

"We're hardly expecting snow this trip."

"Well, you can't never count on weather. 'Sides, these specs are handy for cutting glare, summer or winter. Have a look."

Deke rode up and tried the goggles, and though everything turned a kind of daguerreotype brown, he had to admit that, after the first surprise, they were easy on the eyes. Nate's thoughts lingered on Bill Jackson, roving these mountains with his mule Gimlet, piled high with glass plates. William Henry Jackson had got his picture-making start in Matthew Brady's Washington studios during the late civil unrest. He was now bent on recording the West before it got wholly tamed. He'd demonstrated for Nate the way of flashing a bulb, exposing chemical-coated glass plates, then bringing up the picture inside his dark little tent. Now and again he dropped and smashed a precious plate. "Had me another siege of mountain fever, hands aren't steady yet," he explained. "Can't find anyone eager to assist me in this operation."

"Had Indian trouble of late?"

"Nope. Arapaho or Apache, Kiowa or Cheyenne, they'd rather have their picture taken than bugger a yellow-haired white girl. Except for the Utes. Had those chiefs lined up half-a-dozen times—and dadblame it, the heat lightning and blue thunder struck every time. Now they think I'm a shaman—heap bad medicine. When I show up for a picture, they turn their backs—or raise their umbrellas." Jackson had scratched his head. "If you were ever to turn Injun again, Phipps, I could surely use your help with those hard-headed Uncompahgres." Though Nate briefly considered the proposition, he doubted he'd have the patience to sit the day until the light came around right. Not only wasn't he cut out for hunkering down and waiting, he expected he'd strew the mountains with broken glass.

In Stillwater and Difficult Creek country, Deke cautioned the younger, greener drovers and guards that, even with the low morning run-off, some animals would balk at crossing. "Push, pull, whistle, whatever it takes to keep moving. Jake, Ellsworth, Nate, and I will be there to lend a hand."

Jake drew ahead so he could fish in his pockets for toll at the first of many crude bridges. Willard, dispersing two-bit pieces for every mounted man, one dollar for every wagon, ten cents per pack animal at each bridge, had howled at the larceny. "Fifteen toll bridges, and all them toll-takers done was fell a tree or lay down a few planks!"

"Do you want us to fight every bridge man up the pass, or what?" Nate had asked. "Let's see here…that could amount to a dozen or more skirmishes, every dispute holding us up a good quarter-hour." He had pulled a pencil stub from his pocket. "H'it could delay us, times fifteen, now let me figure this on paper."

"One thing about you, Nathaniel," Willard had snapped, "when you have said all there is to say on a subject, you can always find a few additional words."

Occasional animals crow-hopped or reared, and there were scattered cases of jitters as the young Cattle Creek and Springs hands, accustomed to flatlands, maneuvered the first narrow, makeshift bridges with rushing water to all sides and towering cliffs at their backs. Yet the train made the initial fordings in jig time. When one of Shotgun's younger recruits jumped from his horse to cross a log upstream, then slipped and went under headfirst, his heavy haversack dragging him down in rough water, Jake trotted up, fished again, and pulled the sputtering boy from a tangle of alders. The train then began an ever-steepening climb where the passage grew tight and walls of granite and conifers began to close in.

Traffic was blessedly light. "That notice we put in *The Chronicle* must have done the trick," observed Nate. *The Leadville Chronicle* piece had read: "LARGE, HEAVILY ARMED PACK TRAIN CROSSING THE DIVIDE MONDAY THROUGH WEDNESDAY NEXT. KINDLY DEFER ANY BUT URGENT FORWARDING."

Deke squinted into the sun-glare, scanning the cliff-sides. Men afoot or horseback coming the other way, forewarned by Ike and other point men, awaited the train's passing in small out-thrusts. Only two groups pulling freight wagons had refused to heed the scouts. One old swamper, at sight of Iacono bearing down on him, had drawn a bead and fired off a shot. The bullet glanced off walls of rock, sending shock waves through the train. Ike

215

pounded back to the major to report. "Man think me *nagoto tawats,* big war chief," he grinned. "Bad shot. I win."

When the oncoming wagoneers got a good look at the giant train and gun-toting outriders, they swore and backed awkwardly downhill to the nearest pull-off, muttering about the stink of Indians and meat-hunters. Late in the morning, the four-horse Carson Stage waited by the Curtis Way Station, passengers assembled beside it.

"I God, boys, it's a good thing you're big as advertised," roared the wall-eyed driver, who glared at the mountain with one eye, the other on Deke. "This here stage is a half-hour behind schedule."

"We thank you, sir, for your consideration," called Deke.

"Don't thank me, buster. These passengers of mine don't care to be tromped flat. Oughter charge you with delayin' traffic," the driver answered sourly.

As the climb grew steeper, the burros plodded along at an even pace. Horses and mules paused more frequently to blow, flanks heaving, loudly passing gas. Deke chastised a drover he caught frantically laying on a whip. "There'll be no more of that! These animals are doing the best they know how," he said with one of his hard looks.

They hit heavy timber, and the dark and pungent smell of spruce and lodgepole was cooling after the scorch of the sun. Scooper shuddered. "Feels blacker'n a grave."

"The animals sure like the shady. Look at old Gracious step out."

"Me, I like wide-open spaces," shivered Scoop. "Don't care none how hot the sun burns. Black timber always give me the spooks. Even without bushwhackers around." He peered apprehensively at jagged rock rising into the sky. "Looky up there. Prospect holes on them flanks I wouldn't think a mountain goat could get to."

"Beats all," said Lute, "how men will climb like critters with hooves to get to silver."

"Don't seem called for, not when Mr. Phipps located his strike right handy to Mill Street." He leaned out from the seat to spit. "Don't know why any man would take it in his head to prospect anyway. Too damn lonesome. A season or two up here, and I'd pine away."

"A body can be lonesome even with a crowd around," said Lute. "I was lonesome for plenty of years."

"You're pulling my leg!"

"I ain't—I'm not." Lute whistled to the brindle mule on the left lead. "Step out there, Seneca! After Ma died in Leadville, I had no one to do for me. If the line girls hadn't taken me in, I'd have been put in the orphan home down in Denver."

Lute rummaged in his mind a minute. "The whores did their best. Not a one ever lifted a hand to me. But I wasn't theirs, and I didn't belong. In school, I was the bummer lamb. Boy named Biggy Weller pushed the others to beat on me any time the schoolmaster was nursing himself over a spell of bottle fever."

"Hell, Lute, I never suspicioned. I had my ups and downs with Pap and his drink. But I expect it was some better than bein' a orphan."

"That's how come Frankie and I were friends. Neither of us had family." Lute's face grew strained.

Scoop cleared his throat, hoping Lute wouldn't choke up on him again. "I been back to see Jamestown Jess. She's cork-pullin' with these drovers. Meaner than a cross bear, but she ain't dumb, and she don't forget—not a thing that's comin' to her."

"She's certain Frankie had that chunk of Pearly stock from Mr. Klausmeyer?"

"Swore that's what Frankie told her. Jess got her dress back, water-soaked and shrunk up. But no Pearly paper."

A summer-fat whistle pig scuttled across the trail, sending the team into a lively dance. Lute was firm on the reins, steadying the animals by name. When they'd resumed their pull, Scoop said, "What I ain't had a chance to tell you…" His little black currant eyes gleamed. "Had me a talk with Old Lady Klausmeyer. I waited for her to come out of Beck & Bishop's, offered to tote her groceries.

"'Why Scooper Hurd,' says she, 'whatever is the world coming to?'" He mimicked the woman's fluty voice.

Lute grinned at the vision of Mrs. Klausmeyer's perplexity.

"Told her we learned more than just geography at our school. We learned about 'do onto others.'"

"She believed that?"

"She thought on it. But she thought on that grocery basket more. Heavy as pig iron."

"We talked some, and I worked up to the Pearly strike and how it's taken over this camp. How half the town is gettin' rich."

"'Don't make no never mind to me,' she says. 'The Klausmeyers aren't mine stockholders. We're honest working people.'"

"If working is what she wants to call lugging a few groceries and belly-aching."

"That Herman ain't overworked, neither. Spendin' money in the saloons and cribs like it was free snowfall. Jess says he's went to her four times in two weeks—his pizzle and a world of cash bustin' out of his pants."

"We've got to have more than this to go on, Scoop." Lute leaned over to check his wagon's left front wheel. "Folks have bought and sold and traded so much Pearly stock it's like trying to track down the head of a crick with eighteen branches."

"Don't forget the pig-sticker. The son of a bitch is skilled with a sticker. I ain't sure we ought to bait him."

"Don't you worry, Scoop. I'm beholden for your help, but I won't have you riskin' your neck over something that's my lookout."

"Shucks, Lute, that's what friends are for. We *are* still friends, ain't we?"

"Course we are. Why would you ever ask?"

"I been a little put out lately, the way you spend so much time with that Injun Ike."

"Now why would you be put out by Ike?" Lute was incredulous. "In the first place, he'll soon be back on the reservation. In the second place, I'm getting the hang of that Ute palaver."

"But Tubby Mimser was robbed bare by Utes up on the flattops. Them Indians is all light-fingered."

"They ain't—aren't—neither. Ike would sooner starve than help himself to a thing didn't belong to him. Shame on you, Scoop."

"Now don't fly off the handle. If you say Ike's a honest Injun, I warrant he is."

"You're the best friend I've ever had, always will be. But I went without friends so long that now I can hardly get my fill. You know what Mrs. Lavinia says, 'He who has found a friend has found treasure.'"

The climb steepened and the boys deepened their concentration, contrite that they'd been chattering, their guard lowered. In this section, the stumps were so high that Lute swore the trees had been cut when the snow was seven feet deep. Jack strings rippled around the stumps like water pouring around rocks in a stream. But Lute had to back and cut, gee and haw, to get his big team and load through. Men and animals panted upward through stark white stands of aspen, shivered in the dank chill of black timber and, emerged onto hillsides of scrub oak to again pour sweat in the searing, close-hanging sun. At last, to everyone's naked relief, it was time for nooning.

Deke called a halt beyond Deane's Camp in a broad, open meadow nodding with thousands of luxuriant, nodding clumps of velvety blue and cream columbine. Lute braked the wagon, tied his team's reins, and hurried to lend a hand to the farrier, a businesslike Augsberger named Miles Gephardt. Five or six mules had already thrown shoes. The smith was a sequoia stump of a man, but mules have a hard lean and Lute eased some of the load from Miles's back. Cleaning a left front hoof with a wire brush, he said, around a mouthful of nails, "I thank you kindly, son." Using a curved hoof knife, he trimmed the frog down to the white. "I've shoed this Junus mule before, on a trip to the Butte. Junus would as soon fall on a man as look at him." Miles clipped a rough spot on the hoof and smoothed it with a rasp. "Don't think much of cold shoeing, but we'll replace these ringers tonight when we have us a hot fire."

Outriders loosed their mounts' cinches a hair, hobbled the more undependable ones, and let the animals graze. Olvera kindled a quick fire and put on a pot of leftover breakfast coffee. "It's only lukewarm. Some better than slap cold," he said to men lined up with out-stretched cups.

Camp robbers, the plump, dove-colored Canadian jays swooped down and alighted boldly for scraps. A bounty of redwing blackbirds, their sooty bodies shimmering with silver highlights in the sun, reminded Lute of this red-shirted ore outfit. Nate had removed his dress jacket and loosened his Piccadilly collar and pushed the outsized sun specs up on his head. As he hobbled one of the more fractious mules, he remarked to Shotgun, "Some of the boys say there's gold up that Lincoln Gulch Trail."

"Christ, Nate, they been rumorin' gold up every damn gulch since we first climbed the hump."

"You're right. Look at Conundrum. Musta been two hundred panners found gold drift up that crick. Never any mother lode."

"She's a conundrum all righty."

Nate looked pensive. "Gold recovery is mean work. Tried my hand over in Oro City. Figured leastways the job was above ground. But a man operates sluice boxes in water so cold it turns his legs blue." He dismissed Hazel with a friendly smack on the rump. "Gold panning is as confounded inconvenient as silver mining."

The two men sat eating Nate's lunch of bacon and baking powder biscuits. Ellsworth lifted his gun, raised the hindsight, and took aim at a distant outcrop.

"Save your ammunition, friend. Listen to this here." Nate hurled half a biscuit down a deep ravine falling off the edge of the meadow. There was a crack like a pistol shot. He smiled. "I once sailed a biscuit at a mountain quail, a bird dumber than a fool hen. Cut off his head slick as lard. That biscuit flew on down the mountain and struck like rimfire. Made my first strike there on that outcrop."

"Baking powder's near as powerful as blasting powder," he went on. "Every now and then Harry Bishop gets him a batch with near four hundred pounds of pressure to a square inch. Have to sleep with your boots on and be ready to jump."

Far up the pass, in the gloom of a stand of needled trees on a cutbank above the Little Narrows, Fess Felcher, at the sharp report of the biscuit, pulled up short drawing his sidearm.

"No one's shootin' at us, damn jackass," snarled Shoat irritably.

Fess decided that Shoat boiled up quicker than any man he ever knew. "You unlimbered your gun fast as me," he muttered mutinously under his breath.

"That shot was way down-valley. They won't reach us 'til late afternoon."

"Seems like this was too easy," said Fess uneasily, eyeing the big rocks the gang had piled at the lip of an overhang.

"Give me a hand with this here boulder, Junior. A few more of these, and we'll be all set fer 'em."

The brief lull of the train's nooning was interrupted by pounding hooves. Ike pulled into camp. With the fluid motion of an otter, he was off his pony in front of the major. "Trail at...L'il Nar-rows...this side...Weller Lake..."

"I know the place. The spot where the trace moves up the cliff-side to skirt the floods through that deep cut."

"That place." Ike's look was piercing. "Trail cut...away...underside...no can see..." He struggled to locate the right words. "Cover in brush...h'it'll...cave...first heavy load."

"Well now," said Deke thoughtfully, "I thought to have dealings with the foe later in the day. Maybe at the grottos. If he's done us dirt at the narrows, he may be somewhere nearby. Any sign?"

"Me smell."

"Beans and onions?"

"No, boss...Utes say...Mean white man...smell like—weasel."

####

CHAPTER TWENTY-SEVEN

THE HUMP

Deke explained the undermining to his men. "Dead center in the Little Narrows. Mudgett's men no doubt cut down from the top, went at their work through the night…Ellsworth, I don't guess you've hunted that particular steep."

Shotgun glowered. "Ain't fit for bald eagles up there."

"Well, spread your wings, old man. Find those birds and scatter them."

"If they're roostin,' I'll find 'em," declared Shotgun around his plug. Motioning for two of his shooters, he spat contemptuously and rode straight at the heights.

Deke and Nate directed all available hands to chivvy timber-and-rope-toting burros around the train and up the hump behind Ike. Deke paused for a quick check of his gun loads as animals clattered over rocks and stumps, hauling lengths of iron bar and plank lumber lashed to wood pack saddles.

"You go on ahead, D.K. I'll move this train along," Jake said.

When Deke poked where Ike directed, there was a slow crumbling, followed by a rapid rush, as rock and dirt collapsed in waves down the mountainside. What had looked to be solid ground evaporated into nothingness.

"Good job, son. I might not have spotted it, I guess." Deke's voice was steely, though he was boiling inside. The break was on a treacherous drop-off, a mean place for repairs.

Under the major's direction, every man not standing guard set to work. Some heaved boulders. Axes felled trees for a meshwork of timber tight enough to hold thousands of pounds of freight. Nate and Jake led a crew cross-hatching logs. Ike, tied in heavy rope, was belayed off the side of the cliff to prop stiff planks and iron against the weaker underpinnings. Alternating on a big axe with Scooper, Lute puffed, "Cut some timber last summer. This lodgepole's a…schoolmarm."

"Say that again?"

"Schoolmarm…has two forks…" The rhythm of the axe did not break as

221

Lute talked. "Over there…Tubby Mimser's tree…that's a professor…three forks." Scoop took his turn swinging, his mind puzzling over schoolmarms and professors.

Deke was everywhere, bare-chested, heaving rock and timber, directing the addition of a tree trunk here, a network of limbs there. He glanced often at the looming cliffs, though the riflemen were scanning so hard they did not blink.

From their vantage point far overhead, using a monocular, Fess groused, "Thet damn Injun caught us out."

"I'm gonna snare that fat brownbelly and cook his guts," snarled Shoat. "Weren't fer that black bastard, the train'd be hauling mebbe four wagons and eight dead outa that cut." He'd turned purple with rage. Fess had known older men came out of the rebellion with their dispositions frayed. But Shoat—Shoat had come out of his ma's belly with a ragged temper. Fess owned a long list of things he never dared mention around the man, including the name of Tite Pomeroy, the rancher who'd bent up Shoat's neck. Fess felt spooked. "That Injun is worse'n a ha'nt—can't never see where he's coming from."

"One of these days I'm gonna take me a scalp. Has a good two and a half feet of hair on him."

"Ain't nobody buyin' scalps nowadays, Shoat."

"I ain't sellin'. I'm agonna wear it." The notion brought a grim, unpleasant smile to the scarred face.

Repair work at the narrows took the better part of two hours. Scooper, swinging an axe on an overhang, lost his footing and tumbled onto a narrow ledge of shelf rock. He was retrieved when Ike swung on his belay rope, caught his arm, and hoisted him to safety. A felled tree bounced and caught a swamper on the leg. The snap of breaking bone echoed down the ravine like the snap of a brittle twig. Nate lowered the man from his horse and sliced off the pant leg with a skinning knife. "H'it's a good thing she didn't break the skin," he said as he splinted the break. "That leg of yours is none too clean, boy." Nate held with Doc's ideas about the efficacy of hot water and strong soap.

In mid-afternoon, as the sun had begun its descent in the western sky, with the trail set for testing, the sky darkened, lightning crackled and thunder boomed up the canyon. The train was now stalled between a tumult of water below, sheer rock rising above, and rain pouring down needle-sharp. No one bothered scrambling for oilskins. Drenched to the skin in seconds, they sat like ducks in a carney gallery, water sluicing off hat brims as if they were rain spouts.

"Geezus," wailed a swamper, "we're exposed top, bottom and all four sides. Hope this war crowd ain't settin' over us with a Gatling gun."

Though Deke finally pronounced the trail passable, he clung to a tough old scrub oak on the cliff-bank below, eyeing every trickle of gravel, slip of a mule's foot and dip of a wagon wheel as the progression eased tentatively overhead. Rain and runoff gushed atop him before pouring on into the defile.

The torturous passage sobered everyone. Nate's exultant feeling of the morning was as damped down as his clothes. There was silence except for the rain, the snorting and clopping of animals, the creak and squawk of wagons, and the intermittent rolls of thunder.

A shot, followed by two more, broke the hush. In seconds, one of Shotgun's boys swept down the steep pitch from above. At Lute's wagon, his horse veered off to one side, while the rider leaped from the saddle and across the seat, sweeping Lute and Scoop to the wet ground. The three crouched behind the wheels while rocks in the rider's wake ricocheted off canyon walls, struck trees, bounced to the water below. Because the train hugged the cliff close, most flew harmlessly overhead, in the main missing wagons, men, and animals. One outsized boulder struck directly over Deke's head, flew high, and went on into the ravine. A lone mule was crushed in the barrage. In the distance, shots still reverberated.

"Jake! Jake, answer me!" In a terrible fright, Nate shook his friend's shoulders. Jake lay crumpled on the soggy trail, his spectacles hanging from one ear, Heinz sprawled across his legs. Nate shook him harder, a desperate look on his face. Jake groaned, then opened an eye to squint into the rain. "If you'll maybe get this fat horse…off me…I will rise like Lazarus, amazing one and all."

Nate was so relieved he nearly wept. Deke, helping to hoist Heinz, turned to the horse's owner. "Jake," he said reluctantly, "Heinz took the blow. I'm afraid he's gone."

"Tarnation!" gasped Jake as many hands lifted the dead horse from his pinned legs. He peered half-blind through wet specs and stroked the horse's head. Sorrowfully, he said, "The boys and Bertha set a deal of store in this animal. Mothered him like an old dog."

"Reckon they'd prefer you home safe over the horse," said Nate.

Jake turned away, his eyes wet with rain and tears, as Heinz was rolled off the side after the dead mule.

Shotgun's young man stood waiting for Deke, water streaming off his hat. "Two men," he reported laconically. "Rocks piled high on the edge, levers under 'em. Caught 'em setting off the first barrage. Took off down here. Shotgun give em a load of lead in the gun arms, let 'em scoot. Said you wanted no killing." The boy's expression was disapproving.

"I'll just bet they scooted," said Nate.

The narrows trap safely bypassed, the train started a series of hairpin turns and ess curves leading to the grottos, deep pools surrounded by house-size boulders where the east fork of the Frying Pan cut loose at its wildest. The place was one more bottleneck where the cliff-sides rose high and the water roared—two small boys and a woman with a baby on her back had drowned here not a month past. The day was dying off, the water would be high. In the downpour's wake, a slow drizzle fogged the sky. There'd be no sunset this night.

Arrived at the pools, mules and jacks hunched, blew and plunged into water so cold Scoop insisted it froze his toes fast to his boots. Riders who couldn't swim mostly trusted their mounts—although Deke had to dash into the water to snatch up a lad who'd gotten in front of his horse. Grabbing the boy by his collar, Deke hauled him, spitting and coughing, to the other side. "Don't ever get in front of an animal in the water, son. He'll think you're a foothold. Paw you under."

Jake, who disliked any water not confined in a tub, was plunged into the frigid pool to his neck by a low-in-the-water, mud-colored horse from the remuda. The mud horse had no style, but he was a strong swimmer. On the far bank, his rider announced through chattering teeth, "I've about used up my own prayer. If we make it through the Devil's Punch Bowl, I may embrace the Pope."

The Punch Bowl lay a mile up the trail. Mules, horses, and jacks, their blood racing from the rain and the cold plunge, moved with renewed vigor. Scanning the escarpments overhead, Deke holstered his pistol. He doubted they were in for more trouble. Ike had declared the bad smell gone. His mouth tightened as his thoughts flew. What he feared now was devilment at the Pearly. Sutton knew they were atop the hump—and that Calvin was short of men at the mine.

In what seemed no time at all, those at the forefront were engulfed in the roar of a fifteen-foot waterfall pounding into a deep-rock cauldron beneath fifty-foot walls: the Punch Bowl, dead ahead. As they started downslope, Lute felt a vicious jerk on his reins, heard the squawk of rending wood. "Can't hardly hear myself think!" he yelled to Scoop over the crash of water. It seemed to him the elements up here were a good deal noisier than those in camp. Pulling mightily on the handbrake with one arm, he sawed on the reins with the other as the lee mules skidded toward the cauldron. *This is plumb daft*, he thought, fighting for control over something he could not comprehend. He threw a quick look at Gracious the trouble-maker. When he did, he caught a glimpse of the wagon tongue, crazily askew. *Why, it's broke*, he decided. The fore-section was about to cut loose.

"JUMP, Scoop! Jump clear!"

Scoop dropped his reins and hurtled from the wagon. Lute clenched his teeth and pulled on a brake already set tight. The locked wheels had become runners, sliding downward as if on ice instead of dirt. Just as he was readying himself for a plunge off the side into rock and boiling water, Gracious stopped dead. Cramping the wagon's two thousand pounds of silver matte, the mule stood spraddle-legged, chewing reflectively, gazing placidly at the stony sky.

"Quick!" called Lute to those nearest, "Plug these wheels!"

Men rushed to get handy rocks wedged under wheels. Lute and Gracious held the load with pure sand as the boys put shoulders to the wagon, rolled rocks, and braced the wheels. One swamper, catching his breath, said in an awed voice, "Only thing held this load was that boy's sand—and a son of a bitchin' loco mule."

"Calvin always did…think a lot of…that critter," grunted Nate. "He'll no doubt retire him to green pastures."

"I'm the one needs a soft berth." Scooper dusted off his sore behind. "If I hit the dirt another time or two, my backside'll be broke."

Everyone had his say, shouting over the Punch Bowl din. The major, examining the wagon tongue, found it sawed half-through, patched and smeared with wattle. He turned to Lute, sitting stunned on the wagon seat. "The test of a man's mettle is his resolution in time of trouble. You passed the test fine." He raised his voice so all could hear. "Let's get this wagon off-loaded. On the double! Re-hitch these mules! Night's coming on!"

Much later in the day than planned, under a darkling sky dim-lit by the remnants of a murky setting sun, the ore train at last circled into Lost Man Basin. On the far sides, buttresses of granite rose, scattered bristles of coniferous trees protruding from harsh gray faces. Deep carpets of wild hay and grasses, thick from summer rains, covered the broad expanse of mountain meadow. Deke was relieved they had not had to halt somewhere in deep timber. The men too heaved a collective sigh of relief.

Guards were positioned, the stock baited with oats toward picket pins. Olvera peeled spuds into a large kettle of simmering beef. He produced a supply of biscuits and a jug of molasses from a flour sack and brewed the coffee strong. Men watered their animals at streams, then stretched pants and shirts to dry around three or four fires. Stripped near naked in the deepening cold, they waited patiently for their clothes to warm. High on the hump, a man best sleep dry. Lute assisted Miles with shoeing, then collected pincers, awl, rasp, and hammers as Ike and Scoop hobbled or picketed the re-shod mules. After supper, Olvera threw wood ashes in cooking pots to cut the grease while Nate, his perky self, returned and questioned him about his recipes. "That son-of-a-gun stew was mighty flavorful. What's your secret, Olvera?"

"Muchas *ajo*," said Olvera. "Garlic beats onions. Didn't have no elk liver, though. If someone shoots me an elk, we have liver next time."

"Can you make a vinegar pie?" Nate asked the old Mexican hopefully.

"Pies is for women. Pete's girl Tacy makes pies."

"How about oatmeal? Ever try cooking oatmeal?"

"Gringo eats," muttered Olvera suspiciously.

"It don't do to turn your back on good feed," advised Nate. "I come across oatmeal with a bunch of Kansas boys prospectin' up the Frying Pan. They carried the meal in sacks. Used a big kettle. Added water." Nate grew dreamy. "Cooked it three days and every evening 'til they went to bed."

"No good on the move," huffed Olvera.

"When it was done, the stuff stood up like jelly. Eat it, and it slides down and kerplunks when it strikes bottom. Holds a man up through a day's work as good as fatback and beans. I have it with milk and molasses when I can get them."

Olvera sniffed again. "Mule fodder!" Those nearby nodded agreement. Not a one of them had found food to stick to a man's ribs like sowbelly, beef and beans.

The light drizzle no longer built big puddles. Men laid rubber ponchos on the soaked grass to keep bedrolls out of the wetness. A few savvy hunters spaded out rough hollows in the dirt for a dry bed. Deke had seen to it that everyone had good blankets and coats. Full of hot food and strong coffee, wrapped warm, the men picked up. They leaned back on elbows by the largest fire, sipping from bottles, yawning. The moon was thin as a fishhook, the sky a million miles deep and filling with stars. The night turned bone-cold. Up this high, winter was on them. Playing cards were shortly folded away, hands nestled deep inside pockets.

Shotgun had arrived in time for supper, saying only, "Them cut-throats is on the run—thet good-for-nothing Yankel and his runt of a pard."

"Just the two?" asked Deke.

"Give 'em both a load in their gun arms." After his eats, he pulled out a pint, uncorked it with tarnished teeth, poured it in his coffee, and surveyed Iacono, sitting cross-legged beyond the fire. "Thet wild Injun look sets my teeth on edge," he growled at Nate. Harking back to his cavalry days out of Tucson in the Apache raids, he said, "Down at the Presidio, the hostiles crept in naked as newborns, that same black hair hanging past their hinders. Them they caught they carved out and cooked the guts with the poor bastards still alive watching. Took wives and young'uns and made 'em slaves."

The memory was so hard it turned Shotgun's eyes watery. "Wisht that Injun'd visit Cowpie, get his scalp barbered," he mumbled. "Too blamed Apache for my liking."

"Now don't be holding his hair against him. Lookit Jim Bridger and Joe Culver...and don't forget old Samson. Wore hair to their knees, the lot. Indians think like Samson, think hair gives 'em power. If it was the major asking, that boy'd shave his pelt off—though he'd lose a sight of power and feel doomed."

"Small of me, I reckon," admitted Shotgun. "Boy seen after this train at the Little Narrows. It's only that wild look goes agin my grain."

Nate resisted the urge to inform Shotgun that his own tangled hair, filthy beard, and blood stink made him wild as any Indian.

The din of burros braying in chorus reminded everyone that Nate Phipps might take it in his head to sing. Before he could tune up, Scooper went to playing requests on his Jew's harp. Those who knew the words sang along. Olwen Davies, who spoke little, was not shy about singing. His clear, true voice rang out across the peaks.

"Oh a pretty maid she drove
Me to the top of the hill
Where I plunged to my death
Where I plunged to my death
Loving her still..."

The swamper with the broken leg, laid out on a blanket with a saddle under his head, proved to have a fair voice himself and harmonized with Olwen on the choruses. "Kindly shut your yap, Phipps," he ordered Nate when he joined in. "You're throwing me off the tune."

The swamper and Olwen conferred, then sang:
"When I was a student at Cadiz,
I played on the Spanish guitar.
I was always a friend of the ladies
And I think of them now from afar..
Ring, ching, ching, ching, ring, ching ring out ye
Bells, ring out ye bells...Oh, I played on the
Spanish guitar, ching, ching. Spanish guitar, ching, ching,.."

During the "ring-chings," Miles Gebhardt pinged lightly on a horseshoe, and one of the drovers rang three or four whiskey bottles with his knife. The effect was so pleasing the men felt it an outstanding performance. Nearby, an elk bugled, and talk turned to hunting and game. The cougars had grown so thick on the hump that when a man shot a buckskin he had to pack it directly home. Even hung high in tree, it would be dragged off by pumas. "Hope no dang cats jump us this trip," said a drover. "Nothing a mule hates worse than cougar. They'll stampede surer'n hell."

"Them cougars is bold as house cats," said another. "McClaren caught one sneaking up on his bear. Didn't have his gun on him, but he chased it so hard it lit out with its tail between its legs."

"Hell, I don't mind a few panthers and bears. It's Grandma Tecoucic's bull that worries me," said an Aspen man. The Tekoucic bull, Wellington by name, was the camp's most feared escape artist. When his temper was hot, he yanked up his chain, tore out fences, ripped off porches, and terrorized small children with his roars. Yet when someone ran to fetch Grandma Tekoucic, who was ninety-three, she rose from her rocker, trudged after Wellington and led him home by his nose ring, docile as an old dog.

"It's skunks bother me," said one of Shotgun's hunters. "Raise ned with my wife's chickens."

"Skunks ain't so bad," said another. "I was taking a midnight piss in my backyard last week when I felt this brushing up agin my leg—and there was Mr. Woods Pussy."

"Did he have his hose primed?"

"Never looked. I redirected my own hose and pissed on him first." The man cackled delightedly. "Always did hanker to piss on a skunk."

"Well I'll be hanged," Jake marveled. "Polecat stink was put on this earth to repay us for our transgressions. Your good deeds must have piled up, sir, to permit you such privilege."

Lute sat looking into the fire, so tired his eyes kept shutting down. He tried to focus on skunks and Wellington the bull, but couldn't order his thoughts. Scooper got a blanket roll from the wagon and gently eased his friend atop it. Nate turned away from the fire and stretched out on his back in his blanket so he could watch the stars winking across the sky. Others might take comfort in a bottle. He took comfort in the night sky. It was the one time he harked back to either young wife. The first had been killed by a Kiowa arrow in a horse raid. Lillian, his second, had gone slower of lung fever. They'd had no children; the Utes turned half-breeds out of their tepees. Before she died, she'd asked him to look for her at night in the polestar. "I am your family, Nate. I'll watch over you." He didn't guess he'd ever forget Lillian up there in her star.

Deke rode the periphery of the camp, checking on rope corrals and picket lines, speaking with each guard. At last he too hunkered down by the fire and allowed his thoughts to drift. They drifted straight as string to Emma. The night was vast, the stars like curtains, and he wished now he had invited her to ride along. His heart raced at the notion of her being so near he could nestle his head in her cloud of hair as he pointed out lesser constellations, Vulpecula and Delphinus. He'd be doing nothing of the kind, not for a spell. Emma's solemnity had deepened as she'd lain in his arms two mornings ago. "Deke, I care for you deeply," she'd said with one of her straight-on looks, "and I expect you care for me. But it's not right for us to come together. Not while I am bound by marriage vows…Hush now," she murmured when he tried to speak. "Those vows have chained me like prison fetters, but they are vows all the same. I only pray the Lord will hold with my divorcement."

Her eyes grew clouded. "I'm no longer certain I'm a credit to myself. I cannot trust my appetites. And I am not secure about my judgment. How could I have given myself to a man as bone-bad as Garrett?"

"You were young, Emma."

"I'm still young. And I'm foolish. But I'll not run off again, Deke. You can't be holding a silver strike together and worrying about me. When I am free of Garrett…if you're of a mind to come courting…"

"Oh my dear," Deke had pulled her closer, "what you ask is hard. When I come courting, I'll drink you in like water at an oasis."

She had lifted her face to kiss him sweetly. "All of it will keep, Deke. True love will always keep."

Looking into the starlit sky, he felt suddenly unsure of his powers. Fighting Sutton's camp was like battling a nest of angry hornets. His companions were good hearts, not constructed to deal with evil that struck like grapeshot, hitting from the back, in the dark. Emma was right to think he'd need every bit of his savvy. As the men drifted into bone-weary sleep, Deke remained deep in thought. He was interrupted by the clatter of a buggy turning off the trail.

"Hold your fire, Deke Burdine! Company coming!"

Deke rose and squinted into the night beyond the fire. "Why, is that you, Wyatt?" he called as a man and woman bounced into camp, lanterns swinging, harness horses high-stepping.

"We been easing along in the dark, thought we'd never come on your fire," said Wyatt Earp, jumping down from the buggy, lifting his dainty companion to the ground, then clasping Deke's shoulders. "Josie and I hoped to throw our blankets down with your army. Hear there's calamity loose in these hills. What held you up?"

As Wyatt's woman, declaring that way stations on this pass weren't fit for vermin, got busy unpacking supper and bedrolls. Olvera poured coffee and Deke told Wyatt about the sabotaged trail. "But that's water over the sluice," he said. "What brings you atop the hump, my friend? And at this hour? The silver strike's all taken."

Wyatt moved closer to the fire. Nate, noticing his fine fur-lined gloves, regretted he was not sporting his new silk cravat—though it'd look a mite silly for sleeping out. Still, he'd have liked Wyatt Earp to know someone else on this hill had style.

"I've given up silver mining, D.K. This is a bounty hunt. Sent you a wire early this morning. The keyman wired back it was you headed over the top with an expedition." Wyatt blew on his coffee. "I'm after two bad customers. Lifted a lady's savings and broke her old man's head on a ranch north of Taos. Low-life brothers. Name of Hoople."

Deke clenched his fists and whispered, "Damn! They're multiplying!"

"Who is that?"

"The hornets." Deke filled Wyatt in on the strife over the Pearly, on Garrett Sutton and his foreman Bull Mudgett, and on their depredations of the past weeks.

"These Hooples you're after, they're balloonists, I expect?"

"One and the same. Thieves and killers."

Deke looked bleak in the firelight. He was faced with one more hard decision—and wondering if he'd make the right choice. "I must think a minute, Wyatt. I don't know whether to turn back—or stick with this train 'til we hit Granite. The Hooples could mean unexpected peril for the Pearly."

Luther, awakened by the rattling buggy, sat wide-eyed beside Scoop as Deke and Wyatt talked. Even the older men were awestruck. Wyatt Earp, the noted gunfighter, sat by their fire, common as grass, with his woman clucking like she was about to serve at a garden party. Having Marshall Earp—and a female—in their midst gave the night a new dimension.

Deke got around to introducing everyone who was awake and within reach. "Nate here's the balloon expert. He can supply you with particulars."

"They been flying around Aspen and over the Pearly for weeks," said Nate. "How come you to just now strike their trail?"

"The ranch wife's memory was slowed by blows to the head."

"Well, that machine of theirs is slowed too. Most mornings you can hear the Hooples cussin' her out. They ain't got the right air...or their fire is not hot enough...or they can't steer her where they want her to go." Nate's voice was anxious. "We never thought of the old bag in the same breath with trouble. Thought they was jest borrowin' our mountain air."

Wyatt looked in Deke's drawn face and said, "You get your outfit over to Granite. Josie and I will light out before sunup, fast as that buggy of ours will roll. I'll have those *banditos* in irons before you can say 'jack rabbit.'"

Though Deke felt easier in his mind with Wyatt on the job, he was not wholly mollified. "These are trying times, Wyatt. Trying times."

Iacono materialized in front of the major and waited for his attention. "Weather come, boss."

Deke looked at the sky, so clear that he could see the outline of the Collegiate Peaks in the distance. He lifted a puzzled brow.

"Weather come," Iacono insisted.

#####

CHAPTER TWENTY-EIGHT

THE MINE

Calvin had barely shut his eyes against the night before it was morning. In the last dark before dawn, he crept from bed, gathered his clothes and tiptoed down the steep, narrow steps to the kitchen to dress. He groped for the box of safety matches on a shelf, lighted the kerosene lamp, shook down the ashes in the wood side of the stove where the night-fire had been banked, and added splits of pine to rekindle the flame. He pulled on his pants and primed the sink pump. He toted a basin of water out to the back stoop; he liked a cold splash in the morning. He placed the coffeepot, ready to go, over the fresh fire and hurried to the outhouse before his bladder burst.

He explored gently under Vinnie's sleepy hens for eggs, filled the coal skuttle, and gave himself a brisk wash. His thoughts were with Deke and the boys high on the hump. The cold this morning was sharp. There was a stiff breeze—he expected the train had hit snow. There'd be trouble of some sort, that was certain. But he was confident of Deke's abilities—the man was unwavering in face of tribulations.

There were tribulations to try Job himself, some of a breed even Deke could not put down. Only last evening Calvin had had word that Sutton was counter-suing his wife over her bill of divorcement, seeking stays, claiming the woman young and half-witted and unfit to own or operate a mine. For the life of him, Calvin could not figure how Sutton financed his endless litigation and legions of lawyers.

Well, if nothing more, the lady would have her share of the strike take. And he himself would be grateful when this whole affair was done. He was dog-tired when he flopped in bed at night, and he did not feel rested on rising. After a long stretch of giddy euphoria, a body longed for even one dull, uneventful day, for more than scant hours of sleep each night. *I am feeling the wear and tear*, he admitted silently. He'd been taken aback by the differences between locating a comfortable streak—and striking a full-bore bonanza. Hitting millions carried a power of worries—far more than *angst* over a mortgage. He was appalled at the numbers of men who came begging after money. Not jobs of work. Handouts. Some few grew mean-spirited when he referred them to Willard. In his own former condition, near to dead-broke, he would have shot himself before asking for charity. Nor was he at all certain he liked his present condition. Daily he climbed out on another limb which could break off beneath him. He had hired two of the state's ablest attorneys to plead the sideline suit. He'd staked dozens of old pards to grub or equipment. Both the Midland and D. & R.G. railroads were pestering for his investment, arguing the added prosperity their lines would bring. Suppliants swarmed like mayflies. He rarely had time to get down in the cathedral to share in finding a wondrous new streak. He could no longer indulge in the joy of discovery; he must deal with its seamier consequences above-ground.

Sitting down to the table, he cut a thick chunk of Vinnie's potato bread and waited for the coffee to boil. He'd been so sure that a good find would bring him more time for Emerson, the leisure to sit back and ponder the mysteries and byways of life. Yet here he was, in some way more dissatisfied than he'd been as a failure. Was it Plato or Aristotle said both wealth and poverty were the parents of discontent? He'd surely been caught in the teeth of both.

Visions of marble-topped tables and Turkey carpets were gone. Re-fortified was his long-held view that little in this world is given us to keep. Nathaniel had chortled when he'd long ago expressed that notion aloud. "You could be pure Ute or Cheyenne, Calvin. That's their whole idea. That's why they puzzle over the whites' addlepated drive to own so many parcels of land." He spoke a phrase in Ute, then translated: "Manitou says land belongs to everyone—and no one."

Nor does a thing we create belong to us either, thought Calvin. He had only to recall his two small boys to remember that hard lesson. Creation was the Almighty's work—and that included the coupling of a loving man and woman. A painter's art, a philosopher's thought, soon belonged to the larger world. In the same manner, his sons, this mine, the strike, his marriage, none were his forever—or for long. A man's very life was on loan, and no man could ever know when a loan would be called in, a loved one taken, his own life hanging in the balance.

Calvin had the on-edge feeling he got when the weather was set to change. He poured himself a tin mug of coffee, blew into the cup, took a careful sip and dipped in a chunk of bread. He had just leaned over to button his boots when Vinnie appeared in the doorway, starched and combed.

"Why, you look gloomy, Calvin."

"I am feeling my age, madam. It's my penance for marrying a beauty in the bloom of youth."

"Go on with you."

Quelling his unsettled feeling, Calvin rose to nuzzle the soft, ticklish spot behind Vinnie's ear. He opened the back door to look out at the first red-lavender streaks of dawn, his mind on the myriad concerns he'd face this day. The trail over Pearl Pass had caved again. Coking coal was in short supply. An out-of-the-ordinary number of freight wagons were in for repair of broken wheels. It wasn't only these irritants that troubled him. He was distressed over the consequences of the silver rush for his town. The most orderly saloons had suffered an influx of trouble-buying strangers. Long-time companions had again strapped on pistols. Good men had turned wary. Women fastened locks on barns and houses where no locks were used before. The peeping tom was reported more frequently. His strike had changed the entire complexion of his camp. He was sorrier for this than he could say.

Calvin split a stack of fresh kindling and carried it to the basket by the stove. Vinnie, busy frying sausage from the last hog butchering, looked up to smile at Needle, who'd appeared at the table, his eyes heavy with sleep. "I'll have your eggs in a minute, boys," she said.

"Don't bother with eggs for me, Vin. I've had coffee and bread."

Vinnie frowned. "Bachelor rations, Cal. You've a wife to cook for you."

"Save my eggs for one of your custard pies, my dear. I'm hungry for a custard pie." And with a preoccupied peck on her cheek, he was out the door.

Needle sat at the table with knife upraised in one hand, fork in the other. "If h'it ain't too much trouble, I'd take kindly to an egg or two, ma'am." He was such a simple soul with the look of a small, hungry boy, that Vinnie broke a few extra eggs into the skillet.

Josie and Wyatt awoke to find themselves in four inches of snow. "Be an early winter," muttered Wyatt, wrapping his wool muffler twice around his neck and donning his fur-lined gloves to shake out their blankets. They'd grained the horses last night, and while Wyatt watered, Josie bundled herself up and packed, her movements sure in the dark and the cold. Wyatt was annoyed. The snow would make for slow going until they got lower. He spoke little when he was annoyed.

Jolting down the Aspen side of the pass, there was no chance for chatter anyway. Neither Wyatt's severe look nor the rattling of their teeth in time with the spinning buggy wheels invited talk. Josie held firmly to her hat and the side of the gig. They'd crossed this divide on snowshoes in winter, waded deep mud in the spring. She knew the hazards. When they finally outran the snow, Wyatt tore down the dark, rough trail on sense rather than sight. Even

Josie had to clamp her mouth shut hard to keep from crying out. Her calm was the reason Wyatt seldom left her behind; she was a better comrade than most men, never troubling him with talk when he was in no mood for talk. On the descent, he was able to focus all his faculties on a dangerous business.

Shortly before his seven o'clock shift, Aaron Beard pounded up Mill Street in a tizzy. He was reporting for work—and he was reporting trouble. Stump Clancy, on night guard at the big Hopkins Street dump, was so sick that Aaron suspected appendix. Appendix was one of the camp's worst killers. Doc Alderfer was so disgusted with its death-dealing that he threatened to start cutting "that blasted little worm out of the next belly." He hadn't tried it though. His saw was trouble enough—patients were not ready to accept knives on top of saws.

Aaron was anxious, and not only about Stump puking his guts out, twisted in a corkscrew of pain. Of late Aaron had been drinking his drinks in the Chloride Saloon. Harking back, he guessed it started the night he'd had more words with Young Frank. Calvin's wife said he and Frank were like two billy goats fighting over the same trash. Denver Bob Bisbee had clapped him on the back and offered to buy him a busthead and beer. After that, he'd taken to drinking with Bob, surprised at how congenial the fellow was. Bob had further astonished him by hinting at a superintendency in the Little Robin Mine.

"With this boom, there's a shortage of good help, Aaron. We've lost two assistant superintendents. I've asked around, hear you have sand. I'm the foreman on those works, and we're about to tool up for bigger production."

Aaron Beard had never been offered a job of work in his life. He'd had to beg, hat in hand, for every job he'd ever had—or else move in on Pete's coattails. The prospect of a superintendency had given him a prime feeling. At the same time, he felt somehow in the wrong. Bob Bisbee was no friend of Calvin's camp, and he'd helped beat Young Frank half to death. Frank was cantankerous, but he'd never deserved a whipping like that. Aaron knew that demon drink loosened his tongue 'til it wagged like a snake's. Sheepishly, he suspected he'd talked overmuch. He picked up his pace. He'd sort out the right and the wrong later. Stump, an old companion of Calvin's, appeared sick enough to check out. Worse, Cal might scold if he was late. He was in no frame of mind for a scolding. He rushed into the shafthouse and called, "Man down, Calvin. Stump Clancy at the Hopkins dump. Puked up his voice box and is set to lose his insides."

"Mercy!" breathed Calvin. "Deke and Nate are on the hump, Willard has got a burial. We're short a man below and two guards here at the shaft." He wondered irritably why Aaron hadn't thought to summon Doc Alderfer himself. There wasn't enough of Pete Beard's good sense in this world, and that was all there was to it. "I thank you, Aaron. If you'll get to work on the mucking below, Needle can run the cages while I locate Doc."

He turned to Needle. "I just signaled a three-count. When the load is hoisted, you can finish lowering those supplies." Needle knew the drill, and he was steady. "Most of your shift is already below, Aaron," Calvin said dismissively. "Needle, if I can't find Doc, I'll fetch Aggie or Lavinia. Be back directly."

Climbing into the cage as Needle signaled two whistles for lowering, Aaron mumbled in an injured voice, "'Get to work on the mucking, Aaron.' That's what I hear around here. 'Shovel, Aaron. Swing that pick, Aaron.'"

What Pete heard was Calvin and others deferring to him. "What is your idea about blowing that hind wall, Pete? How many spitter holes should we bore, Pete?" Aaron was sick and tired of having Pete treated like a high-and-mighty poobah, while he was the one ordered around like a sweeper. *Well sir,* he decided, *if they offer me that Little Robin job, I might take it I guess. I'll show Calvin and Pete a thing or two.*

Calvin hurried past the Clarendon veranda where Aggie stood wrapped in a clan-plaid shawl, shading her eyes against the rising sun, watching the big balloon drift silently but steadily toward the Pearly. The air was stirring more than usual. Aggie had rushed from the hotel kitchen, pulling Emma after her. The flying machine had never come this close before. They could make out every patch and dirt clod on its sun-bleached fabric. Aggie's face was rapturous.

"Anyone seen Doc?" Calvin called. "Stump Clancy's taken sick at the lots."

Her eyes fixed on the balloon pilots, Aggie called back, "No, but if you need me to doctor, Cal, I'll come."

On the broad front steps of the hotel, Young Frank Parker clasped Bridgie O'Reilly's plump hand in one of his and shyly traced the arc of freckles across her nose.

"It's only a six-hour shift, Bridgie," he promised. "She'll warm up by afternoon, and we'll take a picnic to the cemetery." Bridgie did not think a pile of headstones a proper place to court, but she did not demur. "I'll pack us lemonade and raisin cookies, Frank."

He gave his bride-to-be a hungry look and trotted uphill past the Pearly's blacksmith shop, a place that put him in mind of a devil's forge. Fires blazed, sparks flew, anvils rang so that the clanging resounded as far as Pratt Mountain. The work of sharpening drills, forging horse and mule shoes, honing picks and shovels was never ending. This morning, three smiths were on the job.

Inside the shafthouse, Pete Beard went over the inventory of black powder at his feet and cached in the underground magazines. Needle checked their spitters. Young Frank nodded a greeting and signaled Needle to lower him to the main tunnel.

Pete was deep in thought as he rolled coils of wire around his arm. "My two youngest can't shake off them summer coughs," he said worriedly. "And the middle girl, Ellamae, was stung by yellow jackets, her arm's swole big as a punkin. There's days I need a woman's hand, Needle."

"Your Tacy has a good head on her."

"Time is a cruel thief. I won't have it snatching her sweet smile, burying her in an old woman's worries. She didn't have all them babies. Her mother and I did."

As Needle and Pete talked, the last remnants of the night shift emerged blackened and chattering from the cage and started noisily downhill to boardinghouses and shacks. Pete, his powder, wire, and rope double checked, pulled up suddenly and said, "Dern! I forgot we're short of blast caps!"

"Go on below, Pete. Soon's Calvin gets back I'll hightail it down to Thompson's for more."

Pete finished filling both arms with supplies, paused for a final mental inventory, then stepped into the cage. Needle grasped the big lever and started to lower him. As he did, a sudden large shadow enveloped the shafthouse, a kind of eclipse pierced by strange, darting shards of light. He looked up through the yawning holes in the roof. The danged balloon had never come this close before. He hoped those pilots wouldn't bang themselves on the sides of the building.

As the cage neared bottom and Needle began pulling on the brake, there was a heavy thunk. He peered over his shoulder, startled. Bouncing off a joist and swinging straight toward him was a thing he had never seen: a very large bundle, a bundle with both ends spitting fire.

Outside, Emma and Aggie stood motionless, their eyes riveted on the strangely antic balloon boys, first tossing a long rope with ballast from their

237

basket, then another, then hauling one up to hurl it again. *Why, they look like they're fishing*, Aggie thought. Bridgie stood open-mouthed at the hotel entrance. The balloon was so near it appeared bigger than a block of buildings. Drovers moving downhill braked and ogled the sight from their wagon seats. The anvils in the forge quieted as the smiths turned toward suddenly shadowed windows and doorways.

Emma was the first to speak, breaking the disquieting hush. "Those don't look like the usual ballast bags." Her hand flew to her mouth even as her feet started to move. "They look like…they look…oh my God, Aggie!"

At the silver dump, Calvin knelt beside the crumpled-up Stump, now wracked by wrenching, unproductive heaves.

"Can you talk, Stump? Help is on the way." He felt of the man's head. Stump heaved and moaned. "Got…coffee…off'n a boy…poisoned me."

In one terrible instant of recognition, Needle discerned that the hissing and sputtering he heard was from lighted fuses which had somehow descended from the sky. He leapt for the nearest swinging, deadly package, caught it in both hands, gathered it in and rolled with it across the floor toward Calvin's big desk, beating at the fuses as he rolled. He never saw the identical package which, with the devil's guidance, dropped straight down the cage shaft.

When the explosions came, they were so powerful some insisted they shifted the whole of the Elk Range. The blasts blew all the windows out of the Clarendon Hotel and shivered floors and walls as far away as Woody Creek. Sadirons flew from stoves. Pots clattered to floors with the noise of crashing cymbals. A nearby ore wagon was hurled in the air, bounced off the hill, and burst into shards, firing off its load of slag like cannonballs. Jerry-rigged shacks buckled in on themselves, collapsing in heaps of kindling. On the Row, doors heaved, buckled, and fell from their hinges. Outhouses tumbled. Chickens along Durant Avenue dropped dead of concussion. The Pearly shafthouse dissolved in jagged splinters, large spears of wood flying for hundreds of yards. Benchboy Rheumanalor Wilson was impaled where he sat. Enrique, the cinnamon bear, was wounded; he cowered in a porch corner, his roars of pain adding to the pandemonium.

The Pearly's blacksmiths were unconscious, their fires beginning to ignite the rubble. Down Mill Street, Angus McClaren was hurled in the air. To his astonishment, he landed upright some six feet away. Tacy Beard, in the act of packing wet baking soda on Ellamae's yellowjacket stings, dropped the poultice and sat motionless, her heart pounding visibly through her bodice. Vinnie Krueger, hoeing her garden under a big slat sunbonnet, was jolted headfirst into a hill of potatoes. She got her bearings, staggered grey-faced to her feet, and began running for the mine.

Overhead, the Hooples were stunned by the enormity of their destruction. Dynamite blows upward—yet this load appeared to be blowing everything from a hundred feet below ground. They had no way of knowing that a bundle had plummeted into the bottom of the shaft, where it blew like confined cannon fire, igniting a large load of black powder by the open cage. The explosion's initial backdraft had threatened to suck the balloon into its vortex. Half-a-dozen jagged spears of wood had punctured its bag. Then successive shock waves blew their machine past the Silver Queen's flowing, aspen-tree locks. They worked frenziedly, using their bellows on the fire and pumping more hot air to loft themselves higher. They rocked the basket in mute desperation, their muscles taut with the effort to catch enough breeze to push them more rapidly north and west. Slowly the balloon drifted out of reach of the Pearly. Neither man uttered a word. Their lives, like their machine, were at the dubious mercy of whisper-thin, undependable currents of air.

Rattling down off the hump, Wyatt and Josie were too distant to feel the mighty gusts of massive concussion. Even so, they recognized the explosions as something out of the ordinary. Wyatt, who seldom used his whip, drew it swiftly from its socket and laid it on the flanks of his team.

Long before the last echoing roar had subsided or the smoke and dust drifted to ground, Calvin tore for the mountain, praying as he ran.

Aggie and Emma rose dazedly to their feet, shook their pounding heads, picked up their skirts, and stumbled uphill toward the mine. Neither could hear, though they were only vaguely aware they'd been deafened.

One good look assured the bench boys that old Nailhead Wilson was dead. A splintered wooden spike protruded, still quivering, from the center of his thin flannel shirt. The point had gone through his breastbone, pinning him to the back of the bench. His mouth and eyes were wide open in indignation.

"He'll keep," grunted Henry Gant as the boys found leg power they didn't know they owned and scrambled for the Pearly. Trouble whistles shrieked, the firebell clanged and from across the camp, beginning with a ripple and gaining the force of a flood-tide, men snatched up picks and shovels and raced toward the explosions.

Emma and Aggie were the first to reach the smoldering smithy, then the shafthouse. "Get the fireboys, Henry!" shouted Aggie to Henry Gant as she and Emma began yanking aside twisted fallen joists. Her voice sounded whispery in her ears, though she knew she'd yelled at the top of her lungs. Nor did Emma hear herself weeping as a heavy cross-timber was seized from her grip and she looked up to see Mr. Krueger and Mr. McClaren, their faces the faces of death.

Aggie was startled to find Calvin heaving tangled lumber and broken machinery beside her. "Oh my friend!" she cried.

Calvin, his voice breaking, asked, "Needle? Pete?" The question was another prayer.

####

CHAPTER TWENTY-NINE

PETE AND NEEDLE

Down in the number one tunnel, Young Frank had just greeted Mike Medjeric, his hand in a half-salute, when there was a monstrous roar. All the candle lamps were snuffed out. The mine rocked like a berserk bronc. Frank was thrown so high he bounced off the tunnel roof. More than thirty crewmen working on the new Lavinia outlet, along with those in the cathedral, were hurled against headwalls, flung to the ground, struck with rock that whacked them like sledge hammers. Aaron Beard was slammed to the floor of the tunnel. Like Mike and Young Frank, he expected he was dead.

In the aftermath of Armageddon, Frank, on his knees, prayed to the Holy Mother that what had struck was the end of it, that similar detonations would not follow. He'd be a goner if his system took another rattling like the first. Somewhere nearby, Mike made muffled sounds. His mouth had been open, ready to speak, when the blast came. He had to spit and claw out clods of dirt before he could get his tongue around any words. Down the tunnel, Aaron sat keening, a high-pitched noise that sounded more Indian than white.

Young Frank was the first to speak, in a voice that did not sound like his own. "Must be alive. Don't know why."

Still spitting dirt, Mike groaned, "I'm here, pard. Though my head pains me." The two young men groped their way toward each other in the dark, managed an awkward embrace. Mike located a candle, got it lit, and moved shakily through fallen debris toward the keening noise.

The Vinnie Tunnel crew lay stunned or in a faint. Those who recovered first lit candles and stumbled to their feet, astonished to find the timber had held. They'd figured the whole mountain had blown sky-high. In the vug and drifts, men crouched in the pitch black, unable to comprehend what disaster had struck. Underpinnings had trembled and bent, scaffolding collapsed. The blasts broke open an underground lake and spawned a fresh waterfall that poured out of once-solid rock into the deep-level, number four tunnel. Two diggers there blundered across a partly demolished ladder, raised it, and clambered through pouring water to the Vinnie excavation above. Men everywhere groped for light. Heaved those still stunned to their shoulders. Headed for the Vinnie exit. Prayed it was still there.

With impossible speed, hundreds of rescuers made short shrift of the above-ground wreckage. Not only was the shafthouse gone, but most of the floor with it. Generators and boilers were blown to the heavens, shards of wood and metal spread far up the mountain and into the streets of town. Legions cleared the smithy, doused the fires, and pulled out the unconscious but still-breathing smiths. Calvin tore at the wreckage like a man gone mad, he and Mac horror-struck by the gaping cage hole which now held a jumble of cable, metal, and pulverized wood.

"Looks like a deep charge blew out the shaft walls below," said an old-timer from the crowd. In the aching silence, a young boy handed Calvin one of Needle Newsome's worn boots, the one with the hole he'd cut to ease his troublesome corn. "Found it up the hill," said the boy, his face gone gray.

Calvin turned the boot over in his hands, found part of a bloodied foot with splintered bone, shards still inside and sank to the ground, his body heaving with unutterable grief.

When the mine crews dug out through rubble and began stumbling from the Vinnie adit, shielding reddened eyes, jagged cuts, and terrible headaches, a shout went up. With the appearance of each man, there were exultant cries from wives, children, and cronies. Bringing up the end of the tattered procession were Mike and Young Frank, supporting Aaron Beard between them. At sight of her man, Selma Medjeric fainted.

Aaron had ceased his keening. He wasn't hurt, but his legs wouldn't hold. "Pete?" he croaked. "Pete?" They led him to a seat on a stump and eased him onto it like a brittle old man.

At the base of the hill, Bridgie O'Reilly had lost her wits. She sobbed so hard that she gulped and hiccupped, as wracked as a drowner fighting deep water. Young Frank Parker had never in his life seen anyone take on so, and as he approached, he wasn't at all certain Bridgie's convulsions were for him. Shy about the many gaping onlookers, and mindful of his mud-and dirt-caked hands, face, and clothes, he tapped carefully on Bridgie's shoulder. Finally he found his voice. "It's me, Bridget. I'm here,"

Bridgie looked up through tears, let out a howl, and clutched him to her breast. "Oh Frank," she wailed, "how could you give me such a fright!"

Wyatt Earp, following crowds streaming for the mountain, pulled his team up short at the scene of destruction. "Lord!" he said, after one look at the smoking ruins, at boilers blown far up the hill, at broken remnants of machinery hanging from roundabout roofs, and at hundreds of men and women digging desperately in a blur of flying hands. "Is that the Pearly?" he asked an old codger with his arm around a weeping girl.

"It once was."

"What caused this?"

The man looked bewildered. "Beats me. Weren't like Pete Beard to go careless with powder."

"Didn't you hear, Blackie?" interrupted another oldster. "It was them son of a bitchin' balloon boys—pardon me, ma'am. The women at the hotel seen them do it. Threw packs of lighted powder."

Wyatt scrambled up on the buggy seat. In the distance, to the west, he sighted the balloon—so far gone it was down to the size of a small skein of wool. He did not question any of the half-crazed crowd further. Bounding to the ground, he lifted Josie from her seat. "I'll be back," he called tersely, already whipping the team out Durant Avenue. His pair were high-strung, sometimes too jittery with their prancing. But the rough descent down the hump hadn't winded them; they were still raring. They raced through town and across a toll bridge abandoned by a keeper who thought the world had ended. Wyatt urged them up the steep bank—"Pull, PULL!"—to the Wozniak pasturage. At the top, he could just locate the balloon lying in folds on the ground at the far side of five or six fields. Around it were horsemen. Four of them, he judged. They must have spotted him, for they set off down-valley at a fast pace, moving like tiny antelope in the distance. Wyatt raced across the first field, his eyes searching for the gate through the fence. There'd be maybe a half-dozen more gates. He'd lose time. But he was persistent. Persistence always paid.

Late in the afternoon, they dug Pete Beard from the tunnel immediately adjacent to the shaft, piles of rubbish pulverized atop him like grain. Though his body was grievously crushed, there was more peace than pain on his face. When solicitous hands carried and laid him on cleared ground, Aaron, dry-eyed, took Pete's big, broken hand in his. Calvin knelt beside the brothers, his grief so crippling he could scarcely breathe.

In the quiet, a woman murmured, "He shouldn't have died alone. No family man should be without kin at his dying."

Questions had flown along with shovel blades. "Jest cain't hardly believe Pete Beard or Cal Krueger would go rash with black powder."

"Doubt they did." Word was spreading that this was the work of the balloon boys. Yet there was bafflement. How could a machine in the air set off such a ruckus deep in a mine?

"Hard to credit. Did they fire a cannon, or what?"

"Heard Miz McClaren tell Krueger—she and Mrs. Sutton seen them…"

"Seen what?"

"Seen them fiends throw lighted powder sticks into the shafthouse."

"I swan."

"Little Emma ain't one to see things that ain't there."

"Threw the spitters through holes in the roof. Then came the blows. One load musta dropped straight down the cage shaft."

"Them dirty, rotten shit-heels!"

"Where's the sheriff?"

Mutterings and threats grew until the crowd noise was ugly. Sheriffs Harwood and Thatcher were surrounded by men clamoring for a posse. Strident voices demanded the Hooples be strung high.

"And while we're about it, might's well track down Bull Mudgett!" a voice bellowed.

"Him and Bisbee!" howled another.

"They was thick with them pilots—the pilots was put up to this!"

A little lady in a big hat spoke up, her voice clear and carrying. "Never you mind, boys. Wyatt Earp is in pursuit."

People could hardly trust their own ears.

"I am Marshall Earp's helpmeet. He took after the killers a few hours back. Wyatt is on the job—he'll bring in your perpetrators."

Sheriff Harwood, though relieved to be freed of a hard carriage ride, was in a fever of anxiety over this terrible turn of events. The fight for the Pearly had reached unexpected—and scarifying—dimensions. What he had here was no longer a skirmish. It was full-blown war. If Mudgett and Bisbee were at the bottom of the dread deed, that meant Sutton, and maybe Tacker, were on the fringes. For a disaster of these proportions, they could all be lynched. Feeling frantic, Harwood tried to recall how often he'd appeared in public with Garrett Sutton of late. Determined to pursue his duty with as much vigor as he could muster, he hurried off to speak with the bench boys. They'd dug with the crowds 'til they were pooped, then tottered back to their seats beside Nailhead. Dirty was appalled at the sight of Rheumanalor Wilson. Nale looked like a cigar store Indian, his body rigidly upright, his eyes popping. The sheriff was not conditioned to violent crime. His job in this camp was dealing with drunks and keeping whores in line.

"You boys held a front-row seat," he rasped. "See anything suspicious?"

"All we seen was thet Christly balloon, derned near ready to drop in our laps," said the outraged Henry Gant.

"Our sight ain't what it was." Potato John mopped rheumy eyes with an old rag to emphasize his point.

"Heard the blow though," marveled Bob Dinkel. "Flushed out both my ears."

Harwood turned to the onlookers gawking at the dead bench boy. "Think a few of you could quit yer gapin' and help ease old Nale off this seat?" he asked irritably.

In front of the Clarendon, two ranch hands roped and hog-tied the cinnamon bear. The bear was mad, and he was active, but they got him trussed so Angus could yank the big wood splinter from his rump. Aggie examined the wound and flushed it out with hot water, soap, and solomon's seal, ignoring Enrique's furious attempts to rake her with his claws. "He's na' able ta' reach around to pick at it," she announced over his roars. "It'll heal."

Angus was proud of his bear. He'd raised it since he'd found it orphaned up the hump. "Hope that wound don't hurt him too bad," he said anxiously.

"'Tis mostly his mad makes him yell, the big blether," said Aggie. "I doubt the spear went through his outside layer of lard. Now get ye back ta' the desk, Mac. I'll be looking in on those poor fatherless Beard girls."

Calvin and Lavinia sat huddled by Pete's body. Vinnie was in conflict—deliriously grateful that Calvin lived, wrenched with sorrow over Needle and Pete. Calvin's grief was so penetrating that his whole body ached. Though the Kruegers had promised Aaron to see Pete down to Willard's mortuary, neither of them could seem to move.

A strange transformation had come over Aaron. Placing a sheltering arm around Tacy, he said to her sisters, clinging in terror to her skirts, "Let's go to the place, ladies. You little ones ain't had lunch. Olvera won't be worth a plugged nickel. I'll just rustle us up something to eat." Aaron had walked off with Pete's sorrowed family, the two youngest, each with a hand in one of his, looking up at him with mingled hope and fear. To the faint-of-heart, nothing is more frightening than a child's naked need. Yet the girls' need caused him to stand straighter. His voice had firmed. Though few had yet noticed, Aaron Beard bore a marked resemblance to his brother Pete.

Willard had rushed back to town from the graveyard. He said quietly to Calvin, "It's time, old pard. Time to move Pete off this hard ground."

Calvin felt no more able to move than if an ice storm had frozen him where he sat. Lavinia took his hand and half-lifted him to his feet. As she did, some of the numb feeling left him. In its place, a prodigious sense of anger began to rise.

Far down-valley, past the Catherine turnoff, Wyatt spied a ranch house where he might leave the buggy and a tiring team and rent a fresh horse. He turned into the wagon trace and, around a corner at a cluster of tall cottonwoods by the creek, reined up sharp. Two men lay across the trace, one's head resting on the other's leg. They'd been shot in the back. Wyatt got out his bounty poster and pulled up their heads by the hair. It was the Hooples, all right. They wouldn't murder again.

There was no sign of their horses, nor of other riders. Wyatt lighted a cigar and drew in a deep puff. No use chasing after local men long gone up some little-used line-camp trail. Well, he'd collect his bounty, though D.K. wouldn't have his satisfaction. Dead men can't point a finger. He heaved the bodies into the buggy, watered his flagging team at the creek, and turned at a walk back toward Aspen.

When Wyatt drove into camp with the Hooples, he reported first to the sheriff's office, then routed telegrapher Werner Kuster from his supper to send wires. Men gathered around his buggy to glare at the dead evil-doers. Marshall Earp held off until the town had its look. The town was largely disappointed. The Hooples weren't much of a size, and their undistinguished faces showed nothing of murderous minds. They looked shriveled, their chicken necks protruding from ragged undershirts. It was hard to credit that two such puny scarecrows had done vicious killing.

Folks also ogled Wyatt Earp, the lawman and gunfighter. After Wyatt located Josie at the Clarendon, the Earps had to push their way through a heavy crowd to reclaim their carriage and ride to the Krueger place.

"It's been a spell, Calvin," said Wyatt, shaking hands. Calvin's mind was on death, his jaw set, his voice cool. "Marshall," he said, not able to soften his curt tone.

"I've got the two murderers who did for your men, shot before I reached them. Shot so they'd never talk, I'd wager."

Calvin's shoulders slumped, his sense of ineptitude so strong his eyes looked hopeless. Wyatt hurried to add, "Camped with Deke Burdine last night, up at Lost Man. Promised I'd report to you. The train's safe; they expect to pass Twin Lakes tomorrow."

Flustered by her husband's harsh look and inhospitable tone, Lavinia fluttered over Josie, offering to warm up some ham and green beans and ready the spare room. Though Josie looked longing, Wyatt refused. "We must store the killers in the ice house. And Josie's rented us a room at the Clarendon, though we thank you kindly." He looked close at Calvin. "You'd best send a man across the hump to fetch the major."

"I'll go," blurted Young Frank.

"But it's coming on dark," protested Vinnie. "You've been on your feet since early morning."

"More murderin' could be waitin' on the hump." Frank was in a fury.

"It's my idea," said Wyatt, "after this black deed, that their bunch will be on the run. No malefactor chooses to face a noose-knotting mob. And that's what you have in your streets, Krueger, men of a mind to hang."

"Lord God…"

Wyatt thought he had never seen a face so torn, pain fighting with despair and wrath for a place there. He'd had his own experience of underhanded murder. He was understanding. But he held firm. Calvin Krueger was in no condition to tend his fort. "You'll need D.K. here. He knows conditions—and he's a cool head."

"I'll get a horse and lantern at the livery and start now," declared Young Frank.

Calvin thought on it. The boy was a capable rider, he'd ride off some of his heat. He nodded his head, saying no more.

"Guard your back door," Deke had warned. Well, he'd left his door unguarded. He'd failed his friends, rushed off after the first diversion offered him. If he'd stayed on the job…if he'd been watching as he ought…

Vinnie hurried to wrap a lunch of cold ham as Frank snatched up a coat and poncho and rifle. Calvin managed to thank Earp, though his look was far away. *Sutton is responsible for this*, he thought for the hundredth time. *I may have to deal with that villain myself. It's only right. Needle and Pete must rest in peace.*

That evening, hundreds of dog-tired miners and townsmen climbed the steep Ajax incline in the dark. Above Spar Gulch, they regrouped, turned, and trudged down-slope single file, carrying candle lights in tin cans with welded handles. Since there was nothing of Needle Newsome to bury, this was tribute from those who'd worked the cars and downed a drink by his side. The camp stood at attention below: men, women, and children. The women wept tears for the dead and tears for the men miraculously safe beside them. Death was these women's constant adversary. They were forever holding it at bay. It came at them from falling trees, from unreliable machinery, from rearing horses; from mine accidents, high water, and lung sickness. It struck down children with diphtheria, men with consumption, and ranch hands with ornery animals. Though they thrust death aside, fought it away, this was an hour when they must admit its ever-presence in their lives. Candles in the night softened the awful face of death.

There were no prayers from pulpits, only silent prayers from those who knew the words to a prayer. Needle Newsome was put to rest the best way a mountain mine camp knew how.

In the back room of the mortuary, Willard had finished washing Pete Beard, had stretched his stiffening body on a wood pallet under a thin cotton blanket. He'd held off taking the juices from him, for that was when the last of a man's mortal soul departed, the time he turned rock-like and petrified. It was just as well folks considered undertakers heartless. Willard was grateful no one could see the tears leaking down his face as he worked. "Oh my Lord," he groaned. "Oh Lord…"

Just as he straightened Pete tenderly on the pallet, there came a knocking on his back door.

"It's me, Mr. Arey. Tacy. Tacy Beard."

"You don't want to come in here just now, sis," he called warningly. If there was a complication he could do without, it was a caterwauling child of the dead.

"But I do, Mr. Arey. I promise I won't bawl and take on…"

Reluctantly, Willard opened the door. The Beard girl appeared composed, even womanly, though he doubted she was more than sixteen.

"I've come to do up Pa's hair," she said. She held an old comb in her hand.

"His hair?" Pete's hair was nothing but raggedy fringe around his mostly bald pate.

"Well, his beard," said Tacy. "He set a deal of store in that beard. Liked me to comb it for him." She walked over to the pallet and smoothed a hand down her father's cheek. Then she set to combing tangles from the long, wet whiskers.

For once in his life Willard Arey was speechless. He stood with his head bowed as a young girl lovingly tended her dead father. She had brought thread, which she used to tie the ends of the neat plaits she wove, all in a row.

"Pa would have wanted his beard tidy," she mused. "The girls are fine, they're with Uncle Aaron. He's telling them lies about fighting Indians. Uncle Aaron is all the kin we have left. I expect he'll do fine."

"You tell your Uncle Aaron there'll be no charge for your pa's burial." The words, and his voice, sounded peculiar in his own ears.

Tacy finished her handiwork and stood back to survey the results.

"I don't guess I'll kiss him goodbye. Pa wasn't much for kisses, though he was partial to a good hug." She touched her father's cheek once again. "I thank you, Mr. Arey," she said, and turned and went out through the door.

####

CHAPTER THIRTY

THE BURIAL

Deke and Nathaniel, Jake and Young Frank galloped into Aspen in time to join Pete Beard's funeral procession. Each man led a spare mount. It had been a hard thirty-five miles of back-tracking over the same treacherous terrain. Frank, who'd done twice that distance, was close to dropping. The skin across Jake Levy's cheekbones was so tight he looked skeletal.

Young Frank had struck the silver train as they were breaking camp. Spurring and stumbling up the night-black hump like he was fleeing devil's milk, he'd pulled up to the wagons at sunrise. Deke heard him coming, his look wary.

"They're kilt, Major," Frank blurted before his horse was reined in. "Pete and Needle..." He swallowed hard. "Them balloon flyers...blasted the Pearly all to hell."

"The others?" Deke's voice was barely audible.

"Ain't hurt. But they're cross. Never seen Mr. Krueger so bull-mad. He wants you should come home. Funeral's late this afternoon."

Frank had changed horses and gulped down a plate of beans in the saddle while Deke conferred with the men, gave Shotgun curt instructions, then rode over to the stricken Lute.

"You'll assist Shotgun taking this train in, Luther." He pulled a pack of papers from his saddlebag. "This first stack, the one tied in blue twine, is for the station master in Granite. Double check the weight of every load of Denver-bound matte on the depot scales, have the train guards sign these papers, get the station master's signature here and here." Deke continued his instructions for the flabbergasted boy, "You know which wagons go to the Maxwell Smelter in Leadville. The foreman, Larry Patterson, is expecting us."

Lute was dumbfounded. He'd been about to burst into tears over Mr. Pete and Needle and his old comrade Nale Wilson. Now he'd been given a job of unthinkable dimensions.

"You're soon into open country, son. We doubt there'll be more trouble.

250

But mind you keep your guns unlimbered." He about-faced Buford, beckoned to Jake and Nate, and with a *Vaya con Dios* to Lute, headed for home.

Some of those left behind with the ore train complained that Pete Beard had been as much their companion as anyone's. Nate had reassured them, "Pete will taken it kindly if you stop by the grave next week." He struggled to control his voice. "It'll be lonesome then."

On the Aspen downside of the trail, the small group of heavy-hearted riders encountered Wyatt Earp. After one terse look at the corpses the marshall carried, Young Frank felt the same bewilderment as those in camp. There was little to hate in the shell of a man. He would have welcomed a place to lay down his hate. He was so full of it he could have choked.

"That town of yours is in a mean frame of mind, D.K.," said Earp, "and Krueger is undone."

"Any sign of the two varmints Shotgun winged at the narrows?"

"Not a sniff nor a sighting. I put out the word. The whole camp is baying after them."

"Nor any sign of Mudgett?"

"Not him nor any that ran with him. They've lit out for the Gunnison Country, or I miss my guess. The hornet's nest they stirred up is about the size of Kansas. I'll strike your train around Granite, ride them on into Leadville." Seeing Josie wrinkle her nose toward the rear of the buggy, he said, "These polecats stank when they were alive. Dead, they can't smell worse."

Pete's procession was the lengthiest in camp memory, longer even than the July Fourth affair. A good man—widower, father, friend—had died as a result of mortal wrong-doing. Folks needed to draw close in face of an incomprehensible valley of death. At the forefront of the cortege, the Hamtown Band marched in solemn lockstep, instruments stilled. Two drummers rapped a soft tattoo as they moved east on Cooper toward Spring Street. Willard, dressed in a tall silk hat and his mortician's suit shiny with wear, rode the seat of the black hearse wagon beside Rob Skinner. Both were uncommonly quiet. All business enterprise had shut down. Mine superintendents walked beside trammers and ranch hands. Visiting engineers rubbed shoulders with Serb and Bohemian muckers whose English was as broken as the nails on their hands. The men of Aspen entertained savage notions of beating the living daylights out of the sons of bitches behind this. Their women were saddened by thoughts of man's malevolence toward man. Pete's younger girls, in fresh-starched dresses and pinafores, which Tacy had spent half the night washing and ironing just so, walked beside the coffin, their eyes wide and dry. Tacy had instructed firmly, "Don't you disgrace this family and your pa, bawling and taking on. Hold your heads up and stand straight. Ellamae, stop that blubbering. Those wasp stings are about healed."

With every livery in town short of animals and rolling stock, Willard had scavenged a motley assortment of buggies, springwagons, and mismatched teams which carried those too infirm to walk, including three Pearly hands with concussed heads and the one with the broken hip. Behind the coffin walked Lavinia and Calvin. "Cal and I will walk, though I thank you, Willard," said Vinnie. "We'd as soon take our time. Once Pete is in the ground, he'll be gone from us for good."

Though it was a sweltering August day, wives who owned a long-sleeved black bombazine dress wore the dress and suffered for it. Emma, despite the heat, was icy cold. She walked unseeing, her fading bruises hidden under a black lace head shawl, her black silk moire dress whispering around her feet. *The damnable silver is not worth this*, she thought. *All I could think of was my own freedom. I babbled about maybe paying a high price—never thinking, never thinking. I did not vision men dead. I didn't for a minute picture Mr. Beard white as wax in his coffin. Oh Lord. I talked it, but I never saw it.* She lifted her head despairingly to the Sawatch.

She was only fleetingly aware that Deke and Uncle Nate had ridden into the rear of the procession. Her heart gave one feeble jump, then settled back in its place of care. Her anguish for the dead and her wrath at Garrett consumed her. She had no doubt that Garrett was behind these killings. None. If only she had handed over the stock. Yet if she had, she knew that outcome. Her husband, twisted with hubris, would have driven away hosts of good people. Yet again, she argued mournfully, he might not have killed. Emma could think no way clear of escalating destruction. Garrett was too slippery to be brought to law. But he must be stopped. He was *her* husband; it was *her* should stop him. How? Shoot him down? The notion of calculated killing was so repugnant that she turned colder than before, shuddering in the hot sun.

Mrs. Ollie Davidson's mind was on the Fourth of July at Hallam Lakes. Self-righteously, she reviewed her warnings to Sheriff Harwood. "That balloon trash must be run out of this town," she'd bristled.

The Sheriff was a user of tobacco and strong drink, too muddle-headed to heed the sound advice of a sharp-witted woman. Now look! Her buttonhole mouth tightened. Harwood would lose his tin star over this. While Ollie was about it, he could also repossess the Pickering buggy he'd loaned the fat fool, who was too blubbery to hoist himself into a saddle.

Pearly crews marched to the cemetery in disbelief, many nursing powerful headaches. Doc Alderfer had brewed headache leaves 'til the vapors dizzied him. He'd finally escaped his treatment room to carry Grandma Tekoucic and her neighbor lady in his buggy behind Dolly.

Polly Panakarpo drove the Reverend Campbell's wife, who suffered a discommoding weakness of the bowels. The squaw had marched on the Bullion Row stable, swept the dust from the rig's seat, hitched up the sorrels, and taken reins in hand. She was incensed to find the team unexercised and willful. She could hardly countenance a man who mistreated his woman. She despised one who neglected his horses.

There was little sound but the drums and the leathery creaking of horse tack and bumping of buggy wheels through the silent town. The stifling smell of stiff canvas in hot sun was overpowering. At last the Hamtown trumpeter began playing a slow, melancholy refrain. The notes started low, reached out, faded off, then rose high to hang in dusty air stirred by hundreds of feet. The sound was so sorrowful that Young Frank rode up to the sobbing Bridget O'Reilly, dismounted, and caught up her hand in a reassuring grip. Nate Phipps was the picture of misery. Arrived at the grave site, Deke's face was set in the frozen lines of a marble carving.

"Yea, though I walk through the valley…" intoned a voice by the grave. Deke could not think of the silver train just now—his mind was on the deep, unrelenting hole before him. Looking into the grave, he wondered bleakly how many rides he might make this way. He gazed achingly at the stricken Emma. He was faintly aware of Apostle Thatcher's mellifluous voice, "…deliver us from evil…" Of the horn's clear notes sounding hymns. From a far remove, he recognized a favorite from Lavinia's childhood: "Jesus loves me, this I know, for the Bible tells me so…"

The Reverend Campbell was miraculously brief, as directed. Aaron Beard spoke a few words. "Pete always did like being underground." His voice was tender. "He'll be tucked in safe now. He can rest easy."

Calvin pulled himself free of his brown study to place a big hand on Pete's coffin. "Peter Beard was my friend. I valued him above all the riches of Araby. He relished life, cherished his children, prized his comrades. Thomas Carlyle said, 'The courage we desire is not the courage to die decently—but to live manfully.' No one I've known lived more manfully than Pete. Now he is consigned to the ages—and to this earth. Mother Earth sheltered him while he was alive. She will nurse him while he sleeps." With a few soft words of

German, Calvin reached for a fistful of dirt, scattered it gently over the box, and signaled for the coffin to be lowered.

Nate swallowed hard again and muttered to Jake, "Dern, this dog's hard to get over." He was so shaken he could scarcely be heard in the singing of "Nearer My God to Thee."

Apostle finished leading the assembly in the Lord's Prayer. Dr. Campbell gave the benediction. Nearby, Bridgie O'Reilly hid her eyes in her sopping-wet hankie. Young Frank guessed she could not endure the sight of Pete's cold grave. He was taken aback when she reached up and muttered low in his ear, "Don't you dast read any headstones, Frank. A man who reads a tombstone will lose his mind."

#####

CHAPTER THIRTY-ONE

SHOAT YANKEL

After the funeral services, with dusk settling over the mountains like a shroud, the Widow Wickersham alighted from her carriage at her back stoop. She broomed herself off, removed her plumed hat and walked down the center hallway to find the beechwood doors to her side parlor latched tight.

Suppertime stood in the hall, his face filled with fright. "Mr. Tacker in there," he stuttered. "Him and Mistuh Sutton. Tetchy as Grandma's bull, Mistuh Tacker."

Leorah went to a peephole in the flowery wallpaper. Gabe Tacker was so heated he'd risen from his chair to tromp up and down the room. Eyes bulging, wattles shaking, he turned to the younger man. "I've cheated and I've short-changed," he bellowed. "I've side-stepped and close-dealt. But I never committed murder. I won't be a party to it!" Snorting like an old buffalo, he appeared set to paw the carpet.

Sutton's eyes were unreadable. He sat stiffly and he spoke stiffly, his words as articulated as his starched collar. "I have only tried to reclaim what is rightfully mine," he said levelly. "No cause for you to jump to the conclusion I was behind this. I wasn't."

"Don't try to hoodwink me, you furbelowed fop. You're the only one in these parts could have bought and paid for killings. Or profited from them."

Hugging the wall, Leorah listened as Gabe ranted. "It's a good thing for all concerned that the bastards that done this is dead and gone. But I am serving you notice, Mister. If any more of your murderin' bunch show their faces, I'll be the first to sound the alarum. I have posted a reward notice on the bank door: Five hundred dollars for information leading to that alley scum Bull Mudgett."

The color left Garrett's face. He grasped the chair arms so hard that his knuckles whitened. His voice rose high. "How dare you! You have no proof Mudgett had any part in this."

"No proof—but a whole world of suspicion. Amounts to the same. Mudgett was thick with them flyers, and this whole camp is talking. By camp, I mean Mudgett's landlady, Mudgett's cronies, Mudgett's whores." Gabe glared. "If he is not guilty, let him come forth. I might add that plenty around here wouldn't be against stringing you up with your foreman. Tar sticks to the brush that dipped it."

Garrett leaned far forward on the chair, his pointy beard quivering. "You turncoat son of a bitch! You were quick as me to want Pearly production slowed!"

"Slowed, I'll admit to. Never blown to hell. Never with men inside her. You have not only brought down the wrath of God and these townspeople— but those flocks of reporter fellas I warned you about are lighting like magpies over fresh kill."

Gabe pulled out a large linen handkerchief, examined it irascibly, blew hard. "Well sir, the newsmen are your misery, yours and Harwood's. I am leaving on the morning stage for Central City. The apex question is ready to go to law. If we win, it'll be fair and square—leastwise, legal. I will then investigate doing business with your feisty wife. You, sonny boy, can go to the devil."

At the church, Emma helped the Reverend Mrs. Campbell wash and store away the cake trays. All the coffee was drunk, the last of the wake gatherers gently shooed on their way. Cappie waited beside Harriet at the hitch rail. Polly was cooling out the sorrels, slowing them from a light trot into a walk. When they'd laid off the heaviest of their sweat, she pulled up at the Sutton stable, where the mister's big black nickered a greeting. The old woman, sweating in tandem with the horses, unhitched and walked them out. "Guess you ain't ruint," she grumbled. She got out their curry combs and brushed and smoothed them down. As she led the first mare toward her stall in the gloom, a shadowy arm reached toward her, then withdrew. Polly stopped, sniffing. Mingled with the familiar horse smells was an oniony man's smell. She drew her knife and placed it between tight jaws. Watching over her shoulder, her good eye circling the shadows, she dippered oats into the feedbins, latched the sorrels in their stalls, and with a last scornful glance, marched away on foot.

Emma surveyed the many bouquets of flowers, which overflowed tables and hung from lintels. She collected the perkiest to tie on hers and Cappie's saddles. She'd sink them in water with a little sugar and early in the morning ride out to Mr. Beard's grave. A fresh grave looked raw as an open wound, as if the earth had been gashed and left undressed. She'd blanket it with a few colorful bouquets.

Next door, Leorah Wickersham hastened to wait on Big Gabe. That upstart Sutton had stalked out of her house, collar wilted, face thunderous, leaving Gabe fuming. Shortly, she had him settled on her bed for a rest, his fit of pique soothed by sympathetic crooning and a tot of hot sourmash.

In her parlor, Orey loosened her whalebone corset, exhaled in blessed relief, and leaned back on her fainting couch to think. She was as irate as Gabe. Mine camps went from boom to bust overnight. It wasn't always because the ore petered out, either. Mine men were a superstitious lot. A bad-luck mine would send plenty running like a bogeyman was after them. Murder could scare more. Just as her nest was being well-feathered, one wrong-headed conniver was trying to turn a bonanza into a bust. Leorah could not tolerate Garrett Sutton. His woman-killer smile and oily good manners had never fooled her for a minute. Now the despicable man might just have destroyed the town's—and her own—fine prospects. She could have too many eggs in the Aspen basket. At the funeral services, Cal Krueger had looked a beaten man. If this setback took all his starch, his crews could lose their grit, the court injunctions take hold, the bonanza and the Pearly sink slowly in a sea of troubles.

Who was to say the railroads would invest millions to reach a camp with a dawning reputation for hard luck and hard conduct? Without the rails, silver strike or no, Aspen could start on the downhill slide. If Gabe pulled out, he might take her with him—and he might not. She wasn't one for hanging on after a goose was cooked. She poured herself a whiskey, downed it straight, thought some more, then went to the kitchen and ate a cold, silent supper. Usually she turned to Gabe for perspective. She thought another spell, then came to a decision. She rose and rang a bell pull. When the dark, mottled face appeared at the door, she said, "Keep yourself handy, Suppertime. I'll need you to carry a note across town. Much later."

Garrett Sutton sat slumped in his front parlor drinking straight from the decanter of imported Mercier cognac. He'd long been leery of strong drink. It fogged his wits, and he prided himself on having his about him. But this night he needed to dull his thinking. His dismal boyhood feeling, the old sense of abandonment, had returned. He'd thought the feeling done with, yet here it was, like a long-lost cat stalking home out of the past. All those who'd wronged him flitted through his head like specters: his own father, who'd done nothing to give him a leg up in a harsh world; childhood chums, sniffing down their noses at his bare-bones family—until the day he'd ruined the business prospects of two or three; the Denver City partner who'd plotted to bilk him—before Garrett beat the man to the draw; a half-literate Quaker prospector who'd cheated him on not one mine, but two—the son of a bitch must have known the Pearly's secret and prodded Krueger to get it under lease; his wife, whom he'd pictured presiding regally over a table of fine china and high-toned guests—far from being the helpmate he'd envisioned, she'd proved willful and traitorous, questioning his judgments, abandoning his house.

Now Tacker was berating him as if he were a common criminal. Even the once-reliable Bull Mudgett—hinting at mayhem, never murder—had botched matters, his botching leading to this damn kettle of fish. Mudgett had been a convenient bully boy, but sometimes, like a feral animal, he had to be whipped into line. Well, the hyena was out of the cage, out of control, and on the loose. Garrett too admired a man who was clever. He felt nothing but contempt for one who got caught. Mudgett hadn't been clever, he'd been rash. If Bull were taken, he planned to declare him fired weeks before, discharged over the despicable poisoning of defenseless livery stock. He'd deny any recent dealings with the low-life. He'd removed the man from the payroll a year past, when he'd jumped the Conundrum claim. Had dealt with him in cash only. Serve the bollixer right if he hung.

As for himself, he'd be inconvenienced for a spell—but he'd been inconvenienced before. Despite what that old peckerhead Tacker said, few would be provoked into hanging a prominent mine owner. Nor would he be brought to law. He had nothing on paper to link him with the Pearly calamity. The claim itself was in his wife's name, not his. There'd be no one to point a finger at him but a common thug.

It eased Garrett's mind to picture Bull, alongside Bisbee, racing out of Colorado at breakneck speed. Garrett untied his cravat and unbuttoned his vest. The cognac—and no doubt the encounter with Tacker—had soured his stomach.

Or maybe it was last night's fracas with Yankel and Felcher. The unsavory pair had had the effrontery to knock on his door, two shot-up wild dogs, coated with trail dirt and leaking blood on his peachblow limestone front stoop. Though it had given him satisfaction to face them down, he'd been disquieted by the Yankel fellow's threats. The man was known to be unbalanced.

"What do you want?" Garrett had snapped, answering the door pull.

"We're wanting our pay, Mister," snarled Yankel.

"I know nothing about pay, not for the likes of you."

"Well sir…" Fess began.

Shoat had shoved his way through the door. "You'd better know about it, Sutton," he'd barked, the eye on the front side of his twisted head black as creek mud. "We been peppered doin' your dirty work on the hump."

"They caught us out," Fess Felcher's voice was a whine. "Cain't stay in this town. Gotta move on." Fess thought longingly of his scrawny wife and bawling babe. He might never see either again. What he did see was Shoat's temper rising up to the blue vein in his forehead, which pulsed with the surge. *Oh Christ*, he thought.

"Mudgett's been payin' us, but Mudgett ain't at hand. You owe us foremen's wages. And two or three bonuses."

Fess could tell Shoat meant to bring his gun into play. But with only one good arm, he wasn't quick about it. The mine-owner was faster. In his hand was a small derringer, glinting in a businesslike manner. "You're not on my payroll. I owe you nothing." His tone, even with the fine sugar coating, was as deadly as Shoat Yankel's.

Fess's whine rose to a howl as they were ushered at gunpoint to the back of the house and out the kitchen door, his shot-up arm banging on the door frame. "W-we'll take you to law…" His voice was the squawk of a dull saw as he stumbled on the dark porch steps.

Sutton laughed. "Try explaining those bullet wounds to a judge, simpleton. You'd best light out for old Mexico, both of you."

Shoat Yankel spoke with the hiss of a cobra. "I won't waste a fart on you tonight, Sutton. But someday I'll even the score. You won't never know when I'm coming. But I'll come."

Garrett had slammed the door, although he had not shut out the memory of the man's menace.

In the alleyway at the end of the Sutton backyard, Fess had collapsed against the side of the stable, moaning piteously. "This arm hurts like hell, we got no money and we got to ride."

"Shut yer yap, yellow-belly." Breathing hard, Shoat filled two oat buckets from the bin. His movements hampered by his injured arm, he hung them over their horses' heads, then, while the animals ate, filled several large gunny sacks with oats and laced them with latigos and rope to the backs of the saddles, wincing at the pain. "Now we got us horse feed fer travelin'."

"My shoulder hurts."

"You got a bullet through it, knot-head. I got one through mine."

"Yours ain't yer gun arm."

"Pains me all the same. Have a belt from this here bottle, quit your belly-aching—and mount up."

Struggling into the saddle, Fess choked back his weeping. "Which way we headed?" he asked unsteadily.

"Got us a stop to make before we leave Pitkin. Cain't settle with that shitheel Sutton tonight. But I got me one I *can* settle with."

Tite and Annie Pomeroy's cart bounced into their barnyard, lanterns bobbing. "I'll jest warm us some of that corn soup for supper, Tite," said Annie. Her heart and her head were heavy.

"I'll put Elmer up. Make sure that hired boy stripped the cows. Be along." Tite removed Elmer's blinders, unbuckled harness, and carrying a lantern in one hand, a load of tack in the other, went into the barn.

"Evenin,' Pomeroy," greeted Fess above the bore of a rifle. His drink-slurred voice creaked. He was barely visible behind the stanchion door where he'd propped the gun. Tite knew a weapon in the hands of a pint-sized drunk as more dangerous than most. He stared at his runty neighbor, his own hands full, his gun out of reach, knowing he was caught out. Then he was seized from behind and goat-tied with baling rope.

"I'm leavin' town, shitepoke," gloated Shoat in his ear. "but not before I give you back that beating you give me." Grimacing, Shoat trussed the big rancher to a barn upright. Then he positioned the lantern, gave him a long, satisfied look, pulled back, and threw a punch so hard it drew a groan from deep in Tite's insides. The sound of the blows that followed made Fess Felcher's arm wound ache something fierce. Once the old galoot was trussed, Fess had dropped his rifle to accommodate the bottle, and he stood in the dim light pulling on the last of the whiskey, trying not to watch.

Before long, Tite Pomeroy's face was a pulp. Fess could hardly abide blood. He was never one for the butchering at the Miller ranch. Nor could he believe how Shoat could do so much damage with only one good fist. He was battering Tite to splintered bone and raw meat. With every crunching blow, Fess felt sorrier for himself than he could say.

"Hain't got that mad of yours worked off yet, Shoat? No use beatin' the life clear outa' the man." Fess was more than ready to quit this and ransack the ranchhouse for likker and valuables.

"Don't...crowd...me," Shoat warned, his voice still dangerous despite his labored breathing.

Drink had dulled Fess so he scarcely felt a swift, headlong rush. His arm was jostled so hard he screeched in agony—and Annie Pomeroy raced past. Shoat had just drawn back for another bone-cracking blow when, running full-tilt, she stuck him with a pitchfork square in his behind. Tite's farm tools were honed to a good edge, the tines of his pitchfork sharp as needles. Shoat shrieked and fell forward, clawing at what felt like a clutch of arrows in his backside. Annie left the fork in him and turned on Fess, down on his knees, holding his arm and wailing. She snatched up his gun and sobbed, "Git! Git, or so help me, I'll shoot the both of you!"

Fess lurched to his feet and managed to plant one foot on his partner's backside and yank out the fork, which had gone deep.

"Don't you provoke me!" yelled Annie. "You git! And git fast!"

The jostling and yanking had stirred up Fess's wound so he could barely lay a shaking hand on the horses they'd hidden in back of the barn. Shoat was pouring blood like a turned-on faucet, and the animals, spooked by the fresh blood smell, danced and backed. "Hold still, goddam you," he blubbered. For a minute he thought to leave Shoat behind. Only some misshapen shred of comradeship impelled him to heave his pard belly-first over a saddle. With Shoat clutching the saddlehorn in a near-faint, and Fess's gun unsteady in Annie Pomeroy's hands, the men turned haltingly north and west and rode out.

####

261

CHAPTER THIRTY-TWO

THE WIDOW WICKERSHAM

In his room behind the Elephant bar, Deke struggled through the quicksands of a troubled dream. As he was about to be sucked under, a timid knock brought him up like a bung popped from a barrel. Shaking off the dream, he raised the big Colt from beneath his pillow and asked huskily, "Who is it?"

"Powerful sorry to put you out, Major suh." Suppertime's voice was muffled. "Miz Wickersham wants she should talk with you. Mighty important, she says."

Deke cleared the rough sleep from his throat. "I'll be there directly."

"If h'it's all the same, sir, she'd as soon you come a hour before first light." Suppertime's tone was anxious. "Mistuh Tacker is in—uh, in residence. Miz Wickersham as soon he snorin' full-bore when you come."

Though Deke was puzzled, he said, "Tell the lady I'll be there." He shook himself awake, lit a lamp, and examined his pocket watch on the night stand. Two o'clock in the morning. Well, he'd slept a good four hours. He rose, splashed his face from the washstand bowl, sloshed his mouth with baking soda and wild mint paste, dressed and went to Buford, stalled across the alley. Fordy whinnied softly, his satiny nose exploring the familiar shoulder for a potato peeling. Avoiding his saloon, still throwing out noise and light, Deke chucked the big bay into a slow walk. He'd have a word with the guards at the ore dumps, the Clarendon, and the Pearly adits. When he'd made the rounds, he'd head leisurely for the Wickersham house.

Next door to the widow's, a hulking figure sidled out of the Sutton stable and moved up the yard to the big house. Finding the back door bolted, the man crept to a lighted parlor window, waited, then peered inside. Sutton was asleep under the yellow light of a lamp with a painted china globe. His head lolled on the cold, marble-topped table, his tidy beard bent to one side. He looked more an incompetent store clerk than a dandified mine tycoon.

The prowler tried windows and found them securely locked. He located a rock and used it to break the lock on the slanting, ground-installed cellar door where coal was off-loaded from a delivery wagon. He dropped into the coal bin below. There were muffled expletives. Then silence.

When Bull Mudgett materialized in the Sutton parlor, he was black with coal dust and filled with disgust. Fess and Shoat had failed to keep their rendezvous down-valley. Bob Bisbee was on his way south to Arizona Territory, where he had him an Apache half-breed in a silver camp. She was in love with Bob's pretty face, and he was primed to sit in a saloon and gamble and have him some fun with his Apache whore. Bull had no whores who cared about him. He used them too hard.

He had circled back from down-valley, keeping to the river, had ridden in at this hour last night and eavesdropped by the back-alley clubroom entrance of the Chloride, where church deacons slipped in unobserved for a hand of cards. Had he suspicioned that the Pearly bombing had gone grievously wrong, or that he himself was hunted, he'd never have come near this camp. He'd expected folks might have a mad going. What he hadn't figured on was full-out catastrophe—or the spiteful, hate-filled, of-a-mind-to-hang talk he heard from the cardroom. With that complication, Bull had spent the better part of the last twenty-four hours under the hay in one of Sutton's empty horse stalls. His nose ran, his skin itched, and he'd had to choke back countless sneezes. Hay-choked was worse than wet-soaked.

He could scarcely credit how the Pearly shots had so misfired. His plan had been to sicken the guard at the East Hopkins silver dump, draw off Krueger. The timing was to coincide with the shift changes, leaving the shafthouse empty, the fewest observers on hand. The steam engines and cage hoists and other machinery were to become wreckage. That was the plan.

The Hooples must have miscalculated at every step: mistimed the arrival of their balloon; employed more than five times the explosives he'd prescribed. And their luck had been bad. Some of their charges had plummeted down the cage shaft, striking a cache of black powder at the bottom. Men claimed the explosion was as big as Krakatoa.

Feeling the power of the blasts thrum through his legs far out on the Wozniak ranch, Bull suspected the flyers had overstepped. Their bravado, as they raced down-valley, had aggravated him beyond reason. On the back road leading from the Catherine stage-stop to the Carbondale coke ovens, when they had at last eased up and halted to water the horses, they'd stepped up their braggadocio. When they turned contentious over their pay, Bull had finally exploded. "You've no doubt turned the whole camp against us," he roared. By the time they'd neared the far creek coursing through the

Cottonwood Ranch, he'd ordered them on their way, lacking the extra pay they demanded. They'd turned ugly, laid about with threats. Their retreating backs beckoned like bulls-eyes. So he shot them down. He'd lost his head and killed two. And as he'd learned since, those two had murdered in turn. At least five were dead. If he was discovered, the camp could hang him twice.

Bull might be on the scout, but he did not plan on being caught out. He intended to ride hard into the La Sal Mountain country, go to ground at Brown's Hole, then light out for Frisco. He'd had all of Aspen he could stomach. The Hooples' money was on him. But as long as he was in camp, he would just help himself to an extra mount and some easy boodle. He knew where to find both. While he was about it, he meant to take care of the only man in these parts who'd trouble to chase after him.

He paused a moment, considered waking the boss, thought better of it. He suspected what Sutton might have to say, and he didn't care to hear it. He'd noted the empty cognac bottle, the wet, gulping snores. He lifted the derringer from the outstretched hand curled on the cool marble. When he removed the diamond watch fob and its thick gold chain, Sutton never moved, though his breath rattled. He stirred only slightly when his foreman dug in the vest pocket which habitually held his purse.

Moving fast but sure, Bull gulped down dinner scraps from the kitchen, paused to listen for the adenoidal snores of the hired girl in her room off the pantry, then ransacked the bedrooms above and removed items from pantry bins below. At length, carrying two large linen pillow slips, one filled with goose feathers, the other with the Sutton woman's valuables, he slipped out the back way and mounted one of the sorrels, saddled and waiting. On a lead rope was a nondescript animal he'd lassoed from a mid-valley pasture. Sutton's black gelding with the white spur slashes was too familiar to risk riding. But no one would be quick to recognize a ranch workhorse or one-half a span of harness horses. The harness-broke sorrel was a fair saddle mount, she'd do. He'd checked the mare's crow-hopping, reining her in sharp, then rode easy through back streets, his head in an old derby hat slumped low as if he were half-asleep. It was maybe an hour before dawn. When he reached the elephant's back alleyway, he tethered both horses to a water barrel, securing the pillowcase of loot under a tattered serape across the mare's withers. Then he stepped silently up to the window of the room where Deke Burdine slept, muffled the bore of his pistol with the feather pillow, and fired four shots at close range into the major's bed.

At the appointed hour, Deke tied Buford to a clump of young aspens near Mrs. Wickersham's entryway, knocked lightly, and was greeted as cheerily as if he'd arrived for afternoon tea. Putting a finger to her lips, Leorah led him to the kitchen and closed and latched the door. "I thank you, sir, for calling at this contemptible hour. I had to be certain of seeing you before you left again for the smelters, and this is a meeting best unobserved. May I pour you a drink?"

"Coffee would be a boon if you have it, ma'am."

Leorah beamed. She dearly loved Southern courtesies. After she'd served him strong coffee and a hefty slice of lemon sponge pie and decorously rearranged the folds of her dressing gown, the widow recounted Gabe Tacker's and Garrett Sutton's heated argument of the afternoon. "If Gabe says that polecat paid for killing, then he paid for killing. If he's put up bounty for this Mudgett, then Mudgett's rightly wanted. I thought you and Calvin Krueger should know about the killers. They've fallen out with the thieves. Won't do a spit of good to talk to that bootlicking Harwood."

Deke gazed glumly into his coffee cup.

"Major, this town has suffered terrible tragedy. My troubles are as nothing to those of others, but I am a lone widow who must make my way through the slings and arrows of fortune." She poured a jigger of whiskey into her own coffee cup. "I'd be more than grateful for your notions on how matters stand—in the Pearly and in this camp. Has Cal Krueger lost his sap? Will he stick? Does Sutton own the force to try another attack?"

Deke recollected Emma's words. "Sutton will fight like a cornered she-bear with cubs," she'd declared.

"Oh, he'll walk on eggs until the uproar dies down," he said aloud. "And from what you say, he won't have Tacker's millions behind him. But he's bound and determined to have that ore. I doubt murder will stop him."

"As for Calvin," he said, "he's shaken. But he's never walked away from an unfinished proposition in his life. He won't start now." He finished the pie, surprised at his appetite.

"But," persisted Leorah, "you'll have hard times getting the goods on that mountebank Sutton. He's slippery as sleet."

Deke said only, "A man who's cornered loses his edge. He doesn't always think straight, doesn't take time to reason matters through. Sooner or later he'll 'hoist himself on his own petar'."

"What of that hard case Mudgett?"

"Mudgett's as good as jailed. Wyatt Earp'll be hunting him down, and

Wyatt's a one-man wolf pack. He'll dog his trail if it leads to the mountains of Tibet."

As they talked things through, Leorah gazed longingly at the major, wishing a moment for what could not be. She was impressed with the man's grasp of everything from the Indian situation to the railroaders' plans. Gabe had been right. Both the D. & R.G. and the Midland lines were preparing to race into Aspen.

"And I can promise you this: there'll be one more Ute uprising before we're through."

Leorah was shocked. "My word! I thought we were done with Indians."

"They've been treated rough, and they'll rebel. But it'll be put down. After that, the railroads will scrap their way to our door."

Considerably heartened, Orey insisted on cooking Deke's breakfast. "Gabe's dead to the world. And you look peaked, Major. You've thinned down. Responsibility will do it. Worry a man to a shadow."

She'd chattered gaily, refilling his cup and his plate, lingering over talk of Lute Kellogg's bright prospects, regaling him with amusing stories of other camps. One tale concerned a fallen woman going by the name of "Silverheels" across the mountains in Buckskin Joe. She'd recently nursed a passel of men through a bad epidemic of the pox. "Then she came down with the plague herself," sighed Leorah.

"Did she live?"

"Nobody knows. She left town. They named a mountain for her. I could understand naming a mountain for someone big as California Catton," she chuckled, "though it'd be confusing. She already has her a state."

Leorah Wickersham filled the room with cheer, lifting his spirits. *There's more than one reason Tacker values her hospitality*, thought Deke.

The sun was well up when he let himself out on the porchway, took a deep breath of morning air, and turned to lean into the transomed front door and again thanked the widow for her hospitality and information.

Emma had ridden to the cemetery at dawn, before any of her shadowers would think to follow, the bouquets for Mr. Beard wrapped in wet rags in containers and tied to hers and Cappie's saddles. The old sourdough guard had looked furtive the entire ride. "Never fear, Cappie," she'd assured him, "none of your pards will catch you toting posies like a bridesmaid. Not at this hour."

Infinitely sad, she'd arranged sprays of zinnias and daisies, delphinium and larkspur in cans filled with water from the Ute spring. Satisfied the grave looked its best, she'd felt better for her busy hands. As they headed back through Mrs. Rowland's sheep pasture, its grass heavy with night dew, she wondered at the ways women busy-bodied over a death: baking, cleaning, making calls, serving food, arranging flowers. *It's because we haven't learned to value silence*, she answered herself. *We feel swallowed up by the grave and its dead. We fear its silence, so we buzz around like worker bees.* One of the Greeks said, "I have often regretted my speech—never my silence." There were many times Emma welcomed quiet, and it seemed an eternity since she'd last sat in contemplation over the pages of a book. Lost in thought as Cappie opened the gate for them to cross and return containers to the church, she glanced at Leorah Wickersham's place. Aggie McClaren was partial to the widow, and Emma herself had come to enjoy her, though she was a little disconcerted by the woman's syrupy voice and come-hither ways. *Silly of me*, she thought. With a practiced eye, she looked over the widow's flower beds, a-riot with sweet williams and early asters. She noted judiciously that the bridal wreath, its airy blooms gone, could use a good pruning. As she looked, she became aware of a familiar horse. Buford, his big head lowered, tail switching, munching greenery by the front fence. She was so surprised that she was only dimly aware of a man opening the fly-screen door. Then, her head beginning to swim, she peeked harder. The man leaned his big frame into the doorway, saying his goodbyes. Such a wave of dizziness swept Emma that later she could not recall Harriet's silent tread across the timothy, could not recollect Cappie leading Harriet through the gate under the thick cover of young cottonwoods, or of sitting stunned in the saddle as he latched the gate behind them. She did not look back, she couldn't have seen. In an instant of time, Emma's eyes, like the heart beneath them, had turned to stone.

####

CHAPTER THIRTY-THREE

CLEAN SLATES

Calvin stood on Deane street gloomily surveying the extent of the Pearly disaster. He looked up to find Mike Medjeric at his side and thought drearily, *He's here to give notice.* Then he noted the crowd behind Mike. His old companions were there. And hundreds of townsmen, equipped for business.

"Ain't no goons gonna spook us, Mr. Krueger," Mike announced. "The Pearly's shook up, but we can make do without that shafthouse."

"Don't need cages, neither!" called Aaron Beard.

"Nor machinery." The bench boys were lined up at the ready with picks and shovels.

Calvin felt a flutter like nestlings' wings. The heaviness weighing him down began to lift. Already townspeople, including a pack of miners' wives, had set to work. They kept at it far into the night, installing bellows and pipes for blowing in fresh air, replacing twisted iron tram rails, shoring up weakened timber. They moved a shack up to the Vinnie Tunnel entrance to serve as a temporary mine office. Although smaller repairs would be ongoing, in a day or two most of the explosion trash was cleared, full crews were again picking silver, the cars carrying out ore. A broom the size of a mountain town had swept the site clean.

Willard Arey had been confounded. "Ain't a-one of them people being paid," he marveled. "And they've worked like the resurrection is on us."

Only two men had given notice. One had the broken hip. The other's sand had sifted. Calvin straightened his shoulders and set to work. He forced himself to stop pondering over and over the outcome had he stayed at his post: an exercise which led nowhere and profited nothing.

From the pillow beside him in their bed at night, Vinnie sought to ease his anguish. "You can't go blaming yourself for what happened, Cal. It was the fortunes of war."

She smoothed his hair from his brow. "Though you're sick of bloodshed and weary of death, when the next fight looms, you'll stand. You'll nerve yourself, stand, and go at it again."

Calvin wondered how Vinnie, who'd never been to war, had found that thought.

"Your training will keep you going 'til your faith comes home. And it'll come, after you've done with sorrow."

Calvin lay in their bed searching the dark. "I wonder," he said, "if my span of years will be time enough to learn all life's lessons."

"Of course not, husband. That is why we're given eternity."

Three days later the empty ore wagons and jack trains came clattering down off the hump. Men tended the stock and set about re-provisioning. Olvera rushed to Pete's house to hold each girl tight; then, his round face wet with tears, groped his way to Beck's to replenish the train's grub. Deke, Skinner, and Nate turned mules, jacks, and horses out in the big Cowenhaven pastures to roll sweat and work knots from their backs. Farmers assisted Miles with checking sore feet and correcting shoeing. Wagons were repaired, harness mended. Skinner ran knowing hands over the animals' flanks and legs. "These critters are wore a little. No worse than you fellas. They'll have a good rest tonight."

Deke assembled a meeting of the outfit at the pastures. After commending them for a fine job of work, he brought them up to date. "Appears Mudgett's troublemakers are scattered to the winds. From here on, trains should roll out and back in a non-stop loop. But," he warned, "there'll yet be trouble. For one, we'll have less charity from oncoming traffic."

"That wall-eyed stage driver does not plan on standin' back for us more'n once," agreed Nate.

"Nor them Leadville drovers, neither," muttered Shotgun. He leaned on the railing beside Deke, his beard dirtier by half, mouth tight with fatigue. "Got to do something about that corduroy section at the crest," he said, spitting explosively. "The one where the drivers duke it out." The prize ring, as it was called, had slipped Deke's mind. It was a long, near the summit stretch of trail with room for only one-way traffic. Two drovers meeting there customarily climbed down and fought each other with their fists. The winner then drove his team over the narrow corduroy surfacing. The loser must wade, push, whip, and cuss his animals through the ugly mud wallow alongside.

"Lute fought some Leadville drover to a draw," said Shotgun. "Took him near a quarter of an hour. 'Bout that time Olwen Davies unlimbered his pistol, told the sumbitch we wasn't about to lose no more time. Nor ground neither.

When that Cornisher gets around to talk, he's what you'd call forceful."

Deke was pleased that Olwen had showed grit, though not half as pleased as Luther.

Shotgun persisted. "Cain't have no boxing match ever' trip. Takes too much starch out of the boy. Adds too much time to the haul."

"Mayhap we could schedule a fight match in town, settle the passage ahead of time." Nate looked at Luther and winked. Lute took no notice. He was nodding on the wagon seat beside Scooper, sound asleep sitting straight up. Not a few drovers and riders had laid down in the pasture, too dog-tired to eat or to hear the major out.

Lute had been startled by the work of riding a wagon seat. On a hard trail, a driver must stay as alert as the scouts. He'd never minded work, but this job took all his grit just to hold down the worry. After unloading in Granite and Leadville, they'd turned right around and gone at it again. He'd never been so played out in his life. When the major got to checking over the receipts in his charge, he could scarcely prop his eyes open.

"Superintendent Patterson wired me," said the major. "Said you made him give you his best price—and here I thought I already had it."

"Understand you had to box the train through in the bargain." Deke's look was serious, though there was a glint in his eye.

Lute was weary, and he was choked with trail dust. "Yes sir," he said.

"Why don't you and Scooper have a swim at the ice pond," said Deke. "Lavinia's expecting us at their place for supper. I'll see you there."

Amid the to-do of the ore train's return, Garrett Sutton appeared suddenly on the streets of camp. Well-pressed and stolidly erect, he rode his black to the Tacker bank, to the telegraph office, up to the Columbine, then to the offices of Dunbar & Black, allowing himself one brief, hard look at the Pearly. A few nodded his way. Many glared or stared past without speaking. Mrs. Ollie Davidson, who'd considered the handsome mine-owner a community pillar, was so flustered she stammered—an unheard of condition for her. Even Judge Duckworth hesitated, though he mumbled a grudging, "Howdy, Sutton." The bench boys made loud, pointed remarks about Nale Wilson's killers.

Willard was beside himself. "Will you look at that shitheel—on the street, bluffing his way through this like a bad hand of cards," he blustered. "Didn't lift a finger to repair his wife's mine, neither."

Calvin felt torment. *The man'll not come to justice. It'll fall to me to render it*, he thought once again.

Though Sutton's bland expression did not betray him, he too boiled beneath the surface. He was appalled by the wreckage strewn far across the mountain, by butchery that had set his own town against him. The only ones eager to greet him were swarms of news reporters. He spurred the black 'til he'd lost them, then settled back in a slow trot. Doffing his hat to old associates, he made a mental note of every last person who acted chilly or rebuffed him. As he rode past the train pasturage, Deke noted how the man had altered. He wasn't as spear-thin as Doc Holliday, but he looked far deadlier.

The reporters, not a whit affrighted, would not be turned aside. From Sacramento to Philadelphia, the Pearly strike—and Pearly warfare—were thunderous news. Though Sutton might be tempted to lash them out of town with a whip, the town welcomed their presence. Aspen folk wanted their anger aired to the wide world. Newsmen themselves found fresh stories by the hour. Balloon murderers. Opulent bounties. Men hunted and men hunting. Mudgett and Bisbee, Yankel and Felcher, as notorious as the James gang, disappearing like curls of thin smoke. Wyatt Earp was a reporter's answered prayer, Apostle Thatcher a find of pure gold. Old war records and Indian skirmishes were copybook fodder. When a nosy newsman sniffed out Annie Pomeroy, watching over her battered husband in Doc Alderfer's surgery, the doc flattened him with his fist and threw him down the back stairs. Then he ambled over to the horse and mule pasture to report to the ore crew on Tite's condition. "His head is bad scrambled, but he'll live."

"Well, fiddle me for a fool," muttered Shotgun. "Knew I shoulda dropped them two up the mountain."

"Mrs. Pomeroy finished off one varmint for you, Shotgun," said Doc. "Pitchfork wounds are injected with manure, they fester fast. Shoat Yankel will be dead in a few weeks."

"Fess Felcher is as good as finished too," said Nate. "He's on three different wanted posters. Bounty hunters is after the little runt like starved wolves."

Willard, examining Lute's pack of receipts, peered over his reading specs. "Hear tell Felcher's skinny wife is on her ranch porch in a vale of tears."

The men shook their heads. It was hard times for a woman with a fatherless babe.

"Aspen's bad element is thinning out fast," remarked Doc, helping himself to a tipple from one of the hunters' ticklers.

Deke didn't see fit to mention the bullet holes in his bedding behind the saloon. He wanted no chasing after shadows. Wyatt would track the malefactors—to the Andes or to the Alps.

Scooper and Lute stood by Pete Beard's grave, their hats over their hearts. "I never knew the man well. I'm sorry as can be for Tacy," said Scooper.

"Mr. Beard had a way with the young." Lute's voice was woebegone, thinking of the Beard girls' orphaned condition. "Not only his own. He guessed my mind before I half knew what I was thinking."

"He has a good plot, under this here big fir tree. Most cemeteries is so damn bare the dust devils blow round and round."

"Mr. Beard misliked the wind. Guess they wouldn't put him where he'd be pestered with wind."

The boys stood a few moments in tribute, then picked up their shovels and heavy chestnut marker and trudged past the fancier headstones to Frankie's grave. They dug a trench for the headboard, tugged it in place and looked it over from four sides to correct the angle. When Lute was satisfied, he tamped in the marker and stomped the ground down hard. He'd spoken with Sister Coon about the inscription.

"Thet girl nevah had no family name she could claim. Jus' Frannie Mae, that all she knowed. She a good heart, Mistah Lute. What you reckon I best do wid her money?"

Lute had thought on that a few minutes. "I guess she might want you to find kin, leastways another orphan or two, maybe help them west."

When Sister Coon spoke, it was as if she'd learned a fine thing. "Why, reckon I mought find me a stray or two at that."

After several minor adjustments, the boys stood back to survey their handiwork. The carved words stood out plain in the polished wood:

Frannie Mae

Born in Kentucky

Home to her Savior

July 4, 1885

At last Lute flopped on the grass. His eyes, to Scoop's relief, were dry. "I'll give the plot a good weeding come fall," he said in a composed voice. "Mrs. Lavinia promised to help plant flowers." The August afternoon was calm. No thunder clouds were building. The sky was still and clear. Lute leaned back on his elbows and looked at Little Ute Mountain directly ahead. "See that trail winds up Little Ute?"

Scoop didn't have his friend's keen eyesight. The mountain looked like a wall of solid timber. Jake Levy's saws hadn't reached this far. He nodded anyway.

"The Major collected me one day to go lie up along that game run. We watched a bull elk step past, so close we heard his breath whistle. Had his harem following. Eight cows. That bull moved like he was lord of the hill. Prettiest sight I ever saw. The Major told me a secret: he's about the only man in these parts doesn't kill big game."

"Noooo!" exclaimed his friend.

"Expect he would, if he was starved out. He said, 'I'd rather watch wapiti than eat them any day.'"

"What about all them elk he directs Shotgun to kill fer hides?"

"He's even got Shotgun worried. Says at this rate the elk'll be cleaned out of here in two years."

Such a notion seemed so absurd that neither boy gave it much credit. They rolled over on their bellies to watch a wolf spider laying her eggs in a wild raspberry bush. She wove careful little covers, like tiny cottony bolls, for the eggs.

"Reckon you and me'll ever have young'uns?" Scoop asked, chewing on a wad of spruce gum. He ordinarily dreamed of Svea Hoaglund in a soft bed with his head buried deep in her bosoms. The unexpected idea of her with a babe suckling there and two more yelling for supper at the table consternated him. He harked back to Bessie Felcher biting off those wood spoons. When he turned his head, Lute was asleep, his breath coming at deep, restful intervals. Scooper let him snooze a spell, then pelted him with pebbles.

"Rise up, deadhead! You ain't ready for this graveyard nohow!"

Using a shortcut through the woods, the boys raced to the ice pond, skinned out of their clothes, and jumped feet-first into the cold, clear water.

With the stock pastured and the mine going, Nate Phipps paid a visit to Pie Burkhardt, had Sister Coon spot-clean and press his good suit, and wearing his sun goggles and a half-pint of rosewater, rode up to the Clarendon with Injun Ike in tow. He and his girl Emma had hardly had a word at the funeral or during long hours of mine cleanup. He found her stirring a batch of soap in the sideyard by the telegraph office.

"Why, you stylish scalawag!" she cried, standing back to admire him.

Ike she saluted with solemnity. Utes frowned on womanly displays of affection.

Holding her at arm's length to look her over, Nate was pleased to see she'd lost her peaked look. Her skin was honeyed, her hair sun-bleached, her green eyes bright. "Only lady I know looks as fetching in a apron as a ballgown."

Ike lounged on his pony in the warm sun while Nate filled her in on the many happenings with the ore train, talking Ute so Ike could savor his words of praise. "That tadpole did a fine job on the hump. Spotted a big break, saved a few necks. Earned his keep."

Emma too spoke in the guttural tongue. "Born to be a chief."

"Knows his mind. You'll note that pony is the only animal not yarded up with the outfit. The boy may love horseflesh—but he don't pamper it."

Iacono had one leg thrown up on his pony's neck as she munched contentedly on a clump of lambstail. "She eating," he said placidly. "Like company when she eat."

Deke had ridden up, feeling shy, wondering how he might go about speaking with his girl. He did not care to break his word; yet he was filled with joy at the sight of her, so proud of owning her affection he could have burst his seams. When she turned toward him, he doffed his hat. All his heart's feelings were in his eyes.

"Perhaps you can watch young Ike at work yourself, ma'am." His tone was bantering. "As owner of the Pearly Everlasting mine, you might want to accompany an upcoming silver run over the hump." He looked at Nate, who nodded agreement. "The trail will be safe, we figure." He did not add that they had decided Mrs. Sutton would be safer out of this camp and than inside it. Her husband still rode these streets.

Deke expected to see Emma's eyes spark, her face fill with eagerness. Instead, her eyes were empty, her tone cold as she answered, "I think not, Major." She stared through him as vacantly as though he were a passing pack mule.

Deke felt as if he'd been struck. Of course they'd agreed not to court, but that was hardly reason for her dismissive tone and icy look. Nate too was taken aback.

"Why, Emma, honey, you're the proper Pearly owner—by rights you should see some of your silver to them capacious Leadville smelters." He looked at her carefully. "Can't believe you ain't still champin' to get out of this camp."

"My trip through the mine will be excursion aplenty," she said shortly. Mr. Krueger didn't hold with superstition about a woman in a mine being bad luck and stirring up tommy-knockers. Tommies were the stuff of children's tales, scapegoats for misplaced mine tools and underground carelessness.

Emma held her head high. If she looked into Major Burdine's eyes she feared she would catch fire and go up like dry kindling. Deke stood confounded, Nate with a baffled expression. It was simply not Emma's way to turn huffy and act disgruntled.

"I have my soap to see to," she said abruptly, "before it clouds over again." Although she would have liked to fell a tree, wrestle an eight-mule team, chop a cord of wood or jump on Harriet and run off, Emma had been sweating out her misery over the soap-making. Her eyes awash with tears she did not care to shed, she picked up her skirts and headed for the kettles.

Nate turned to the stunned Deke and said, "B'lieve I'll just lend the lady a hand, D.K. See you at the Kruegers'."

Deke, his usual taciturn expression given way to bafflement, turned Buford and went away up the street.

In the side yard a big iron kettle was warming over a fire, Emma's soap ingredients readied. She picked up a box of red devil lye, then put it back down to mop at her eyes with her apron. "Got a speck in my eye," she said, her voice muffled. "Uncle Nate, would you kindly g-get me some chicken feathers from the henyard at Mrs. Lafferty's? Her place is t-two doors down."

"Course, honey."

When Nate returned with a small nosegay of discarded feathers, Emma had a ten-gallon can of grease leavings warming over one fire and was stirring the lye in boiling water over another.

"Whew, that grease stinks!" Nate sniffed at the pot of rancid stuff.

"Five months of hoarded hotel kitchen fat." Emma was all business.

"Hard to figure how a thing gone so bad could turn into something that makes a body clean."

"This is powerful soap; it'll peel the skin off the snout of a wild hog."

"What do you do with that lye?" Nate pulled his sun goggles down over his eyes to peer curiously into the simmering kettle.

"Double, double, toil and trouble. Fire burn and cauldron bubble," she teased. "Soon as the lye is dissolved, we let it cool. When the grease is hot, we add it, along with some borax, a pinch of sugar, salt, a little ammonia, then throw in the eye of a newt and the toe of a frog." Emma's wicked sense of fun hadn't deserted her. "Why don't you take over for me, stir this while I mix up my paste?"

Nate peeled off his coat, hung it on the fence, tightened his sun goggles, and began stirring. When he looked up, Amos Blackwell was beside him, peering curiously into the pot.

"Thought you went home to your ma, sonny. " Amos leaned closer. "Now see here, bubby. This lye is caustic. I want you to scat. Go play under them horses at the hitching rail."

Amos' face puckered up. "Got no place to go."

"How about yer own backyard?"

"Ma won't let me in the gate."

"I can see why. The woman no doubt prays daily for release from her mortal coil."

"What's a mortal coil?"

"H'it's a cross-grained, trouble-making little devil like you sprung full-blown from a unsuspecting woman's loins."

Emma, concentrating on her mix, said, "You can set that kettle over there on the dirt to cool."

As Nate lifted the heavy, boiling cauldron from the fire, Amos, quick as a darting bug, dropped a rock into the bubbly mix. Hot lye splashed up in Nate's face.

"That's how Ma tests her taffy mix," announced the boy proudly.

Abruptly, Nate lowered the kettle to the ground. He sat down by the vat, his face pale as death. "Why, h'it might have put my eye out. Hadn't been for these sun specs, it could have blinded me. Blinded me sure as creation." His voice was awed.

Emma knelt, wet her apron in the water bucket and rinsed away a spattering of lye that had raised welts on Nate's cheek. Then she ushered Amos firmly into the street and locked the gate. "I'll run get Aggie's green ointment," she said in an unsteady voice.

"No need. It's only a speck."

"That little scamp is headed straight for hellfire," said Emma heatedly. "Or the house of corrections, one."

"He's smart, Emmy. And he's lively. I was the same way as a sprat. Worried my good mother half sick. Amos Blackwell will no doubt live to become a rich dentist. And you will have young'uns as smart and as lively yourself."

Emma, still shaken, poured them cold apple cider from a jug in the hotel springhouse. "I don't plan to marry again, Uncle Nate."

He started to speak, noted the stern set of her jaw and held his tongue. They sat in the shade of the fence regaining their calm while the soap mixes cooled.

In face of Emma's resolve and his own close call, Nate was rattled. Dazedly, his mind sorted over the condition of women. He had long felt that they owned more sand than men. They bore the infants—a business men could never tolerate. When diphtheria or cholera struck, it was women tended

276

the sick and the dying. *Why, even a woman's kitchen ain't safe*, he thought. *It is not only rat poison and red devil lye, but that danged baking powder will blow a iron kettle lid sky-high.*

When Emma set to work again, Nate added the heavy borax mix. After the soap was stirred smooth, she took a feather to it. The quill was immediately eaten clean. "Too much lye," she said. She added more borax, stirred and tested until her quill emerged with its feathers intact. "Just right." She and Nate then tipped the big kettle over large flat pans waiting on the ground. When she had smoothed the soap with her paddle, she covered the pans with cheesecloth against flies.

"That's it?" asked Nate hopefully.

"When it's close to hardened, I'll score off the cakes so they'll break clean."

Nate could scarcely wait to get back to ore-training over the hill. He'd had about enough of this hazardous homefront. With a last hug for Emma, and a fleeting instant of pity for Major Burdine, he hightailed it from the Clarendon premises.

####

CHAPTER THIRTY-FOUR

AUGUST DAYS

Emma, leaning on a tram car deep in the Vinnie Tunnel, scraped the sides of her boots against a small outcrop and said to Cal Krueger, "Only a few more days 'til court convenes. How do you figure the decision will go?"

"Historically, only juries rule for the sideliners."

"My instincts tell me things will go our way." She narrowed her eyes, trying to judge Cal's expression in the wan candlelight. "Mr. Krueger," she asked, "do you think you might see your way clear to continue directing operations here after your lease is done?"

She looked down at her muck-coated boots. "I'd be more grateful than I can say. I cannot operate a dig, sir. But if you'll mine out this silver over the winter, I can do a sight of good elsewhere. I have it in mind to go to newspapering, where I'll keep the sideline cause in the public eye."

Calvin's head was bowed; he seemed gone away inside his mind.

"Garrett Sutton will be taking me to law. His deposition declares me unfit as a mine operator—true enough. But if I could boast the finest superintendent in the business…" Her voice trailed off. "I know you'd need to think on the matter some…"

The candles in their miners' helmets cast dull, yellowish half-light on the glistening rock as they waited by the Sugar Maple cut off. Young Frank had climbed a ladder to the number two tunnel above to check on a load of carpentry supplies.

The two men had spent the morning escorting her through what Emma would later describe to Aggie as "a fiendish serpentine." Though metes and bounds were marked on mine district maps in neat, symmetrical quadrangles—albeit at a jumble of angles—underground, away from the strictures of slide rules, they seemed to tilt and rise, fall and jog off in all the jumbled configurations of a crazy quilt.

Emma had asked that she not be limited to the easy confines of the Vinnie and the number one tunnels. She tucked up her skirts and followed the men along narrow passages, over chiseled rock walkways twenty feet above the floors of tunnels. Sometimes a rope-hold had been strung along narrow catwalks. Sometimes not.

At the rich mother lode, she'd been visibly disappointed. Under a tangle of trestled scaffolding, men heaved inconsequential-looking ore into a yawning hopper that funneled into a waiting tramcar on tracks below.

"Why, it's not how I'd imagined the apse of a cathedral. There's no silver shine anywhere."

"The air has oxidized it," explained Calvin. "The stuff is tarnished now." He picked up a clump of ore and held it in front of a lighted cache candle. "Argentite," he said. "Silver, in the main." The rock was as black as the inside of a hat.

Seeing her chagrin, Calvin guided her to a far corner, where he held a lantern high. Emma's eyes were dazzled by a sudden brilliance.

"A fine sight. Except this is not silver. This is a nest of quartz crystals, as faceted and refulgent as diamonds, and hardly worth a red cent. There's no place like a mine," he'd added with the hint of a smile, "to learn how deceiving the look of a thing can be."

Leading Mrs. Sutton through the works had been a tonic for Calvin. She was a keen observer. She asked penetrating questions that reminded him afresh of why he'd fallen under the spell of the mine game. She'd even had him bring out his old blowpipe kit, show her the method of an on-the-spot assay taken by men out in the field.

As they'd moved away from the vug and toward the Vinnie Tunnel, they'd passed stopes where other crews swung picks. "Right here we are improving our odds," Calvin explained. "Any of these locations could hold an extension of that big main lode."

"Would you kindly explain why you carve out so many steep stopes?" Though familiar with silver mine terms, Emma owned very thin knowledge of the actual processes. Garrett had not approved mine talk for women's ears.

"Well, there's some say miners are lazy, though I think of them as inventive. When a man strikes a good vein, he figures some method of tunneling beneath it. That way, he can shovel the ore downhill into a chute, with gravity as his partner. A lot easier on the back."

They had walked and climbed and twisted back on their steps, Calvin pointing out the cross-cuts which ran east-west, and the short shafts running up and down to connect with other levels: the winzes.

"There's a hundred or more miles of tunnel under this town. A greenhorn's been known to lose his way and be running low on grub before he was found." Cal clucked at the very idea. He himself knew the camp's underground pathways as he knew the course of the blood running in his own veins.

"Think of it!" marveled Emma.

"Here in the Pearly, Nathaniel devised us a code for tenderfeet." He pulled a dog-eared square of paper from his shirt pocket and smoothed it on the side of the tramcar. "See here, the red cherries mark the number one tunnel and its drifts and stopes. The oranges do the same at the number two, where the vug lies. The yellow bananas demarcate the number three level, where your Vinnie tunnel egresses the mountain. The green aspen leaves lie deep, at the number four where you saw that new lake with the waterfall—the one that sprang up when the explosion hit." For an instant his face clouded.

"This map shows the basic layout, with matching symbols in color painted on the rock so that a new man can right away get his bearings." Cal pointed to a bright yellow banana on the wall behind them. "In addition, the boys have put a name to most of the winzes and crosscuts, just like town streets."

Indeed, Emma had noticed small signs announcing "Elm Street Winz" and "Sugar Maple Crosscut."

"That waterfall is pretty as a picture. Who would have thought?"

"There are underground streams and falls beneath all these mountains. Had a man drown in one, up at the Smuggler Mine."

Emma shivered at the reminder of death.

"I regret I did not think to have you bring a heavier coat, Mrs. Sutton. The temperature down here is just right for a man at work. Around fifty-five degrees. But if you're not swinging a mattock, it's on the chilly side."

"Are all mines this cool?"

"Depends on the depth—and the terrain. Out in the Comstock they have tunneled a quarter-mile deep. Delved so close to the underworld that it is hot as Hades—120 degrees or more."

"Land!" breathed Emma. "How can the workers endure it?"

"They could not. They were being cooked alive," he said. "Of late, they work a twenty-minute shift, go in a cooling room, are packed in ice for a half hour, then go back for more."

Emma felt melancholy. "How that must tell on a man's constitution."

"Killed more than a few, they say."

Stretching her back against the rock facing, Emma had looked into Mr. Krueger's lamplit face. Tragedy and travail were etched deep as rain runnels there. Though the strong-jawed, clear-gazed engineer of two months ago still went about his work with determination, he seemed disconnected as if some part of him dwelt in another place.

Hesitating over the intrusion on his private feelings, she said softly, "I expect you miss your companions." She quelled the urge to put a comforting hand on his arm. "Not a day goes by that I don't miss Pa," she said sadly. "And it's been almost four years since he traveled."

"Death," she sighed, "is powerful hard on the living." She gazed at the cool, seeping walls of the tunnel. "So is mining. This is a hard business, sir. I have learned great respect for those who dig deep for the earth's bounty."

Calvin had drifted away. He had not answered her proposition. Emma wondered if he had even heard her.

Not until the next morning, over another of Lavinia's estimable breakfasts, did Calvin conclude that he could not answer Mrs. Sutton's request just yet. He had first to conquer the turmoil within. In all his battles with the rebs, he'd never hated one of the men he fought. Hate was new to him. He knew of no way to halt its evil erosion. Not short of killing the animal that roused it. Before he could reorder his life, he must wrestle this demon for a fall.

Willard had breakfasted daily at the Kruegers'. Swallowing the last of his molasses bread, he pushed back his chair and picked up the copybook beside his plate. "Cal, I have here our up to the minute financial report. She's a ripsnorter, and I'd like everyone's full attention. Don't see no sense in awaiting a meeting of stockholders. Enough of us principals is at hand this minute." To Lute's astonishment, Mr. Arey winked at him.

Willard was a schoolboy bursting to share a perfect report card. "I have justified all my ledger sheets, and they tally with Luther's shipment accounts. Willard actually beamed at his young assistant. Lute felt a welling of pride as Young Frank nudged him tauntingly. Mr. Arey was stingier with praise than with money.

Nate, spooning out a third bowl of oatmeal cooked by Vinnie under his direction, said, "Understand you've brought Calvin to heel on the expenses."

"Despite some ill-advised grubstaking, and a surfeit of legal expenditures, he's a sight more heedful nowadays." Purring like a cat by a kitchen fire, Willard surveyed his account book. "I am pleased to report that our total net profits as of this day, and I underline *net*, amounts to $389,261.73."

Lavinia sat down hard on the rocker in the corner by her stove. "I declare!"

Nate burned his tongue on a mouthful of hot oatmeal. Lute swallowed hard. Young Frank was seized with a fit of choking. Even Deke shook his head in disbelief.

Willard's cheerful voice rose for added emphasis. "That is on smeltered silver alone. And we ain't smeltered and sold but mebbe one-fourth of the take to date."

Calvin said, "We must begin parceling out proceeds to the partners. Pete's full share will go to his girls," he reminded his treasurer. "And Mrs. Sutton must be in need of ready money. Would you kindly see to it, Willard?" He straightened in his chair. "I don't know as I've mentioned upping the reward money for Felcher, Yankel, Mudgett, and Bisbee," he said.

"I ain't calculated it in. We will pay that toll when we come to the bridge." Willard licked his pencil point.

"Apostle and Harwood have printed up flyers for camps from the Arizona Territory to California: REWARD, DEAD OR ALIVE, FOR THE PEARLY GANG!" He interrupted himself to mutter, "Hate like thunder to have a pack of murderers named for our mine," then continued. "We're offering two thousand dollars apiece—eight thousand for the lot."

Young Frank whistled. "Added to Tacker's reward, that'll be reason to turn in a man's own mother."

Willard said hopefully, "Maybe the whole kit and kaboodle will sail for Australia—and sink into the sea." He could see no sense in paying out good money for justice he was certain God in His heaven would dispense free of charge. Moving along, he said, "Now Calvin, in case I myself should meet with unexpected affliction, these here accounts are kept in the new safe in back of my salesroom. Nate knows the combination. Also the major and Luther." Willard was not about to give Calvin the key to his own money. He had told him so.

He looked around the table, then back at the copybook entries, and reported, "I have invested the Kruegers' shares. As of yesterday, Calvin and Lavinia own letters of credit in the First Union Bank of St. Louis, in the Spalding Bank of Cincinnati, in the Fourth National Bank of Denver, and in the Lake Superior Trust of Chicago." He waited for this announcement to sink in. "They also possess five thousand shares of Cornelius Vanderbilt's New York Rail Line. They have holdings—detailed herein—in Wells Fargo, in the Denver & Rio Grande railroad, and in the Great Lakes Steamship Company."

Willard mopped his brow and closed his book. His report made, he was not fully as triumphant as expected. Some of this was due to the glaring absence of Pete and Needle. The remainder he could not put a finger on.

"Willard, Lavinia and I are more grateful than I can ever say. No man in this world would have safeguarded our affairs as well. Not by half."

It was the mortician's turn to color. "Oh yes," he added hastily, "the balance of your share is in gold bullion, held by the Kansas City firm of Booker & Naismith."

"Gold?" questioned Nate, scraping the last spoonful of oatmeal from his bowl. "This here's a silver camp, partner."

"We ain't putting all our eggs in any one basket," Willard said determinedly. "Them rattlebrains setting in the U.S. congress might taken it in their heads to move us off the silver standard, put us wholly in gold." Willard placed no trust in a government known to be peopled with freebooters and men with unreliable heads for business.

Deke had been deep in thought. "As long as you are diversifying so ably, Willard, might I suggest a small infusion of cash in Gabe Tacker's bank?"

Willard was appalled. "After that sorry son of a bitch—I beg your pardon, Lavinia—backed Sutton in his dirty schemes?" he railed. "And after his bank near diddled us when this strike took off. After…"

Deke held up a hand. "He might have once. He doesn't plan on the same mistakes again."

"Thet reward he's offered is nothing but bluster. Worming his way to our good sides now that he sees where this camp's bread is buttered."

Deke said calmly, "This is my first meeting since the…since Pete's services. I haven't owned the opportunity to tell anyone except Calvin of my surreptitious meeting with Mrs. Leorah Wickersham."

Willard's mouth hung open as Deke described his pre-dawn conference with the widow, her account of the confrontation between Tacker and Sutton.

"I swan!" said Willard. "Breakfast cooked by the woman's own hand." He had longed for the widow's company himself. There was a certain light in the lady's eye. "In the dark of night, you say? Did…er…" Remembering Lavinia's presence, he reddened to the tops of his ears.

"No, you old rooster, I did not indulge in any of Ms. Wickersham's many charms, except only her cooking and company." Deke struggled to maintain a businesslike expression despite the look of naked envy on Willard's face.

Vinnie glanced up from her rocker, where she was darning Calvin's socks. "How is Leorah feeling, Major?"

"She sent you her affectionate regards, Lavinia. She appeared in splendid health."

"I promised her some of my kinnikinnick tea. More than a month ago. Aggie and I have been meaning to call, but with the strike and all the comings and goings…"

D.K. had a merry look in his eye. His smile spread downward from his eyes, and it had been some time since anyone had seen a smile lighten the major's face. "It might be a good idea for you to call on Mrs. Wickersham yourself, Willard," he said to the now speechless undertaker. "Get her ideas on the future of this camp. She's partial to talking investments, and she'd be pleased to receive you."

As Deke pushed back his chair and took down his belt and pistol from the eight-point buck antlers where he'd hung them, Willard finally thought to close his mouth. Deke strapped on the gunbelt and reached for his hat. "My point is, Tacker has divorced himself from Sutton. And it would appear prudent, since we are taking so much wealth from this town, to invest more than a mite back in."

"D.K.'s idea seems sound," said Calvin. "If we have no faith in our own camp, who will?"

"Expect we'd sooner slide down Tacker's tail than have a dogfight with the man," said Nate, recovering from his own surprise and helping himself to one of the toothpicks from the jar by Vinnie's sugar bowl.

"While you're about it, Willard, you might look into Aspen's new electric power and the telephone company," added Deke. "They are intent on investors."

"They've spoke to me. Nothing but fly-by-night gadgetry!" Willard's spleen had resurfaced.

"I beg to disagree, my friend. So does the widow. She's already invested in both. The woman has a head for business."

Willard was taken aback. The notion of a widow woman getting the jump on him money-wise shook him to the bottom of his prosthesis.

"The ore train is set to leave. Nate and I must bid you farewell. Thank you for another fine breakfast, Lavinia."

"It's been good to have you take a few meals with us," said Calvin wistfully. "Been a spell since we had a conversation about a thing but guns, silver, or cantankerous mules."

"There's no telling how Judge Percy will decide," said Deke. "When he does, we may be forced to ground by a storm of injunctions. Should that occur, you and I will hold more conversations than we know what to do with."

Deke's head was full of rejection as well as injunctions. Unable to comprehend Emma's peculiar behavior, he had kept up a fast pace as though unceasing motion would make him alert and hot-blooded again.

Once more the ore wound out of town. As the last of the jacks plodded east past the hotel, Emma counted the change in the cash drawer, made a notation in a ledger, then removed the paper cuffs protecting the sleeves of her starched shirtwaist. She fought not to succumb to memories of hers and Deke's morning in Sterner Gulch. As for blotting out the picture of him in the widow's doorway, she wrestled with that memory each day. Nights were worse. She suffered from a recurring dream of running through a dark, underground travertine, calling to someone who could never hear her. Often she leapt from sleep awash in tears. She felt not only misery, but ridiculed and a fool, her pride in tatters. The Reverend Campbell might excoriate pride as a mortal sin, but without her pride she would be nothing, as she had been nothing to two men who'd professed to love her.

Emma did not plan to remain nothing. Nor did she plan to do nothing. Unbeknownst to a soul, she had set Polly to stalking Garrett. "Sauce for the gander," she said to the squaw. "Look close and listen hard, under his windows, through doors. If he should catch you out," she'd directed, "make like you're in search of some trifle from the house. He may bark, but he won't bite. I want to know where that low-down dog goes, every move he makes. When he leaves town, we'll send Cappie up the trail behind him."

Polly's look had been scornful. She'd fingered her knife knowingly.

"None of that now," warned Emma. "First we must puzzle out Garrett's schemes. Then we will lay our plans."

Afoot or horseback, wearing a man's work clothes and hat, Polly had been on the prowl for days.

The sun pouring in the front windows of the hotel warmed Emma's face, and she turned to meet it, drinking it in like honey. Although the ranchers needed rain, she was grateful for these last bright August days. Without the crashing interference of rainstorms, chores were easier. Even her dismal mood eased off. And the fine weather made for easier treks over the hump. With each trip, more of her future was secured. She'd never again be chattel for any man. She'd spoken with Aggie about her notion of buying the newspaper down in Telluride. "The editor is troubled with palsey, wants to retire. But he'll wait 'til I'm trained. I've written to Mildred Thompson, publisher of the *Manitou Springs Gazette*. She'll have me as an apprentice next spring."

"But I dinna think…" Aggie was wholly taken aback. She could have sworn Emma Sutton and Major Burdine were on the path to betrothal.

"You don't think I'd be a wonder at newspapering?"

"T'is na' that, lass," said Aggie, sputtering.. "T'is only that…we could ha' sworn…oh, bother!" Aggie threw up her hands and marched off to her kitchen, meaning to ask Nate Phipps what on earth ailed those two. She'd talk to him the instant he trailed back into the hotel, all mud and dust from the hump.

####

CHAPTER THIRTY-FIVE

PEEPING TOM

Nate Phipps sat in the Clarendon's side parlor, freshly barbered, wearing starched linen and his good suit. There was a merciful break in the relentless ore-hauling, he'd slept on a good bed with a mattress, and for a change he wasn't as beat as a run-out coon hound. He basked lazily in the dying warmth of the sunset through a side window. He was about to deliver Emma's first letter of credit from the Pearly take.

"Uncle Nate! I never expected you on a Saturday evening." Striding into the parlor, Emma peeled off her celluloid cuffs. "I've been updating accounts. My fingers are inky, or I'd give you a hug."

Nate cleared his throat and said a little formally, "Madam, I hereby have the honor to present you with your first share of the Pearly silver spoils." And with that he handed her a bank letter. Emma looked at the amount and gasped. "My stars! I can buy a bandicoot. A pachyderm. A Paris wardrobe...Even a newspaper," she added as a hushed afterthought.

Nate wasn't certain he approved any of these notions. He said in a tone of some severity, "We boys have been discussing investments. I'd like to think you'll seek advice from any one or all of us. Willard is a whiz at planning for the long run; he has the Kruegers positioned like potentates—in rail lines, boat outfits, bank stock, gold bullion...and the Major has some right smart ideas. He spent half a night at the Widow Wickersham's and she divulged some of that crafty Tacker's ideas on futures and Aspen propositions."

"Half the night?" Emma was shocked.

"Thunderation! That didn't come out sounding right," said Nate hastily. "The widow summoned him by the dark of the moon to divulge things about the enemy camp. May not sound fittin' but neither is spending a clear afternoon closeted with a widow lady—as if D.K. ever had an afternoon...She wanted Cal to know that your worthless husband and Tacker had parted company and the parting wasn't pretty. Tacker come close to strangling him with his bare hands. She also needed an old friend's advice on whether she could count on Cal Krueger to stick. They talked finances and futures and what-not. She's a good woman, Emmy. Helped Calvin over his thorny path, even while keeping company with Tacker. And now that old reprobate's enlisted with us."

Emma was speechless.

"D.K. thinks it might be smart to put some money in Tacker's bank, in the town's telephone and electric. That's what the widow's done—and the woman knows how to set a dollar to work."

Emma's head was in a whirl. She gripped the arms of her chair to steady herself. "I...I was being facetious about Paris wardrobes, Uncle Nate...but oh, dear God, I thought...I thought..." Her face was chalky.

She looked so stricken that Nate reached over and clasped her hand. "I know all this is a shock to the system, honey. And I don't mean to snoop in your affairs. Just want to make sure you plan smart for your years ahead."

"I've got to find Deke. I have to say—oh, where *is* he?"

"This minute? In Denver City dickering with the smelter people. Be home in two or three days."

Emma slumped back in the chair, her face drained. Nate felt terrible. "Didn't mean to spring this on you so sudden," he murmured, feeling he hadn't handled the disbursement as delicately as he might.

"It isn't the money. It's *me*! I've been a fool!" Emma rushed out of the parlor, leaving Nate Phipps thinking he'd grown too set in his ways to ever more understand the ways of women.

Luther and Scoop were at loose ends. They'd eaten a fine pot roast and raisin pie at the Kruegers', but supper and table talk were done with early. Mr. Cal looked dead to the world. They didn't care to overstay their welcome. Lavinia sensed their restlessness. It was hard going for boys too young to court, not welcome in card games or men's clubs, nothing to settle them down.

"Boys," she said, "I have an errand needs doing. Might I call on you?"

They both beamed. Any reason to get out on the town suited them down to the wire.

"I promised the Widow Wickersham some of my kinnikinnick tea weeks ago. But I haven't found a free hour in all my days. Would you mind delivering her a jar? And I'd like to send along a raisin pie and a book of Calvin's she had it in mind to borrow."

"We'd be pleased to make delivery," said Lute eagerly. Not only did he like lending the missus a hand, but he knew good and well they'd be offered something special from the widow's own kitchen. He might be well-fed at the Kruegers', but he often wondered if he'd ever get filled the whole way to the top. Besides, he'd been telling Scoop for donkey's years about the widow's fine house and furnishings. Now he'd see for himself.

Pie basket, tea jar, and book in hand, the boys said their goodbyes and headed across town.

Herman Klausmeyer was another at sixes and sevens. He'd already been to visit his current whore girl, a slat-sided woman with a wen on her nose, and he'd found the encounter unrewarding. Now he traveled one of his back alley routes, looking for lamplit windows where churchgoing women were readying themselves early for bed. Saturday was bath night to boot. He'd had a long, satisfying look at the young Medjeric woman as she'd dropped her shift and soaped herself good from the pitcher and basin on her washstand. She'd pulled her curtains tight, but they were thin and he could see the very pores in her skin. Aroused, he'd headed for the widow's. The woman had gotten cautious about her curtaining, but maybe fortune would smile on him.

Leorah Wickersham, freshly bathed, was settled on her fainting couch with a fresh novel from back east, fanning the cool night breeze from her window with a bamboo fan. With Gabe in Denver, she felt on the empty side. She turned up the flame on her table lamp and had just unwrapped a foil-covered chocolate when there was a pull on her door ringer. Now who? She fastened the front of her dressing gown high and went to the door. She was delighted to look through the glass door panes and see young Luther and a companion.

"Why, Luther Kellogg! What a pleasure! Come in, come in. I don't believe I've met your friend."

The widow soon had them settled at the kitchen table. As she warmed up the supper coffee, set out a plate of oatmeal cookies, and brought half a chocolate layer cake from the pantry, she chattered gaily. "Now I want to hear every last story of your adventures over the divide," she said as she settled herself in a chair beside them. Scooper Hurd peeked around him and decided he had maybe found a vision of how the hereafter might be. Even the kitchen, with its rows of glass-fronted cupboards, fresh-cut flowers on the table and marble counter tops and Turkey carpet was one of the grandest sights he ever hoped to see. He barely managed to compose himself as Lute launched into tales of grouchy stage drivers, Injun Ike, and Gracious the mule.

After awhile, Scoop yearned to get an oar in the water too. When Lute had his mouth full of a second helping of chocolate cake, he blurted, "Not only that, we seen murder done. Or dern near!"

Lute nearly choked on his mouthful of cake. "Dang it, Scoop, it's not fittin'…"

But the widow was enthralled. "Oh my, I *must* hear all about it…"

And before Luther could stop the outpouring, Scoop had eagerly told the widow about the start of the fire on the Row, about hauling out Frankie—right down to their suspicions about Herman Klausmeyer and the mine stock.

Much later, Scoop would protest, "But she's so nice to talk to, Lute. A fella just wants to go on and on."

"You went on and on all right. If I'd had a handy gag, I'd have knotted it around your waggin' tongue."

"Well!" the widow said, on hearing the tale of Frankie, "I wouldn't put it past that oaf Klausmeyer. Man gives me the whim whams." She looked pensive. "Cal Krueger and the major are right. This silver strike has brought out the best in good people—and the devil incarnate in those no better than they should be."

By the time the boys, stuffed to groaning, headed out the door, it was well past ten o'clock. Scoop threw himself down on the widow's soft patch of front lawn, put his hands behind his neck, and inhaled the sweet smell of climbing roses. He did not wish to take leave of the place. "When I get me a wife," he said, "I'd like a place this fine."

Lute stretched out beside him to let the widow's baking settle in. They talked in low murmurs of times to come. Above all, they longed to pass into manhood. They hadn't come around to thinking how near they were to that state already.

The widow, her spirits buoyed by the two youngsters—she loved nothing more than entertaining—blew out her parlor lamp, picked up her book, and drifted sleepily into her bedchamber. Her head was filled with the boys' stories. They'd shared experiences that no stuffy man would have thought to let loose of. She dropped her dressing gown on a chair, loosened her hair, and suddenly smelling the wisteria climbing outside, remembered she'd not closed and latched her window or pulled her draperies tight. In her thin night shift, scolding herself, she stepped to the window sash.

"Ach, lieber Gott!" shouted an apparition before her, and Herman Klausmeyer lunged at the window sill and scrambled to pull himself into the bedroom.

All the widow saw was a slobbering mouth and a look of unmanacled lust;

the face of a crazy man. She ran to her bedside drawer, snatched up the pocket pistol, turned and as the maniac climbed into her room, shot him square in the face.

Lute and Scoop, hearing the shot, pounded on the front door until the widow finally staggered out in her night shift to unbolt the latch. Then she sank to the floor. "In…in there," she pointed.

They found Herman Klausmeyer spread-eagled by the widow's bed, eyes bulging, a crazed expression on his face.

"Son of a bitch!" breathed Scoop.

The widow was awash in tears and shaking from head to foot as they supported her to her couch, covered her with a crocheted throw, brought her a glass of water. "He…he leaped through my window; he was going to…going to…Did I kill him?" she ended with a sob.

"You needn't say it, ma'am," Lute assured her. "Anyone can see what was on that lunatic's mind."

Scoop patted the widow's trembling hand. "Now don't you worry, ma'am. Lute will stick right here by your side. I'm running to fetch the doc. He'll know just the thing to do."

####

CHAPTER THIRTY-SIX

ROSE KLAUSMEYER

The Appalachia Club adjourned from their Armory meeting room on a note of acrimony. Willard Arey, on noting an error of $37.18 in Cowpie Burkhardt's treasury report, had demanded to see the club's books. Burkhardt, under pressure, consented to an audit by committee. Willard was the duly appointed chairman of the committee.

Their meeting done, most of the members departed for home. As Cowpie locked the door, he protested heatedly, "Dammit, Arey, I'd think your plate was full with a million-dollar silver operation, without bothering your head over a measly few dollars in a social club account."

"Thirty-seven dollars and sixteen cents ain't no light matter, Burkhardt."

"You don't say!"

"Penny-wise is dollar-wise, and don't you forget it."

"I am not simple, Arey. I am a certified graduate accountant of the Millard Fillmore College of Business in Buffalo, New York."

"That weighs but little with me, Burkhardt. I taken Millard Fillmore's measure, and he come up short. I'll be only too pleased to take yours."

"Will you now!" Cowpie's neck wattles, red as an old buzzard's, quivered alarmingly. The two men, inflamed with righteous wrath, were interrupted by a heavy thumping on the door.

"It's me. Doc Alderfer. Who is in there?"

"Willard Arey, certified mortician, and—" Willard raised a scathing eyebrow, "one grad-u-ate of the Millard Fillmore School of Abbreviated Bookkeeping." Willard had to hop quick to escape Cowpie's fist.

"Well, unlock the door! I got you a customer, Arey."

Later, Willard looked down at the deceased pile of blubber on his mortuary slab, the bullet hole no more than a pin prick—and felt monumental satisfaction. The Sons of the Black Forest were not cheese-paring. For one of their own, they would provide the finest services and accoutrements money could buy. At last he'd unload that overpriced Brazilian mahogany casket that had been eating at his craw.

Doc and the sheriff having provided him with the particulars of Herman Klausmeyer's demise, all had agreed there'd been enough scandal for a month of Sundays. They'd settled on a story that the beefy butcher had died doing his citizen's duty. He was shot down while chasing an intruder intent on breaking in a side window of the widow's. Herman would not set off any choruses of mourning. But half the souls in town would turn out for the Hamtown Band concert, the first-class food, and the declamatory eulogies. It was Willard's favorite brand of memorial occasion.

All in all, this had been a banner week. He not only had that powdered and perfumed sharpster Burkhardt on the ropes, but just this morning he'd survived one of the most near-calamitous confrontations of his life. The confrontation could have left him a broken man. Instead, he felt oddly exuberant.

Bright and early he had unlocked the front door of his establishment, and raising the green roller shades, looked up to see a vaguely familiar figure. Arbella Arey's hair had greyed, and the figure corseted inside a watered silk dress in a comely shade of violet was fuller. The Arbella of old was on the angular side and customarily wore black. But it was her, right enough. She took two steps inside and looked around, gazing at his impressive inventory. Her expression had been hard to decipher.

"I've found you, Willard," said she.

"Oh hell," declared Willard.

"Well now, husband, will you invite me to take a seat?" she asked pertly.

"Take a seat, have your pick, Arbella. These here are the Morris Company's latest catalogue items."

Arbella put down her carpetbag and arranged herself decorously on an overstuffed davenport in mulberry repousse priced at the astronomical figure of $28.50.

"This is quite a town," she said pleasantly, looking out on Cooper Avenue, where dust was beginning to rise in puffballs around bustling men and animals.

"Let us not talk all around this, Arbella. I ain't afraid of you for a minute. Why have you come?"

"I have come to make you a home, Mr. Arey."

"I got me a home," he said irritably, "right in the back of this here store."

"I mean clean, cozy furnishings and home-cooked meals, Willard. Home-baked pies and home-style housekeeping."

"Do not lay about with your sugar-coated talk, Arbella. I've lived the bachelor life for a good spell, and I've come to fancy it."

"Now don't tell me you haven't missed my prime cooking."

"I eat anything that's put in front of me. Have for years."

"You never hunger for my lemon meringue pie or my raisin-stuffed küchen?"

Willard stifled a groan.

"No one knows your sweet tooth like me, nor all the receipts you are partial to—the schnitz und knepp, the paunhaus, the Dutchy corn relish."

"The one thing I ain't missed a iota is your home-baked sermons and all them raisin-stuffed prayer meetings."

"I have left off attending prayer meetings, husband. The minister of the First Lutheran Church of South Philadelphia left a wife and four small children to run off with the Widow Eichelberger. My faith in prayer flew away in his wake."

"Well," said Willard grumpily, "I ain't changed in the matter of church-going. I believe in the Lord God Almighty, but I don't care a thing for prayer meetings. Although," he added grudgingly, "I don't mind a prayer to two regarding my leg, which I hope to meet up with so I may walk the Streets of Glory on two good feet."

Arbella smiled, put aside her dainty violet reticule, and began peeling off her gloves. She looked at Willard with a look he hadn't seen for years. "Church socials and services are not as fulfilling as I once thought. I have been lonely, Willard. I am sick and tired of lonely. I need a man to do for."

Willard looked Arbella over, his interest tweaked. She had not stalked in and taken charge in the way of the Arbella he remembered. He paced the floor, thinking. His wife sat serenely, an affable expression on her face. Willard peeked at her as he paced. She was not a bad-looking woman.

"How did you find me?" He would not be mollified in a wink.

"Why, on the front page of the *Philadelphia Inquirer*. You gave a reporter an interview about the great Aspen silver strike."

His mouth had done for him again. He should have known.

They talked of old friends, neighbors, and eventually, of their courting days. Willard even spotted something of the Widow Wickersham in Arbella's eyes. About that time, it came to him that every rooster needs a hen to crow for. In the end, visions of light-as-a-feather lemon meringue pies got the best of him. He had found himself showing off his embalming room, his gilt-lettered sign, his new Hurley safe with the painting of the Brooklyn

Bridge on the door. Arbella's admiring clucks and looks had done the rest. He had summoned a boy to carry her traps in the door.

He had, however, made himself clear. "I know I ain't done my duty by our marriage vows. But when a man is making his fortune, the weeks slips by and the years follow. I am wearing three or four hats, Arbella, and I must high-step to be in five places at once. Your big mine operators do not have the leisure for social calls on preachers. I want it understood that I pick the music and call the tune."

"Yes, Willard dear," she said meekly.

And though Willard knew he had the hook in him again, he felt surprisingly little pain.

The Sons of the Black Forest had indeed voted to lay on a full sauerbraten dinner following elaborate funeral services. Fritz Hartlieb's brewery donated the beer. The Hamtown Band rehearsed four new numbers for the concert at the lakes. Everyone was invited, including the Irish, the Pollacks, the Eyties, the Serbs and the Croats. It seemed the whole camp, starved for entertainment, came.

To the newshounds, Herman Klausmeyer's passing was welcome diversion from a lull in the action. The Denver lawyers had wound up their arguments, Judge Percy was brooding in chambers. During this interlude, the reporters had something to trumpet besides guesswork. Though Klausmeyer had not been directly connected to the silver war, they eulogized him as one more battlefront casualty. ASPEN PIONEER LAID TO REST, announced the *Daily Times*. OUR GERMAN FRIENDS BUILT FIRM FOUNDA-TIONS.

Rosie Klausmeyer was in a place she had never experienced in Herman's lifetime. Hog heaven. She held court for a steady stream of visitors in her dark little parlor. The city newsboys had lighted on the story like screeching magpies, and Rosie did her best to accommodate every Aspenite who wanted his or her name in print. "Lena dear, meet Mr. Joseph Flynn of the *Boston Herald*, and this here is Mr. Gene Knecht of the *Cleveland Plain Dealer*. Gentlemen, my dearest friend, Mrs. Ollie Davidson. She knew Herman well, and I expect she'll be tickled to answer your questions." Mr. Gene Knecht had plenty of questions, though mostly he supplied his own answers. Daily, he wired fevered, fanciful installments of Herman's life and times to his paper, later to be reprinted as a dime novel with countrywide readership. Rosie herself talked non-stop to the Ohioan, waiting with his pencil whetted.

"As I was saying, Herman and I come down to Leadville directly before General Custer's troop was ambushed. Escaped with the hair on our heads, you could say. We knew old Chief Sitting Bull, of course. Herman did some beef trading with the Sioux. Always traded the red hostiles fair, Herman did." Fanning herself and extolling Herman's virtues, Rosie finally drove Lena Davidson to mutter, "The woman's insufferable. Next she'll claim the Klausmeyers are descended from Holy Roman emperors."

Reporters spoke with the Lutheran Men's Guild, the Sons of the Black Forest, even the Appalachia Club, whose fraternity elected not to mention that Herman had never been one of their own. Instead, Pie Burkhardt used the opportunity to tout the many exclusive amenities of Aspen's most distinguished men's club. Discreetly, he made a number of inquiries about prospects for a first-class bathhouse in Cleveland, Milwaukee, and Baltimore.

With each syndicated episode from *The Silver Lining—A Tale of a German Immigrant Boy's Quest in the West* by Eugene B. Knecht, newspaper circulation in eastern cities with heavy German populations skyrocketed. *The Aspen Daily Times* ran the same episodes, though not a soul recognized the fair-haired, stout-hearted young Teuton of fiction as the Herman Klausmeyer known to them in life.

"I have stepped in dogshit," snorted Potato John. "I have worked in cowshit. And I have read bullshit aplenty. But this here 'Silver Lining' shit is about the smelliest I have encountered to date." Barely containing himself, he downed a snort from his tickler and concluded reading a paragraph aloud: "…and so Klausmeyer went on to take his place as community leader in the phenomenally rich silver-mining camp of Aspen high in the heart of the Colorado Rockies."

The boys on the bench cackled so hard that two of them peed their pants.

Rose Klausmeyer never saw nor heard about the Pearly stock in Herman's possession. Vinnie Krueger had paid a visit to the widow, and they had had a good long talk. Knowing Leorah's affection for Lute, Vinnie told her of his strange grief over a murdered woman of ill repute. After hearing the story, Leorah called the boys to her parlor. When she handed them stock from the dead man's coat pockets, it was almost as good as a live confession. "There's not much left," she said. "And what there is, is dirtied money. Mind you don't let it rub off on you." The widow had a strong superstitious streak. Blood-tainted money could be worse luck than a white horse.

Rose Klausmeyer received several small royalty checks from *The Plain Dealer*, and these, in addition to the startling wads of cash money she discovered in the toes of Herman's old galoshes, were more than enough to transport her to her sister's in Kansas City for an overdue visit. There she entertained offers to speak on the Chautauqua Circuit the following summer, although she adamantly refused to appear on the same bill with Chief Ouray's guitar-plucking widow, Chipeta.

Not until weeks later did Lute and Scoop get around to the cemetery's latest grave. They came down off the hump, grabbed the pigsticker, went to check Frankie's plot, and stopped by to see Klausmeyer's. "Looky there at that headstone," sniffed Scoop irritably. "Polished marble. With a Angel Gabriel fat as old Klausmeyer on top. It ain't right."

"These things hardly ever have tidy endings," said Lute sadly.

"The bastard's turned up some kind of hero. By rights he shoulda been strung up by his balls."

"Nothing will bring Frankie back. Besides, Mrs. Lavinia says to let the Lord handle the vengeance department. Klausmeyer took away Frankie's life, so the Lord, by way of Ms. Wickersham, took away his."

"Well, it burns my ass the way the papers make the man out a cross between that Sir Lancelot and the Pilgrim fathers."

"City writers will say anything to peddle papers, Scoop. People in these parts know better. They think it's a prime joke."

Scooper thought a minute, then pulled out his clasp knife.

"Chunk me that board, Lute boy. The one fallen over in that next plot." His face earnest, he began scratching out words in the half-rotted wood. When he'd finished, the boys pounded the makeshift marker in front of the Klausmeyer monument. The letters were cockeyed, and in a few years the shallow carving would be worn away. The inscription read: "Here lies a merdering son of a bitch." Buried deep in the board was Klausmeyers's pigsticker. When winter snows arrived to blanket the graveyard, the boys noted that no one had bothered to remove the makeshift marker.

On the bluff where she had first seen off the Pearly ore party, Emma waited in the saddle for its latest return. Beside her sat Polly. "Mr. Billy Goat come down mountain. Same time," she'd grunted in warning.

"You're certain he's been to Leadville?"

"Cappie send word. Mister come back. Bring new shooters."

"You can't know these men he's hired are gunmen," protested Emma. "He must tread with care. Even Sheriff Harwood is watching."

Emma looked anxiously up the pass. "Oh, where *is* the major?" She was beside herself over her mistreatment of Deke. She'd dragged Polly along to meet the train, unable to wait 'til it reached camp.

She rehearsed again the words she'd say. Apologies. Endearments. She was still running them over in her mind when Polly said, "They come." At sight of Iacono's high-crowned hat, Emma's heart pounded harder. Behind him clattered the first of the empty wagons. She searched each approaching face, her anxiety plain. As more wagons and jack-lines poured past, her impatience grew. At last she spurred Harriet down the embankment to Luther's wagon. Startled at the sight of her, Lute said, "Why, hidey, Miz Emma. Didn't expect you on the trail."

"Lute, where *is* the major?"

Lute looked alarmed. "Is there trouble?"

"No, no trouble. But I must see him."

"Why, he stopped off at the Weller Way Station. He's hiring two of the Weller boys to work on the trail, places it's breaking down." Emma's look was so dismayed that he hastened to add, "He'll be along right smart. Said he'd see us at the pasturage."

"Tarnation!" exclaimed Emma. "Why is it that one or the other of us is forever in the wrong place?" She could have wept with frustration.

Back at the way station corral, Deke finished his instructions to the Weller boys. They were not ones he would ordinarily hire. Both had rotted teeth, and their manner was as slipslop as their hygiene. The younger wore two different shoes on his feet, and his breath was foul. But they'd agreed to fell timber and corduroy the worst sections of road. If he waited for the county work crews, he'd be held up 'til spring.

"I'll check the repairs the beginning of the week, stop by with your pay," he said to them, heading Buford back onto the trail. He had just sheathed his rifle and ridden out of the turnoff when he looked up to see Garrett Sutton accompanied by two heavily armed men. Deke's hand was on his holstered pistol as he drew to a halt and, resting easy in his saddle, watched them approach. In a minute or two one or the other party would need to give way.

Sutton looked the major up and down. His thoughts were: *So, here is the arrogant upstart who's panting after my wife. I could inflict an ugly wound, claim Burdine drew first.* He motioned the men behind him to rein in.

Deke looked them over. They were an ugly pair. "Headed for a war, Sutton?" he inquired in his easy drawl.

"If I were, the news would not be in a public bulletin."

"I'd agree. Bushwhacking from the rear is more your style."

Sutton's hand jumped to his gun. Before it got there, Deke's Colt was pointed his way. The men to the rear paused. None had gotten more than halfway to his weapon.

"I wouldn't, boys. You'd be stone dead before you ever hit me. Now, how was it you answered my question, Sutton?"

"What I'm about is no affair of yours, Burdine." His eyes were as merciless as a red-tailed hawk's.

"It is if it concerns the Pearly Mine."

"Not after the court issues an injunction against further operations."

"Should the court rule against us, you'll have no need of an army. Cal Krueger abides by the law."

Sutton was not appeased. He glared at the gun in Deke's hand. "Well then, holster your goddamned pistol."

"H'it's all right, Major. I got 'em covered," called a voice. Gordon "Cappie" Barnett sat his horse behind Sutton's men.

"Afternoon, Cappie," said Deke, his eyes not moving from Sutton. "We'll ride on into camp soon as this platoon retires from the front."

By the time Garrett approached Aspen, he had rehashed the encounter with the Southerner until he was ready to eat tailings. Then, at the wooded bank by the ice pond, his teeth still grating, he looked up to see Emma directly in his path.

"Tramp!" The word exploded from him unbidden. Faster than a drumroll, Polly's knife was in her hand. She edged her pony closer to the Missy. Expecting Deke, Emma was stunned to silence.

"Get out of my path, Emma, before I take a whip to you—as any husband would have the right."

"I don't…"

"Do not blush and stammer and act the innocent with me! You're a common slut, and you are thieving my silver. I want you out of sight, out of my mine. Out of this camp!"

His anger was so volcanic that Emma's tongue remained tied. Polly glowered at the shooters grinning malevolently behind the mister.

In those fleeting moments Emma saw that Garrett was as removed from her as a carved likeness on a tombstone. He dwelled alone in a place where all his troubles were the fault of others. She stared full in his face and knew he still thought he could have anything he craved—if he must kill to get it.

Polly grasped Harriet's reins and, wheeling both mounts, headed them back toward camp.

"If I cannot have my own silver," her husband shrilled after them, "I promise you, neither will you!"

The two women put their horses into a fast gallop and fled the doomsday screech of his voice.

####

CHAPTER THIRTY-SEVEN

THE DECISION

When he was old and bent over with rheumatism, Aloysius "Scooper" Hurd's feet still jigged at the memory of the night of September 4, 1885. That evening, swept up in the jubilation of the western mine world, he danced Svea Hoaglund down Cooper Street in Aspen in a manic, hip-hop capering.

Around suppertime, lingering orange and purple streaks were dissipating down the sky to the west. Werner Kuster, the telegrapher, had rushed onto Durant Avenue squawking the news that the Denver judge's decision had come down. The bench boys, about to meander to boardinghouses and barrooms, scrambled instead to spread the word. Saloon crowds poured into the streets. Households abandoned their supper tables. Men hoorahed and bonfires illumined the sky as far south as Crested Butte, north and west to Mount Sopris and the Flattops, up the Frying Pan River past Seven Castles, on beyond Ruedi and across miles of mine country, from Fairplay to Oro City, from Tincup to Ashcroft.

At that, the sideliners had not won.

They had been reprieved. For now, the apexers were stood off. Kuster sat by his key, relaying bulletins to those waiting outside. Judge Percy had ordained that a decision so momentous should be handed down by a jury of miners' peers. He had been set to rule for the apex—until given pause by the murderous mayhem in Aspen's Pearly Everlasting Mine. He then figured he had just cause for obfuscation. The judge was not ordinarily a pussyfooting man. But he knew the temper of his state. He too was mindful of his neck.

"The matter needs more than mere adjudication. We must have intensive deliberation," he'd announced on the courthouse steps. "We will empanel twelve good men on the third day of April next."

As reporters rushed to wire offices, and his non-decision poured out across the West, the weary judge climbed into his carriage and trotted gratefully home to the sheltering arms of his wife and nine children.

There would be no stop-work orders for now. In Aspen, the Pearly silver could be plumbed to the end. Young Frank Parker burst into Vinnie Krueger's kitchen, lifted her in the air, and bussed her soundly. He pounded Calvin on the back and embraced the nonplussed Lute. Though he was too run out for lengthy pronouncements, his exultant grin told the story. Luther huzzahed and Vinnie wept. A smile—like faint, uncertain sun emerging from clouds—spread across Calvin's face.

Jake Levy's boy Daniel popped up like a hobgoblin at Willard and Arbella Arey's kitchen window. He was nine, he was excited, and he lisped. "Pa seth come quick! It'th a jubilee!" Willard looked longingly at the beef brisket and dilled cabbage just served him.

"Supper won't spoil, Willard," said his wife, rising to grasp his hand and go with him into the streets.

The Clarendon dining room was in an uproar. Big Gabe Tacker stared glumly at his plate of wild turkey embellished with fresh garden peas and buttery sweet potatoes. They'd done it to him again, ruined a good hot meal he was about to pile into. Young Frank twirled Bridget O'Reilly down the hall, out the open door, and into the crush that spread from Durant to Cooper to Hopkins. Jake Levy and his boys clasped hands in a dizzy hoedown. Clamorous drum rolls clashed with hurrahs and hymn-singing. Scooper and Svea were caught in a clutch of dancers capering to a discordant "Turkey in the Straw" rendered by two Slovenian ocarina players. Scoop, without a by-your-leave, had taken the big girl in his arms to join the frolicking. Hair flying, eyes bright, she danced as exuberantly as if her partner were the mighty Paul Bunyan.

Emma ran into the street. This night she *had* to find Deke. She pushed her way through the mob, pine-knot torches beginning to blaze around her. Spying his tall figure framed in the saloon's swinging front doors, she called, "Deke! Oh, Deke…!" She raised her voice high above the din; she reached out her arms in an invitation as old as time. Deke's own eagerness rose in him like the swell of a wave, and he plunged hungrily toward her.

At that moment, from the corner of her eye, Emma spied another figure. By the last rays of a fading sun and the spreading light of torches and bonfires, she glimpsed a familiar paint streaking at a full-out gallop up Mill Street, headed for the mountain. Polly!

Emma turned back toward Deke, then wheeled around, eyes and heart racing in time with the headlong flight toward the Vinnie Tunnel. Why hadn't she thought to call Polly off? An awful realization swept her. The frenzied pursuit meant Garrett was headed for the mine. On this night, no man would stick by his post. The place would be unguarded. Her maddened husband would have the workings to himself. His words on the trail echoed in her head. "If I cannot have my own silver, Emma, then neither will you."

She did not care about the silver. Let him have it. But Polly…Garrett would not tolerate an old woman's interference. He would shoot her down. Emma searched frantically for Uncle Nate, for Aggie or Mr. Mac. With a last desperate look at Deke struggling toward her through the crush, she turned away into the press of people. Once out of the crowd, she stumbled up the steep incline toward the mine. On all fours, she scrabbled along the trace to the tunnel mouth. At her approach, the Indian paint, standing obediently beside a pile of slag, nickered a greeting.

On the ground by the entrance lay a young guard, motionless, gun drawn, face turned to rest against the dirt. Emma felt for a heartbeat, found it, though it was faint. Beyond a stack of timber she could make out Arsenic, the gelding's sides still heaving with exertion. No light came from the tomb-like cavity before her. Dreading the pitch black of her nightmares, she felt fear swoop down, an encircling bat in the night. Oh, *why* hadn't she called Polly off? An old woman was no match for a man possessed with animal malice. *Was she*? she wondered.

She thought then of her Pa, heard his strong voice. And in a whisker felt suddenly solid and sure—like good river bottom in fast current. She would do what she had to do. Searching hurriedly through the downed man's shirt and pants pockets, she found a scattering of loose safety matches. She longed for a miner's lamp, but the matches were better than a handful of nothing. She tucked up her skirts and held her pistol close to her face to check its load, the steel cold in the settling night chill. Then she stepped into the tunnel.

Feeling her way along the crossties of the tram tracks, she pressed forward until blackness finally stayed her. Every wall candle had been snuffed out. She struck a match and rapidly scanned the walls. On her right, a cheery banana gleamed. Some thirty feet along, there'd be another. She cupped the match in one hand and groped forward. The winz she remembered here was the Oak Lane rise. The first cross-cut should be the Sugar Maple. Her match sputtered out, and Emma shut her eyes to accept the dark. She leaned her forehead against the tunnel wall, thinking hard to recall the location of the nearest cache holding reserve miners' lamps. The crosscut where she had paused to talk with Cal Krueger held such a cache. Garrett would not be aware of the new street names, the fresh stopes, the colorful codes. But he would know every cranny of the mine far better than she. She could not think of worse ground to engage her husband than this hellish, unlighted underworld.

Mine darkness was unlike any she had ever experienced. It was not a darkness to hide in. She felt as exposed as a cadaver on Mr. Arey's embalming table. Her heart was a ramshackle door banging in a hard storm. She stretched her free arm out to the tunnel wall. Hard rock under the hand was more reassuring than cross-ties underfoot. She crept between the wall of the tunnel and the ends of the crossties, her shoulder brushing the rock, gun at waist level. She stopped to light another match. Minding her frail flame and the places she put her feet, she scuttled toward the crosscut sign. The brief, hot spurt of dying flame singed her fingers. She groped along rough-blasted rock 'til her hand struck a declivity with a wood door, felt her way to the hasp, and found the cache padlocked tight. Her frustration had the dry, bitter taste of one of Aggie's tonics. She felt desperately for any spot which might shelter a key—in the rock above, to the sides, along the floor around the cache. As her fingers moved along seams and shelves, her foot came down on a sharp stone. She grunted, leaned over to remove it from her boot sole and discovered a candle stub, dropped and not bothered about. Hoarding it like a gold nugget, she dried the wick on her skirt. After a few false tries, got it lighted so the flame held. She allowed herself to whisper what she had feared when she first spied Polly's paint: "The powder magazines. He'll blow this mine to hell, if he must send himself with it."

There was a powder magazine on the banana level. Garrett had no doubt strapped on a miner's lamp. He must be around a bend or on the level above. Polly would be on his heels; Polly's good eye pierced the night like a long-legged owl's. She prayed that the Ute woman would not come upon Garrett before she got there.

Shielding her puny flame, she worked her way into the main tunnel, heading for the dogleg that led to the stope by the silver-laden cathedral. She'd passed the Oak Lane and Elm Street winzes when she detected a shimmer like lantern light on dark water. Snuffing out her candle stub and tucking it deep in her pocket, she prepared to encounter her husband. She blinked her eyes. Open. Shut. Open. Her gun arm just under her sightline, she moved toward the shimmer.

Then she heard the thrumming, like wind humming through telegraph wires across winter fields.

Deke stumbled, caught himself, and feared he had trampled a child. He halted to look down. When he looked up again, he caught only a glimpse of Emma's disappearing back. Could he have misunderstood her look of entreaty? He hesitated, once again uncertain. Finally he thrust his way to the Clarendon, where he found a jubilant circle of friends and well-wishers surrounding the Kruegers. Aggie's yellow face glowed. "Och, Major, t'is a grand night!" Nate and Cal grabbed his hands and pumped as if they were bringing up a barrel of well water.

"It is indeed, Mrs. Mac...Er..." Deke looked pleadingly at Nate. "I've gone and lost Emma again. She beckoned me, and then she was carried off in the crowd."

"Ah. She's been searching for you, Major. Searching ivery-where. She's been about rehearsing her excuses fer...well, the lass will tell ya' wi' her own lips." Aggie beamed her fond hopes for her young friend and the major. "When ye locate her, the both of ye' are expected here. We'll be after havin' cake and coffee and singin' to beat the band."

Nate broke into song on the instant, his voice roaring through the hotel doorway. "*I'll take you home, Kathleen...to where the fields...*"

"I'll just search out Mrs. Sutton," said Deke, hastily taking his leave.

The thrumming sound, thin as fine tissue, hung tremulously in the dank mine air. Half-song, half-chant, it noodled Emma's skin like a pond rippling from scooted pebbles. She followed the sound into a sidecut where she came on a bundle of scraps propped against rock headwall. She knelt beside her lifelong companion. Tracing the gnarly, beloved face, she found atop the bristly head of still-black hair, a deep, jagged wound pooled with blood. A crooked hand reached for hers, clasped it weakly. The thin voice did not alter. Leaning close, Emma could decipher only a few words: "I...come...come now...earth...mother..." In all her years of knowing the Utes, Emma had never heard a death chant. Yet she knew not to interrupt the cadences of a song as sacred as Christian prayer. Certain her heart would crack, she lowered her head to Polly Panakarpo's breast. In a little time, the singing ceased. She heard the rattles of a distant bear dance.

Rising unsteadily, she dashed at her eyes with her sleeves and gripped the butt of her gun so hard her fingers ached. She took one step, then another, nearing the corner by the cutoff. Sliding along the wall, she held the gun with both hands, arms out straight, easy pressure on the trigger. Quick then, every nerve end alive, she sprang around the bend.

Garrett was less than thirty feet away, huddled over a mess of wire and hemp, intent on preparing fuses. The broken door to the powder magazine dangled above him.

Emma took a solid breath, stepped out in plain sight, and ordered, "Leave off, Garrett. Leave off your murderous work." Her words reverberated around the rock chamber, falling back on themselves.

She might have been a bug that Garrett could not be bothered to brush away. Intent on the business at hand, he continued twisting fuse wrappings as if she had not spoken. In the silence, Emma heard every intake of her own breath.

"Do not crowd me, Emma," he said at last, his voice preoccupied. His indifference was more chilling than his tempestuous outbreaks.

"Put your hands up," she ordered, her voice rising. He continued wrapping fuses, eyes a-glitter under his headlamp.

"I mean to see you to the jailhouse, you murdering filth."

"I wouldn't advise shooting into this powder, Emma. You'll blow both of us—and your precious Pearly—over the top of Gold Mountain."

Emma had never known a killing rage. One rose in her now, like water boiling over in a pot. "You've murdered Polly!"

Garrett looked up. "I should have erased that nuisance when I first ran afoul of it," he said coldly.

Emma fired.

With an animal grunt, Garrett dove and rolled.

Emma moved closer, trying for a surer shot. She had been over-cautious about the powder. The last thing she saw before Garrett smothered his lamp was the splash of bright, arterial blood over fuse makings. Furious with her blundering, blinded once again, she would need to grope once more through the insoluble maze that baffled her in troubled dreams. The darkness darted around her ears and nose, threatening to swallow her in toothless jaws. Though she heard footsteps stumbling away down the dirt corridor, she didn't risk lighting her candle.

The blood! she thought. Swiftly, she tucked her gun in her skirt, tore off one of her boots. With her thin-stockinged foot, she felt for the trail of warm stuff across the jumbled fuses, then shuffled along until she came upon the next wet dropping, following it like spoor.

In the moments illumined by Garrett's lamps, she'd half-noted the narrow, low-ceilinged passage with breaks where crude ladders led upward. From somewhere in the distance came the sound of falling water. Sliding her foot from one blood-splotch to the next, she came to the first ladder, explored splintery rungs, and moved on. Then the wall stopped abruptly, and she caught herself as she started to fall. Dipping to her knees, she felt for and found a ladder descending to the Aspen Leaf Tunnel below. It held a stickiness. She turned and lowered herself rung by rung. At the bottom, the sound of the waterfall became a crashing. Somewhere a stream rushed, searching its way down the mountain. She found the blood spoor and hurried forward. Then her unshod toes struck timber, and the explosion of pain was so sharp she could not still her cry. Doubled over, she was suddenly buffeted by a blaze of light. She dropped flat. Bullets barked past. *Ghhh-raang. Ghhh-raaang.*

She had run into a small stack of mine timbers, which she now crouched behind, blinded in the brilliant light and shaking like a small, hairless dog. She was concealed but—her gun was gone. Adjusting to the glare from what appeared to be pineknot torches, she spied the pistol on the tunnel floor a few feet distant. This deep, crudely carved-out tunnel served as storage for lumber and tools. She did not think Garrett could see the pistol. He must be on the rough scaffolding at the foot of the stope above the waterfall. She waited.

"Aha! Little Emma strikes out!" The words, shouted over the tumult of water, were followed by lunatic laughter, which like a swallow of ice water, made her teeth ache. She realized, chillingly, that Garrett was overcome by derangement. Yet, though his brain might be skewed, his gun arm was steady. The light blazed. She held her tongue.

"When I unleash the rest of this river, the Pearly will flood, and the famous child entertainer will drown," he cried. "Lucifer will have him one more bony stewing hen for his cauldron." The crackbrain laughter rang out again.

Emma's head pounded and her toe hammered. Though she yearned to shout back-talk, she would not be baited. She removed her other boot and raised it slowly above the timber. More shots whined past. The boot quivered. Garrett was almost as good a marksman as she. But he had little patience for awaiting the sure shot.

With the motion of a carpet roll thrown to the floor and unfurled, she rolled across the passage. A bullet whizzed so near she could feel the heat of its trajectory. She rolled back to the safety of the lumber, retrieving her gun as she went. Two more shots rang out.

I'm damned if I'll drown or be shot in a mine hole, she told herself grimly as she tipped her pistol, twisted, checked her loads, clicked shut the cylinder.

Clinging close to the wall, she rose to her feet and took careful aim at the outline on the scaffold. She squeezed the trigger and the outline slumped, then slid torturously along a scaffold railing. Emma waited, her breath thready. She made a feinting movement, her eyes glued to the downed figure. Delayed again. Then, crouched low, she moved toward the scaffold. By the trestlework, she looked up at the man slumped against the wooden support. She could not hear gasps or moans over the thundering waterfall. At last she climbed hand-over-hand up the cross-hatching, eyes glued on her tormenter. At the top, she drew her pistol and moved close. Garrett lay face down, a rattail fuse and powder bag beside him. Delaying the moment of looking in his face, Emma picked up a bent driller's steel and moved it aside. It felt oddly heavy, like a fallen tree. At last she sank down to stare at her husband in the eerie flare of the pine torches. She had broken yet another of God's commandments, had killed the man who had caressed her and sworn vows of fidelity. She felt no compunction for the man, only a terrible sorrow for the deed.

At that moment her arm was jarred with a bolt so paralyzing that her pistol clattered away, bouncing downward from wooden crosspiece to wooden crosspiece. Like a downed animal, Emma found herself clawing, kicking, punching. When her arm struck the cast-off driller's steel, she clutched it, leaned into Garrett's ear, and bit down savagely. When Garrett shrieked and threw up a protective arm, she brought the steel down on his head. The blow sent him half off the scaffold, where he clawed at her skirts, his strength ebbing. At last he hung head-down over the lip of the waterfall. He lay still.

Emma felt rather than heard the sobs wracking her. Though she had an odd notion of closing her eyes, a longing to sleep deep, she willed them to stay fixed on the man below, a man so devil-possessed he might not stay dead.

Deke found her there, staring wide-eyed at the figure on the falls in the blaze of pineknots secured in the stope holders. He was so afraid for her that he scarcely dared hazard a touch to her pulse. "Emma? My darling!"

She turned at the sound of his voice, her eyes listless. "Why Deke," she murmured, "you've—you've come underground."

####

CHAPTER THIRTY-EIGHT

THE WEDDING

Emma lay back against her pillows, her book drooping unread in her hands. Grasshoppers clicked lazily amid yellowed cottonwood leaves beginning to sag with frost. She did not note the hoppers nor the fading leaves but stared out her window unseeing, adrift in an in-between place. She sensed she bore some affliction, though she could not fathom the nature of it.

Aggie spoon-fed her nourishing broths, assuring her, "The sap will rise in you again, lass." Yet Emma was not able to consider life at all. Such a weight burdened her that she could not imagine how tomorrow would feel, let alone a time as distant as next week. She wept easily and often. She slept the night and far into the day, a listless, sweat-soaked sleep. Food had a sameness, flat as wood shavings, though Aggie tempted her with every delicacy.

When she'd finally comprehended that she had not done murder, that Garrett was convalescing from his injuries in the Glenwood Sanitorium, she'd been released from the onus of killing. Even so, she could not seem to get around to living. Like a new-foaled colt struggling to stand, she was too feeble to find equilibrium. Deke came for long hours to sit by her bed. With the court postponement and Garrett's incapacitation, the ore trains were now routine. Deke had even joined Shotgun's troupe in bagging an occasional buckskin for Emma's Ute Reservation enterprise. But he was only content near a woman mostly asleep or dazedly half-awake. When tears pooled in her eyes, he reached to enfold her hand in his. With a bottomless inner composure, he waited. Somewhere inside, Emma's life force was re-gathering itself, though her grief for Polly was as smothering as a blanket of snow. One day when the quakie leaves turned sere, curled into small black fists and blew rattling away, when following early high country snows, Indian summer returned on soft, moccasined feet, he felt they might ride at last to the Crystal River Springs. Perhaps Emma would recover to make one trip over the hump under crisp, porcelain-blue sky before winter settled in to stay. If not, they would hold on for spring.

Nathaniel Phipps wished he owned the major's certainty. He who had always considered hindsight pure foolishness now wrung his hands in chagrin. "I never seen Emma like this, D.K. Not ever. When the judge went under, she did not shed a tear for others to see. She suffered, but her head stayed high. This is a perilous state she's in. Like she's lost her good mind."

"Maybe she has, for a spell. She'll find it again, Nate."

"Promised her pap I'd watch over her. And I've been no more use than teats on a boar hog."

Following church services on a warm late September forenoon, all the men were gathered on the Clarendon porch, rocking in Aggie's new rattan porch rockers, feeling awkward in their idleness. Inside, Lavinia, Arbella, Bertha, and Leorah Wickersham sat with Emma while she slept.

"Perhaps she'll sense friends by her side, Major," they said.

It was an enigma to Vinnie how everyone deferred to the major when it came to Emma's care, him a man she'd thought cold and uncomforting as a winter sea.

"Has anyone give her news of the Pearly Gang?" Willard asked brightly.

"I doubt she'd give a tinker's dam," said Nate.

Willard's face fell. If it was *him* sick, he'd be pleased as punch that the varmint brigade was dying off.

Jake Levy shook his head over the report they'd had from the sheriff in Orem, Utah. Shoat Yankel had died harder than he'd lived. "Say Yankel swole up bigger'n a prize squash. Turned coal black," said Willard with satisfaction.

"Hear all his teeth fell out."

"Never heard of the blood poison acting such a way," said Nate skeptically. "Are we sure them Mormons know their symptoms?"

"Coulda been his own poison rising up in him," conjectured Willard.

"What about that runty Felcher?"

"Think the Paiutes et him."

Willard looked a little green. "That tribe's no better'n starved dogs, livin' on grubs and worms."

"Fess musta looked about like a skinny woodchuck to them."

Calvin said, "I'd hoped the dying was done with. How much more dying do you guess we can expect?"

Deke could imagine what was in Calvin's mind: columns of casualties, good camp or bad, adding up like battle statistics. "I'd wager we're about done, Calvin."

"We've got over that dog," agreed Nate. "We'll slide down the tail."

Deke changed the subject. "Hear Tacker's set to compromise, Calvin."

"We're meeting the end of the week. You're all invited. Has it in mind for the mine operators to come together, run the electric into the mountain, build a communal tunnel, put up a bigger smelter. I've held off, hoping to get Mrs. Sutton's ideas."

"She'll trust your judgment, Cal."

"Word is that Tacker will prod the railroads in here if we can guarantee an end to bicker. Nothing would suit me better than an end to bicker."

What finally brought Emma to her senses and her feet was duty. When Bridget mentioned that she and Frank Parker were postponing their wedding, hers was such a sad, hungering look that Emma croaked, "Won't hear of it. Help me to my feet." Within a few days she was planning menus and decorations, hiring musicians, laying in china and linens. She tired quickly, and she worked in spurts, but bit by bit she grew steadier. She brought out a closeted Paris gown, ordered as a surprise by the judge not long before he traveled. Now it went to Lily Angstrom to be cut down and let out, reshaped from tall and slim to short and plump. Bridgie chewed her nails to the quick, aghast over knife-bladed scissors slashing through beautiful satin and lace. Leorah Wickersham had taken charge of the bridal cake. Aggie, with Arbella Arey's assistance, would be directing supper preparations. The church women were harboring late-blooming asters and sweet alyssum.

Deke blessed Bridget O'Reilly to the skies.

On the October Saturday of her wedding, Bridgie rose with the dawn, felt eagerly of her face, dashed to the looking glass and shrieked, "Jesus God, I'm skinned!" Snatching up the M.O. Hughes home formulary, she ran down the hotel hallway to pound on the missus' door. Inside, she collapsed against a wall, her cries stricken. "Holy Mother preserve me! I wanted to be rosy pink fer me Frank—and I'm as scalped as a red Indian!"

Emma, who'd fallen asleep over a copy of the novel *Ramona,* took one look at Bridgie's skin hanging in tatters, dropped the book, and threw aside the covers. "What on earth?"

"Twas that home formulary, Mum…"

"Land! I hope you didn't use the recipe for removing silver tarnish!" Emma was horrified.

311

"I...I...I...r-read under the part about r-removal of f-freckles." Bridgie hiccupped in anguish.

"But Bridget girl, your freckles are a blessed part of you."

"I l-looked like a speckled trout!" Bridgie protested around tics and gulpings in front of the bureau mirror.

Emma pulled her over by the window in the dim morning light. "Did you mix this confounded brew yourself?"

"I—I t-took the formulary to Mr. Hughes at th-the pharmacy and asked h-him to mix me up a batch. First he said n-no. Then he stood me in his front window and t-taken a good hard look. After th-that he stirred up the medicine."

"Drat the man!" Emma drew on her clothes and went to search out Aggie.

Aggie examined the bride closely. "What are the ingredients of this—er, formula, lass?"

"Mr. Hughes taken sweet almonds, then bitter almonds...p-put 'em in that aqua pura...l-like it says in the recipe."

Aggie put on her reading specs to read the formulary. "Purified water? Malarkey! No doubt from the filthy pump in his back alley."

"H-he stirred him up an e-mul-shun...He dis-solved him some—"

Emma read over Aggie's shoulder. "Hy-drarg- bi-chlor-corros. A corrosive?!"

"H-he melted the stuff in alcohol. It s-spit out steam—like the d-divvil himself."

"T'is a wonder you didn't ask Miles Gephardt to take his shoeing rasp to your phiz," sniffed Aggie as she set to work mixing a paste of orris root and cornstarch. For the next hour she and Emma gentled away Bridgie's peeling skin until she emerged more or less smooth-faced but in mottled shades running from picket fence white to peppermint pink.

Bridgie again peered in the mirror. "L-looky here. There's more of the d'dam freckles b'neath!" she howled.

Emma knelt down and reached under her bed. "Hush, girl. You'll only redden your eyes. I am making a plan." She searched deep and pulled out a pile of folded mosquito netting.

Aggie, wearing a stern expression, said, "I intend to give Oliver Hughes a piece of me mind. As for you, Bridget O'Reilly, I have another piece. The good Lord gives each of us a cross t'bear. Me, I ha' not a hair on m' head. Amos Blackwell is missing half a hand. You ha' nought but freckles on your fair face. There's worse trials. Take up your cross, girl. Bear it."

"Well, she needn't start 'til after the wedding," said Emma gaily. "Her hands will be busy with her nosegay. What's more, she'll be the most temptatious bride this side of County Kerry." In her lap ballooned the pile of mosquito netting. In her hand were the scissors from her sewing basket. "Sit on this stool, girl, I need to measure."

Later, when Aggie had given the bride comfrey tea to settle her hiccups and stretched her on her bed under a mask of fresh cucumber slices, Aggie and Emma looked at each other and collapsed in helpless laughter. The freckle folly proved the jolt needed to galvanize Emma, who was now fully alive with urgency.

The following Monday, *The Aspen Daily Times*—starved for social fodder for months—stumbled effusively over its own type. "In the foremost social occasion of our autumnal season, Mrs. Bridget O'Reilly, widow of the late Paddy O'Reilly, appeared at the font of St. Mary's Church at four o'clock of this Saturday afternoon past. The bride was exquisitely attired in a gown of province satin and Brussels lace in the latest style directly from Paris, France. Crowned with a multi-tiered veiling reminiscent of that affected by doges' wives of seventeenth century Venice, she floated down the aisle to meet her betrothed, Mr. Frank Seamus Parker, Jr. in a perfect aureole of cumulus clouds. The groom was the picture of speechless joy as he waited to lift the voluminous veiling and bestow the nuptial kiss on his glowing bride. The ceremonies were conducted by the Right Reverent Michael H. Downey, M.E. By special dispensation from his Eminence the Archbishop of Kansas City, the bride was given in marriage by Mr. Nathaniel Phipps. She was attended by…"

Emma finished reading the verbose four-column panegyric and leaned back on her pillows with a sleepy smile. Aggie had ordered her back to bed. "Ye've still a touch of the jaundice, lass. Under the kivvers wi' ye." Emma was grateful. She had jumped back into life so fast that the leap had used about all her grit.

At the armory reception Deke had guided Emma carefully across the floor, mindful of her fragility, though he'd roared at her account of the bride's skinning. She'd been a wisp in his arms, no bigger around than a child. Lily Angstrom had tucked up another of her Denver City gowns, all the while clucking and scolding. Emma herself was so taken aback at her peaked appearance that she'd said boldly to Deke, "I'm as thinned down as a dog nursing twelve pups."

He'd vowed, "You're the most beautiful woman in the Wild West." Indeed there was a spark in her eye, color in her cheeks. But he'd slowed his steps so she wouldn't tire. He wanted no part of her to break.

As they danced, Shotgun Hayes slid by, steering a path with his elbows for the Widow Wickersham. Smells of toilet water and talcum powder surrounded him like a heavenly aura. He was so barbered that Emma's mouth dropped.

"First bath he's had since Garfield was shot," commented Deke. "The new man at Burkhardt's Bathhouse swears the job took three full-sized bars of soap and a pack of red devil lye."

Emma smiled. "I hear Mr. Burkhardt left town in the dark of night," she said.

"He did. Taking the treasuries of five or six organizations with him."

"No!"

"They claim the man would be at his petty pilfering still—if Willard hadn't caught him out."

Deke was holding her scandalously close, shutting away the dancers around them. Though he had sworn to keep his desires in check, he could not stop the words from spilling out. "I promise I will never leave town, Emma, by day or by night. I cannot lose you again." He looked into her eyes. "Will a waltztime proposal of marriage be acceptable, Ma'am—or shall I carry you back to the Clarendon and ask properly on bended knee?"

Color rose in Emma's face. "Deke, you know I may not consider such a proposal now."

"You'll be a free woman shortly," he reminded her gently.

"I wonder, will I ever be free in my mind?" Her face was so mournful that Deke wondered if he had erred in his timing again.

"A bond must work two ways, my dear. If one-half of the bonding breaks away, there's no sense trying to hold it together. Your husband dishonored you—and he would have taken your life."

"Two good men are dead in the pursuit of my silver. My oldest, dearest friend is killed. A man lies in the hospital, grievously wounded. Death and guilt are not easy companions."

"Emma dear, you were caught in the trap of a man turned lunatic."

"Nevertheless, I am not blameless." Emma's face was wishful. "I do thank you for the lovely proposal. But I am still burdened with shame—and with sorrow."

"Sorrowing is not the way of Polly's people. You well know that a Ute leave-taking is a time of joy."

"Oh, I don't mean to wear black and lurk under heavy veils, or I would not be here on this dance floor. But I must finish my farewells, say to Polly's spirit all the loving things I neglected to tell her in life."

Polly had been packed in ice, wrapped in canvas tarpaulins, placed in a buckboard with Iacono on the reins. He had carried her to the Four Corners country, where she would be placed in an unmarked cache deep in the San Juans with her favorite possessions—her elk-bone-handled skinning knife, throwing hatchet, beads and her pony. As Ike prepared for departure, Emma had stood by the wagon, looking desperate.

"It was her time," said Ike. "She die good. Not many die good."

"My head tells me Ike's words were true," Emma said to Deke on the dance floor. "But my heart aches with emptiness. Without Polly, some part of me is missing. I am alone, and I am bereft."

"You are not alone, Emma. Though I should have known not to rush you so thoughtlessly—to take one slow step at a time."

Thinking to change her line of thought, he said, "The first step is the trip to the reservation. We've bagged game and those young squaws have stockpiled pemmican. We'll soon be ready to go. It was my hope that you'd be strong enough to accompany your expedition."

Deke felt a tap on his shoulder and Nate slipped into his place. "Got to have my turn before you're danced down to a nubbin, Missy."

"Oh, Uncle Nate, remind me again this is a happy day."

"The best," he said, walking her cautiously across the floor. "There's been a time or two I didn't think we'd get over the derned dog—it was a buster." He tried a careful dip—Nate liked a good dance step almost as much as a song. "You going to marry that major? Make the man happy at last?" he asked.

Seeing Emma flag, he suspected he'd put his foot in his flapping mouth. "Let's have us a cup of punch. You're my fifth go-around and my knees are giving me fits."

He seated her next to Willard and Arbella and hurried away to the punch bowl.

"This is a beautiful affair, my dear," said Arbella.

The fall had been warm, and Aggie and Vinnie had again besieged every garden owner for late-blooming sweet peas, pearly everlasting, baby's breath, asters, and climbing roses. Young aspen trees were artfully clumped

315

in corners in buckets of water. "The room is a picture," said Arbella admiringly. She herself wore delphinium blue taffeta cut daringly low in the bodice, and the smitten Willard made no bones about who he thought made a picture.

Lavinia rustled in a new gown of her own, and though it was a respectful black in deference to Pete and Needle, its ruffles and furbelows made her feel like a cock pheasant.

At the dessert table, Nate found himself battling an otherwise tamed Amos Blackwell for the last of the angel food cake. Amos had been carrying cake to Ellamae Beard like he was resupplying an army of defenders.

On the dance floor, Scooper Hurd, looking natty in his first store-bought suit, exercised his new-found passion for dancing. He'd stepped out with Gwyneth Davies, with Grandma Tekoucic, with the youngest Beard girls, and with Svea Hoaglund, who hung above him like a half-masted flag. Scoop did not mind having his feet trod by small girls, holding the bones of an old lady, or having his nose smothered in Svea's enveloping bosom. "Hell," he proclaimed cheerily to Lute, "I'd dance with a bull moose, I guess."

Lute's main intent was not to mash his defenseless partners with his outsized feet. Flushed with effort, he doggedly shoveled Mrs. Krueger and Mrs. Wickersham and Mrs. Arey around the floor. He danced with the bride and remembered to pay her the proper compliments. Anxiously, he inquired of the widow, "Am I too fumble-footed to invite Tacy Beard to dance?"

Tacy sat at the bridal table in a gown she'd dyed herself. It wouldn't come black, so she'd made do with the resulting silvery grey. She looked worn but womanly, and she made Luther's heart act up in his chest.

"I believe it would be more fitting if you carried her punch and had a nice talk, Lute. She is mourning for her father."

Lute reddened. "Dang it, I near forgot!"

At the table, Willard announced out of the blue, "That preacher was some sight, him in all those skirts and satin and lace." He had been brought to a standstill by the parade of acolytes, bell-ringers, incense-wafters, and candle-lighters. "Man had more gold on him than Goldtooth McGonaghy over to Breckenridge." Goldtooth was a gambler known for the gold nuggets displayed prominently in his front teeth, his watch chain and fob, cuff links and shirt buttons.

"Seen Indians dressed in finery like that, never whites," said Nate. The sight would have turned his Quaker mother into a pillar of salt.

For most of them it had been their first visit inside a Catholic church. "The marriage vows were about like the Presbyterians'," observed Vinnie.

"After they finished all that commotion over water and wine and wafers and basins," harrumphed Willard. "And why does the man talk Greek a body can't understand?"

"Not to put too fine a point on it," said Calvin, "we were hearing Latin, not Greek."

"A little high-toned Greek or Latin might be good for your system, Willard," said Nate.

"H'it may surprise you to know," said Willard huffily, "that I have it in mind to take up instruction in French. I'll want to order a few tony items when I take Arbella to visit Paris, France, in the spring."

"I knew it," murmured Deke in Emma's ear. "I wonder if he's found a portrait painter yet."

Lavinia felt as flustered as a young girl when Calvin asked her for the pleasure of the next dance. "Why Cal," she stammered, "you haven't had your arms around me in so long it's…it's like being courted again."

"About time I remembered I have the comeliest partner in this camp." He looked into her face so long that she colored. "You're all the treasure I need, Lavinia. And I'm ashamed to say it's taken a world of trouble for me to come around to that truth."

By this time, a quantity of home-brewed grappa had been slipped into the raspberry shrub. Though the fights would not break out 'til later, the groom was already besotted with drink, as was his bride. As toasts resounded and the grappa took hold, the menfolk were unable to keep to their feet, and Scoop and Lute found themselves hard-pressed as dance partners. The women had eyed Emma Sutton enviously. Major Burdine, in his sprucely tailored uniform of the Colorado Volunteers, his tall figure imposing, was the finest dancer in the room. They danced with each other, then vied for the attentions of the two young, eager foot-stompers.

Deke took care to do his duty by those widowed and alone, then returned gratefully to Emma's side. Though she had thought only to go through the motions, she was now caught up in the music and the gaiety. She found her feet prancing, her skirts flying. Suddenly, surrounded by friends and music and happy chatter, it came to her that her eyes might again drink in the world. She pictured community sing-songs, the watchful eyes of aspen groves, creeks racing eagerly down-mountain, winter sleigh rides through snow white as sugar. Only now she did not picture these wonders alone. In her fancies, a loving man was by her side. She thought she might be half-pagan, to worship the power of sky, of snow, of sun. *No*, she thought, *for those were the places God dwelled. He lived in the trees...in the flowers...in rushing streams...in the snow-capped peaks surrounding her. And in this man who loved her.*

She felt a surge of the old joy that lay at the core of her being. She threw back her head, and her laughter bubbled up like a fresh-sprung spate of creek.

THE END

EPILOGUE

The Widow Wickersham grows rich, invests in the railroads, gives Aspen a school and a hose company and has a street named for her.

The last Ute uprising occurs in 1887. Aspen volunteers, including Sergeants Kellogg and Hurd, ride off to fight under Colonel D.K. Burdine. The colonel and Sergeant Major Ellsworth Hayes, along with a Glenwood Springs sheriff, are the only three men killed in action. Colonel Burdine leaves a wife, Mrs. Emma Burdine, and an infant son, Dalrymple Knowles Burdine IV.

During the celebrations following the arrival of the D&RG rail line in town in 1887, Gabe Tacker over-indulges in a dinner of roast pork and potato dumplings, suffers apoplexy and dies in the armory banquet hall. Shortly afterward, Garrett Sutton returns as a railroad superintendent on the D&RG Line.

Widow Emma Burdine takes over as editor of Aspen's newspaper and is instrumental in bringing women's suffrage to Colorado.

Calvin Krueger never fully recovers from the mind-numbing catastrophes of the Pearly strike. Within a year, Mike Kastelic has stepped in as the Pearly superintendent.

Nate Phipps is fitted with bifocals and eventually settles in with the bench boys to watch Durant Avenue's passing parade.

Willard Arey trips over a new prosthesis and barely escapes falling overboard from a trans-Atlantic steamer.

Denver Bob Bisbee fathers six children by his breed, is secretly scalped and roasted by White Mountain Apaches after he cheats in a card game.

Bull Mudgett is knifed to death by Aussie Outbackers in a San Francisco brothel.

By 1891, Aspen is one of the richest mining camps in the West, with a population of 13,000, several trolley lines, a stunning opera house, a showplace hotel, and elegant hot springs excursion trains. The great Modjeska appears at the opera house. Trains carry in circuses and potentates. Elephants lumber through Aspen's streets.

In 1893 the country goes on the Gold Standard, silver collapses, and entire households stream out of Aspen, bound for the new gold finds in Cripple Creek, Colorado.

In later years, Aspen men get together to repopulate the hills with elk, the trees grow back, the mountains heal over and are as breathtaking as ever. Over the years, the town settles into decades of quiet neglect until 1948, when the great Albert Schweitzer, under the impression he is traveling to Chicago, emerges from Africa and ends instead in Aspen to celebrate the Goethe Bicentennial. He is joined by Tenth Mountain veterans of World War II, who build one of North America's great ski areas over the old adits and tunnels of forgotten silver mines.

Today Aspen is populated by the rich and famous, jets streak in and out, and humble miners' cottages like the Beards' and the Kruegers' sell for a million or more.

Below ground, a handful of young Aspen men keep mining alive. They pick and tram and guide tours through their "workings" and live in a past they wish were the present.

Martie Sterling—2004